MISSING EXES

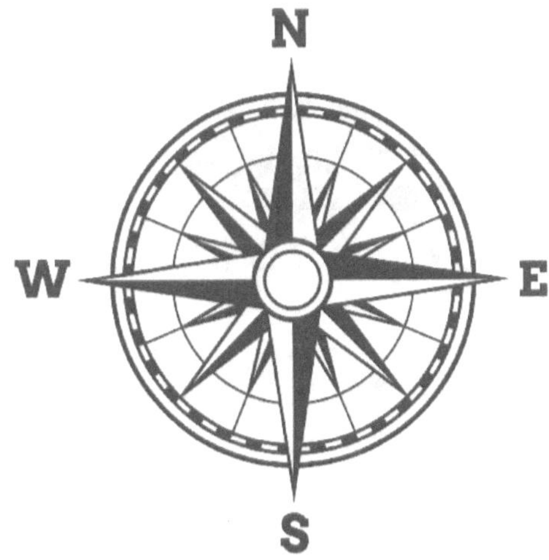

Missing Exes
Copyright © 2025 by Ben Cooper

Paperback ISBN: 978-0-9663548-3-6
eBook ISBN: 978-0-9663548-4-3

Library of Congress Control Number: 2024923408

Edited by: Robin Cain

First Edition

Author contact: heritageproductionsltd@gmail.com

Published by Heritage Productions, Ltd. Houston, Texas

MISSING EXES

A Novel

Ben Cooper

For Jody and Robin

1

For Alexander Christian, fishing was his sanctuary. A chance to disconnect and enjoy the peacefulness of the ocean. His escape from the harsh realities of life. Wade fishing in the Gulf required complete focus and attention. The sea was a merciless predator, capable of taking lives in an instant. Riptides were its deadliest weapon, claiming more victims than sharks, stingrays, and all other sea creatures combined.

Being a decent swimmer, he knew if ever caught in a riptide, he should swim parallel to shore until he'd cleared the pull of the current. When fishing, he wore long pants and a long-sleeved shirt. His attire was not suitable for long swims, so he wore an inflatable life vest. The vest was unobtrusive but would save his life in a pinch.

Usually, he fished for pleasure. More recently, Alexander found solace in this perilous dance with death. A solace that would, if even for a short time, take his mind off his ex, Bonita. She'd been gone for five and a half months. The relationship was over, but he still cared for her.

The Gulf of Mexico looked more like a lake than an ocean. Small swells gently rolled in, broke along the beach, and disappeared into the sand. The normally brownish gulf water looked almost blue in the early afternoon sun. Standing on the second sandbar, Alexander cast his orange-bellied MirrOlure Poppa Mullet Surface Popper past the third sandbar. He slowly retrieved it, twitching the rod tip, making the lure pop, which simulated a fish feeding on the surface.

He twitched, reeled in enough line to take up the slack, and twitched again. Nothing had attacked the lure, and he wasn't expecting anything to attack it. Top-water lures worked best in the early morning and the late afternoon. A spinner bait might have fared better, but when a big speckled trout hit a top-water lure, the experience was re-markable. Usually, Alexander released any fish he caught. Once in a while, an unlucky trout or redfish would end up on his grill. Catching fish wasn't important. Standing in four and a half feet of semi-clear wa-ter and watching his lure pop across the water was therapeutic.

On this Wednesday in late May, the temperature of the water off the Bolivar Peninsula was a comfortable eighty degrees. Warmer than usual for the time of year, thanks to an early summer along the Texas coast. Eighty degrees was more than tolerable. It wouldn't be long be-fore stepping into the Gulf would feel like stepping into a hot bath. He enjoyed tepid water and a semi-deserted beach.

A small swirl in the water appeared next to the lure. Alexander low-ered his rod slightly and counted to five. Nothing. He twitched the rod tip, and the lure popped. Again, he counted to five. Nothing. The fish that had checked out the bait had moved on. He shrugged and retrieved the big MirrOlure.

Whenever he made a cast, Alexander would take a glance to be sure no one was behind him. He knew he was alone in the Gulf, but he checked anyway–out of habit–then made his cast.

The lure hit the water with a pop. Ripples moved away from the splash and disappeared. Alexander didn't retrieve any line. He stood still, staring at the sea. He tried to make sense of what he had seen when he glanced behind him before he made his cast. He shut his eyes and tried to recreate the image.

He thought he saw a lone figure standing on the beach looking at him. It was possible. People walking on the beach will often stop and watch fishermen for a few minutes. Nothing seemed normal about this person. Perhaps it was because of his uncertainty about the person's gender or stance.

It would have been easy enough to turn around and look. What he saw, or thought he saw, was a woman with blonde hair. Had she had dark brown hair, he would have quickly turned to see if it was Bonita.

This was not her. He didn't want to turn and look because that would have acknowledged her presence. She may want to chat, and he wasn't in the mood to be social.

Without twitching his rod tip, Alexander quickly retrieved the lure. Using his normal casting routine, he glanced behind and then launched his lure into the gulf. He only got a glimpse, but now he was positive it was a woman with blonde hair. Whoever she was, she was in the same spot. She wasn't casually strolling along the beach.

Alexander retrieved the lure, turned sideways, and cast parallel to the shore. From the corner of his eye, he got a good look at the figure. Tall, thin, wearing a crop top and blue jean cut-offs. Her blonde hair flowed with the slight breeze from the Gulf. She stood with her hands on her hips and stared at the lone angler.

The instant the MirrOlure landed, an explosion of water greeted it. The large speckled trout engulfed the bait and headed toward deep water. Instinctively, Alexander set the hook.

"Shit," he yelled. His mind was on the figure watching him from the beach. At the moment, a fish was the last thing he wanted. The fish was determined to take its meal out to sea and Alexander was determined not to lose a twelve-dollar fishing lure. The big fish tired quickly and was soon close to its captor, but before he could grab the fish, it made one last attempt at escape. Several feet of line stripped off the reel until the fish gave in and allowed itself to be pulled close enough to be picked up.

Alexander grabbed the trout behind its head and lifted it out of the water. The fish gave a cursory flip of its tail, but there was little energy behind it. The fish was beaten. After unhooking the lure from the corner of the fish's mouth, he held it up. A Spotted Seatrout, commonly called a spec or a speckled trout. This was a female. She measured two feet long and weighed at least five pounds.

After Alexander cradled the fish in the water for a few seconds, she flipped her tail and disappeared. He rinsed his hands in the saltwater and glanced toward the shore. The woman he had noticed earlier was standing in the same spot, hands on hips, watching him, apparently waiting for him.

Alexander considered his options while he inspected the line near the lure to see if the big spec had nicked it during her battle to survive. He could continue to fish and hope the woman moved on down the beach, or he could wade ashore and see what she wanted–if anything. It was possible she liked to watch people fish. Or did she have news about Bonita?

He reluctantly made his way toward the shore, shuffling his feet across the sandy bottom to avoid stepping on a stingray. When he got closer, he took a good look at the woman on the beach. She was pretty, with the legs of a dancer. She stood in his path and didn't move. Alexander, with no choice but to acknowledge her, nodded when he got close.

The woman's head tilted quizzically as she checked him out. "Are you Alex?"

"Yes ma'am," he said. Not only did she know him, but she knew him well enough to call him by name. Only his friends called him Alex. Maybe Bonita had sent her and told her to ask for 'Alex.'

"You're a private investigator, right?"

"I was. I'm not taking any clients right now."

"Too busy?" The woman glanced at his fishing pole.

"Funny. No, I have a lot on my mind. I'm sorry."

The woman frowned. "I understand. But I wanted to meet you anyway. I'm Jana."

Alexander hadn't forgotten that the woman had called him by name, as though she knew him. "So, we haven't met?"

"Not in person. Maybe not at all."

The woman he now knew as Jana was one he would not forget. Her blonde hair hung to her breasts with bangs cut even with her eyebrows. She had the bluest eyes he had ever seen. They were a bright blue, like the Caribbean, unlike his own eyes, which were a deeper blue. Her lips formed a natural grin at rest, with slight corner-mouth dimples.

"I'm sorry. Like I said, I've got a lot on my mind. Do I know you?"

"I'm Jana." She said this as if he was clearly missing the point.

She could tell that her name still didn't ring a bell. "Jana Wilson."

"I'm sorry, I—"

"You talked with my boyfriend last year. Reymundo. He was being forced to smuggle girls in from Cuba. You helped him."

The lightbulb went on in Alexander's head. "Oh, my God. Yes, I remember you. I'm so sorry."

"That's okay. I didn't expect you to remember me. I don't know if we ever actually talked. Plus, I'm probably the last person you'd expect to be standing on your beach."

Alexander shook his head. "You got that right." He stuck his hand out toward her. "It's nice to meet you."

Jana leaned in so only her upper body lightly touched his then wrapped her arms around his neck. After a lengthy hug, she backed up a step and said, "It's nice to finally meet you." She hesitated for a second. "Rey is missing. I was hoping you could help, but I understand. Can you recommend anyone?"

"Forget what I said. I'll help you. Let's walk to the house and you can fill me in."

The two walked across the beach and up the sandy road to the second row of beach houses. Alexander pointed at the white Lexus in his driveway. "Is that yours?"

"Yes, it's a rental," Jana replied.

When they reached the steps, Alexander said, "Go on up. The door's unlocked. There's beer and wine in the fridge if you'd like. I need to rinse my gear off. I'll be up in a couple of minutes."

"Thank you." She didn't leave immediately. Instead, she studied Alexander's attire. He couldn't help but notice her quizzical expression.

"Suit pants. I wear long pants when I wade fish and I haven't worn a suit in years. I believe the pinstripes attract bigger and more refined fish."

She turned and went up the stairs without speaking. Alexander noted a slight change in her expression. Her natural grin seemed to turn into a smile, albeit a forced smile. Her boyfriend was missing. He didn't know the details, but he understood what she was going through.

2

Alexander rinsed the salt water off his rod and reel, the cool droplets splashing against his warm skin. He cradled the combo in the custom-made rod rack. The ground floor bathroom was basic. A toilet, shower stall, sink, and mirror. A small vanity contained the basics–extra toilet paper, soap, shampoo, and bleach. A makeshift closet stood outside the bathroom. In it, he kept several complete changes of clothes, including a collection of well-worn Hawaiian shirts, that each told a story of a past adventure.

He quickly showered, dried, ran a comb through his sandy brown hair, and dressed. Barefoot, he climbed the wrought iron circular staircase that entered into his master walk-in closet through a secret door. When he walked into the living room from his bedroom, he surprised Jana, who was sitting on the couch with her legs curled under her.

"Damn! I didn't expect anyone to come through that door. I thought you'd come in through the front door."

"Sorry. I added a private staircase when I built the house. It's nice to have when the weather's bad and, if I ever need it, I could use it as an escape."

"Escape from what?"

"Bad guys. Crazy women. You never know when you'll need an escape hatch."

Jana giggled. He was glad to see her mood lighten, if only a little.

"Do you have to escape from crazy women often?"

"Not too often. I'm usually a pretty good judge of women. I see you found the liquor cabinet."

"I did. You mentioned beer and wine, but I noticed the scotch, which looked good. Especially the twenty-year-old stuff. I hope you don't mind."

"Not at all. That's what it's there for. It's early, but I may join you."

"It's five o'clock somewhere," Jana said.

"You got that right. What would Jimmy Buffett do?" Alexander said without hesitation.

"He'd pour something tall and strong," she said and smiled. It didn't seem forced.

"If he was still alive," Alexander lamented.

Her smile disappeared. "That was so sad."

"And unexpected."

"I didn't take you for a Parrothead."

"I'm a big fan. I can't tell you how many times I saw Jimmy in concert. Occasionally I bought tickets, but usually I'd show up at the venue, flash my FBI credentials, and they'd let me in. Rarely would I get questioned, but when I did, I'd tell them I was investigating an interstate drug trafficking lead. That was back when getting busted for pot could get you time. Nobody questioned me."

"That's crazy. I bet they flushed so much pot down backstage toilets they were clogged for weeks." Jana laughed at the thought.

"I hope not. I didn't care. I avoided contact with anyone connected with the band as much as possible. I didn't want to upset their normal routine or have them worry about whatever they might have been doing backstage. I usually went into the crowd and found an empty seat or stood at an out-of-the-way place to enjoy the show."

"That's cool. I only got to see him in concert a couple of times. For the past few years, whenever he did a show in South Florida, I said I'd go 'next time.' There won't be any more 'next times.'"

"Nope. He'll be missed. But you didn't come here from Florida to chat about Jimmy Buffett. You said Rey was missing?"

Jana sipped the now slightly watered-down scotch and said, "He is. I came here hoping you could help me."

After several seconds of awkward silence, Alexander said, "I hope I can. What's up?"

"Rey is missing. Probably dead. The cops insist he isn't even missing.

They say he's out on his boat."

The frankness of Jana's tone surprised Alexander. She blurted out that her partner may be dead. Most people whose significant other is missing hope that they're still alive and that they'd be found alive, or that they would come bounding through the door one day and say, "Honey, do I have a story for you!"

"It's only been three days, but it's not like Rey to disappear. He spends a lot of time on the boat, but he always calls or texts. He texted at about ten in the morning and said he was going to do maintenance on the *Miss Jana*. We hadn't taken her out in a while and the engines needed to be run. He usually lets me know when he's finished. When I didn't hear from him after a couple of hours, I texted him but didn't get a reply. When I called, it went to voicemail. I guess it was around five, and I still hadn't heard from him. I went to the marina. The boat was gone. He never takes the boat out alone."

Jana took a healthy drink of scotch and glanced around the living room of the beach house. Nautical-themed décor, including pictures of seabirds and paintings of boats, adorned the living room of the beach house. She looked back at Alexander. "He never takes the boat out alone."

"That's when you called the police?"

"Yes. I told them what I told you. They said he likely took the boat out and didn't have cell service. I told them he never takes the boat out alone. They said, 'There's a first time for everything.'"

"And that's all they said?"

"Yes. They asked if it was his boat. I told them it was. They asked how old he was. I told them twenty-eight. They said he was a grown man out on his boat and there wasn't much they could do. I called back forty-eight hours later. They said they would keep an eye out for the boat. If they spot it, they'll let me know."

"It hasn't been long, so I doubt you've heard anything?"

"No. I called on the way here and told them I wanted to make an official missing person report. They said they'd file a report and look into it. I don't expect to hear from them. Never expected to. That's why I'm here."

"At the risk of giving you an aneurysm, I need to ask. Is there any chance Rey would take the boat out alone?"

Jana glared at him. "NO! He never takes the fucking boat out alone!" She took a deep breath, seemingly to center herself, then asked, "Can I have another scotch?"

She was off the couch and halfway to the kitchen before Alexander could reply. He watched her as she filled the glass with ice and twenty-year-old.

"This is good scotch," she said, sitting back on the couch. "I'm sorry I snapped at you. I'm sorry I cussed too. My language used to be much worse. I had a dreadfully dirty mouth. It came from working in strip clubs and hanging around with the wrong people. I made a vow that I'd stop cussing, or at least cut down on my cussing."

"That's okay. I riled you up a little. Maybe on purpose." Alexander wanted to add that the scotch better be good, considering the price, but he was just glad she appreciated it. "You said you think Rey may be dead, not just missing. Why?"

She cocked her head slightly. "I think someone saw him on the boat, killed him, and stole the boat. If they took the boat but didn't kill him, he would have gotten in touch with me. Oh, his truck was still at the marina, too."

"I need another drink." Alexander went to the kitchen and refilled his glass with ice and scotch. He returned and sat down. "You think someone forced him to take the boat out and then killed him and took off with the boat?"

"Yeah. I mean, that's the only thing I can imagine."

"Last year, a guy made him take the boat to Cuba, pick up a bunch of young girls, and deliver them to Texas. Could that have happened again?"

Jana sipped her drink and thought for a bit. "It's possible. But he only did that because they were holding me. He wouldn't do it unless he had no choice."

"Maybe some people needed a ride to the Bahamas, or Cuba, and commandeered him at gunpoint to take them. Took his phone. He couldn't call."

Jana looked around the room as she pondered the question. "None of those places are that far. Cuba is about a day. It's been almost four days. The boat might be in the Bahamas or somewhere in the Caribbean, and it most likely is, but I doubt Rey is on it."

Her lack of emotion puzzled Alexander a bit. Four days was not that long. "Are you and Rey married?"

"No. We lived together."

"Was everything okay between the two of you?"

Jana shuffled on the couch, crossing and uncrossing her legs. "Yes. Fine."

"Fine? Your body language told me differently."

"Well, maybe not fine. I mean, we got along okay, but I like hanging around, watching the tele or movies, or reading a book. I didn't get to read much in the past few years, so I was catching up. Rey couldn't sit still. He didn't watch TV much, and he didn't like to read. He had to be doing something. I know I loved him, and he loved me. But we have been drifting apart. We never talked about splitting up or anything."

"At the risk of getting cussed at again, I need to ask. Would he take off with the boat to get away from you?"

Jana's forehead wrinkled. "That's a reasonable question. No cussing. To answer, no. He wasn't like that. He had to be the most straight-up, honest guy I've ever met. If he wanted to leave me, he'd talk to me about it."

"I noticed you refer to him in the past tense. You must feel strongly that he's dead."

Jana nodded. "He wasn't a tall man, like you, but he was muscular. His brother owns a gym, and Rey worked out there a lot. He knew judo or whatever you call it. Funny, Rey loved the *Miss Jana*, but we were talking about selling her. He wanted a sport fisher. He wouldn't have protected that boat with his life, if you know what I mean. He wouldn't have risked his life for it. If someone boarded the boat and tried to steal it, he'd have gotten the hell off it."

"And reported it stolen. That's why I hate to admit it, but you might be right. If the boat was stolen, they wouldn't have gotten far after it was reported."

Jana stretched her legs out. "Well, fuck. My brain kept telling me Rey was dead, but my heart was holding on to a flicker of hope. You blew it out."

"You're a strong woman and you put on a brave face. You were bracing yourself for the worst but still hanging onto that thread of hope. Keep hanging on. There are other possibilities."

Jana stared at him while she waited for the other options.

"How hard is the *Miss Jana* to drive?" he asked.

"Not hard. Easy if you've ever driven a large boat with twin screws."

"What if a person had never driven a big boat like yours? Or even a much smaller boat? Could they do it alone?"

"No, not without instruction."

"Could a person with little or no boating know-how get your boat out the slip and into the Atlantic?"

Her expression went blank for a few seconds. "No. Our slip is tight. We always back her in, but you have to ease out of the slip and as soon as the stern has cleared the pilings, swing hard to starboard to avoid boats on the other side. After that, it's easy. You stay in the channel until you get to Stranahan Inlet. The inlet can be rough, but it's nothing compared to the Haulover Inlet. When we had the boat in Miami, Haulover was the closest cut to the Atlantic. It would get crazy rough. Even in a boat that weighs over eighty thousand pounds like the *Miss Jana*, Haulover could be treacherous. There are sandbars, rock walls, strong tide currents, and gusty onshore winds. Even the most experienced boaters can have trouble getting through Haulover. Besides being close to my new condo, it's much easier to get into the Atlantic from Bahia Mar."

"I'm not saying Rey was alone, but if he was, could he get the boat out of the slip and into the Atlantic alone?"

"Absolutely. It helps if you have a hand to get out of the slip but once you're out, it's a one-person job."

Alexander rubbed the stubble on his chin. He looked at Jana, whose bright blue eyes were staring back, waiting for him to say something. Her piercing blue eyes were hypnotic.

"What are you thinking?" she finally asked.

"Any idea how many boats are in South Florida?"

"Huh?" It was not the question she was expecting.

"Roughly, how many boats are in South Florida? Any idea?"

"Lots. I've no idea how many. It's one of the highest concentrations of boats in the States."

Alexander pulled out his phone and did a quick Google search. "Wow, there's over fifty thousand boats in Fort Lauderdale alone."

"That doesn't surprise me. There's at least that many or more in Miami, too."

"That's a lot of boats. Is the *Miss Jana* an expensive boat? Is there anything special about her that would make her more likely to be taken?"

"She's not an overly expensive boat. My ex sold her dirt cheap–that's how Rey could buy her. On the market today, she'd fetch a couple hundred K. She's in great shape and has an extended range, but other than that, nothing special. She's an older boat."

"So, with fifty thousand boats to choose from, what are the odds the *Miss Jana* gets hijacked? Especially with a stout man who's trained in self-defense on board?"

Jana's eyes narrowed. "Not likely, I'd say."

"I agree. My feeling is Rey and or his boat were targeted. And not by experienced sailors. They need Rey to drive the boat."

"But why Rey?"

"That's the question. It could have been random. Someone needed a boat to get out of the country and saw Rey and got the drop on him. Again, not likely, considering the number of boats in the area."

"There's a lot of boats. But if you walk around the marinas, you rarely see a lone person on a boat. It's usually empty or there are several people on it. Maybe they saw Rey alone and thought it would be easy."

"That's possible. Did Rey have any enemies? Anyone that might want to harm him?"

"No. He was a friendly guy. The only person who might have had a reason would have been the guy who was forcing him to traffic the Cuban girls last year, but he's at the bottom of the Atlantic."

"Are you sure?"

"Pretty sure. A couple of Rey's brother's friends took him several miles offshore, wrapped him with chain, and threw him overboard. They said he disappeared faster than a Twinkie at a Weight Watchers convention."

Alexander ignored the metaphor. "Did that guy have any friends or relatives?"

"His 'friends' took off. I don't know about relatives. He was Cuban, so most likely he has some in the area."

"It's possible his relatives were seeking revenge."

"But why go to all the trouble of taking the boat?"

"Good question. I have a feeling someone wanted either Rey, the boat, or both."

"You know, there's more to a boat than just driving it. It has to be maintained. If they were planning to use the boat, they would need Rey to keep it running. I mean, it would run fine for a while, but Rey could convince them it needed constant maintenance to run for a long period."

"Rey sounds like a resourceful guy. Unless they grabbed him to kill him simply for revenge, I'd say he's still alive."

Jana exhaled a deep breath. "Thank you. I feel like there is hope. When he didn't call or text, I kinda lost all hope of seeing him again." She took another drink and emptied the glass. "I should be going. Where's the closest hotel?"

Alexander laughed out loud. Jana gave him a sneer.

"I'm sorry," he said. "There aren't any hotels on Bolivar. There's a few motels, but you wouldn't want to stay in one. Besides, you've had too much to drink to drive. There aren't many Ubers here either. I have a spare room. You can stay here."

Jana was taken aback. "Stay here? Don't you have a girlfriend? What's her name...Bonita?"

"Yes. Bonita."

"Briana talks about her. I used to see Briana quite a bit at the women's shelter. Where's Bonita? Wasn't she pregnant?"

"She was. She lost the baby, fell into a deep depression, and disappeared."

3

"Wait. What? Did you say Bonita is missing?" Jana was beside herself.

"She's not exactly missing. I know where she is, or where she was. I haven't heard from her in several weeks."

"That's crazy. What happened?" Jana covered her mouth with her hand.

"How much do you know about Bon?"

"Very little. Briana mentioned her a few times."

"Bon got trafficked as a child." Alexander looked at his empty glass and said, "I'm going to need another drink. It's a long story. Would you like another?"

Jana nodded and handed him her glass. He moved slower and with a little less spring in his step than the last time he refilled the drinks. She wondered whether it was the alcohol he'd consumed or the untold story that was causing his sluggishness. Based on his expression when he returned and handed her the drink, it was undoubtedly the latter.

Alexander had been sitting on a small loveseat perpendicular to where Jana was sitting on a long, leather sofa. This time, he sat on the couch next to her. Not so close that she would feel he was invading her space, but close enough to surprise her.

He twisted to face her, sipped the whiskey, and sat the glass on the coffee table in front of him. Using his thumb and forefinger, he wiped the corners of his mouth, then wiped his fingers on his shirt sleeve. "You know about Briana, how she was smuggled into the US and trafficked."

"All too well."

"And when her sister, Mayte, came looking for her with the traffickers that commandeered your boat, they raped her. She was afraid they were going to kill her so she jumped off the boat. That's when I found her."

Jana nodded. They both took sips of their drinks.

"I agreed to help Mayte find her sister. Finding an attractive trafficked Hispanic girl in Houston is easy. Finding a specific one is not. There are thousands. Then we got a break. The two small trackers Rey gave the girls led me to several bars on the near east side of Houston that were fronts for prostitution. I planned to go in just to see if I could get information. I was asking a worker at the bar about Cuban girls when this guy came in from a backroom dragging a small, frail-looking girl. He slapped her around and was about to punch her with a closed fist when I stopped him. I figured the guy would kill the girl when I left, so I took her. I asked the girl at the bar if she wanted to come with us. At first, she said, no. Then, as I was about to leave, she agreed to come. She was a big help too; the other girl was a mess."

"The working girl was Bonita?"

"It was. After Bonita made the girl comfortable in the guest room, we had a couple of drinks. I'm not ashamed to say I was smitten with her. She was beautiful and, to my surprise, quite intelligent. She stayed with me that night and ended up living with me. A few months later, she was pregnant. I was shocked. She was ecstatic. She always wanted children. We talked about selling the beach house and moving to Houston. Getting a nice house in a nice neighborhood with good schools. About four months in, she miscarried—"

A loud gasp from Jana interrupted him. He blinked a few times to regain his train of thought.

"I'm sorry," Jana said. "Continue."

"We did all the prenatal stuff. Everything looked fine. One morning, Bon woke up in deep pain bleeding profusely. I got her to UTMB in Galveston as quickly as I could, but it was too late. The baby was gone. It turns out she had been pregnant several times when she was young–maybe as young as fourteen–and someone performed abortions on her that did significant damage to her female parts. The doctor said it was amazing she even got pregnant. He said there was less than a one percent chance she would ever carry a child to term.”

“Oh my God, that must have been devastating.”

“It was. For me. For Bon, it was beyond devastating. After all she’d gone through, she thought she was about to live the American dream. A husband–we had talked about getting married–a house, kids. She wanted a dog too. When she lost the baby, she blamed herself. She believed I didn’t want to be with her if she couldn’t have kids. I told her that wasn’t the case, but she wouldn’t listen. She spiraled deeper into depression, refusing to see a doctor or talk to anyone. I did what I could. I even tried giving her space, but nothing worked. One morning, I took a walk and when I got back, she was gone. She left a note that read, ‘Alex, I love you and I’m so sorry.’ I called her phone and texted, but she didn’t reply. The next day she texted me and said she was okay, not to look for her, and she’d be in touch. Of course, I kept texting her. Occasionally she’d reply and say she was fine and ask me to stop texting her. I didn’t text as much, but I did text. I haven’t heard from her in a month.”

“Oh, Alex, that’s awful. Do you know where she is?”

“I have a good idea. Bat, my neighbor and IT guy, tracked her phone to the east side of Houston. The same area where I found her. Which means she’s gone back to her old life.”

“Are you going to look for her?”

“I thought about it. Every time I text her, I tell her she can come back. I thought I’d give her some space.”

“Alex, when you say you’re giving her some space, does that mean you’re giving up on her?”

Alexander stared at the blank television that hung on the wall. After several long seconds, he shrugged. “Not that I want to, but I feel it’s time to move on.”

Jana instinctively put her hand on his bare knee. When she was a stripper, it was a gesture that, when done after hearing a hard-luck story, would typically guarantee a bigger tip. She would have kept her hand on the client's knee, massaged it provocatively, and rubbed the inside of the man's thigh. This time, she realized it was a mistake. So she just patted Alexander's knee, then removed her hand. She hoped there was nothing provocative about it, just the actions of a concerned friend patting him on the knee. If he read anything more into it, he didn't show it.

"Again, Alex, I'm so sorry. I'm sorry I asked about her."

"Don't be. It's fine. I need to decide what to do. For now, we need to find Rey."

"I agree. Any ideas?"

"A few. In the morning, I'll ask Bat to check Rey's phone and see if he can find out when and where it was last used."

"He can do that?"

"He can. The guy's amazing. Scary, but amazing. I rarely ask how he does things. Plausible deniability. I do know what he doesn't know about the ins and outs of the dark web doesn't need to be known. From what he tells me, you can get anything from the dark web."

"What do you mean 'anything'?"

"Bank account numbers with PINs, email addresses, website account IDs, all with passwords, hacks or backdoor codes into corporate servers, and anything from child porn to firearms."

"Whoa, that is frightening. More than frightening, to be honest."

"Yeppers. That's why I don't want to know too much about it, and I never go there."

"You were with the FBI. Why don't they shut it down?"

"No single person or organization controls the dark web. It's a decentralized network that uses Tor. Tor is like a web browser that's used to see sites on the dark web. Tor links are generated using cryptography. Last I heard, the feds can't crack today's cryptography. Then there's jurisdiction. If the host is outside the US, the feds would need to work with other agencies. Most countries don't give a shit about it and others, like Russia, encourage the use. To answer your question, it's literally impossible to shut the dark web down."

"Wow. I had no idea."

Alexander flashed a quick smile. "Most people don't. Even fewer know how to use it. That's a good thing."

"So, Bat uses tools and stuff from the dark web to hack things? Is that legal?"

"Is it legal? Let's say there's a fine line between legal and illegal when he works. That line is blurry at best."

"I got it. The less you know about it, the better."

"That's my philosophy. Don't ask, don't tell."

Jana giggled and then smiled. It was her first truly wide smile. Alexander thought she had a beautiful smile.

"What's the plan for tomorrow?" Jana asked. "We see what your friend can find out?"

"For starters." Alexander knew the little information Bat would give them was important, but it wouldn't sound like much to Jana. He bought a little time with another sip of whiskey. "We need to go to Florida. I want to get boots on the ground. Talk to people at the marina. There should be witnesses."

"When?"

"The sooner the better. It's been four days already. People forget quickly."

"Tomorrow morning?"

"That would be good. I'm sure Southwest has flights to Fort Lauderdale or Miami all day." Alexander took another drink.

"Southwest? I have a plane. We can go when we want."

Alexander choked on his drink. "You have an airplane?"

"Well, it's not mine. I'm a member of a private jet service. I call them and tell them when and where I want to go, and a plane is usually ready within a few hours. Sometimes it takes a little longer. I'll call them in the morning and book it. What time do you want to leave?"

4

Jana made the call first thing that morning and after she was assured that an Embraer Praetor 500 aircraft would be available, she drove her and Alexander in her rental from Bolivar to Houston's south-side airport. Traffic was light. There was no wait for the ferry. While Jana drove, Alexander had his friend Bat on speakerphone. After they filled Bat in on the details, Jana answered his questions: What was the name of the marina where they kept the *Miss Jana*? What pier and slip number? Rey's cell phone number. Did the boat have any devices onboard that would transmit the location of the boat to the Coast Guard or local authorities? Unable to answer the last question, she would have to research it and get back to him.

Confident he had enough information to get started, Bat said he'd text or email if he needed additional information and would update them if he found anything, then hung up. Alexander pressed the button to end the call and said, "Bat will dig and he'll find a crumb that will lead him down a rabbit hole, which he will have more questions about. He—"

"Oh, my God," Jana interrupted. She glanced over her shoulder and yanked the steering wheel. The Lexus swerved from the far-left lane to the far-right lane. At the intersection, she slammed the brakes and made a right turn.

"What the hell?" Alexander yelled, holding on for life.

"Jack in the Box!"

"What?"

"There's a Jack in the Box. We don't have 'em in Florida. I have to get tacos."

"You almost killed us for tacos?"

"Jack in the Box tacos."

"You almost killed us for Jack in the Box tacos? That's even worse. Good tacos, I might get it but—"

"You know they're the best," Jana said when she eased up to the speaker in the drive-thru lane. "How many do you want?"

"I guess I could eat a couple."

"A couple? Ha." Jana pressed the button and the Lexus' tinted window lowered. She leaned half out the window and shouted at the speaker. "I'd like four, no, five orders of tacos, please."

Alexander watched and listened, as she ordered. "You're going to eat three?"

"I got five orders. That's ten tacos. I bet you eat five."

"Five? I doubt it."

Jana pulled to the window and handed the cashier a credit card. She turned to Alexander. "Have you ever had a Jack taco?"

"Honestly, no."

She laughed and said, "You're in for a treat."

Several minutes later, the cashier handed Jana the bag of hot, crispy tacos. Jana passed the bag to Alexander. "Damn," she said. "I forgot to get curly fries. Oh well, next time." She put the SUV in drive and turned onto Airport Boulevard toward the QuickJet office. "We're close. We'll eat on the plane."

The QuickJet office and hangar were at the far west end of the airport. Jana pulled into the small parking lot.

"This is it?" Alexander asked.

"Yes. Grab your bag."

"What about the car?"

"They'll take care of it."

Alexander got out and stretched. He glanced at the nondescript building before grabbing the small bag he'd packed for the trip. Inside, the combination office, waiting room, and check-in counter were as plain as the outside of the building. A coffee pot against the back wall looked like it contained freshly brewed coffee, and a small refrigerator held bottles of water and sodas. Instead of hard, standard waiting room chairs, sofas and cushioned chairs filled the lounge.

After a brief exchange with the attendant at the counter, Jana returned to Alexander. "The plane's ready. Let's go."

Before he could respond, she grabbed his arm and led him out the rear doors of the office and onto the tarmac. "That's our plane," she said, pointing to the Embraer Praetor 500 sitting twenty-five feet from the back door.

A female flight attendant met them halfway and took Jana's bag. She reached for Alexander's bag, but he waved her off. "I got it," he said. The pilot greeted the pair when they got to the steps of the aircraft. Before Alexander could refuse, the pilot took his bag and gestured toward the steps. Alexander obliged and walked up onto the plane.

"Let's sit here while we eat," Jana said, pointing to the two club seats. "You can move to a single seat later if you need more legroom."

Jana and Alexander sat facing each other, with a small table between them. The flight attendant, eyeing the paper bag from Jack in the Box, asked if she could get them anything.

"Water for me," Jana said.

"I'll have water as well. Thank you." Alexander said, also checking out the fast-food container.

Jana handed Alexander a handful of brown napkins, several small packets of hot sauce, and a small paper bag containing one taco. When she ripped the bag and pulled out the taco, he followed her lead.

"This is a taco?" Alexander asked after studying the crispy shell for a few seconds.

"Shut up and try it."

He did. "Well, I'll be a suck egg mule. This ain't half bad."

"What?" Jana asked. A small piece of lettuce hung from the corner of her mouth.

"This looks like crap, but it's not half bad."

"No, before that. What'd you say?"

"Oh, I said, I'd be a suck egg mule."

"What the hell does that even mean?"

"No idea. A character in a John Wayne movie said it. I like it."

"Cute. John Wayne, huh? Are you a fan?"

"A big fan. You?"

"I've never seen one of his movies."

"You're kidding? Not one?"

"No, I'm not. He died before I was born. Plus, I'm not into Westerns or war movies. That's what most of his movies are, right?"

"Right, most were. Fair enough. Can I have another taco?"

Jana flashed him a smug grin. "Certainly. I got you five."

By the time Alexander finished the fifth taco, the Embraer 500's two Honeywell HTF7500E jet engines had pushed the aircraft to forty-thousand feet and a cruising speed of five hundred miles per hour. The cabin was quiet.

Alexander took a sip of water from the bottle the flight attendant had brought. He shuddered slightly when his phone vibrated. "My phone buzzed. I didn't realize we'd get text messages."

"Yep. We have full internet service too. Is the text important?"

Alexander retrieved the phone from his pants pocket and scrolled through the message as he read. "It's from Bat. He found the last time Rey's phone pinged off the tower closest to the boat. He's downloading the numbers of every phone that pinged off the tower around the time Rey's last pinged. He's going to play around with the numbers and see if anything jumps out."

"That's amazing. Any idea what he hopes to find? There's a lot of boats in that marina, not to mention hotels, condos, and townhouses. It's got to be a gazillion phone numbers."

"He said it was a lot of numbers. I don't know what he's looking for. Maybe any numbers that ping off the same towers as Rey's phone did before it went silent. Any pattern, maybe."

"Hopefully, he'll find something useful."

Alexander tried to reassure her that Bat would find something useful. After he considered the number of phones that would be hitting off the towers in Fort Lauderdale, and not being overly optimistic, he guided the conversation back to Rey. He asked Jana about his habits, friends, anything he could think of—except whether or not he'd take the boat out alone. Jana answered his questions the best she could. In the end, no useful information was ascertained, but the dialogue made the flight go by fast.

The flight attendant approached them. "Is there anything I can get you? We have food, but I saw you were eating, so I didn't offer."

Jana said, "That's fine, we had tacos. I can't get them in Florida."

"I noticed," the attendant said enviously. "We'll be landing in about thirty minutes. Let me know if I can get you anything."

"We will. Thank you," Jana replied.

The airplane touched down at Fort Lauderdale Hollywood International Airport on time. It took three minutes to taxi to QuickJet's hangar area, where a black Lexus was standing by. The driver introduced himself, put his passengers' bags in the trunk, and opened the rear door for Jana. Alexander climbed into the other side of the SUV.

"You're going home, to your house?" the driver asked.

"Yes. The address is—"

The driver interrupted. "No worries. I have it."

The driver pulled into the condo which was located on the Intracoastal Waterway and a block from the Atlantic. He parked under the awning in front of the eight-story building. He jumped out, opened the door for Jana, then removed their bags from the trunk. She thanked him and handed him a hundred-dollar bill.

Jana had sold the house her ex owned in Coral Gables, a spectacular ten thousand square foot Mediterranean estate on a one-acre lot. The house, although beautiful, was too large for her and Rey. Seven bedrooms and eight bathrooms were too many. The house was also a reminder of a time she would rather forget.

When the house sold, Jana bought the small three-thousand-square-foot condominium in Fort Lauderdale. The condo, a south-facing corner unit with four bedrooms and four and a half baths, had breathtaking views from every room. Before being listed for sale, the unit had been completely remodeled. It was a turnkey home and exactly what she wanted. She loathed dealing with contractors and was happy to pay a three-thousand-dollar monthly maintenance fee to avoid ever having to talk to a roofer, HVAC, yard man, pool man, or any other contractor.

Jana entered her code into the keypad and led Alexander through the lobby to the elevators and up to the fourth floor. She stepped out of the elevator into a small foyer, unlocked the white French doors, and motioned for him to go in. He took a couple of steps, stopped, and looked around in awe. He ignored the living room on the right and the kitchen on the left and went straight to the large door leading to one of the three terraces. He turned and looked back at her.

"Wow. That's all I can say. Wow! This place is gorgeous. And the view. Wow."

"Thank you. I love it. The pool isn't private. There are sixteen units in the building, but it's not bad. I bought the condo exactly as you see it. All the furnishing came with it."

"This is amazing."

"It's not too feminine?"

"Too feminine? No." Alexander took another look around the unit. Jana gave him a gentle hug. "Thanks. Rey says it is. He doesn't like it that much. He also thinks it's too sterile. There's a lot of white. The walls, the shiny white tile on the floors, the kitchen, and most of the furniture."

Alexander looked into her eyes. The bright light coming through the large double glass doors constricted her pupils and highlighted the blueness of her irises. Jana stared back at Alexander. He wondered if she felt the same heart flutter as he had.

"Well, I love the place," he said, breaking eye contact by looking toward the kitchen.

Jana grinned slightly and bit her lower lip. "Thanks. What do we do now?"

He thought of a couple of things he'd like to do but suppressed the thoughts. "I'd like to go to the marina and take a look at the slip. Is it far?"

"Not at all. Give me a minute to change and we can go. Do you want to change? Let me show you to the guest room."

5

"We'll take my car," Jana said while she and Alexander waited for the elevator. She wore a blue backless halter neck tank top that exposed a bit too much of her small perky breasts, and a white pleated mini skirt. She'd pulled her blonde hair back into a ponytail.

Alexander took a deep breath and exhaled slowly, trying to avoid looking at the bare patch of skin between the thin straps of her halter top.

The elevator doors opened, and Jana pressed the button for the parking garage. Her parking spots were halfway up the ramp. When they got to her car, she unlocked the red Alfa Romeo 4C with her remote.

"I have a MINI Cooper and can squeeze in it semi-comfortably. This thing is about half the size of a MINI."

Jana laughed. "I didn't think about that. You're a big guy. How tall are you?"

"Six-four." He opened the car door and looked in. Not only would it be tight, the floorboard was barely five inches off the ground. He shook his head and eased himself into the seat. His shins hit the dashboard. Jana was in the driver's seat, trying to suppress a laugh.

"There's no way I can get my legs under the dash," he said, his knees resting against the car's glove box.

"We should take Rey's truck. I have the key."

Jana watched as Alexander tried to extricate himself from the front seat of the little Alfa Romeo. He eventually rolled out of the seat onto the driveway and crawled away from the car. Jana couldn't contain herself and burst out laughing. "That was one of the funniest things I've ever seen." She took a few seconds to catch her breath.

Alexander sat on the pavement. "You did that on purpose, didn't you? Just to see what would happen when I tried to get in the car. I should…"

Jana walked around and stuck her hand out to help the big man up. "You should what?" She grinned as she helped him to his feet.

Alexander smiled and shrugged. "I'll come up with something."

Jana smiled again, stepped up to him, and kissed him on the cheek. "I'm sure you will," she said. "Come on, the trucks up here."

The truck was a silver Ford F-150 STX Crew Cab. Jana unlocked the doors, and Alexander climbed in. "This is more like it."

"I thought it would be. Sorry about the Alfa. But we had a laugh and now we have a story to tell."

"We do. How far to the marina?"

"It's close. Only about a mile down A1A. We could walk. When Rey didn't come home, I walked and got his truck."

Traffic was light, and they didn't have to stop for any of the three signal lights between the condo and Bahia Mar Marina. The drive took less than five minutes. Jana turned the truck into the Bahia Mar DoubleTree Hotel. The attendant recognized her and motioned her in.

"Is there always a guard at the gate?" Alexander asked.

"I think so. He's always there when I come through."

"The same guy?"

"Maybe. I wave and he waves back. He seems to know me."

"We need to talk to him. It's been a few days, but maybe he saw something."

"The guard's here at the front. We keep the *Miss Jana* moored near the back of the marina. Slip F-18." Jana wheeled the big truck through the parking lot until she found a space near her pier. She turned the engine off and jumped out of the truck. Alexander scanned the parking lot and made a mental note of the number of vehicles and any that stood out. Rey's truck was the only anomaly. Most of the vehicles were high-end: Lexus, Porsche, Mercedes, and the like. He even noticed a couple of Bentleys. This wasn't the Bolivar Peninsula.

"This way," Jana said. She stuck her hand out toward him and the two walked together toward the pier. She stopped midway down the pier and pointed to an empty slip. "That's ours. That's where the *Miss Jana* should be." She let go of Alexander and covered her mouth with her hand.

Alexander put his arm around her and tenderly pulled her into his chest. Her cheek rested against his collarbone. After a few seconds, she pushed herself away and wiped her nose. "Thank you. I'm sorry, I guess seeing the empty slip again got to me."

"No need to apologize." Alexander turned and walked along the narrow pier between the slips. She followed. "The lines, are they always like that?"

Jana leaned over the pier and looked at the ropes dangling in the water. "Oh my God, no. Rey would never leave them like that. Those are spring lines. He'd remove them first and coil them on the dock." She raised her hand to cover her quivering chin.

"So, he left in a hurry or someone else took the boat out?"

Jana nodded, pulled Alexander close, put her lips close to his ear, and whispered, "When you hugged me earlier, I saw someone watching us from the boat two slips up the pier. Don't turn around, but he's still watching us."

Alexander put his hands on her bare shoulders. She felt nice, but he shook off any amorous feelings. "Is he still watching?"

Jana stretched higher on her tip-toes to look over him. He dropped one hand to her waist to help prop her up. Again, he shook off the feelings that were trying to distract him from his business at hand.

"I don't want to stare at him, but he seems to be watching us. I think it's a 'he.'"

Alexander put his other hand on her hip and pushed her away. "We should go introduce ourselves. Whoever it is might be able to answer a few questions."

Jana glanced toward the boat again but didn't see the person who had been watching them. "Let's go."

They walked down the pier to the boat where they had seen the person watching them.

"Ahoy the Serendipity," Alexander read the name of the boat off its bow. The boat was a wide-beamed center cockpit sloop. He estimated it to be sixty-five feet. When there was no response, he called out again. This time, a man stuck his head out of the open hatch.

"What can I do for you?" the man asked. He seemed to be tight-roping a fine line between suspicious and paranoid.

Jana spoke up. "I keep my boat in the slip over—"

"I've seen you before. I don't recognize the big guy."

"He's a private detective. He's helping me. My boat's missing."

"I noticed. It's been gone several days."

"It has. Did you see it leave? By the way, I'm Jana and this is Alex."

"Hi," the man said.

After a short but awkward pause, Alexander said, "Did you see the boat when it left?"

The man, who looked to be in his late thirties, balding, with several days of beard growth, dramatically squeezed his eyes closed, opened them, and said, "Couldn't say. Lately, that boat hadn't been out much. It used to go out all the time. I'm trying to remember if I saw it the last time it left."

Alexander said, "It would be a big help if you could remember."

The man glanced at Alexander and then at Jana. He stared at Jana longer than he should have. "I can check my cameras and let you know. Give me your phone number," he said, gesturing to Jana, "and I'll let you know what I find."

"Here's my card." Alexander handed the man his business card. "You have cameras? Do you have the video from when the boat left? Can we see it...I'm sorry I didn't catch your name."

"It's Ronald. I have video. And, no, you can't. I don't let anyone on my boat." The man glanced around the marina and the parking lot. "People are after me. I know too much."

Jana and Alexander exchanged looks, then Jana said, "The people after you, are those the people that took my boat?"

The man laughed. "No, whoever took your boat is probably small fry. Big-time bad people are after me. And not just one group."

"Tell me about it," Alexander said. "Maybe I can help."

"I doubt it. But one group is a bunch of skinheads, led by Adolf

Hitler's grandson."

Jana coughed and put her hand in front of her mouth to hide her laugh. Alexander kept a straight face.

"You know Hitler's grandson?"

"I do. I met him a few months back. I'm bald on top. I used to shave the sides, so I was completely bald. I was at the Galleria in Fort Lauderdale and these guys came up to me and said they had someone that wanted to meet me. I thought it was a little odd, but I went with them. We went to a corner of the mall where there weren't many people and they introduced me to this guy. He said his name was Carl. He said his mother was Hitler's daughter. The guy looked a lot like Hitler."

Alexander and Jana looked at each other in wonder. They didn't know how to respond. Alexander broke the silence. "So, why is he after you?"

"Because I had a shaved head. They thought I was a skinhead. They wanted me to join the Nazi Party. I refused. They weren't happy. The Freemasons are after me, too. I have to watch my back everywhere I go."

Again, Alexander and Jana exchanged another wide-eyed glance. Jana said, "Oh my God, that's terrible. You must always be on high alert."

"Let's say I'm prepared. I have dash cams in my car and close-circuit cameras on the boat."

"The cameras you have on your boat. Do any show the pier area around the *Miss Jana* or the boat itself?" Alexander asked.

"Um, no. And I don't let anyone on my boat," Ronald repeated.

"Rey and the boat are missing. It would be a big help if we could look at your video. They disappeared four days ago. How long do you keep the recordings?"

"I upload the video to the cloud. I never delete." He looked at Jana, paying particular interest to her exposed cleavage. His lascivious leer didn't go unnoticed by Jana or Alexander. Jana stepped to the edge of the pier and leaned on a stanchion, which gave Ronald a more vivid view of her breasts.

"It would be a big help if I could look at the videos," Jana said in a soft, slightly sexy voice.

"Maybe I can show you, but not today. I have top-secret projects laid out that I need to cover. Come back tomorrow, and I'll let you come onboard and see the video. But just you. I've seen you on your boat. I know you're okay. What day do you need?"

Jana squeezed her upper arms together against the sides of her breasts, forcing as much cleavage as possible from her thirty-two Bs. Ronald noticed. "Thank you. He left four days ago, late morning or early afternoon. Can we come by early tomorrow? We got a late start looking for him and time may be running out."

"How 'bout ten in the morning?"

"We'll be here."

Alexander said, "From the back of your boat, I'm going to take a few pictures of our slip, just to get a perspective of where it is in relation to the other boats and the parking lot. Do you mind?"

"No, that's fine. Just don't take any of my boat. Thanks for asking."

Alexander walked down the pier between the boats to the main pier. Using his cell phone, he took several pictures of the *Miss Jana*'s empty slip. He motioned to Jana he was ready to leave.

When they reached the parking lot, Jana asked, "Why did you take pictures of the slip? Is there anything useful there?"

"No, not particularly. I wanted to get the exact GPS coordinates of Ronald's boat. I'll send them to Bat. He should be able to hack this guy's cloud and download the videos."

Jana looked at him. Her eyebrows rose slightly. "That would be great. I don't want to go on his boat alone. He's creepy."

"He is. And he met Hitler's grandson? I'd like to hear more of that story."

"Personally, I'd rather not," she said tentatively.

"True. Mind if I ask a semi-personal question?"

"Not at all."

"Are the slip fees here expensive?"

Jana's head whipped around toward him at the question. "Yeah. They're quite expensive. Why?"

Alexander ignored the question. "And Ronald's sailboat. It's huge. I'm guessing it's expensive."

"I couldn't tell you exactly, but it's in the neighborhood of a million. Give or take a few thousand."

"Jiminy Christmas! How does that crazy bastard afford it?"

"I see what you're getting at. Rumor around the marina is his father is a billionaire and bought him the boat and pays for everything."

"Ah, that makes sense. Daddy buys him a yacht and sticks him in a marina where he's out of sight, out of mind."

"Sounds about right," Jana said, clicking the remote to unlock the truck.

Once inside the car, Alexander said, "I wanted to talk to the security guard on the way out, but I don't see the point if Ronald has video."

"So you want to wait and see the video?"

"Yeah. Plus, I did like those tacos we had for breakfast, but they didn't last. I'm getting hungry. How 'bout you?"

"Definitely. What are you in the mood for?"

"Anything but tacos."

Jana gave him a go-to-hell grin. "You like seafood? Steak? Fort Lauderdale has some great restaurants."

"As we left your condo, I noticed a Señor Frogs. That sounds interesting."

Jana laughed. "Hell no. That's a tourist trap and a meat market. I have a better idea."

6

While Jana drove, Alexander sent the pictures he took near Ronald's boat to Bat. A few seconds later, his cell phone rang. He put the phone on speaker. "Hi Bat. You got the pictures?"

"I did," Bat replied. "They're pictures of an empty slip. Are they supposed to be artistic?"

"Very funny. No. I was standing in front of a boat two slips down when I took the pictures. The owner of the boat is kinda strange—"

"Kinda?" Jana interrupted.

Alexander continued. "Okay, he's extremely strange."

"In what way?" Bat asked.

"Lots of ways. He seems paranoid. Won't let anyone on his boat. He says he met Hitler's grandson—"

"Adolf Hitler?"

"That's the one. He said the kid looked like Hitler. And now the Nazis are after him. Along with the Freemasons. I didn't catch why the Freemasons are after him."

"And you call me strange."

"Not anymore. Anyway, he has video cameras all over his boat. At least one, maybe more, point at the *Miss Jana*'s slip. He wouldn't show us the video, but said he might tomorrow. He stores all the videos on the cloud. I took the pictures I sent you standing next to his boat. Can you get the location from the picture's metadata and see if you can hack into his computer?"

"Should be easy. I'll get on it and get back to you shortly."

"Thanks." Alexander disconnected the phone. "Hopefully Bat will get the video and we won't have to pay Ronald another visit."

Jana turned the truck into the driveway of the Fort Lauderdale Weston and pulled up to the valet. Alexander looked at the hotel. His forehead furrowed.

"We'll park here. The restaurant is a block up A1A."

Alexander glanced at the hotel. "I didn't know why you were pulling in here. I thought you were going to drop me off and say good night."

Jana grinned. "No, I have a guest room for you." She hopped out of the truck and handed the keys to the valet. The young man in a black suit took the keys, admired Jana, then handed her a parking ticket. Alexander was waiting in front of the truck.

Jana took him by the arm and led him up the street. "The restaurant is the Casablanca Café. It's pretty cool. The house was the first home built on Fort Lauderdale Beach and is the oldest remaining structure. The food's good, and for this area, reasonable."

Alexander listened politely as she shared the history of the restaurant. His stomach was growling from hunger. Of everything she'd said, only, "The food's good," registered.

They arrived at four-thirty in the afternoon. Late for the lunch crowd and early for the dinner crowd. A few people, all of whom looked like tourists, sat sipping fruity drinks and snacking on boiled shrimp and calamari. Jana requested a table on the patio with a view of the ocean.

Jana opened the wine menu and glanced at it. "Are you a wine drinker?"

"On occasion."

"White or red?"

"How 'bout both? I'm in a surf and turf mood." Alexander wondered if she would take his request seriously.

"Maybe a sweet red? It'll go with both."

"Works for me. I knew you liked good scotch. I didn't know you were a wine connoisseur as well."

Jana shrugged. "I'm not. I prefer white. When I drink red, I like chilled."

"Blasphemy," Alexander retorted.

"In public, I try to be socially correct."

"Bullshit."

"What?" Jana's eyes widened with surprise.

"If I'm paying good money, I get what I want. I couldn't care less if the server or some biddy at the next table thinks I'm gauche."

"Wow. That's the most worked up I've seen you."

"I'm sorry. It's not a big deal. Was I that worked up?"

"You cussed. I've noticed you aren't a cusser. You're a positive influence on me."

The server approached their table. "Good afternoon. I'm Josh. I'll be your server tonight. Can I start you off with a cocktail, wine, or beer?"

"I'll have a chardonnay," Jana replied.

"Make it two," Alexander said. The server nodded and walked away.

"What happened to sweet red?"

"I prefer white. You convinced me."

"I'm an excellent influence," Alexander said with a wink.

"You are." Jana's smile broadened. She glanced at the menu. "What looks good to you?"

Alexander set down his menu. "Everything. But I'm going with the grilled New York Strip. The Blackened Florida Grouper looks interesting. I was in a surf and turf mood, but I think I'll just have steak. What about you?"

"I'm going with the yellow tail snapper...since I ordered white wine." Jana laughed.

The server brought two glasses of chardonnay and set them on the table. Alexander gently swirled his glass, smelled the aroma, and took a sip. "This isn't bad."

"It's not. Their house wine is decent," Jana replied.

Alexander stared at the glass of wine for a few seconds, then looked at Jana. "If you don't want to talk about it, that's fine, but I know little about you. I know you put up a lot of money to create a shelter for trafficked and abused women, and you flew me here in a private jet. If I remember correctly, your husband died, and you inherited some money. That's what I heard, 'some money.' Again, it's none of my business, but obviously, it was a large sum of money."

"You don't think I could have made the money on my own? Is that what you're saying?" Jana's bright blue eyes stared at Alexander.

"Oh, hell no. That's not what I meant. I'm sorry if it sounded like that. I—"

"You know, you're cute when you blush." She smirked at her dinner companion. "I'm sorry, I couldn't resist. Yes, I inherited a large sum of money. There's no way I could have made that on my own. My ex was a lawyer. He walked a fine line between legal and illegal. He made a shit-ton of money. When he died, it came to me."

"That's nice. I'm sorry for your loss."

"Don't be. I had left him. It's a long story."

The server returned to the table with the entrees. After setting them on the table, he asked if they needed anything. Jana ordered two more glasses of wine.

"What about you, Alex? What's your story?"

"There's not much of a story. I went to the University of Houston and joined the FBI right out of college. Most of my time with the Bureau was in Phoenix, with a couple of years in DC. I put in my twenty years and retired."

"You're right, that's not much of a story. There has to be more to it. That's a decent beach house you live in. You can afford that after twenty years?"

"Like you, I inherited a little money. My dad saved and invested all his life. Most of his investments turned out to be very good. He died unexpectedly and his estate came to me. I'm an only child and my mother passed away when I was young."

Jana patted his hand.

"It's fine. It's been a few years since Dad died," Alexander said, his voice cracking ever so slightly. He took a sip of wine and asked, "Are you from Florida?"

"No. I grew up in San Antonio. I went to UT for two years, but college wasn't my thing. A girlfriend felt the same as me and suggested we go to Florida. We ended up in South Beach. We had no money, so we got jobs in a strip club. The first club we worked at was a dive. As we learned the tricks of the trade, so to speak, we moved to the nicer clubs, the 'gentlemen's clubs,' if you want to call them that. That's where I met Robert, my ex. He begged me to go out with him and I finally did. He begged me to marry him and I did. For a while, it was great. Then he started treating me like shit. I was his trophy wife...that he wanted to share with other girls—"

"I got the picture. You don't need to go on."

Jana flashed him a smile. "It's fine. Like you, it's been a while."

"Well, hasn't this been a fun and stimulating dinner conversation? I didn't even get to tell you about my wonderful love life."

Jana laughed. "Next meal. Your love life. I can't wait."

"You'll be disappointed."

The server refilled the water glasses. "Can I get you anything? Dessert?" he asked.

Jana looked at Alexander. "Key lime pie?"

"Is it made with Key limes or Persian limes?"

The server cocked his head and stared at Alexander. "Uh...it's Key lime pie, so Key limes?"

"Why don't we wait and have dessert another time? I'm pretty full," Alexander said.

"I am too," Jana agreed. "Just the check, please."

A few minutes later, the server returned and left the check. Alexander reached for the check, but Jana stopped him. "I've got it."

"Are you sure?"

"Yes. I'd let you pay, but you'll add ten percent and bill me. I assume you're charging me a daily rate plus expenses. We never discussed your fee."

"I don't charge friends. So far, I've had no expenses. You're good."

Jana lightly bit her lower lip. "You consider us close enough friends that you're not going to charge me for your service? We've only known each other for a little more than twenty-four hours."

"That's true, I haven't known you long. Mayte talks about you and what you did for those girls we rescued. I feel like I've known you for a while."

"That's sweet, but I still feel like I should pay you."

Alexander glanced around the restaurant. "Tell you what. If I ever need cash, I'll send you a bill."

"It's a deal. Are you ready?"

"Yeppers."

The restaurant had become crowded. As Jana walked toward the door, she got more than her fair share of admiring glances. Her tank top helped considerably.

In Alexander's eyes, Bonita was the most beautiful woman he'd ever seen. She was tall, nearly six feet, with high cheekbones and full, firm cheeks, a sharp jawline, and a well-defined chin. Her eyes were large, wide, and dark—almost black. She was quite well-endowed. He thought Jana was as beautiful. At five feet ten inches, she was shorter than Bonita and had much smaller breasts. Her eyes were as blue as the Caribbean, set off by shoulder-length blonde hair. Her facial features were softer than Bonita's. Her nose was slimmer and more pointed. When Jana's lips were at rest, small creases formed in the corners of her mouth. Even the slightest smile turned the creases into large smile lines. They looked like parentheses bracketing her mouth. Both women had sacral dimples on their lower backs—a feature Alexander found extremely sexy.

Alexander held the door open for Jana. He took a last glance at the people looking at her. When he was out with Bonita, men would stare at her, but this was Fort Lauderdale. There were more beautiful women in South Florida than teens at a Taylor Swift concert. When he closed the door and followed Jana to the sidewalk, he couldn't help but glance at the dimples in her lower back, peaking out above the white skirt.

It took two hurried steps for Alexander to catch up with her. They strolled back to the hotel where they'd left her truck without speaking. The sight of the Atlantic engrossed Alexander. The setting sun cast a golden glow across the sky that reflected on the ocean, creating a dark blue that looked like an oil painting. He was still staring when they reached the valet stand.

"It's beautiful, isn't it?" Jana asked.

"It is. In the evening, the Gulf of Mexico looks blue. But nothing like this."

"We still have a little time. Wait until you see it from the apartment."

It only took five minutes to get from the hotel to Jana's parking garage. They took the elevator to the fourth floor. "See," Jana said, "the sun hasn't set yet. I'll get wine and meet you on the patio."

Jana's condo had two porches, both with large sliding glass doors. He didn't know which patio to go to, so he stood between them and waited.

"This one," Jana said, pointing to the door facing west. When they stepped outside, she handed him a glass, put her arm around his waist, leaned into him, and rested her head on his shoulder. "Do you like?"

7

Jana came from the bedroom wearing a cream-colored, waffled pajama top and loose-fitting poplin shorts. "You surprised me," she said to Alexander who was sitting at the kitchen table. "I didn't expect you up this early."

"I'm an early riser and we didn't go to bed late last night. It had been a long day. I hope you don't mind, I made a pot of coffee. A walk along the beach sounded good, but I realized I didn't know the code for the main doors and I couldn't remember your last name. I'd be stuck outside until you got up, and I didn't know if you were a late sleeper."

"I'm glad you made coffee," Jana said and poured herself a cup. "My last name is Wilson. It's my married name, and I kept it. With Robert dead, there was no reason to change it back to my maiden name. Oh, and the code to get in, in case you ever need it, is two-one-zero-two-one-zero. It was my area code when I lived in San Antonio, doubled."

"Got it. I shouldn't need it, but it's nice to have. And I apologize for not remembering your last name. I'm usually good with names."

"No problem," Jana said. She gestured to him scrolling on his phone. "What's up?"

"It's not good news. I got a text from Bat at three o'clock this morning. He said he found Ronald's boat and searched for Wi-Fi coming from it. There were two strong signals. Both have robust encryptions, way beyond the normal encryption for Wi-Fi. He said he can hack it, but it'll take a while."

Jana's shoulders slumped. She cradled her coffee cup with both hands. "I guess that means we pay him another visit."

Alexander nodded. "If we, and by we, I mean you, are going to get a look at his video, going to him is the quickest way. Time is of the essence."

"I agree, but will he let me see the video?"

"Judging by the way he was looking at you yesterday, he will."

"I hope I don't have to blow him to see it."

"What?" Alexander's eyes bulged.

"I'm kidding," Jana said. Alexander wondered if she was.

"Speaking of going down," Alexander said, "you know sailboats have steep stairs going into the cabin. If you wear a skirt like you did yesterday, either going up or down the steps, Ronald will be below you looking up. Shorts or long pants might be a better wardrobe choice."

A slight smile came to Jana's lips. "What a clever segue, especially this early in the morning."

"I've already had a cup of coffee."

"Right. Anyway, if I wear a short skirt, I won't have any trouble getting on the boat."

"But do you want to do that?"

"Alex, I was a stripper. It's not a big deal. I may even wear a G-string–give him a thrill. It beats giving him a—"

"You're right about that," Alexander interrupted.

"When do you want to go?" Jana asked.

"He said to come by at ten. If we get there early, he might be cranky."

Jana sipped her coffee and said, "We don't want that. Maybe we should go to breakfast, then pay him a visit."

"Works for me. I'll get dressed."

"Me too. Give me twenty minutes to get pretty."

"You're beautiful. You don't need two minutes." The words were out of his mouth before he realized what he had said. Jana took it in stride. She was used to being complimented.

"Awe, you're sweet," Jana replied. "Give me twenty minutes."

It took Alexander five minutes to brush his teeth, comb his hair, and put on socks and shoes. He was waiting for her when she came out fifteen minutes later. His heart jumped when he saw her. She wore a pink lace-trimmed crop top and a black miniskirt with a slit running up one leg.

"How do I look?" she asked.

Alexander made a soft whistling sound. "Amazing."

Jana lifted the skirt, exposing a small patch of material covering her pubic area. She spun, still holding the skirt up, exposing her bare butt.

"What the hell, Jana?"

"Relax, Alex, it's a bikini bottom. I wear it to the beach all the time."

"Maybe so, but this ain't the beach, darlin'. And I wasn't expecting you to flash me. You could've given me a heart attack. Or something else."

"I'm sorry. I'll warn you the next time I flash my ass at you."

"That would be nice."

"Warning or flashing?"

Alexander's face turned a slight pink. "I'd say both, but I don't think you should be flashing me at all."

"You're right, I probably shouldn't. It wasn't appropriate. You blush easily, don't you?"

Alexander turned redder. "Do I? It seems you have that effect on me. I'll admit, if you have the same effect on Ronald, you'll get the video."

"That's the point," Jana said. "Shall we go?"

***

Jana and Alexander enjoyed a leisurely breakfast at a local pancake house. The food was good, and the coffee was strong. When they finished one last cup of coffee, they decided it was time to visit the man who knew Hitler's grandson.

It didn't take long to get to Bahia Mar. Ronald was sitting in the cockpit of his boat when Alexander and Jana approached. He stood and walked to the starboard lifeline to greet them.

"Good morning." Jana flashed a wide, toothy smile.

Ronald didn't seem to notice her smile. He was too busy checking her out. "Morning," he replied. "I guess you want to see the video."

"We'd appreciate it," Jana replied.

"I went through the archives and I found the date you mentioned.

Three guys showed up at your boat that morning and about an hour later, the boat left with them still on it. It hasn't been back since. Follow me and I'll show you."

Ronald held out his hand to help her over the lifeline. She took his hand, lifted one leg, then the other over the plastic-coated wire. He went down the companionway and waited. Jana turned and backed down the narrow ladder. She moved slowly, allowing the perv a long look. When she was halfway down, Ronald grabbed her waist. "Be careful," he said.

Jana reached the bottom of the steps and turned around. Ronald kept a tight grip on her as she spun, he grasped her breast. She wanted to knee him in the groin but smiled and pushed him away. It had been a long time since she got paid to let men grope her.

It took a few seconds for Jana to acclimate to the dark interior of the sailboat. When she could see, several assault-style rifles, pistols, and what looked like large pistols with long magazines, all mounted on the sides and bulkhead of the boat, came into view. The hair stood up on her arms.

"Over here," Ronald said. He grabbed her by the arm and pulled her close. "Here's the first video. Three guys are walking down the pier and they stop at your boat."

Jana squinted, but couldn't make out the men's faces. Ronald reached for his mouse and slid his arm along her chest as he did so. He clicked the mouse twice and a video of the men standing on the aft deck of the *Miss Jana* began.

"Can't you zoom in a little?" Jana asked.

Ronald moved the mouse around the screen, brushing up against her breasts with each move. "Here ya go."

"Oh my God," Jana said. "I know one of those guys." She held up her phone to take a picture of the screen, but he pushed her hand down.

"What are you doing?"

"I need to get a picture of that guy."

"Um, I don't know if I want you doing that."

Jana spun and glared at him. "Look, you little fucker. I let you look at my ass when I came down the steps. You've done nothing but try to feel my tits since I got here. My boyfriend is missing and I need a picture of the guys who are with him. I'm taking pictures of the video and you're going to give me a copy of the whole video or I'm going to scream and the detective with me will be here before you can get close to a gun and he will beat the shit out of you."

"Whoa, babe, calm down," he said, noticeably shaken. "I'm sorry. I don't get much female companionship."

"That's because you're a fucking pervert. And don't call me 'babe.'" She snapped several pictures of the zoomed image and stepped back. "Put all the videos on a thumb drive."

Ronald fumbled through a drawer and found a thumb drive. He inserted it into the computer and, a few minutes later, ejected the drive and handed it to her.

"Thank you," she said. "Let's go. You go first."

Ronald obliged and went up the companionway first. Jana followed, quickly stepping out of the cockpit and off the boat.

On the pier, she gave Alexander a thumbs-up and said, "Got it. Let's go."

Alexander turned to Ronald. "Thanks."

"Fuck him," Jana said, walking away.

"Damn! What happened down there?" Alexander had to hurry to catch up to her.

Jana's face was red. A vein bulged from the side of her neck. "The little fucking pervert looked at my ass as I came down the ladder, just as we thought he would. Then he spent the whole time trying to feel my boobs. He showed me the video, and I recognized one guy. I wanted to take a picture, and he said I couldn't. I knew he wanted something from me to let me take the picture, and I kinda lost it. I called him a fucking pervert and told him if he didn't let me take a picture and give us a copy of the video, I'd scream and you'd come kick his ass. That worked."

"Had you screamed, I would've been there in an instant. I'm glad it didn't come to that."

"Me too. Guns were hanging from every wall of his boat. You could've gotten to him before he got to a gun, especially with me pounding on him, but it would have been risky."

"Geez, he must be paranoid. And a little creepy."

"More than a little creepy."

"Would you have pounded on him?"

"Hell yeah. I've been working out and training at Miggie's. Miggie is Rey's brother. He owns a gym and teaches martial arts. I could've beat the shit out of Ronald myself, but I thought he'd feel more threatened by you." The red faded from Jana's face. Her breathing normalized.

Back on the boat, Ronald hopped down the companionway, yanked an AR-15 from the wall, and confirmed one bullet from the thirty-round magazine was chambered. He climbed the first three steps of the companionway and rested his elbow on the deck of the boat. He drew a bead on the small of Jana's back. "I'll teach you to call me a pervert, you whore." He placed his finger on the trigger.

Jana stepped in front of Alexander, took a martial arts stance, and kicked her leg in the air, showing him the moves Miggie had taught her.

Ronald lifted his finger off the trigger and watched. Alexander was between him and his target. When Jana stepped to the side of Alexander, Ronald put the crosshairs of the AR's scope between Jana's shoulder blades. He rested his finger on the trigger for several seconds before removing it completely. "You aren't worth it, bitch," he said to himself before slipping back into the cabin of his sailboat.

Alexander and Jana got in the pickup. "You said you recognized someone from the video?"

Jana started the truck and pulled out of the parking lot. "I did. It was Cole. He's a friend of Miggie. He and another guy saved me when I was being held and then they, shall we say, disposed of Rafael, the guy who was holding me hostage." Jana turned right onto A1A instead of left toward her condo.

"Where are we going?"

"We need to talk to Miggie."

<h1 style="text-align:center">8</h1>

Jana drove the pickup truck, weaving in and out of traffic without signaling, accelerating rapidly, then braking hard. With every delay, she pounded the steering wheel with her fist. Alexander held on to the grab handle on the passenger's side of the truck with a death grip and braced himself for the sudden stops.

After one intense braking at a red light, he asked, "Do you have a spatula?"

Jana glanced at him. "What?"

"Do you have a spatula? After that last stop, I need to scrape my face off the windshield."

Jana giggled. The light changed, and she stomped the accelerator. The 5.0-liter V8 engine roared. She laughed again. Loosening her grip on the steering wheel, she let off the gas and slowed to the speed limit. "A spatula. That was funny."

"Thanks for slowing down a little." Alexander released his grip on the grab handle.

"I'm sorry. I'm pissed because Miggie knows where Rey is and he didn't tell me."

"What makes you think Miggie knows where Rey is?"

"Cole is a Mixed Martial Arts fighter. He works out at Miggie's. They know each other, but they aren't close friends. Cole doesn't know Rey well at all. They see each other at the gym occasionally, but they've never hung out or anything. Miggie, Cole, and one of Cole's MMA friends rescued me when Rafael kidnapped me. They robbed Rafael and then kidnapped me. They wore masks, and I didn't know Cole or his friend JP. I thought I was in worse trouble than I was with Rafael, who was a sex trafficker."

"So, you could say you, or Rey, owe Cole?"

Jana stared at the road ahead. She slumped back in her seat and lowered her hands on the steering wheel. "I'd say I owe them my life. He, Miggie, and JP. Rafael told me he was going to rape me. I'm ninety-nine percent certain he planned on killing me." She turned to face Alexander. "Could that be how they got Rey to do whatever he's doing?"

"I'd bet on it."

"But why didn't Rey tell me what was going on?"

"My guess is he wanted to protect you. Maybe he thought he was only going to be gone overnight or at most, a day or two. He knew you'd be worried, but figured it was only for a couple of days."

"Sounds like Rey. If it's illegal or dangerous, or both, he wouldn't tell me."

Jana moved her hands to the ten and two o'clock positions on the wheel. Her shoulders relaxed. Several miles later she said, "I get it. But this has been a crazy few days, and I still don't know if Rey's dead or alive. He should have told me. Someone should have told me. If he's alive, he should let me know. Even if it's just an occasional text. He should let me know."

"You're right. But what if he told you what he was doing and that it could be dangerous, and then, if he couldn't call or text you, you would be even more worried?"

"Maybe. I guess there's no right way to do whatever fucked up shit he's messed up in."

"Eloquently put," Alexander said.

Jana gave him the side-eye. "Funny. I definitely fell off the no-cuss wagon today. It was that fucker Ronald's fault. I was a stripper. I'm used to guys looking at me and touching me, but it was always on my terms. I planned to let him check out my ass. That's why I wore a bikini bottom. Granted, it was a thong and didn't cover any of my ass, but it was my choice. When he kept rubbing against my boobs, I lost it. On top of that, I saw Cole in the video. I knew something was afoot. Rey didn't get hijacked or kidnapped or shanghaied. He knew what he was doing."

"If you want my opinion, you're handling yourself quite well. It's been a crazy morning."

"And it's about to get crazier." Jana turned the F-150 into the gym parking lot.

Miguel Cruz's gym, aptly named "Miggie's," occupied three retail spaces at the end of a strip center in Hallandale Beach. Known for its high cost of living, casinos, and crime, Hallandale Beach is located halfway between Ft. Lauderdale and Miami, with Hollywood to the north, the Atlantic Ocean to the east, and Pembroke Park to the west.

Jana parked the truck and turned the engine off. She sat, staring at the sign on top of the building.

"Are you up to this?" Alexander asked. "I could go in and talk to him."

"No. I mean, yes, I'm up to it. I have to do this."

"Take a few deep breaths and try to stay calm. Miggie's been hiding something from you, but he's probably as worried as you are. And he may blame himself. Tread lightly."

Jana nodded and got out of the truck. When they got to the double glass and steel doors, she paused, took a deep breath, and pulled the door open. Rows of free weights and machines lined the front of the gym with mirrors running the length of the interior. Five treadmills faced the front windows. Only one was in use. Set up for martial arts training, floor mats, and a makeshift ring filled a quarter of the gym. Against the back wall, six heavy bags hung from the ceiling.

An extremely muscular man with bleached blonde hair and a green tank top was doing curls with the free weights. Another muscular man, bald, with no shirt, and covered in tattoos, was looking at himself in the mirror. Jana caught the man's attention, and he watched her in the mirror as she walked to the unmarked door in the rear corner of the gym.

"This is Miggie's office." Jana tapped on the door.

"Come," said a deep voice from within the room.

Jana opened the door and walked in, surprising Miggie. After an awkward hesitation, he jumped from his chair and hugged her. As he hugged her, he studied the man who was with her. He was six inches taller, at least ten or fifteen years older, and big, muscular, but not thick. Not gym muscular.

Jana pushed out of his arms. "Miggie, where's Rey?"

"What do you mean, where is he?" Miggie was not a good liar, nor did he have a poker face.

"Don't fuck with me, Miggie. I'm not in the mood. I know Cole and Rey took off in the *Miss Jana* four days ago and I haven't heard from him since. I don't know if he's dead or alive. Where in the hell is he?"

"Okay, okay. I'll tell you what I know. But it's not much. Rey wouldn't tell me much. He said it was for my own good. And he said not to tell you anything."

"Well, that ship has sailed. Tell me what you know."

Alexander lightly bit the tip of his tongue to keep from grinning. He was sure the pun was unintentional.

Miggie rubbed his chin. His eyes darted around the small office to avoid eye contact with Jana. He motioned to a couple of old wooden chairs and turned his attention to Alexander.

"This is my friend Alex Christian. He's a private investigator," Jana said.

Miggie leaned forward and shook Alexander's hand. "Nice to meet you. You found out Cole was involved?"

"Jana did most of the legwork. I just pointed her in the right direction."

"I'm curious. What direction was that?"

"The nutcase in the boat two slips over from the *Miss Jana*. He has the entire marina under surveillance."

Jana had become fidgety in her chair. She slapped her hand on the desk between her and Miggie. "Enough of the fucking chit-chat. Where's Rey?"

Miggie finally looked at Jana and addressed her with a soft voice. "Jana, I don't know. And that's the God's truth."

"What do you know?"

"Nothing. Rey called me as they were leaving the marina. He said he thought they were heading south. Way south, like maybe the ABC islands or South America, Venezuela, or Colombia."

Jana pounded the table. "South America? What the fuck? Why the hell would they be going there?"

"Like I said, he didn't tell me why." Miggie leaned back in his chair and ran his fingers through his hair.

"Cole was with him. At the boat when they left. What's it all about?" Jana asked.

Miggie hemmed and hawed and finally said, "I don't know the details, but from what I understand, Cole has a gambling problem. He started gambling a few months back and won big the first time or two. After that, he's been losing. Losing a lot. He bet on football, the horses, slots, blackjack, whatever. He got into shady poker games and lost big. Like a couple hundred thousand, give or take a few grand."

"Jesus," Jana said.

"Uh-huh. When he got that far behind, the people he owed said they had a way for him to clear his debt."

"Here we go," Jana said.

"It turns out they needed a boat. A big boat. One that could make an ocean crossing."

Jana closed her eyes and leaned back in the chair. "Oh no. Not again. Are they trafficking young girls?"

"I doubt it, but I don't know for sure."

"Why in the hell would Rey agree to do it? Why didn't Cole ask me for the money? He was with you when you saved my life. I'd have given him money."

Alexander shook his head. "They didn't want money. They wanted the boat. And they know who you are. They may have told Rey if he didn't cooperate, something would happen to you. I'm only guessing, but knowing Rey, that's about the only way they'd get him to go along."

The muscles in Jana's jaws flexed. "You know, I'm really tired of that bullshit. I'm going to tell Rey if anyone ever threatens me to get him to do something, tell them to go fuck themselves. Don't do it."

"He would never do that, you know that," Miggie said.

"I know, but there has to be a way to keep this from happening."

Alexander laid his hand on her arm. "Let's cross that bridge when we get to it. What's happened has happened. We need to find Rey."

"Do you?" Miggie asked. "I kinda assumed when they did whatever they set out to do, they'd come back."

"Do you know who 'they' are?" Alexander asked.

"No. My guess is gangster or mob-type guys. Not big-time players. If they were, they wouldn't need to go through all the trouble to get Rey and the *Miss Jana*. They would've taken Cole out and dumped him."

Alexander agreed. "It almost sounds like they knew Cole had a connection with someone with a boat like they needed and set him up to lose. When he couldn't pay, they made a deal. It sounds very small-time to me."

"Is that good or bad?" Jana asked.

"I'd say good. There probably aren't many of them. That they're watching us is concerning. Not all the time, but enough to track you. There's a good chance they've seen me, so they may know we are digging around. The way you drove over here, I doubt anyone followed us. But there is bad news. If they're small time, they won't want any loose ends. Unless they scared the crap out of Rey and Cole, there's nothing to keep them from going to the cops when they return."

Jana and Miggie looked at one another. Their faces had turned pale. Alexander's scenario was one they hadn't considered.

"So, we need to find them," Miggie said.

"We do. But let me handle it. I know it's not likely, but if you hear from Rey, let us know. Don't tell him Jana knows what's going on. Don't tell him about me. We don't want him doing anything rash."

"Alex?" Jana said, "Why don't we go back to your beach house? Nobody could follow us there unless they had a private jet. They could figure out where we went by checking the flight manifest, but they would never find us in Bolivar. Then, if Miggie hears from Rey, he could let him know I'm safe. Cole is a beast. Rey's no slouch. There are only two guys on the boat with them. I gotta believe the only reason they haven't killed the two guys is they're worried about me."

"I agree," said Miggie.

"But what if they meet up with more guys wherever they are? It wouldn't be that easy. We don't know how many there are or how many are still here. If the people that are still here don't hear from the others, they'll know something's wrong and they'll be waiting for Rey and Cole when they return to Bahia Mar."

"Damn...I didn't think it all the way through," Jana said.

Alexander leaned forward. "And, depending on who those people are, if you run, you might be looking over your shoulder for the rest of your life. You don't want that."

"No, you're right. So, what'll we do?" Jana asked.

"We need to figure out where they went, or where they're going. When we find that out, I'll go there and see what I can find."

"We'll go," Jana and Miggie said simultaneously.

"They likely know you two. I should go alone."

Miggie agreed, albeit reluctantly. Jana shook her head and stood.

"I'm going," she said. "And I won't take no for an answer. I can help. I need to go."

Alexander ran his hand through his hair. "Let's find him first."

9

When they climbed into the truck, Alexander shook his head. "That's not what I wanted to hear. Rey and the boat could be anywhere in the Caribbean. Do you know the boat's cruising range? Since it made it from Florida to Texas several times, it must be huge."

"Topped off. Over thirty-three hundred nautical miles."

"What's that in regular miles?"

"I'd have to do the conversion, but around thirty-eight hundred miles. In the Caribbean, depending on which direction you're going, there's a fuel dock every hundred and fifty miles, give or take fifty. Rey only kept about five hundred gallons in the tanks. Diesel goes bad. Unless we were taking an extended cruise, he'd keep enough fuel onboard for a quick trip up the Intracoastal or to West Palm, or maybe Miami. That way, he always had fresh fuel."

"Which means they'd have had to stop and refuel before they got too far."

"They would. Does that help us?"

"Not really. We could jump on your jet and check every marina on every island within, say, a hundred and fifty miles of Fort Lauderdale to see if anyone remembers a big trawler getting fuel in the past four or five days."

"That doesn't sound feasible."

"Nope. Even if we got lucky and found out where they got fuel, it wouldn't tell us where they're going."

Jana slowed when they approached the drawbridge over the Intracoastal Waterway. "So, what do we do now?"

"We wait. And hope for a break. When they get to a spot with cell service, I'm hoping Rey will text or call Miggie, or you, and say where he is and what he's up to."

Jana eased into the right lane, crossed the bridge, and merged onto A1A. Alexander looked past her at the Atlantic on his left. "We're going south. Didn't we go south to get here?"

"We are. And we did. Since there isn't much we can do I thought I'd show you a little of the area and we'd get lunch."

Jana followed A1A over Haulover Inlet, past Bal Harbour, and into Surfside. After showing Alexander a few of the South Florida highlights, she pulled the pickup into a large, open parking spot. "This is Flanigan's. It's kind of a chain restaurant, but it's laid-back with good food."

"Sounds like my kind of place."

"Do you want to sit outside?" Jana asked.

Alexander looked at the building. A typical storefront in a lengthy line of storefronts. Green awnings hung over tables that sat in front of large windows. He looked up and down A1A. The street was three lanes of one-way traffic with parking on both sides.

"Honestly, it's a nice day, but I prefer to eat my meals without carbon monoxide. Let's eat inside."

Jana glanced at the amount of traffic on the road in front of the restaurant. "You're right. We'll go inside."

The restaurant wasn't busy. The host promptly seated them. While they ate, they rehashed the morning. Alexander decided he needed more information on Miggie, Cole, and JP. When they had finished their meal, the server brought the bill and Jana handed her a credit card.

Jana said, "Are you sure there's nothing else we can do, Alex? It's only been a few days, but it seems like I've been doing nothing but waiting forever. I'm tired of it."

The server returned with the check. Jana signed the receipt and closed the order book.

"There's one thing we could be doing. I'll tell you about it in the truck. You ready to go?"

Jana took a drink of water and set the glass on the table. "Ready."

Alexander nodded, and they walked back to the truck. When both were in, he said, "We need to put a little pressure on Miggie. He might know more than he's letting on. If we don't get anywhere, try Cole's friend. JP, wasn't it?"

"Yes. He goes by JP. I don't know his real name."

"Does Miggie?"

"Probably. But what you said about putting pressure on Miggie? Wasn't he telling the truth? I doubt he knows any more than he already told us. If he knows anything more at all."

"Maybe he doesn't. I'd like to talk to that JP guy. He and Cole were good friends, right?"

"They were. Are."

"He may know the people behind this. Cole had been losing money for a while. He may have told JP where he was gambling or who he was with. If we could find them, they could tell us where Rey is."

"Would they tell us?"

"With a little persuasion. At least we might find out what we're up against."

"I like that idea. I'll call Miggie and get JP's number."

"See if you can find out where he lives. Or when he's at the gym. I'd like to talk to him in person."

Jana made a left turn, then another left, and headed north on A1A. When she crossed over Haulover Inlet, she turned into Haulover Beach Park and parked in a lot near the beach. She pulled out her phone, opened the Contacts app, and pressed Miggie's number. He answered on the second ring.

"Hi, Jana."

"Have you heard from Rey?" Jana asked.

"No. Not that I'm expecting to."

"I know, I was hoping. The reason I'm calling is we, well Alex, would like to talk to JP. Do you have his number? Better yet, where we can find him?"

"I'll have to look up his number and address and send it to you. He used to come into the gym four or five times a week, but I haven't seen him in a while."

"He hasn't been around? Is he mixed up in this, too?"

"Not likely. I remember him saying he had a fight coming up. He might be training for it somewhere else, or it could be an out-of-town fight."

"Hmm. Okay. Send us what you have and we'll decide what to do."

"I will, but be careful. Cole's a nice guy. JP is a loose cannon. He can be cold-blooded. Remember what they did to Rafael. They're trained killers. Your friend Alex is a big dude, but he doesn't want to tangle with JP."

"We will. Thanks. Talk to you later."

Jana hung up the phone. "Miggie thinks JP is training for a fight and could be out of town. He'll send us his address and phone number shortly."

"Damn," Alex said. "We're back to waiting."

"I guess so. Do you want to take a walk along the beach?"

"A walk and fresh air will be nice."

The two followed the paved trail from the parking lot to the edge of the beach. Jana stopped, put her hand on Alexander's shoulder to steady herself, lifted a leg, and pulled her shoe off. She switched hands and pulled her other shoe off. Alexander used one foot to kick one size fourteen tan boat shoe off and then the other. They picked up their shoes and walked toward the shoreline.

The Atlantic was calm. Other than shore break, waves were negligible. As they walked along the edge of the shore, sea foam occasionally lapped over their feet. Terns and sandpipers darted in and out of the shallow water. Larger egrets and herons drifted with the breeze above the ocean, occasionally diving into the water for a meal. Various seagulls drifted above beachgoers, looking for a handout.

"This is nice," Alexander said. "Other than the white sand, blue water, and high-rise buildings, it's not much different from Bolivar."

Jana laughed. "Property values are about the same too, huh?"

It was Alexander's turn to laugh. "Almost exactly the same." He pointed toward a large blue building in the distance. "Is that a hotel?"

"No. That's the Ritz-Carlton Residences. The two buildings behind it are the Trump Towers."

"Trump Towers? He hasn't lost those?"

"I don't think he ever owned them. I read that an investment company owns them. They just have his name on them."

"Interesting. The other building, The Ritz-Carlton, those are condos?"

"They are. Nice too."

"Any idea what they sell for?"

"I do. I looked at a unit there. The building has fifty-two stories. That's too big for me. They have everything from studio apartments to five-bedroom units. I was looking for a two bed, two bath unit. They were in the neighborhood of three to four million. Most units were around two thousand dollars a square foot."

Alexander let out a hoot. "The nicer beachfront houses on Bolivar go for about five hundred a square foot. When you get off the beach a few rows, they drop to around three fifty a foot."

"Three fifty's not peanuts. You made it sound like it was the slums. I know that's not the case. I love your house. Except for that monstrosity of a house that sits between you and the beach."

Alexander stopped in his tracks and squinted at the large green sign rising from the sand in the middle of the beach. "Are you kidding me? 'Attention. Clothing optional beach beyond this point.'"

"That's Haulover Beach. It's clothing optional, as the sign says. Does that bother you?"

"No, I guess not. I've never been to a nude beach."

"Do you want to keep walking?"

"And get naked?"

"You don't have to. It's clothing optional. Normally, if you walked through the area dressed like you are now, people would look at you like you were a perv. But, remember, I'm wearing a thong under my skirt. I can take my skirt and top off and we'd walk together. It'd be okay."

"Ha. If you took off your skirt and top and walked down the beach, no one would notice me."

Alexander glanced at her pink top. A row of lace trimmed the upper hem. She wasn't wearing a bra and the thin top left little to the imagination. She grabbed the bottom of her top and lifted it.

"Don't," Alexander said, pulling her hands away from her top. "You shouldn't."

"No? It's not a big deal."

"I'd rather you didn't. Let's say it's not the time or place. We should head back to the truck. We walked a long way."

"Okies." She looked at Alexander and flashed a smile, but he was looking at a brown and white bird with orange eyes, a vivid red-orange bill, and pink legs walking along the water's edge.

Alexander pointed at the bird. "That's an oystercatcher."

"It's cute," Jana replied.

"Had we kept walking up the beach, we would have likely seen a tufted titmouse. Or maybe a double-breasted swallow."

Jana jerked her head and frowned. "What?"

"What?"

"Did you make those names up?"

"One. The other's an actual bird."

Jana glanced up at Alexander. Before she could comment, her phone buzzed. "It's Miggie," she said, looking at the screen. "He sent JP's number and home address. Should I call him?"

"Hang on a sec," Alexander replied. He took out his phone and called Bat.

"Bat, how long does it take you to do whatever you do to find the location of a phone?"

"You mean a phone that's active?"

"Yes."

"Not long. I've got a nifty little app that I enter the phone number into and it tells me everything."

"I've got a number for you." Alexander read him JP's number from Jana's phone. "It would be nice to know about where he is. Whether he's in town or not would be a help."

"I can do that. As long as the phone is on, I can get you a general area."

"Great. Call me back when you have a location."

"Will do. Bye."

Alexander disconnected the call. "That should tell us if he's in town, and if he is, the general area he's in."

"Like at his house?" Jana said.

"Exactly. When Bat calls, if he says JP is close, we'll go visit him."

The text from Bat arrived at the same time they arrived at the truck. Attached to the message was an image of a map. A dot in the middle of the map represented the location of JP's phone. Alexander zoomed in on the map and showed it to Jana.

"That son of a bitch," she exclaimed. "He's at Miggie's gym. Miggie said he hadn't seen him in weeks and he's there now. I bet he's been there all along."

"Let's give him the benefit of the doubt. Maybe he just showed up after being out of town."

"Yeah, right," Jana said. She started the engine and sped out onto A1A.

The first traffic light they came to was red. Jana pounded the steering wheel. When the light finally turned green, she yelled at the car in front of them, "Damn it, let's go. It's not getting any greener. Fucking tourist."

Her aggressive driving abated after two more red lights. Her demeanor didn't. She had a death grip on the steering wheel and pounded it at each red light she had to stop for. Luckily, they cleared the gates of a drawbridge just before they began flashing. A few seconds later and she would have been caught by the drawbridge and forced to wait until the line of sailboats passed through. Her forehead creased. Her normally upturned mouth was a distinctive frown. Alexander wisely refrained from commenting on her driving or anything other than how they narrowly made the bridge.

Jana pulled the big pickup into the parking lot of Miggie's gym, double-parked behind two cars in spots directly in front of the gym doors, and bolted to the front doors. She was inside before Alexander reached the door.

Miggie and JP were at the free weights; JP was on his back lifting barbells with Miggie spotting him. Jana marched over to them with purpose, neither of them seeing her until she had her finger in Miggie's face.

"Miggie, you said JP hadn't been here in weeks. What a fucking co-incidence."

"Jana! Uh...I...he—"

"Don't lie to me. I'm fucking tired of people lying to me."

"Jana, calm down," Miggie said. He assisted JP in hooking the weights back onto the J hooks.

"Fuck you," Jana replied. She pirouetted and launched her foot toward Miggie's head, exactly as he'd trained her. He caught her calf in mid-swing and held it. Jana hopped on one leg, struggling to keep her balance.

"Let me go, you—"

"Not until you calm down and we can talk about this."

JP struggled to keep a straight face. From his prone position on the workout bench, his view was Jana's exposed thong. He stayed put and watched the show.

Alexander noticed and kicked JP in the foot. "Hey, eyes up here," he said.

JP jumped up, clenched his fists, and stepped toward him. Alexander took a step back and held up his hands. "Hang on there, I don't want any trouble." When JP kept coming, Alexander drew his Glock 43 pistol from underneath his Hawaiian shirt.

Miggie let go of Jana's leg. "Whoa, what the hell! JP, back off," he said. "There's no need for guns."

Jana hadn't seen Alexander with a gun before. "How long have you been carrying a gun?"

"Since we got here. It was in my bag on the plane."

"Please, put it away. There's no need for it. Right, JP?"

"No, no need," JP said, still glaring at Alexander.

Alexander put the gun back in the holster hidden under his shirt. "I apologize for kicking you. It wasn't my smartest move. Instinct, I guess. The gun's a nine-millimeter. Holds six rounds. It might have taken all six to stop you. If I'd brought my three-fifty-seven, it would've only taken one."

The sight of Alexander's gun, knowing he could have killed JP, despite what he said, had a sobering effect on Jana. "Look," she said. "I'm sorry too. But I'm pissed. Miggie, you lied to me. Where's Rey? I want the truth."

Miggie's shoulders slumped, and he looked at the ground. "Okay, I haven't heard from Rey in at least three days. I lied because I didn't want you to worry. A couple of days after they left, I got a text from him from an unknown number. They were in West Caicos getting fuel. He borrowed the dockmaster's phone. All he said was they were heading south. They were planning to go between Cuba and Haiti. He felt they were heading for South America. I told you that earlier."

"Why South America?" Jana asked.

"You know as much as I do now. I looked at a map. There's a few small islands like Aruba and Curaçao off the coast, but there's not much there other than tourists. My guess is they're headed to Colombia or Venezuela. There's a lot of illegal activity going on in those countries. Drug smuggling, human trafficking, you name it."

"It could be any of those and most likely is," Alexander said. "There's money in human trafficking, but is there enough to force Cole and Rey to do it instead of just having Cole repay the debt?"

"Not likely," Jana said. "I don't remember the exact numbers, but it seems like they were getting ten thousand for each girl they smuggled into the US from Cuba last year. They'd have to bring in twenty girls to break even. I suppose they could put forty or fifty on the *Miss Jana*, but that would push it. It wouldn't be a pleasant trip back, especially if they hit rough seas, and they got seasick."

"Which means they're most likely after drugs," Alexander said. "They could carry several million dollars' worth of drugs in a boat the size of the *Miss Jana*. But there's another possibility. They could be smuggling humans, but not trafficking them. A lot of people are willing to pay big money to get out of Venezuela right now. Maybe someone has a relative who's jailed in Venezuela and they want to get him busted out. Or maybe they're political prisoners and the CIA is behind this whole thing."

"It's not the CIA," JP said.

Alexander rested his hands on the edge of his pants pockets, not far from the holstered Glock. "Care to elaborate?"

"I've heard the guys are a bunch of local thugs who think they're big-time mobsters. Cole met them gambling. They approached us about throwing fights and we refused. They seemed to take it in stride, but that's when Cole hit a losing streak. He lost a lot in a short amount of time. They kept giving him markers to cover his debt but when he owed over two hundred K, they called it in. We figured they wanted us to throw a couple of fights. But they knew Cole knew Miggie. They also knew about Miggie's relationship with Rey, and that Rey had a big boat. They said if Cole and Rey would take a couple of their guys and make a delivery for them, they'd call it even. Cole approached Rey, and Rey said he'd ask Jana for the money. He said she'd do anything for us and two hundred thousand wasn't a big deal. But when Cole asked if he could pay off the debt, they said no. Cole and Rey had to either make the trip or they'd kill them, including Jana, just for the hell of it."

"Damn," Alexander said. "These are some unsavory characters. Do you think they'd have done it?"

"They would have tried," Miggie replied. "We didn't want to chance it. We thought they might go after Jana first, her being the easiest target. Kill her to make a point and get Rey to agree to do what they wanted."

"It wouldn't have worked," JP added. "Had they killed you, Jana, they'd have to kill us all and I guarantee you, we wouldn't have been easy targets."

"That's sweet, I guess," Jana said.

"Let me summarize," Alexander said. "You're involved with wannabe mobsters, for lack of a better word. They need something brought here from South America and are willing to kill for it. So, Cole and Rey are with at least two of them, doing what they want."

"That's about the size of it," JP said.

"And you two think when they get back with whatever they went for, these guys are just going to let them walk away."

JP and Miggie exchanged glances and shrugged. Miggie scratched his temple and thought for a moment. "You don't think they're going to let them walk away?"

"Nope. My guess is they'd come after Miggie, too. Maybe Jana,"

Alexander said.

"So, what do we do?" Jana asked.

"Find out who they are and kill them."

10

Jana's restless pacing echoed through the apartment, reverberating off the polished onyx white porcelain floors. Alexander watched from the elegant gray armless curved sofa while he sipped the twenty-year-old scotch Jana had poured him. Its smooth, smoky flavor delighted his taste buds.

Jana plopped onto the sofa opposite him. "I can't believe someone threatened to kill me, and those guys didn't warn me. Didn't say a fucking thing. Hell, I could've jumped on a plane and disappeared. Would these 'mobsters,' as JP called them, be organized enough or sophisticated enough to find me if I went to Orlando or maybe Tahiti for a few months?"

"I hate to say it, but your friends are a couple of tacos short of a combo plate."

Jana snickered. Her mood only slightly lightened. "You're right, they aren't too bright. That could be why they're MMA fighters."

"Getting punched and kicked in the head can't be good for their cognitive abilities. But they seem capable, and we're going to need them."

"Ah, you have an idea."

"I do. Kind of. I need to know more about who we are dealing with. How many are there? Are they local, or are they part of a bigger nationwide or worldwide gang? It makes a difference. Hopefully, JP can tell us how or where Cole got involved with them. I need to meet them."

"You? Is that a good idea?"

"They probably know JP and maybe Miggie. If they have been following you, they know you."

"And you," Jana added. "If they have watched us any in the past few days, they've seen you with me. You are memorable."

"That's a chance I'll have to take. There's no one else to do it."

"What happens when you meet them?"

"Cole had gambling losses. I'll have to do some gambling and see what I can learn."

"They aren't going to come right out and tell you about their organization."

"No, they won't. I'll force the issue, but not too much. That's about all I can do."

"Even if they were to tell you anything, that could take a while. You'll have to earn their trust."

"True. And time is not on our side. Hell, it could take weeks to get any good info."

Jana thought quietly for a few seconds. "I don't know," she finally said.

"Now that I said it out loud, I realize it may not be the best idea."

"You got anything else?"

Alexander got up and walked to the balcony door. He leaned on the glass and looked at the ocean. "We've got muscle. JP and Miggie. We should leverage it."

Jana joined him at the door. "How do you mean?"

"We find one of their guys and ask him."

"Huh? Ask him? Would he tell us?"

"With enough persuasion, he would."

Jana covered her mouth with her hand. "Oh my God," she said through her fingers.

"You got it. They have Rey and Cole. This is serious shit. They're not going to let them walk away when this is over. Would you like to step outside for some air?"

"That's a good idea," Jana said, sliding the glass door open. She and Alexander stepped onto the balcony and walked to the railing.

Alexander took a deep breath. "Nothing like the salt air to clear the senses."

"Maybe too clear. This seems so surreal. Now you tell me you're going to kidnap and torture a guy until he tells you what you need. That makes it real. What happens to the guy if he talks? Or, if he doesn't talk?"

"It depends on how cooperative he is. Hopefully, we can convince him to talk and then leave town. I get the impression Miggie and JP could be very persuasive."

"They can. They've done it before." Jana took another long look at the Atlantic. "I could use another drink. How 'bout you?"

"Always."

They went inside and Jana refreshed their drinks. The thought of what they might do to make the guy talk unnerved her. When they were back on the sofa, she decided to change the subject. "Today at the gym, you kicked JP for looking at my, uh—"

Alexander couldn't help but glance at Jana's private area. "Crotch?"

"Sure, crotch. But I'm wearing a thong. It wasn't a big deal. Why'd you kick him?"

"He didn't look, he leered. It wasn't just a glance. It bothered me."

"That's sweet. But I'm used to being ogled at." Jana had noticed Alexander's glance. It was a fleeting glance, which she assumed was okay. She had to wonder if his reaction would have been different had JP only taken a fleeting glance at her thong-covered crotch.

"When it was on your terms. When Ronald looked earlier today, he pissed you off."

Jana was still thinking about Alexander's glance. She only heard the second half of what he said. "Uh, true, he did. Well, thank you for being chivalrous. I'm glad you didn't shoot JP over it."

"Me too. I didn't realize a light kick in the foot would set him off."

"I'd be careful around those guys. I don't know about JP or Miggie, but some of the guys at the gym take steroids. Roid rage can be scary. It's a good thing JP backed off when you pulled a gun." Jana sipped her drink and cocked her head slightly. "What kind of gun was it? It looked small in your hand. I thought because you have big hands, you'd have a big gun."

"Oh, I have a big gun."

"Oh?" Jana flashed a half smile.

"A CZ 1911. It's a Czech Republic-made semi-auto." Alexander blushed slightly.

It wasn't the first time Jana saw him blush. "Alexander Christian, you're a...uh...different man."

"Oh? What makes you say that?"

Jana had to think about his question. When she commented on him having a big gun, his reply indicated that he picked up on the metaphor. But then he told her about his big gun. Why would he blush if he was talking about an actual gun? Maybe the innuendo did not escape him, but he wasn't comfortable continuing the banter. He didn't approve of JP leering at her, yet he had taken more than a few peeks at her and when she'd catch him looking, he'd quickly turn away and blush. He said she was beautiful, but when he had the chance to see her mostly naked at the nude beach, he turned it down.

Jana didn't know how much of her thoughts she wanted to share with him. "I don't know. When I caught you checking me out, you blushed. It's like you're shy, or even intimidated around women. But I know that's not true. I met Mayte when she was in Miami, visiting her sister. She told me about how you took Briana and Bonita from the trafficker. She said you and Bonita hooked up that night and were together until..." Jana's voice trailed off. She felt she was about to bring up a subject better left unsaid.

"Until she took off," Alexander said. "We got close quickly. I still think about her and care for her, but it's over."

"Is it?"

"Yes, it is. Had she not left, we might've worked things out and been happy. Is she going to come back? If she was, she would've by now."

"And if she did?"

"Right here, right now, I'd say I'd be her friend and help her if I could, but that'd be it."

"Do you really mean that? Briana told me she was gorgeous. Dark soulful eyes, glossy black hair, long slender legs, and large boobs. I have a feeling you'd take her back if you saw her again."

"She was indeed gorgeous. But there's more to a woman than looks."

Jana snorted. "That's what all men say."

"Hear me out. She took off. I get why. She wanted that baby more than anything, and she lost it. The doctor said she could never have a baby. She went down a slippery slope in a hurry. I don't blame her, but she shut me out. Refused my help. Then she disappeared. I got a text saying she'd left me. That was hard for me, too."

"And now you're afraid to get involved with another woman."

"I wouldn't say that. In fact, I feel I'm ready—"

Alexander's phone rang. He pressed the Accept button. "Bat, hi. Jana's with me. I have you on speaker."

"Alex, got a few minutes?"

"Yes. You got anything?"

Jana moved next to Alexander to hear better.

"I tracked Rey's phone on the day the boat left Fort Lauderdale. I tracked it tower by tower until it stopped pinging. Using AI, I checked all the other phones that pinged the same towers concurrently. I got hits on two numbers. Rey's phone stopped pinging, so he must have turned it off, or it died. The other two phones pinged along the coast for a few hours. Those phones last pinged off a tower in Key Biscayne. The next time they were both active was in Matthew Town on Inagua Island. That's a small island near Turks and Caicos. The phones were active for several hours, then nothing. A few minutes ago, both phones pinged off a tower near Cartagena, Colombia."

"Cartagena! Jeez, no wonder they wanted a big boat with a lot of range," Alexander said.

"The movement from tower to tower has slowed. When it stops, I'll send you the last tower the phones ping off."

"That'll help. Knowing where they are is a tremendous help. But, damn, why did it have to be South America? I don't speak Spanish. Anywhere else in the Caribbean, I could have communicated, but not Colombia. I don't even know anyone who speaks Spanish well enough to guide me."

"Yes, you do," Bat said.

"I do?" Alexander and Jana exchanged confused glances.

"Yep. She's even from Colombia."

"Bonita!"

"Bingo. She'd be the perfect tour guide. Speaks the language like a native."

"I don't know about her. Even if I could find her, she may not come with me."

"Her phone pings off McCarty, just north of Clinton Drive. That's where you found her and Briana. Odds are, she's at the same bar."

Alexander hesitated. "I figured she'd be there. She has nowhere else to go."

"Weren't all those bars raided and closed last year?" Jana asked.

"Most of them reopened within a couple of months with a new name, with 'new' management," Alexander replied.

"Are you going to go see her?" Bat asked. "Ask her if she'll help you?"

"Should I get her involved? It could get dangerous."

"I have a feeling she can take care of herself. She's been through a lot. She could be a real asset," Bat said.

"You're right, as usual. If she's working in that sleazy bar, she's hustling drinks and...well, you can imagine what else she's doing. If she'll help us, it might be good for her. I'll think about it. Bat, I appreciate your efforts."

"No problem. I'll be in touch."

"Cheers." Alexander disconnected the call, sat back on the sofa, and closed his eyes for a second.

Jana gently touched his hand. "You should at least ask her," she said. "If she's depressed, it might snap her out of it."

"I wonder how well she knows Colombia. She left when she was young and hasn't been back. But, it's worth a shot."

"I can have a jet ready to go in the morning."

"I could fly Southwest. It would be a lot cheaper."

"I don't fly commercial, remember?"

"You're going?"

"You know it. There's not much I can do here and if those mobster guys are watching me, I don't want to be here alone."

Alexander wasn't thrilled with her going along, but he knew he could use the moral support when he confronted Bonita. "Good point. You may be handy to have around too...just in case."

"Plus, we can go directly from Houston to Cartagena."

Taking Jana to Houston was one thing. Taking her to Colombia was a whole different ball game. He decided to save that battle for a later date. "Let's not jump the gun. We have a lot of pieces that have to fall into place and the timing has to be right. We can't do anything in Colombia until we know JP and Miggie have taken care of the locals. Damn, I should be here for that. We don't know what we're getting into."

"I didn't know finding Rey would be so complicated. I thought you'd find out where he is and then I'd walk right up to him and ask what the hell was going on, and that would be the end of it. Now, we're talking about killing people and maybe getting killed."

"Are you getting cold feet?"

Jana took a sip of her drink. "No. I mean, I wish there was another way. I want to find Rey."

"When I was with the Bureau, we'd plan for weeks, often months, to take down an organized operation. We had unlimited resources, too. Now there are four of us, maybe a few more if we add a couple of JP's friends and Bonita, and we hope to bring down a crime syndicate in a few days."

"Alex, honestly, are we biting off more than we can chew? There's no point of three, or four, or more of us getting killed to save two, who we may not save anyway."

"As I mentioned earlier, we need more intel. We need a plan, too. A solid plan."

"And you have one?" Jana leaned in closer, a look of expectation on her face.

"Not yet. Maybe a little more alcohol will help."

"It always does." Jana laughed sarcastically. "What about food? You hungry?"

"Now that you mention it, I am."

"How does cheesesteak sound?"

Alexander shrugged. "Not as good as ribeye steak, but it's getting late."

"You'll like these. I'll order." Jana picked up her phone and scrolled until she found the Uber Eats app. From there, she linked to Charley's Cheesesteak. She ordered two Kentucky Bourbon Cheesesteaks and closed the app. "Twenty minutes."

"Time for a little ice and about two fingers of scotch," he said, holding his glass toward her.

Jana poured two glasses of scotch. When she returned, she sat cross-legged on the sofa and handed him his drink. "So, we need a plan."

Alexander took a sip. "Yes, we do. I'll let you know when I come up with one."

11

Alexander and Jana sat on the northeast-facing balcony having coffee. The summer sun, rising in the southeast, was obscured by the high-rise condos between them and the beach. The buildings may have blocked the sun as it broke the surface of the Atlantic, but they couldn't block the spectacular morning colors that danced across the sky.

Miggie's gym opened at five o'clock in the morning. Jana texted Miggie at five-thirty and asked if he and JP would meet her and Alexander. Miggie replied that JP was more of a night owl, and he usually came in around noon. "I had to plead, but Miggie agreed to text JP and ask him to come to the gym. No guarantees," Jana told Alexander.

"This is frustrating," Alexander said. "We're wasting time. Time we may not have. Who knows what those people wanted Rey and the boat for, but if they needed Rey to get the boat to Colombia, they may not have any more use for him."

"That's a dreadful thought," Jana said. "Hopefully, they'll need him to take the boat wherever it's going next. Any thoughts on where that might be? Or why they're in Colombia?"

"My guess is drugs. That's where the big money is."

"Makes sense."

"There's so much we don't know. How long will they be there? Are the drugs, if that's what they're after, there waiting for them? Will they pick them up, refuel, and head back in a few hours? Or will they be there a few days?"

Jana held her coffee cup with both hands and took a sip. "All good questions...any answers?"

"Not yet. I have a gut feeling they're going to hang out in Cartagena for a while. A few days, maybe a week. Arriving one day and leaving the next would be suspicious. The local authorities must track boat traffic in and out of the area."

"Are we going to Colombia?" Jana asked.

"We?"

"Yes, we. We're in this together."

"I'm not talking you out of going?"

"Nope."

"Okay then. But if it gets too dangerous, I want your ass on that private jet and gone."

Jana shrugged. It wasn't the time to argue about whether she would leave if things went badly. "Speaking of private jets," she said, "when do you want to go find your missing ex? We'll need her to find mine."

"Your missing ex?"

"It feels like it at times, but no, not ex...not yet."

Alexander wanted to ask her to clarify but thought better of it. Instead, he said, "The sooner the better." He scratched his head. "Bonita was already deeply depressed. If she's doing what I think she's doing, she's also self-medicating. She may need a few days to detox. I'm hoping for the best, but we need to plan for the worst."

"If she is, that's no bueno. I hope she'll come with you and that helping us will help her. Why don't we go get her today, after we meet with Miggie and JP?"

Alexander thought about it. "It's as good a time as any."

"I'll call and have a plane on standby. Will we come back tonight or stay at your place?"

"With luck, we can find her tonight, stay at my place, and come back in the morning. If she's a little messed up, will there be a problem with the plane?"

Jana laughed. "Are you kidding? Those guys fly rock stars and other celebrities all the time. Fucked up passengers are normal for them."

The text from Miggie came in while Jana was making the plane reservations. "Alex, Miggie said he got a hold of JP. He had to call and wake him. JP said he could be there by nine." Jana glanced at the time on the phone. "It's almost six. What'll we do until nine?"

"I'm going for a run on the beach and then maybe breakfast. Do you know a good breakfast place?"

"I do. I could use a run too. Can I come?"

"Absolutely. I'd love the company."

The run on the beach was more of a jog and walk than a run. Jana and Alexander both admitted they were out of shape and vowed to do better. They returned to the condo, showered, and dressed. Alexander wore a different Hawaiian shirt, but the same shorts as the day before. Jana wore a mint-colored romper with teal and orange flowers and flutter sleeves.

Jana studied him. "Do you have any shirts other than Hawaiian shirts?"

"Only a few long-sleeve dress shirts that I wear fishing."

"Why dress shirts for fishing? Never mind, I know. To catch classier fish. Are you ready to go?"

"I am. Not classier fish, fish with good taste." He gave her a wink.

She rolled her eyes and let out a long groan.

Jana loved to drive her Alfa, but with Alexander, it was out of the question. She told him to get in the truck and she would drive. "We're going to Lester's Diner. It's on the way to the gym," Jana said. "There's an IHOP closer, but I thought you'd like this place better. It's like an old fifties-style diner. There are stools at the counter. We can eat there or in a booth. People love sitting at the counter. I prefer a booth."

Lester's was a typical fifties diner with red and chrome chairs, Formica tabletops, and neon lighting across the ceiling. The forty-eight-inch flat screen above the bar didn't fit the motif.

A booth was available. The two sat and ordered coffee. Alexander looked over the menu. The server, a middle-aged, slightly heavyset woman dressed in all black, brought coffee and took their order. Alexander ordered Lester's Big Deal—three eggs, three pancakes, two strips of bacon, two sausage links, and one sausage patty. Jana ordered Eggs Benedict.

When the server left, Jana smirked at her breakfast companion. "The 'Big Deal' huh? You must be hungry from your run this morning."

"At least I didn't add the French toast."

"That'll save the calories."

"I'm six-feet-four and weigh maybe a tad over two hundred. That's not bad."

"A tad over? I'd bet you're closer to two-twenty than two hundred."

"Okay, you may be right. But for my height, that's still not too bad."

"It's not. What worries me is the growth on your hip. Do you carry that around all the time?"

"Most of the time. I shouldn't need it at Miggie's, but JP said someone may be watching you. I like being armed."

"To tell you the truth, I'm glad you are. Is it legal? I mean, are you allowed to carry a gun in Florida?"

"I am. Although in Texas, it's no longer necessary to have a license to carry a concealed weapon—our idiotic state legislature repealed the law requiring one. Don't get me started on that. Anyway, you can still get a license to carry and it has reciprocal privileges in most states, Florida included. Plus, I have my retired FBI credentials, which means I can carry a weapon in all fifty states."

"At least that's one thing I don't have to worry about, you getting busted for an illegal gun."

The server brought the food and refilled their coffee cups. She continued to check on the diners, always topping off their coffee cups. She was pleasant, efficient, and attentive. After placing the check on the table, she said, "I'll leave this here. No hurry."

"Thanks," Jana said. When the server was out of earshot, she whispered, "She's nice."

Busy putting butter and syrup on his pancakes, Alexander just nodded. Jana took the hint and quietly ate her breakfast. When they finished, Jana put a hundred-dollar bill on top of the check. She glanced at her phone for the time. "Are you ready? It's still a bit early, but maybe JP will be early."

"What are the odds?" Alexander chuckled. "He didn't strike me as a morning person, and Miggie confirmed it. But that's fine. I'd like to talk to Miggie a little before JP gets there. I'm ready."

Jana slid to the end of the booth and stood. Alexander gestured at the hundred-dollar bill she'd left on the table. "Do you want to wait for change?"

"No, it's fine. She was good."

The size of the tip shocked him, but he slid out of the booth without commenting. He motioned for Jana to walk ahead of him.

Outside the truck, she said, "We're about fifteen minutes away. Can you drive? I want to check on the plane. I'll navigate."

Alexander drove slower than Jana, and he stopped for yellow lights. The drive from the diner to Miggie's Gym took closer to twenty minutes. They were pulling into the parking lot when Jana confirmed a plane would be ready for them. QuickJet just asked for thirty minutes notice to have the jet fueled, ready, and on the tarmac waiting for them.

It took what seemed like an eternity to Jana for Alexander to maneuver the big F-150 into a parking space. Her impatience showed in her body language.

"You try to park this big son-of-a-bitch without hitting anything after driving a MINI Cooper. It ain't easy."

"I didn't say a word." Jana smiled. *Quit your bitchin'. I usually drive an Alfa Romeo 4C.*

They got out of the truck and walked to the gym. Miggie motioned them toward his office when they came through the door. Once inside, he closed the door and said, "JP texted. He's on his way. Did you want to wait or do you want to tell me what this is all about? We've told you all we know. At least I have."

"I wanted to talk to you before JP got here. I'm hoping he hasn't told me everything," Alexander said, taking a seat nearest the door.

"Oh?"

"To save Rey, for lack of a better word, we have to find out who's behind this. Who and how many? I have no doubt we can find Rey, take care of whoever is with him, and come back. But it wouldn't end there. Whoever these people are, they'd come looking for us. I don't fancy living the rest of my life looking over my shoulder."

"Good point," Miggie said. "Do you have a plan?"

"No. We can't make a plan until we know what we are up against. That's where you and JP come in. Is JP trustworthy? Not in the sense that he'd betray us. I'm sorry if I sound rude or judgmental, but JP doesn't seem to be the brightest person I've ever met."

Miggie contemplated the question as he glanced around the room, at Jana, and then back at Alexander. "You have him well-pegged. He looks meaner than hell because of his size and the tats. You saw how he reacted when you kicked him. No doubt he's short-tempered. Is he very bright? You nailed that one, too. I barely finished high school and I run a gym, but I'd say I'm a brain surgeon compared to him. Cole too. Cole's in a little better shape, but not much. Most MMA fighters aren't too bright. It's a brutal sport, and it doesn't take long for your brains to get rattled. Anyone with half a brain would never get into the sport."

Alexander sighed. "We've been ragging on JP, but he's not a total idiot. What I need isn't anything he can't handle."

There was a loud knock on the office door, then JP stuck his head in. "Hey. I'm here. I hope it's important."

"It is," Alexander said. He stood and shook JP's hand. Jana stood and gave him a quick hug. Once JP was seated, Alexander continued. "We need your help. I've thought about it, and I think Cole and Rey are mixed up with the tail of the snake. We could go find them and bring them home. But to get out of this, we need to find the head of the snake and cut it off."

JP looked puzzled. Alexander hoped the snake metaphor wasn't too much for him. "You with me?"

"Uh, yeah. Unless we take care of the big boss, Cole and Rey will still be up shit creek."

"Exactly. What I need is intel. I need you two, or anyone else you know who might know who these guys are, to find out where they hang out, figure out who's in charge, and how many there are. Also, are they local or are they like the Miami contingent of a much larger organization?"

"Any idea how to find them?" JP asked.

"You said they approached you and Cole to throw a fight. How did you find them? Or did they find you?"

"They found us. They wanted to rig a fight. After I said no, I left. Cole stayed. He likes to bet on fights. We were at a place that held both amateur and pro fights on weekends. Betting on either is legal in Florida, but you have to wager at a casino. The guys took Cole's bets and he won. He bet on several fights that night. He asked them if they took bets on other sports. They said they did, and they asked him if he played poker. Before you know it, he was betting on basketball and baseball, and playing Texas Hold 'em. Then he started losing. It didn't take long, and he was way in debt. That's when they asked about his friend who owned a boat. I don't know how they found out about the boat."

"Do you have any idea who the guys were? Did you ever see them again?" Alexander asked.

"No, I didn't."

"They spoke English good, and they spoke Spanish to each other. I thought they were Cuban. Maybe Puerto Rican."

"Miggie," Alexander asked, "have you heard anything about Cubans or Puerto Ricans running an illegal gambling house?"

"I haven't. But I don't hear a lot of gossip. I try to run a clean place and if any shit like that's going on, I'm the last to know."

"Damn," Jana said. "This isn't like the movies where everybody has an informant that knows what's happening on the streets."

Miggie leaned back in his old wooden swivel chair. "No, it's not."

"That's not to say there aren't people out there that know. But they'll want something in return," JP offered.

"Money?" Jana asked.

JP nodded. "Money, or drugs, or sex."

"Geez," said Jana. She opened her purse and pulled out ten one-hundred-dollar bills. "Will this be enough?"

JP fanned the bills in his hand. "Plenty. I'll break it into twenties. It don't take much."

"Find out what you can," Jana said.

JP slid the wad of bills into his pants pocket. "What exactly do you need to know, Alex?"

Alexander had told JP once before what he needed. Remembering the consensus on him was that he wasn't overly bright, Alexander thought it best to repeat himself. "The more, the better. Who are they? Where's this poker room? Is that where they hang out most of the time?

Home addresses for any would be nice to know. Last, and this is important, I need to know if they're a local group or are they an offshoot of a bigger mob. Like the Mafia. If they are, we may have a problem."

"I'll do my best. I'm curious. What if I can't get the info you need?"

"That was Plan B. Plan A was to find one of them when he's alone, convince him to come with you, and convince him to tell you everything he knows."

"Convince him to tell us? How...oh...I know what you mean."

"JP," Jana hesitated, her eyes narrowed. "You could do that?"

"They've got Cole and Rey. Cole's my best friend. So, yeah, no problem. In fact..." JP dug in his pants pocket and pulled out the wad of cash. He held it out to Jana. "Plan A's a better way. I won't need this."

"Keep it. You'll need it to find out who they are. Find out which one is likely to know the most and convince him to tell you what we need."

"You're right. I'll need cash for that. When do you need the information?"

"ASAP," Alexander said.

"ASAP?"

"As soon as possible."

"Oh. It shouldn't take but a day or two."

"Be careful. They know you and will have a good idea why you're snooping around and asking questions. If you get the slightest inkling that they're suspicious of you, disappear. Go to Orlando and lie low. Just let us know you're okay."

"That's why I like your Plan A better than B. They'll never see me coming."

12

On the way to the Fort Lauderdale/Hollywood International Airport, Alexander turned to Jana. "If you don't mind me asking, how much are you worth?"

Jana glanced at him and then back to the road. "What?"

"I'm sorry, I shouldn't have asked. Or shouldn't have been so blunt. I was curious."

"No, it's fine. The question just surprised me. To answer, I have an idea, but I don't know the exact amount. I rarely look at statements."

"That must be nice," Alexander said, trying to imagine having so much money one didn't know how much they had.

"Believe me, it is. We weren't poor when I was growing up, but money was often tight. When I was on my own, I did well at the gentlemen's clubs, but I knew it wouldn't last. I tried to save, but it seemed like I never got ahead."

"I know what you mean."

"Now, to paraphrase the old Joe Walsh song, I have accountants take care of it all. And a lawyer and a financial advisor. They take a cut, which is fair. I don't worry about anything. Last year I signed the tax and I couldn't believe the amount of tax I paid. The tax was more than I think I ever made in a year before. Next year, I think I'll sign it without looking at the amount. The last time I looked, my investment portfolio was over a hundred million. I've got other accounts too, like checking and savings. My CPA shuffles money around, so I always have enough in my checking to cover my credit card bill, HOA fee, and utilities, which are all on auto-pay."

Alexander whistled. "Your credit card bill has got to be pretty high."

"It will be this month. Private jet charters add up fast."

"You must have a lot of points."

Jana laughed. "I have no idea. Why'd you ask about my money?"

"It occurred to me that the guys who took Rey must not know how much you're worth. If they know where you live, they would know you're doing okay, but they must not have a clue about your net worth."

"That's true. But what difference does it make to them?"

"Since Rey and Cole are in Colombia, we are assuming they're smuggling drugs. Smuggling involves buying the drugs, getting them to the US, or wherever you're taking them, and then selling them. I'm out of touch, but what's the most they could make? A million or two? If they knew how much money you had, they could've taken Rey and asked for a million or two ransom. It seems to me it would be a lot easier than what they're doing."

"You're right. I'd have paid too. But I've always heard the problem with kidnapping people and asking for a ransom is you rarely get away with it. It's the money exchange that gets them caught."

"That was true. Now you can create cryptocurrency accounts and get paid in Bitcoin or another digital asset. Accounts are virtually untraceable. That's why there's so many cyber-attacks on companies with ransomware. They're getting away with it."

"That's really fucked," Jana said without taking her eyes off the road. She turned into the small parking lot of QuickJet Aviation. Ten minutes later, they were sitting in the cabin of an Embraer Legacy 450.

Alexander glanced around the cabin. "This is a different airplane, isn't it?"

"It is," Jana replied. "It was all they had available. They said it flies at the same speed but has a little shorter range. They assured me it had plenty of range for us."

"Nice to know. I'd hate to run out of gas halfway across the Gulf."

Jana gazed out the window as the jet took off over the Atlantic, banked, and headed west. "Alex, what's the plan when we land? There'll be a rental waiting for us."

"I'd like to look for Bonita alone. But it's a long drive to Bolivar and back. I thought we'd go straight to where I think she is. If you don't mind, I'd like you to wait in the car. If she's not there, we'll try a few other places."

"Maybe if she saw me with you, she'd feel better about coming along?"

"I don't know what to expect. She may be fine or she may be fubar'd."

"Fubar'd?"

"Fucked Up Beyond All Repair."

"Oh God, let's hope not."

"I hope not as well," he said, without turning his head. He leaned against the fuselage, his arms crossed, and stared out at the nothingness of the sky.

Jana watched him staring out the window. *What was he thinking? Was it Bonita?* She felt a tinge of jealousy. He said he was no longer interested in her. Jana wondered why it mattered. She was still with Rey, or was she?

A couple of hours later, the captain spoke over the intercom. "We'll be landing soon. Please remain seated with your seatbelts fastened until the aircraft has come to a complete stop."

Alexander glanced around the aircraft. "I just realized there wasn't a flight attendant on the plane."

"They're optional," Jana replied. "I told them we didn't need one. Had we wanted anything, we could have gotten it ourselves."

The airplane touched down and taxied to QuickJet's area of the tarmac. The pilot came from the cockpit and unlocked the cabin door. He stood by while the steps descended, then motioned to his two passengers to exit the aircraft.

"Thank you, Jana," the pilot said when she walked past him. "I hope to see you soon." He nodded at Alexander.

"Real soon maybe," Jana replied.

A sparkling Land Rover Discovery waited for them at the bottom of the airplane's steps. A fashionably dressed woman in her early thirties with a customer service-trained smile handed Jana the key fob. "Thank you for using QuickJet Aviation today. Would you like me to show you around the vehicle?"

"No, thank you. I've driven one before." Jana took the keys, got in the driver's side, and pressed the button to raise the tailgate. Alexander dropped their bags in the cargo space and then climbed into the passenger side.

"Are you ready for this?" Jana asked.

"As ready as I'll ever be."

Alexander directed her to the east side of Houston. Other than his giving directions, the drive was quiet. "Pull in there." He pointed to a pot-holed parking lot on the left.

Jana gazed at the faded purple building with its peeling façade and black iron bars over the door and windows. The front blazed like a giant billboard in the Texas sun. A billboard that would have read, "Do Not Enter."

"Go to the front, next to the door, and back in," Alexander instructed.

Jana looked at the building. "You think Bonita is here?"

"Yes. This is where I found her last year, and her phone has pinged off a nearby tower. If she's not here, she's in a nearby bar." He pulled his Glock 9mm from the holster that was attached to his belt and ejected the magazine. After verifying the magazine was full, he slid it back into the handle of the gun and then pulled the slide back enough to confirm a round was chambered. He put the gun back in the holster, and covered it with his Hawaiian shirt.

"You carried your gun on the plane?" Jana asked incredulously.

"I did. I do like flying on a private plane. It's a real pain in the ass to fly commercial with a weapon."

Three cars were in the parking lot. They were older and had their fair share of dents and dings. The new Land Rover looked out of place.

"Keep the doors locked and the motor running," Alexander said. "No one should bother you, but if they do, lay on the horn. That should scare them away. If it doesn't, haul ass."

"Leave you?"

"Yes. I'll text you when and where to get me."

"Are you sure?"

"Yes. Again, I don't expect trouble. Stay alert."

"Don't worry about me," Jana said. "Go get Bonita and let's get out of here."

Alexander nodded and got out. He leaned against the side of the car for a few seconds. His heart racing, he strolled toward the front door. The lack of an electronic lock on the iron-barred outer door surprised him. He pulled the outer door open, pushed the heavy metal inner door open, and stepped inside.

He closed the door and let his eyes become accustomed to the darkness of the bar. The air in the bar was heavy with the mingling scents of alcohol, cheap perfume, and the faint aroma of a recently smoked recreational drug. When his eyes adjusted, he could see the inside was unchanged since the first time he'd been there. A long wooden bar to his left in the front. Booths along the walls surrounded a dance floor.

The dimly lit bar buzzed with the low hum of conversations, punctuated by beer bottles being slammed on tabletops. During his cursory glance, Alexander noticed a couple of people sitting in the booths, a bartender, and a female patron sitting on a stool slumped over the bar. No sign of Bonita. His first thought was to back out the door and leave. She wasn't there. But he was, and although he didn't expect a straight answer, he wanted to ask a few questions.

Wearing his usual summer fare–Hawaiian shirt, shorts, and boat shoes, he eased up to the bar and nodded toward the older, tattooed bartender. She was standing in front of the woman slumped over the bar. She glanced toward him, then at the woman at the bar. She tapped the woman's arm and whispered. "Hey, sit up."

"What?" The woman looked up at the bartender who, in turn, nodded toward Alexander.

Alexander didn't look away from the bartender. "Uh, no, that's not why I'm here. I want to ask you a couple of questions. I'm not a cop."

"You look like a cop," the bartender replied. She poked the woman who was slumped over the bar. With great effort and little enthusiasm, the woman straightened and swiveled on her stool so she faced Alexander.

"Bonita?!"

The woman looked at him through glazed eyes. "My name's Bonnie and unless you got a hundred bucks, you be wastin' my time."

Alexander moved closer to her and brushed her dirty, unkempt hair aside. "Bonita, what the hell has happened to you?"

She blinked hard several times, then looked up at him. "Alex?"

"Yes, it's me. Alex."

"Go away. Bonita is dead. She died with the baby. Leave me alone."

Alexander's stomach tightened into a large knot. He turned to the bartender. "How long has she been like this?"

"Oh, man, no clue. She showed up a few months ago and asked for a job. The manager, Angel, was here. He pounced on her. She was hot...then. Not like she is now. Anyway, he said he was going to take her to the back for an 'interview.' They came back out a little later and he was grinning ear-to-ear. I can't say exactly what they did, but I have an idea. Angel said her name was Bonnie, and she'd be hustling drinks and that she'd be using a backroom too."

The knot in Alexander's stomach turned into a concrete lump. He was angry, hurt, sad, and wasn't sure what to do about it. Bonita didn't look up when he said her name. He said it again, louder, and grabbed her by the shoulder.

"I said, leave me alone!" She jerked away.

A thin Hispanic man appeared from a side door. "What the hell is going on?" He stopped in mid-step when he noticed Alexander. "Hey man, we don't need no trouble here. You need to be leavin'."

Alexander stared at the man as he put one hand on his hip and the other in his back pocket. He didn't want the man, who he recognized from their first encounter as Angel, to misconstrue his angry tremor for fear. "No, you don't want any trouble, especially from me. I suggest you turn around and crawl back into your hole. This doesn't concern you."

"The fuck it don't. You're in my bar, harassing one of my girls." The man reached under his shirt to his waistband.

Alexander pulled the Glock from under his shirt and aimed it at Angel's chest. With a shaking hand, Angel pointed his Taurus 38 Special Revolver at Alexander.

"You're shaking like Barney Fife. If you pull that trigger, you're more likely to shoot the bartender than me."

The bartender backed against the wall. Bonita rested her head on the bar.

"We're eight feet apart," Alexander said. "You don't have a chance in hell of hitting me. But I can put two rounds through your heart without even thinking about it."

Angel's hand shook more violently than before.

"Try using two hands. It might help," Alexander goaded. He raised the Glock and pointed it at the man's head. "But as soon as you do, I'm putting a round right between the eyes."

Angel stared at Alexander, who stared back.

"Do it," Alexander commanded. "The last time we met, I almost killed you, and I didn't have much of a reason. This time, I really want to kill you. Give me a reason."

"Okay, okay, take it easy." Angel pointed his gun in the air.

"Slowly, set the gun on the bar and back away."

The man did as he was told.

"Slide the gun down the bar to me," Alexander told the bartender. "No need to pick it up."

Alexander took the double-action handgun with a stainless-steel barrel, opened the cylinder, pressed the ejector rod, and emptied the bullets into his hand. He put the bullets in his pocket, closed the cylinder, and set the gun on the bar. "What happened to Bon? Didn't she own the bar or part of it?" he asked Angel.

"She did. The old bar got raided and shut down. They lost their liquor license and several people went to jail."

"You didn't?"

"No, they couldn't pin anything on me. I just worked here," he said, his eyes glancing between Alexander's eyes and the gun he was holding. "I always wondered why Bonnie didn't go to jail. I guess she was shackin' up with you, so they figured she was okay." Angel glanced at the gun again. He wanted to press Alexander's buttons, but he didn't want to press too hard. "That, and I bet she ratted everyone out. And then she came back here looking for work. So I gave her..." He paused, thought, then said, "I gave her work."

"So, how'd she get like this?"

"Why should I answer any of your questions?"

Alexander cupped his left hand onto the gun under his right in a standard firing grip. "Because if you don't, I'll blow your fucking head off."

Angel's demeanor quickly softened. "She was already out of it when she came looking for work. She'd started using again. Mostly meth. She lived on the streets for a while until she needed money. She still looked good, and she could make money. But the more she made, the more she used. It's a vicious cycle. It happens to all the girls."

"And you felt no obligation to help her. You just gave her 'work.'"

"I guess so."

"And when she 'worked,' did you get a kickback, or you just sold her the drugs?"

"She bought from me. Honestly, I thought about not supplying her, but there were other sources, too. Meth and crack are easy to come by. At least she knew what she was getting when she was getting it from me."

"You're a saint."

"Look, why don't you put the gun down? I'm cooperating. If you want the girl, take her. You took her before. Take her now."

Alexander lowered the Glock but didn't holster it. "Last time, I asked her if she wanted to come with me and she said yes. I didn't force her."

"Whatever. Take her. She's messed up. She's no longer discreet. One of these days she's going to proposition an undercover cop or TABC, and we'll lose everything. Take her...please."

The door to the bar opened and two Hispanic men walked in. They went straight to the bar and, in Spanish, ordered beers.

Alexander glanced at them, holstered the Glock, and looked back at Bonita. "Come with me. You need help. I hurt, too. You don't need to go through this alone."

Bonita leaned forward and looked around him at the two men. She smiled and said, "Hola." The men replied in Spanish and laughed. She looked back at Alexander. "I'm not going with you. That part of my life is over. I killed our baby. I'm a worthless piece of shit. Now, leave me alone so I can go fuck those guys."

Alexander grabbed Bonita by the arm and lifted her off the barstool. "Don't say that. You did nothing wrong. You're a good person and I love you. Come with me. I need your help."

The two men at the bar said something in Spanish, stood and stepped toward Alexander. Angel yelled to them in Spanish. They both turned and sat back down, glaring glared at Alexander.

Alexander turned to Angel. "What was that all about?"

"They were concerned. I told them it was okay and to sit down." Angel was glad Alexander didn't speak Spanish.

Bonita shook her arm loose from Alexander's grasp. For a split second, she looked him in the eyes, then turned away. "Alex, I can't look at you. I can't look at myself in the mirror. The drugs make the pain go away for a little while and that's all I want. I want to get high and forget."

"If you keep doing this, you're going to die. Do you want to die?"

One of the Mexicans at the bar yelled, "Oye pendejo, ¿no hablas español?" He laughed, held up two fingers, and in broken English said, "We do her. Dos holes."

Alexander got the gist of what the man said. He turned to face them, his face red, the veins in his neck bulged. They continued to taunt him.

"Sì, dos holes. Five dolla." The men roared with laughter and slapped the bar.

Bonita's head snapped. She screamed at the men in Spanish, picked up the Taurus revolver, put the barrel in her mouth, and pulled the trigger.

13

The two men at the end of the bar froze. At the other end of the bar, Angel stood with his mouth agape. The bartender's face went pale. Alexander gingerly removed the revolver from Bonita's hand. He pulled her close. She buried her head in his chest. He pulled the Glock from its holster and pointed it at the two men at the end of the bar. "This one's loaded."

The men didn't understand the words but didn't argue. Angel moved closer to Alexander and Bonita. "Should I tell them to leave?" he asked.

The two men sat and sipped their beers. Neither looked in Alexander's direction.

"No, they won't be any more trouble," Alexander said. He would have liked them gone, two fewer people to worry about, but he was afraid they might see the attractive blonde sitting outside in the Land Rover. It was best if they were inside, where he could keep an eye on them.

"Señor," Angel said in a soft, gentle voice, "that was the scariest thing I've ever seen. It's a good thing you removed the bullets from the gun. I like Bonnie. She's good for the bar. Was good. I wanted her to stay, but that was no bueno. You take her. Help her. I'd hate to see her dead."

"I'm glad to hear you say that," Alexander said, his tone softer now.

"I'll be right back," Angel said. He turned and left the bar.

Alexander eased Bonita away from him and checked the men at the end of the bar. "Bonita—"

"No. We are done. Adios," she said.

Alexander held the back of her head and made her look at him.

"Listen to me," he said. "If we're done, we're done. That's okay. I can live with that. But we have another problem, and I need your help."

Bonita shook her head, trying to comprehend what she'd heard. "You need my help?"

"We do."

"How? Who's 'we'? Is Mayte in trouble? Bat?"

"No, it's Rey. Do you remember Rey? He was the captain of the boat that smuggled the Cuban girls."

"Kinda."

"He's been kidnapped," Alexander knew Rey was technically missing, but hoped kidnapped would resonate with Bonita.

"Huh?"

"Some people took him and his boat. We think they're in Colombia."

"Colombia?" For the first time, her eyes showed signs of life.

"Yes. We need someone who speaks the language like a native."

Bonita cocked her head "Who's we?"

"Rey's girlfriend Jana. She hired me to find him."

Angel appeared from the back room carrying a small backpack. "This is everything Bonnie has. Her purse, passport, and a few clothes." He handed the backpack to Alexander, then looked at Bonita. "Bonnie, you're a sweet girl. I don't want you to die. Go with this man and let him help you."

Bonita shuddered. "Okay."

Before she could change her mind, Alexander thanked Angel, helped Bonita off the stool, and walked her to the door. He kept an eye on the two men at the bar until he was out of the building. As he approached the car, he heard the lock mechanism click. He opened the rear door and helped Bonita in. After he buckled her in and closed the door, he climbed into the front seat.

"Go," he said to Jana. The Land Rover was already moving.

"Where to?" she asked.

"We'll be okay taking the ferry across to Bolivar. We'll go via Galveston."

Jana glanced at Bonita through the rearview mirror. Bonita was leaning against the window, staring out through droopy eyes that were rapidly closing.

Jana touched Alexander lightly on the arm. "I thought about it while you were inside the bar. Two things were going to happen. You would get her to come with you or you wouldn't. If she didn't come with you, there wasn't any need to stay here in Texas. If she came, why not take her back to Florida?" She lowered her voice to a whisper. "Get her away from the area in case she changes her mind. If we're in Florida, she wouldn't have any place to go. She couldn't run. That doesn't mean she wouldn't try, but it would be less likely."

"All good points," Alexander said.

"I booked the jet to take us back. It's refueled and standing by. I can cancel if you'd rather go to your house."

"No, I like that idea. Angel, the guy who runs the bar, gave me a backpack. He said it was everything Bonita had, including her passport."

"He gave her stuff to you? Why?"

Alexander looked back at Bonita, who was now sleeping against the window. "It's kind of a long story, but she tried to kill herself. She put Angel's gun in her mouth and pulled the trigger. She either hadn't noticed or didn't remember that I removed the bullets."

Jana's jaw dropped. She looked back at Bonita. "Oh, my God. That would have been awful."

"Awful would've been an understatement. That's when Angel decided she needed help."

Jana cocked her head at him. "She saw you and tried to shoot herself?"

"I said it was a long story. Seeing me may have been a part of it. Being messed up was a part. What triggered her was a couple of guys in the bar who wanted to have sex with her and offered her five dollars."

"Five bucks! I would've shot those motherfuckers."

"In her state of mind, maybe she thought they were right. That she's only worth five bucks."

Jana glanced back at Bonita again. "The poor thing. I'm so glad we're going to help her."

"When she wakes up, she may not remember anything. She'll wonder what she's doing with me, with us. She could go ballistic."

"That could be bad if she goes crazy on the plane. Maybe we should go to your beach house."

"She may get a little testy, but I can handle her. If we're on an airplane, there's not much she can do. If we were flying commercial, that would be different."

Jana glanced back at Bonita several times. "She looks emaciated. I wonder when she last ate a decent meal? She needs something to eat."

"Jack in the Box tacos?"

"Right," Jana said. "She tried to kill herself. Jack tacos would kill her for sure. But seriously, I did request food on the plane. I figured we'd be hungry. I didn't ask for an attendant, so we'll help ourselves."

"That's actually good. If we have any trouble with Bonita, there won't be a flight attendant to freak out."

Alexander directed Jana back to the airport. When they arrived, she pulled up to the front door.

"Stay here. I'll be right back." She jumped out of the SUV and briskly walked into QuickJet Aviation. Moments later, she returned and climbed back into the Land Rover. "They're opening the gate." She pulled to the side of the building and waited for a large metal gate to open. When it opened, she drove onto the tarmac and up to the Embraer Jet. A man in a captain's uniform greeted them. He opened the door for Jana, then followed her to the back and pulled their bags out of the hatch.

Alexander tugged Bonita from the back seat. She woke, tried to speak but couldn't, then, leaning on Alexander, made her way up the steps and into the cabin of the aircraft.

"Is she okay?" the co-pilot asked Jana.

"Sort of. She's a trafficking victim. We're taking her back to Florida to a women's shelter. She'll get the help she needs there." Jana thought a little white lie would eliminate a lot of questions.

"You chartered a plane to come and get her?" the co-pilot asked.

"To rescue her."

"Wow. That's wonderful. I'll do my best to give you a smooth ride."

"Thank you. That'd be nice. She's had a rough time of it."

Jana and the co-pilot boarded the plane. The pilot was in the cockpit going over the preflight checklist. The co-pilot joined the pilot, and Jana joined Alexander in the cabin. Alexander had sat Bonita in the back against the bulkhead and strapped her in. She fell back to sleep.

Alexander sat in the seat in front of Bonita. Jana sat in the next seat, facing him. A small table sat between them.

"Did you hear me?" Jana asked. "I told the pilot Bonita was a sex-trafficking victim, and we were taking her to a shelter in Florida. Maybe we should drop her off at the facility and let them detox her."

"That's not a bad idea. Do you know how long it takes to detox?"

"It depends. What's she on?"

Alexander rubbed his chin. "I assume meth or crack."

"That's what I figured. Again, it depends on how heavy she was using and how long she's been using."

"From the look of her, pretty heavy. I bet she got progressively more into it. Angel mentioned she started out using a little, then to make money, she sold herself, which caused her to need more."

"It's a vicious cycle. Hopefully, she can get clean."

"I hope so," Alexander said.

"Then what?"

He looked Jana in the eyes and shrugged. "Let's worry about that when we get there."

It wasn't long before the captain announced the aircraft was at cruising altitude and the passengers could move about the cabin. Jana found the tray of wraps she'd requested. She set the entire tray on the table between her and Alexander and went back for bottled water.

"I've been thinking about it," Jana said once she reseated herself. "We should take Bonita to my place. It'll be weird, but she desperately needs a shower. One of us may have to help her."

"That'll be awkward. I hope once we get to your condo, she'll be able to function on her own. At least enough to shower."

"We need to get food and water in her, too," Jana said, glancing back at Bonita. "Should I wake her?"

"It's a three-hour flight. Let's wait a bit. See if she wakes up on her own."

***

Two hours after the Embraer Legacy 450 took off, Bonita stirred. She slowly opened her eyes and looked around the cabin. Struggling to sit up straight in the seat, she clamped her eyes shut, then opened them gradually, and looked around the cabin again. The seatbelt prevented her from standing.

"Hello," she whispered through dry lips.

"She's awake," Jana said to Alexander.

"Here we go," Alexander said. He unbuckled his seatbelt and went to Bonita.

Again, Bonita squeezed her eyes closed and slowly reopened them. "Alex?"

He knelt next to her, happy she didn't freak out when she saw him. He rested his hand lightly on hers and said, "Hi. Yes, it's me. How are you doing?"

Bonita looked around the cabin, then back at him. "Okay, I guess. Where am I?"

"You're on an airplane on the way to Fort Lauderdale. Do you re-member what happened at the bar?"

Bonita closed her eyes and shook her head. "Pieces of it. I kinda re-member you saying you needed my help?"

"That's right. We do. Rey may be in Colombia and in trouble. Since you speak Colombian Spanish like a native, we thought you could help us."

A slight grin came to Bonita's lips. "You want me to go to Colombia with you?"

"Yes, will you do that?"

Bonita nodded. "It's been a long time since I've been there."

"That's okay. You'll be our translator."

"Okay..." Bonita's voice trailed off. "Can I get some water?"

"Of course," Alexander replied. He stood and went for a bottle of water. He opened it and handed it to her. "Can you eat?"

"Maybe. I feel like shit."

Jana joined the couple in the rear of the cabin. "Hi," she said. "I'm Jana. We haven't met, but I've heard a lot about you."

"I've heard a lot about you too," Bonita replied. She studied Jana, looked at Alexander, and then back at Jana.

"There's no way to ask this nicely, so I'm just going to ask," Jana said. "How fucked up are you?"

Bonita squinted as she tried to focus. "Very." She forced the word out.

"You need to get clean," Jana said. "Not only to help us but for yourself. You don't need to be living like this."

"How do you know what I need? Have you been abused? Have you lost a baby?" Bonita snipped.

Jana immediately recognized Bonita's mood swing. Instead of easing off her, Jana decided she needed tough love.

"You think you're the only person who's had it rough? Let me tell you, I've been there. Maybe not as bad in some cases, but worse in others. We need your help to find Rey and we need it quickly, so drop the self-pity bullshit and make up your mind that you're better than what you've become and buck up."

Bonita scowled at her and Jana returned the look. The two stared at each other for what seemed like an eternity. The muscles in Bonita's neck twitched and she looked away. Her body jittered. "I guess you don't have any ice, do you?"

"I'll check the galley," Alexander said.

"She means meth," Jana clarified.

"I knew that."

"No, Bonita, we don't," Jana said. "You're going to have to go cold turkey."

"Why? I can function okay with a small hit. Especially with a little smack. You wouldn't even know I was high."

"Smack is heroin," Jana told Alexander.

"I knew that one," he replied.

"No, Bonita, no meth, crack, heroin, or even pot."

"Fuck," Bonita said. "You know, when this is over, I'm going to go back to using."

"Hopefully not," Jana said.

"Having sex with guys at the bar is the only way I know to make a living. I can't flip burgers at McDonald's or work at Walmart. Meth lets me do it."

"And then you use more meth to forget what you're doing," Jana said incredulously.

"So?"

"Fine!" Jana said. "If that's what you want, I don't give a shit. But we need you and we need you sober. Get sober, help us find Rey, and I'll give you enough money to stay high for a year."

"That's a deal," Bonita said. "Look, I've tried to get clean. Almost weekly. The first day is the worst. After that, I'm pretty good. Give me a day."

"We will. But damn, girl, if you could go through a day without it, why didn't you stay off it?"

"Because as soon as my head would clear, I'd remember what happened, and I'd need a fix. To get money for it, I'd...well, you know what I'd do."

"I know," Jana said. "Look, we'll be landing soon. Try to eat a little and drink a lot of water. We'll go to my condo and you can shower and go to bed. It's been a long day. Hopefully, you can sleep. Let's see how you feel in the morning."

Bonita nodded. Jana grabbed Alexander by the arm and pulled him back to their seats. When they sat, she leaned close to him. "Since she's tried to stop using a few times, she may be okay tomorrow. Not great, but good enough. I noticed she never made eye contact with you."

"I noticed that too. She didn't want to talk to me, that's why I stayed out of it."

"You should give her some space. Let me interact with her as much as possible. At least for the next day or so."

"I'll do that. I know you can handle her, but I'm concerned." Alexander looked forlorn.

The pilot came on the intercom and announced their approach to Fort Lauderdale/Hollywood International Airport. Jana went back and checked Bonita's seatbelt, then returned to her seat. "Buckle up, Alex. Things are about to get real."

14

The day after the meeting with Jana and Alexander, JP arrived at the gym ten minutes before noon. He scanned the floor for Miggie, who was standing next to an attractive brunette on an elliptical machine. She seemed relieved when Miggie excused himself.

"Did you find anything?" Miggie asked when he met up with JP by the dumbbells.

"Nothing," JP replied. "Drew a blank everywhere I went. I drove around to other gyms where guys I know train, and they didn't know anything about an illegal gambling operation. No one had approached any of them to throw a fight. I thought someone would've approached at least one of those guys."

"Maybe they have, but they don't want to say anything," Miggie said.

"That's possible. Maybe they thought I wanted in on it. If they thought I wanted to fix a fight, and they were straight, they wouldn't talk to me."

"Or maybe they thought you were wearing a wire. Working for the cops."

"I suppose. But, they didn't seem to know what I was talking about."

"You didn't find the guys who contacted you and Cole?"

"I didn't. I worked at the bar last night. Anyone that came in that looked like a fighter, I struck up a conversation with to see if they knew anything. I asked if they knew a place to do a little betting. I didn't mention gambling on fights, just gambling. Nothing. Later, this guy comes up to me. He said he heard me talking to the other guy—"

"JP, you need to be careful. You don't want people hearing you."

JP glanced around the gym suspiciously then lowered his voice. "I know. I got a little careless. Anyway, he says he knows where there's a game if I was interested. He was a skinny dude. Either Puerto Rican or Cuban. Dressed pretty well. I said I was interested, but I panicked. I don't play poker. I'm not a sports fan. I like football, but it ain't football season, so I says I like to bet on boxing and MMA fights. Especially the local MMA fights. Then he says they have a gambling room in West Palm with Texas Hold 'em and blackjack tables. They'll take bets on basketball and football–both college and pro–but they don't bet on baseball, hockey, or boxing."

Keeping a straight face was difficult for Miggie when JP's tone turned covert. He knew no one in his gym would be listening to them. "If they don't bet on MMA, they aren't the guys we're looking for."

"Probably not," JP agreed. "But I snapped a couple of pictures of the dude. I'll ask around and see if anyone knows him."

"Sounds good. Be careful. You don't want to ask too many questions. Whoever it is may hear you're looking for them."

"If they do, they might find me. That would work. I'd say I was asking around 'cause I heard they took bets on MMA. Maybe that's the way I should play it."

"Except they might not like you poking your nose around. You might get it cut off."

"I dunno. I can handle myself." JP flexed his muscles to prove the point.

"Don't get too cocky, JP. Most likely, you'd never see them."

JP nodded his head in agreement. "Maybe not. I'm going to do more digging this afternoon. I'll be careful."

"Glad to hear it."

"What's that big fella and Jana up to? Have you heard from them lately?"

"I haven't. They may be waiting to hear from you. I'll call Jana and give her an update later."

"So, they're just hangin' out? I wonder if he's tappin' her?" JP returned to speaking in a normal volume.

"JP, be careful. That's my brother's girlfriend you're talking about."

"Sorry, I forgot. He got pissed when he caught me upskirting her."

JP smiled as he recalled the image of Jana next to him, her legs spread eagle with only a G-string covering her vagina.

"You're lucky it was him and not me," Miggie said. He was not smiling.

"Come on, man, you woulda looked. I was lying there looking up, and you were holding her leg stretched out. What was I supposed to do?"

"Let's drop it, okay?"

"Okay, but I'd keep an eye on him, that's all."

Miggie thought for a second. "They did seem a little chummy. I hope nothing's going on between them, but if there is, that's up to Jana. I wouldn't like it, but it isn't any of my business."

"Ain't my business either. My business is finding out who Cole was with. I'll do that, then I'm done with 'em."

"Unless they need our help."

"If they need me, I'll help. But I don't like the big guy."

"His name is Alex."

"Whatever. Did he tell you what he planned to do if I found the people he's looking for?"

Once again, Miggie contemplated the question for several seconds. "No, he didn't. I'm not sure he has a plan. It sounds like he wants to find out what he's up against first."

"Hmm, it would be nice to know what he's planning. I'm stickin' my neck out for him. I don't want to be hung out to dry in the end."

"How do you mean?"

"They got tons of money. Let's say they find Rey 'cause of shit I told them, and they disappear. I'm the one those guys will come looking for."

Miggie ran his hand through his hair and scratched his head. "They wouldn't do that. Even if they did, it would be after those people got what they wanted. They'd be getting Rey out of harm's way. If the people had what they wanted, they wouldn't mess with you."

"I hope you're right."

"The next time I talk to Jana, I'll see what I can find out and I'll mention your concerns. If she and Alex were planning to take off with

Rey, they'd take care of you."

"Let me know what she says," JP said. He turned and walked to the bench, where he began his daily lifting routine.

Miggie walked to his office, closed the door, pulled his cell phone from the pocket of his gym shorts, and called Jana.

15

It was a challenge, but by morning, Bonita was able to shower without assistance. She came out of Jana's guest bedroom wearing a white cotton robe. Her long black hair was disheveled but clean. She doddered into the living room where Jana was sitting on the oblong sofa, looking at her iPad.

"Good morning," Bonita said quietly. Her voice was dry and raspy.

"Good morning. How are you feeling?"

"I've been better. My head is throbbing, my mouth is dry, and I can't tell you how much I'd like some crank right now."

"Sit down," Jana said. "I can help you with two of the three."

Bonita sat on the sofa opposite her. She closed her eyes and rubbed her temples. "One would fix the other two." She opened her eyes and tried to smile.

Jana went to the kitchen and returned with four ibuprofen and a large glass of water. "Take these," she said when she handed Bonita the pills and water. "Do you drink coffee?"

"I do, but sleep is the best thing when going through meth withdrawal. If it's okay, I want to go back to bed soon. I better skip the coffee." Bonita swallowed the pills one at a time and washed each down with small sips of water.

"Of course it's okay. Sleep is good."

Bonita glanced out the large glass doors to the empty patio, then around the large living area. "Where's Alex?"

"He went for a jog…or a walk…along the beach."

"Good. I didn't want to see him."

"Bonita, why not?"

"He hates me. I can't face him," she said, her chin quivering.

"Bonita! Alex does not hate you. I know that for a fact. Why would you say such a thing?"

Bonita took another sip of water. "He was so happy when I told him I was pregnant. He doted on me. Gave me everything I wanted. He was there for me. We talked about redoing the guest room, but he said we should sell the beach house and move inland to a house with a proper yard and better schools. Then I lost the baby. I could tell by his eyes that something inside of him died too. He never said anything, but I could tell. He became withdrawn. In the mornings, he sat on the deck and stared at the ocean. He'd come in and get on his computer for several hours. Then he'd turn on a football game or an old movie and sit and watch television. He'd make dinner for us, but we didn't talk much. He'd kiss me and give me an occasional hug, but we didn't make love once after..."

Bonita took several more small sips of water. "I could tell he blamed me for being so flawed I couldn't have a baby. I stayed in bed and watched TV all day. I got bored and depressed. I wanted to talk to him about it, but whenever I'd try, he stared at me with those cold blue eyes, eyes I only saw hatred in. One morning, he said he was going fishing. I gathered a few things, took a thousand dollars from a stash he kept, and took off. I walked to the corner store and called Uber. They took me to the ferry. I rode across and called another Uber to take me to Houston."

"To the bar?" Jana asked.

"Another bar nearby at first. I didn't want to see Angel. I went downhill pretty fast. After a few weeks, I ended up at Angel's. Alex texted me and told me I needed to come home. I asked him not to look for me and I'd be in touch. Angel put me to work. I had no problem with that. He kept me supplied. I was doing okay at first. One rock would last all day. Then the price of ice went up, so I had to work a little harder, if you know what I mean, to pay for it."

Jana nodded. She knew exactly what Bonita meant.

"So, you know what happened. To get me in the mood to make the money, I had to use more. I kept spiraling downhill. I'd try to stop but then I'd have to...uh, you know...and I'd need something to get me through it."

"Bonita, I have to ask, going to that bar, which is a front for prostitution, right? You knew what you would have to do. Why didn't you go to a strip club? You're a beautiful woman. You could have made a lot of money dancing. And, if you wanted to go a bit further, in a private room, you would make even more. A lot more than you made at the bar."

"When I was a teen, I was smuggled into the country. They literally auctioned me off. I was chained in a tiny room and forced to have sex all night. The original owner of the bar liked me and I became a trafficker instead of being trafficked. That's all I know. I thought I'd found the American dream with Alex, and then it all went to shit. I could have tried dancing, but at my bars, I knew the people around me. I guess I was more comfortable."

"I get it," Jana said. "I remember the first time I danced. It was a sleazy bar, and I wondered what I'd gotten myself into. But I made more money the first night than I'd made in a week at other jobs. That's how I got into it. I wasn't happy, but it was my choice and I wasn't forced to have sex with the guys. I can't imagine what you went through."

Bonita looked around the condo at the white furnishings, the gray quartzite countertops with double waterfall quartzite backsplashes, the designer light fixtures, and then out the glass doors at the view of the Atlantic. "I guess it turned out okay for you."

"I can't argue about that," Jana said. "But it wasn't easy. That's a story for another day. Are you hungry?"

Bonita shook her head. "I'd like to go back to bed." She disappeared into the bedroom. Jana made herself another cup of coffee and sat on the sofa. She opened her iPad and browsed the headlines at CNN.com. She looked up when she heard the electronic door lock buttons being pressed. The door opened and Alexander walked in wearing an extra-large T-shirt, shorts, and sneakers. The T-shirt was damp with perspiration.

"How was your walk?" Jana asked.

"Nice. It's less humid here than in Bolivar. Anything happening? Is

Bonita up?"

"She got up for a little while. Drank a little water and ate a couple of painkillers. We had a pleasant chat before she went back to bed. She thinks you hate her because she lost the baby," Jana said.

"That's ridiculous. How...why...?"

She filled him in on the conversation she had with Bonita.

"I need to have a talk with her," Alexander said. "Hopefully, she'll be up to it later. The sooner we put this behind us, the better."

"Will she listen? I mean, she blames herself, which is absurd. She was a victim."

"That's what I plan to tell her. She needs to understand and accept it."

"From what I heard this morning, she doesn't like who she is when she's in the bar, but that's all she knows. We've got to change that, too."

Alexander sighed. "As Ted Kennedy said to Mary Jo Kopechne when she asked what he'd do if she got pregnant, 'We'll cross that bridge when we get to it.'"

"Mary Jo who?"

"Never mind. Have you heard from Miggie?"

Jana picked up her phone and scrolled through the messages and call log. "No, I haven't. But it's still early for JP. Remember, he's not a morning person."

"That's right. I'm going to shower and change. If Miggie calls, don't answer it. No, it's okay, answer it. You can tell me what he said. If he asks what we are planning, tell him you don't know."

"I wouldn't be lying," Jana said with a sly grin. "But aren't we going to Colombia as soon as Bonita is able?"

"We are. But I don't want anyone to know. Especially JP."

"Not JP? Why?"

"I don't trust him. If he gets close to anyone involved, he's liable to mention where we're going. I'd rather no one know about it."

"What about Miggie?" Jana asked.

"I trust him, but he could slip. The key to a successful operation is only those who need to know, know."

Jana shivered. "An operation. That gave me goosebumps. I never thought about it like that. Should it have a name?"

"A name? No. If it did, it might be 'Operation What the Hell am I Doing?'"

"What?" Jana's face scrunched up in a giggle.

"Don't laugh. I'm about to go to a foreign country with a drug-addicted prostitute and a...hell, how should I classify you? Hot blonde chick? No, you won't attract attention," Alexander said, a slight grin on his face.

"At least you didn't say ex-stripper or rich bitch," Jana said.

"We don't know what we're up against. An army could have met Rey and Cole there. And they could have an army here waiting for us when we return. If I fuck this up, you and Bonita could suffer the consequences. This is serious business and it could turn bad on a dime."

"Alex, you've officially scared me. Is this a good idea?"

"If we want to find Rey and Cole, and get them away from whoever has them, going to Colombia is our best shot. Is it a good idea..." Alexander shrugged.

"Alexander Christian, you sure know how to instill confidence in a girl."

"You don't have to come."

"Would you prefer I didn't? Would it be best if just you and Bonita went?"

"If things go south, it would be best if you weren't there. But honestly, I think you can help. We have to find Rey before we do anything, and the more eyes, the better."

Jana smiled. "I'm glad you said that because I'm going. If things go 'south'–I guess there was no pun intended–I should be there. I got you into this."

"I'm glad it's settled," Alexander said. "I'm going to shower. Shouldn't be long."

Five minutes later, Jana's phone buzzed. It was Miggie.

16

When Alexander returned from his shower, Jana was typing on her phone. She looked up and said, "You clean up nicely." She then typed for several more seconds. Alexander sat on the sofa across from her.

"I was giving QuickJet a heads-up," she said. "Colombia isn't much further than Houston, but they can't fly over Cuban airspace, so they have to go around. It adds several hundred miles to the trip. There's also more paperwork involved in filing the flight plan. It sounded like we might go soon. I thought I'd let them know. I said we'd be going to Cartagena. Isn't that where Bat said those cell phones last pinged from?" She finished typing and put the phone on the coffee table in front of her.

"It is. Cartagena's on the coast. It's as good a place as any to start."

"And Miggie called right after you went to take a shower."

"Any news?"

"Nothing. He said JP did some digging last night but didn't come up with anything. A guy in the bar where JP works overheard him asking about gambling and said he could get him in a game, but he didn't take bets on MMA. JP was convinced he wasn't with the people we're looking for. Miggie said JP was going to keep digging. He had a few more contacts he wanted to talk to."

"That's odd," Alexander said.

"What?"

"JP is close friends with Cole but can't find hide nor hair of anyone involved."

"It does seem odd," Jana said. "What does that mean?"

"That maybe it's not a gang or a mob or crime syndicate, but a couple of guys pulling a heist and they conned Cole and Rey into it. The two guys on the boat were bluffing. There might be one more guy locally who took pictures of you and sent them to Rey and said he was watching you. Just enough to get Rey to comply."

Jana pulled her legs to her chest and wrapped her arms around them. "Oh...my...God," she said, "could Rey be in on it? He, Cole, and the two other guys?"

"It's possible. Is Rey too proud to ask you for money?"

Jana rested her chin on her knees while she thought. "Yes and no," she said. "We planned to sell the *Miss Jana* and buy a big sport fisher. He wants to run fishing charters. Not because he needs the money, but because he's bored sitting around the condo. I told him I'd buy him any boat he wanted. It didn't seem to bother him that I'd pay for it."

"So, there's no need for him to risk the boat or his freedom on a smuggling operation?"

"No, that'd be stupid."

"We can rule out that Rey's there under his own free will. We need to go to Colombia, find him, and ask him what's going on. And that's where Bonita becomes important. When we find him, she can walk right up to him and talk to him. Cole doesn't know her, and anyone else involved certainly won't know her."

Jana nodded and pursed her lips. "And I can't wait to hear the answer."

"Don't crucify him yet."

"No, I shouldn't. Rey's one of the most honest people I know."

"But he can be coerced to do something against his will."

"How do you mean?"

"How many young Cuban girls did he smuggle into the US?"

"Oh, yeah, there's that. I see what you mean. But that was my decision, too. We felt like we had no choice."

"Which is why he's in South America, as we speak."

"And that's why we'll be there soon. Speaking of Colombia, we'll go through customs like anyone else entering the country. Since we're on a private plane, customs will heavily scrutinize us. Leave your gun at home."

Alexander nodded. "I planned to. I'd like to have my gun, but it's not worth getting caught trying to smuggle it into the country. The last place I want to see is a Colombian prison."

"No, that's not where you want to be."

"The good news is, whoever has Rey shouldn't have any weapons either—if they bothered to clear customs. They could hide guns on the boat, but if immigration found them, it would jeopardize their entire plan. It'd be risky."

"Without weapons, we may have an advantage," Jana said. "Looking at the picture of the two guys with them, Rey or Cole could take them out fairly easily. Rey is not a fighter, but he's trained in martial arts for years. He can if he has to. Cole is a warrior."

"And the only reason they haven't taken those guys out is they're worried something will happen to you."

"Which means, when we find him and he knows I'm safe, he and Cole can take out the guys and we can all come home." Jana's face was painted with concern. "Unless I'm not safe?"

"I haven't spotted anyone following us and I haven't even noticed anyone who looks like they might be watching us. I'm...almost...convinced no one is watching you."

"Almost?"

"Never say never."

"Alex, I get the impression you aren't telling me everything you know...or think you know."

"That's true, in a sense. My head is swimming with possibilities. I haven't quite worked them all out. No need to share every crazy scheme I dream up. I promise you, when I have something that's solid, I'll share it with you."

"Works for me," Jana said. She was curious about what he was thinking. He told her his most recent idea, that it likely wasn't a large organization behind Rey's disappearance, but she wondered how much he truly believed it. If he was incorrect, and there were ten, or twenty, or even more people involved, they would be heavily outnumbered.

The guest room door opened. Bonita walked out and methodically made her way to the oblong sofa and sat next to Jana. She never looked at Alexander.

"How are you feeling?" Jana asked.

"Better. I ache all over, but my head isn't pounding like it was."

"Are you hungry?"

"A little," Bonita replied. She fiddled with the cotton belt that held the white robe together.

"We haven't eaten either. I'm going to go out to get food."

Bonita's head snapped up and she glared in fear at Jana. Before Bonita could object, Jana lept off the sofa, grabbed her purse, and scurried out of the room. "I'll be back soon," she yelled as she left the condo.

Alexander stared at Bonita, who was still fiddling with the belt of the robe. He walked across to the sofa and sat beside her, gently but firmly grasping her arm, so she couldn't scoot away. He held her with a soft touch, but with enough pressure to maintain control, conveying a sense of reassurance and support without being overly forceful.

"Bonita, we need to talk. At least I need to talk and you need to listen." Alexander placed his hand on Bonita's cheek and turned her to face him. He felt only minor resistance. Her eyes danced around the room, looking everywhere but at Alexander.

"Look at me," he ordered. She slowly made eye contact.

"I should begin by saying I'm sorry."

Bonita squinted. "Why—"

"Please, don't interrupt. I failed you, and I'm sorry. Jana told me what you said. I thought I was doing the right thing, but in reality, I guess I was doing the opposite. When you told me you were pregnant, I was happy. Surprised. Shocked. Scared. But I was happy. Especially happy for you. You were over the moon. You never mentioned wanting a baby, partly because we hadn't been together that long and it never came up, but it was obvious. I was happy, but not as happy as you, so I put on a brave face and pretended to be. Don't get me wrong, I would've come around and I'd have been ecstatic once you had the baby. Then when you lost him, or her, I had mixed feelings. Yes, I wanted to have a baby with you, but I'm older and it was scary. I wasn't relieved, not at all. The tears I cried were real, but I was most sad because of what you were going through. I felt horrible for you."

Alexander relaxed his grip on her arm. She didn't scoot away. "I wanted to talk to you about what had happened, but I didn't know how. I thought if I gave you some time and space, everything would be okay. In retrospect, I should have reached out for professional help immediately and forced you to go. I drifted back into the routine I had before we met—coffee on the porch, on the computer checking the stock market and the news. I watched a lot of football. That was my routine, dull as it was. I thought you were doing okay and the books you were reading and movies you were watching were taking your mind off the baby. I kept hoping one day you would be your old, smiling self. Instead, I came back from fishing and you were gone. That hurt me as much as losing the baby hurt you."

Bonita rested her head on his shoulder. "I'm sorry, Alex, I felt like you were ignoring me. In bed, you didn't touch me. I was certain you hated me."

Alexander put his arm around her and held her close. He expected to see tears, but none formed. He recalled that losing the baby must have hurt her deeply, but she didn't cry. At least he never saw a tear.

"What now?" Bonita asked.

"I love you. I'll always love you. But my routine must bore you. It makes you feel like I'm ignoring you. We could try again, but you wouldn't be happy. I'm too much of an old fogey for you. I can't risk you going back to what you were doing."

"That's sweet, Alex, but that's all I know."

"Let me rephrase. I won't let you go back to that life. Do you remember sticking a gun in your mouth and trying to kill yourself?"

She wore a look of pure terror. "No! I did? Oh, my God."

"Yes. You'd rather be dead than do what you were doing. When this is all over, we'll figure something out. What's important now is for you to know that I could never hate you, I love you...as a friend. Can we be friends?"

"Yes, I'd like that. Thank you, Alex. I feel a lot better. I do miss you, but we should just be friends."

"That makes me happy," Alexander said.

"Me too. You can text Jana and tell her she can come back now."

"What do you mean?"

"I know she left so you could talk to me alone. I may still be a little fucked up, but I'm not stupid."

"That you are not." Alexander pulled out his phone and texted Jana.

Ten minutes later, Jana returned with breakfast tacos. "I walked around the corner to Tinta Breakfast. They have lots of options, but I thought I should play it safe and get tacos. Real tacos, not Jack... They're all sausage, egg, and cheese. I got plenty, too. I didn't know how hungry you all would be."

"More tacos?" Alexander said, helping her with the bags of food.

They sat at the round glass table in front of the second set of sliding glass doors. The view from the table was of the Intracoastal Waterway.

"The water in the Atlantic is bluer than the Gulf, and the sand is whiter," Alexander said. "From a distance, with the sun at a proper angle, the Gulf of Mexico off Bolivar can be almost as beautiful. What we don't have in Bolivar is an abundance of fine restaurants, shops, hotels, and stores. This area is amazing. I didn't realize how close that place we ate at the other night, Casablanca, was. I walked right past it this morning."

"Casablanca?" Bonita asked.

"Yes," Jana said. "It's a restaurant. When we get back, we'll go there...to celebrate."

"That sounds nice. The taco was good, but that's all I can eat. I'd like to go back to bed. Suddenly, I feel exhausted."

"You get your rest. Alex, when do we leave for Colombia?"

"Let's give JP one more day. If he doesn't come up with anything concrete that would keep us from going, I'd say we need to go tomorrow. I'll check with Bat later. He's still checking the location of cell phones. He may have news."

"Bonita, will you be up to it? To leave tomorrow?"

"I should be. I feel much better today. Even better after Alex talked to me. I'm tired, but I'll be okay." Bonita left the table and went to the guest room.

Jana waited until Bonita had closed the door, then she turned to Alexander. "She seems in much better spirits. What'd you say to her?"

"I told her it was my fault. I didn't get her the help she needed. I thought I was giving her space, and she thought I was ignoring her and wanted nothing to do with her. I told her I loved her, but we weren't compatible, so I'd like to be her friend. She accepted that. When this is all over, I want to help her. I can't...I won't let her go back to what she was doing."

"You're a good man, Alexander Christian. But as I've said before, you're a different man."

"And why do you say that this time?"

"Here's a beautiful, exotic woman who seemed to adore you, but she'd rather be smoking crack and fu...uh...having sex with losers than living with you."

"Jeez, Jana, don't sugarcoat it. Give it to me straight. The knife is in. Give it a big twist."

"Oh, I'm sorry Alex. That sounded a little cold."

"A little. You're saying Bonita would rather be a crack whore than live with me? Maybe I'm the one who should've put the gun in my mouth."

Jana shook her head. "That's not what I meant. Now I feel bad."

"Maybe not, but it's true."

"Okay, this has gotten all spun out of whack. She was depressed about losing the baby. She thought you hated her. That's why she left. Also, men have treated her like shit all her life. She has to have trust issues. Had she not gotten pregnant, you two might have stayed together for a while, but she would have gotten bored eventually. It's hard to say. You two may have done more together and been fine. Then again, she might have tired of your routine and left you. Had she, I doubt she'd have gone back to the bar. It was her depression that made her do what she did, not you."

"What you said makes a lot of sense. Nice save," Alexander said, smiling at her.

Jana leaned her head back and laughed. "The FBI agent and the crack whore. The stripper and the fishing boat deckhand. We know how to pick 'em, Alex."

"That's funny. But I wish you wouldn't call Bonita a crack whore or yourself a stripper."

"I thought about that after I said it. I'm sorry. Bonita's had it hard. I feel for her." Jana paused and looked him in the eyes. "Alex, you know how I said I couldn't label you? I said you were different. I think I've got it. It took me so long because I've never met one. You're a gentleman."

17

Alexander didn't need to look at his watch. The sunlight streaming in through the northwest-facing sliding glass doors told him it was early evening. He loved Jana's condo, but the northwest exposure was not ideal. Especially in South Florida. He stood at the patio doors and took in the view.

"I bet it gets hot in here later in the summer," he said to Jana, who was sitting on the couch in the main living room staring at her iPad.

"Uh, what?" she asked.

Alexander walked to the living room and sat across from Jana. "I said I bet it gets hot in here later in the summer."

"It's not too bad. The patio has electric shades I can lower to block the sun. They block the view too, so I rarely lower them. The AC keeps it cool."

Alexander wondered what Jana's electric bills were, but didn't ask. He doubted she knew. "You've been on your iPad for a while. What are you looking at?"

"Doing Wordle."

"Wordle?"

"You haven't heard of Wordle? I thought everyone had by now."

"I lead a sheltered life."

"Yeah, right," Jana said with a smirk. "What have you been doing?"

"Going crazy, mostly. I checked with Bat and he had nothing new. I'd like to call Miggie and see if JP has anything, but I know Miggie will call when he hears something. I thought about hitting the streets to see what I could dig up, but if a local who knows where to look can't find anything, I doubt I could."

"I thought about that too," Jana said. "A few years ago, I'd be able to tell you, but I've distanced myself from that world. I'd like to stay away from it."

"Smart. I emailed a friend at the Bureau in Houston. I asked her if she could check with the Miami office and see if they have anything on anyone running an illegal gambling operation."

"Cool. Will they have anything?"

"Maybe. It would have to be interstate for the FBI to get involved, but they might have something. They'll likely check with the local LEOs. They should have some intel."

"LEOs?" Jana asked.

"Law Enforcement Officers," Alexander replied.

"Ah-ha. They should. There's a ton of illegal gambling going on in the area. Back when I was working in the clubs, I'd hear guys talking about it and see money changing hands. If I saw a guy get handed a big wad of cash, you know where I was going."

"Did that work?"

Jana laughed loudly. "Oh yeah. It didn't take long for his winnings to become mine."

Alexander could only shake his head.

"You don't approve?" Jana asked, her tone a bit defensive.

"No. I mean, I don't care. It's crazy how much a guy will spend on a girl in a strip club."

"You know the old saying, 'The little head starts thinking for the big head.' You never went to a gentlemen's club?"

"I wouldn't say never. And I'm not too different from other men. I made a point to stay out of them."

"You don't strike me as the type that would find it necessary to go to a strip club to find female companionship."

"Oh? Was that a compliment? Thank you. Truth is, my one vulnerability is women. I fall for them pretty easily. It hasn't always turned out well."

"Was Bonita one?"

Alexander glanced over at the guest room where Bonita was sleeping. "You could say that. One look at her and I was smitten."

"And her past didn't matter to you?"

"At first, I thought she might have been playing me, but the more I got to know her, the more I loved her. I know she loved me too...until it all went to shit."

"I'm sorry it ended like it did."

"Luckily, it's been a while and I'm okay with just being friends with her. Who knows what's going to happen when we find Rey and this is all over, but I doubt I'll ever see Bonita again. I wouldn't bring it up, but I was hoping she could go to your women's shelter until she got on her feet."

"That's a great idea. I can arrange it. Briana would love to see her."

"Awe, Briana. How's she doing?"

"Fantastic. She's working on a degree at FIU and co-managing the shelter. She even has a boyfriend."

"Good for her. I—" Alexander stopped in mid-sentence when Bonita came out of the bedroom. She wore the same white robe she had on earlier. She joined them in the living room.

"How are you feeling?" Jana asked.

"Not too bad. I slept well, and I didn't have any muscle spasms. I'm a little achy, but way better than last night, or even this morning."

"Are you hungry?"

Bonita nodded.

Jana turned to Alexander. "I said we'd go to the Casablanca Café to celebrate, but would you like to go tonight?"

"I'd love it."

"We need to find you some clothes," Jana told Bonita. "What you had on and the few things you brought with you aren't wearable."

Bonita blushed and dropped her gaze to the floor.

"It's okay, don't worry about it," Jana said to her. "You're a little taller than me, but you are, um, bustier. I think I can find something you can wear."

"Thank you," Bonita said. "Too bad we aren't at Alex's house. He had a large closet full of women's clothes. All sizes too."

It was Alexander's turn to blush.

"Come with me. Let's see what I've got."

The two women disappeared into Jana's suite. Alexander opened his laptop and Googled Cartagena, Colombia and crime.

An hour later the women emerged from the bedroom. Alexander finished reading an article and closed his laptop. He glanced at the two of them and did a double-take. His heart raced. When he regained his composure, he said, "Wow, you all look fantastic. Stunning."

"Thank you," they said simultaneously.

He looked at one and then the other. Jana wore a vintage blue micro denim skirt and a white sleeveless, plunge neck, cotton tank top with delicate lace trim tied into a bow between her breasts. Bonita wore a black low-waist mini-skirt with a pink short-sleeved ribbed T-shirt. The square-neck T clung tightly to her body and stopped above her navel.

Alexander quickly noticed what looked like the top of a large peacock feather tattoo rising from Bonita's waistband. A small dreamcatcher with gold feather pendants, a ruby gemstone, and a Swarovski pearl bead hung from her navel. The gold ring of the dreamcatcher glistened against her tan skin.

"Are those new?" he asked, unable to stop looking at her.

"Yes. I got them right after I went back to the bar. A guy bought me drinks, and I told him my story—some of it anyway—and he said I should get the tattoo and the dream catcher. He said in some cultures, the peacock tattoo is a symbol of good luck, and in others, it's seen as a symbol of wealth and prosperity. I needed both. Native Americans believed the dream catcher protected sleepers from bad dreams, nightmares, and evil spirits. Again, something I needed. He said he knew a fabulous tattoo artist and would pay if I wanted to get it done. I figured, what do I have to lose, so I did it."

"They're nice," Alexander said. Only the top half of the feather protruded from Bonita's waist. He wondered how far the feather went.

Bonita must have read his mind—or his eyes. "And yes, it goes all the way to my inner thigh. Would you like to see it?"

"No, thank you." Alexander's face turned a pale red but not from embarrassment. He was angry that within a week of leaving him, she allowed someone to tattoo her inner thigh. He shook his head to clear the image from his mind.

Jana picked up on Alexander's mood shift. "Hey," she said, "I'm starving. Let's go. Alex, are you ready?" She glanced at his gray shorts and Hawaiian shorts and cringed.

Alexander turned to Jana who gave him an 'I'm sorry' look. A slight smile crossed his lips. He told her he was ready and gave her a slight nod of acknowledgment.

The three had just left the building when Jana's phone buzzed. Alexander stopped and watched Jana pull her phone from her purse. "It's my accountant," she said. "Hang on." She turned and walked a few steps away.

Bonita put her hand on Alexander's shoulder. "I'm sorry, Alex, for disappearing on you. Please forgive me."

"It's fine. I—"

"No, let me explain. I left because I thought you hated me. I hated myself. When the man at the bar suggested I get a tattoo, I thought it was a perfect way to punish myself. I thought about getting a hideous tattoo on my face, but I guess I wasn't that fucked up. Getting the feather hurt. Especially around the...the other end of the feather. I think he paid for it so he could watch me get it. Funny, for what he spent on the tattoo, the navel piercing, and the dreamcatcher, he could have—"

"Bon! Thank you, but I don't need or want an explanation. I understand and I'm sorry too. I'll admit, the tattoo got to me a little. Looking at you got to me. You look gorgeous. Both of you do."

"Jana did my hair and makeup. I never wore much makeup. When Jana worked at the clubs, the girls would do each other's makeup. I guess I look like a stripper now."

"Actually, you look like a supermodel."

Jana finished her call and walked over to Alexander and Bonita. "Sorry about that. My accountant noticed the Quickjet charges on my credit card. He wanted to make sure it was me jetting around. What'd I miss?"

"Nothing. We were just chatting," Alexander said.

The restaurant was a short walk from the condo, past several high-rise condos and hotels. Jana led them to A1A, where they turned and walked past several more hotels to the Casablanca Café.

"That's a cute little building," Bonita said. "It's close, too. But it looks crowded."

"It gets crowded. Follow me," Jana said. She led them through the throng of people waiting for a table to a young female greeter. She was standing behind a faux wooden stand under a faded yellow umbrella.

"Hi Jana," the greeter said, nodding at them. "Three tonight? Would you like to be seated inside or out?"

"Inside, please," Jana said, slipping the girl a folded hundred-dollar bill.

The girl smiled. "Just a sec." She turned and disappeared inside the restaurant. A few minutes later, she showed them to a table.

"Should we order wine?" Jana asked. "Oh, I'm sorry, maybe we shouldn't," she quickly added.

"It's fine," Bonita said. "It's strange. I do a drug and I need more. But alcohol doesn't affect me like drugs. If I have a drink tonight, it's not like I'm going to wake up in the morning and crave a drink."

"Okay, if you're sure. We'll have one bottle. Red or white?"

"Do they have Sangria?" Bonita asked.

Jana and Alexander looked at her as though she'd committed a cardinal sin.

"I'm joking," she said with a wide smile. "But seriously, I'm not much of a wine person. Get whatever y'all want."

Jana ordered a mid-level white from the wine menu. After the bottle arrived and the glasses were filled, she lifted her glass. "Here's to finding Rey, and to the future." The others clinked glasses and took a sip.

The server came and took their orders. Bonita looked around the restaurant and out the windows as darkness descended on the Atlantic. Jana looked at Alexander as if to say, "What should we talk about?"

Alexander could not get over Bonita's tattoo. "Did it hurt? I mean the tattoo. I've never gotten one."

"Yes, even being a little messed up, it hurt like hell. Especially when he tattooed my labia–"

Jana gasped. "Are you fucking kidding me?"

"No, that's where the feather ends. The guy that paid for it insisted."

Jana crossed her legs, unable to imagine what getting her labia tattooed would feel like. "What if you'd refused?"

"I didn't, so I don't know."

Alexander was disturbed but didn't show it. He didn't want to upset Bonita. "Did you cry when you were being tattooed?"

"No. I don't cry. Why?"

"The man didn't give a shit about watching you get the tattoo. He wanted to see you in pain. He's a sadistic son of a bitch. He wanted to see you cry. You didn't. Good for you."

"You know Alex, you're right. He seemed to be getting off on me hurting. When it was done, he said I should get my clit pierced. I didn't think about it then, but, you're right, I think he just wanted to see me in pain."

"Uh...you didn't..."

"No. I refused and he didn't force the issue."

The food was served. As interesting as Bonita's tattoo experience was, Jana wanted to change the subject. "Bonita, have you been to Cartagena?"

Bonita thought while she chewed a bite of food and swallowed before answering her. "I have. That's where I went to be smuggled to America when I was fourteen. My parents had arranged it and paid a guy to take me. Except the man used me for a while before sending me on. First, for his pleasure. He said it was to train me. Then he said it cost more to smuggle me to the US than my parents had paid. I had to earn the money by working the streets. I was there a year or two before he sold me to other traffickers. What happened after that isn't exactly dinner conversation."

"That's okay, skip the details," Jana said.

"Instead of America, I ended up in Nicaragua. From there, various men bought and sold me. It was a few days with some and a week with others. Then I'd get sold again. All the way through Mexico and finally to the US. I was well-used by the time the man bought me for his bar in Houston. What's crazy is, I was a skinny teenager back then. I had no boobs. If I had had these," Bonita said, cupping her breasts and holding them up, "men might have treated me differently...or worse. You never know."

"So, what happened?" Jana asked. "I know you worked at the bar, but not as a, you know, and you got your US citizenship."

"The guy who owned the bar at the time liked me. Not in the way you're thinking. He genuinely liked me and wanted to help me. He taught me English and helped me get a green card. Then he helped me become naturalized."

"The last part of the story is sweet, Bonita. What happened to the man?"

"He died in prison a couple of years ago."

"I'm sorry."

"Back to Cartagena," Alexander said. "So, you don't remember much about it?"

"I remember a little. I worked the streets so I know the area around the walled city pretty well. It hasn't changed in hundreds of years. I doubt it's changed much since I left."

"I spent time while you all were getting ready looking at Cartagena on Google Maps. The city is big, but not huge as compared to say, Houston or South Florida. From what I could tell, a lot of the coastline is beach, so no marinas. There's a large bay on the southwest side of the city, and it looks like most of the marinas are in that area. If the *Miss Jana* is there, she should be easy to find."

"Miss Jana?" Bonita asked. She looked at Jana.

"That's Rey's boat," Alexander replied. "I'm sorry, we haven't explained what's going on."

"No, you haven't. You said you wanted my help to find someone in Colombia."

Alexander filled in the gaps for her. When he finished, he asked, "Are you still up to this?"

"Totally."

18

A soft, golden glow immersed the bedroom when Alexander woke. It was late. Sleep had come hard and when he awoke, the reason still haunted him. He was about to take two women to a foreign country where he didn't know what he was getting himself into. He knew it wasn't the smartest thing he'd ever done.

Finding Rey, or at least the *Miss Jana*, should be easy. In South Florida, a sixty-five-foot motor yacht is a sapling in a forest. In Cartagena, Colombia, it would stick out like a six-foot-four sandy-haired man. Especially one in the company of a tall blonde with supermodel looks.

What would he do when he found the boat and Rey? That was another question that bothered him. He was flying into the unknown, and he didn't like it. He stood, stretched, dressed, and walked out of the room.

Jana and Bonita were sitting on the oblong sofas near the glass doors leading to the balconies. Jana was scrolling on her iPad, and Bonita was on a laptop. He poured a cup of coffee from the pot on the counter and sat on the sofa that Bonita was on, but at the far end.

"I'm glad you all are up," he said. "I didn't want to mention it last night, but while I was waiting for you to get ready, I did a little research. The drug cartels in Colombia that were prevalent in the eighties and nineties are making a comeback. These are Mexican cartels. The US put pressure on Mexico to crack down on the drug cartels so many have moved from Mexico to Colombia. The reports I read called them 'bloodthirsty.' These people are more brutal and violent than you can imagine. From the little we know, I doubt Rey is involved with any cartels. They have their own networks. But if we go there and snoop around and accidentally ruffle the wrong feathers, we'll be coming back in body bags."

"Oh my God." Jana slapped her hand over her mouth.

"Yes. We need to be very careful."

"Would you like my opinion?" Bonita asked.

"By all means," Alexander said.

"Most Latin men are quite a bit smaller than you, Alex. You're going to stand out. Even the taller guys are not as broad as you. I'm taller than the average Colombian girl. It might have been my height that got me trafficked. I was tall for my age. Anyway, people will notice you. You need to act like a tourist. You and Jana. People will remember her too. You're going to have to be a couple. Rent two hotel rooms. Adjoining rooms with a door connecting them would be best. People should see you two going in and out of the same room. I'll have the other room. I'll be your tour guide, or maybe a friend you brought along. You need to be seen lounging at the pool and doing touristy things. Also, be sure you act like a couple."

"How do you mean?" Jana asked.

"You know, walk hand in hand, go to meals together, hug in public once in a while. You'll figure it out."

"I doubt if anyone would ask, but of all the places in the world to go to, why Cartagena?" Jana asked.

"That's a good question," Alexander replied. "I did a little research. There's a lot of history there. We'll say we're tourists. We can always add that friends said it was a great place to visit. That should be enough. Especially if we're doing touristy stuff, as Bonita suggested."

"Plus, your friend is from Colombia and wanted you to come see it," Bonita said with a wink.

Jana's phone buzzed. She swiped the Answer button, put the phone on speaker, and said, "Hey Miggie."

"Hey. I just talked to JP. He said he spent the day yesterday digging and drew a blank. He couldn't find anyone who knew anything about an illegal gambling operation. He also said he was going to Vegas for a fight. He'll be out of pocket for a few days."

"That's too bad," Jana said. "We were hoping he'd come up with something we could use. Thank him for me."

"I will. What're you planning to do now?"

Alexander waved to get Jana's attention. When she looked at him, he shook his head and shrugged.

"We don't have a plan right now," Jana said into the phone. "Alex and I will have to talk about it and see what our options are."

Alexander gave her a thumbs up.

"Ok. I don't expect to hear anything from Rey, but if I do, I'll let you know."

Jana thanked Miggie and hung up. She looked at Alexander.

"You did well," he said without being asked. "How long does it take to have a plane ready?"

"A couple of hours, if there's one available. I gave them a heads-up, but I didn't say when. I can call them."

"Do that. How long will it take you to pack for three or four days in Colombia?"

"About the same. A couple of hours," Jana said. "It takes a woman a lot longer than a man to pack. Oh, speaking of packing, Bonita has nothing to wear. Some of my stuff fits her, but most of it's too small. She could use a bra or two."

Alexander scratched his head.

"There's a Macy's at the Galleria," Jana continued. "It's only about ten minutes from here. We can run over there and get her a few things. It won't take long. And it won't take me long to pack."

"Go," Alexander told her.

Jana dug into her purse, pulled out an American Express card, and handed it to him. "While we're gone, find us a nice hotel. A touristy place near the marinas."

"I'll see what I can find. Only two rooms?"

Jana shrugged. "I guess. Adjoining."

When Jana and Bonita left the condo, Alexander opened his computer and went to a popular travel site. He checked the location, reviews, and availability of several hotels before he came across the Hyatt Regency Cartagena. It was located on a peninsula along the southern coastline of the city. He checked his watch, he'd spent more time than he planned on finding a hotel.

The city center of Cartagena was east of the coast. The peninsula and the city formed a bay, which looked to him to be where most of the marinas were. It was one of the few protected bodies of water in the area. Close to it was an industrial area, with facilities for large container ships, a cruise ship terminal, and a naval base.

According to Google Maps, the far side of the bay was less than a mile from the Hyatt Regency as the crow flies. Alexander leaned back in his chair and pulled out his cell phone to text Jana.

Do you own a pair of binoculars?

I do. They're on the boat.

I see there's a Dick's Sporting Goods close to the airport. We need to stop and get binoculars.

I know the place. We can stop. It won't take long.

Great. They may come in handy.

Okay. We are doing well here. Should be back shortly.

See you soon.

Alexander put the phone down and went back to his laptop. On the Hyatt reservation site, he entered the dates of his stay. It was awkward putting today's date as the arrival date. He thought about how many nights they would need. Would four be enough? If not, they could always extend. He entered four nights. Two rooms for three people. The only option was rooms with two double beds. "Perfect," he said to himself and, using Jana's credit card, made the reservation.

He leaned back and stared at the wall in front of him, lost in thought. Finding Rey wouldn't be difficult. Getting him out of Colombia might be. Doing it while keeping Jana and Bonita out of harm's way might be extremely difficult. He didn't like it.

He shook off the feeling of impending doom and went into the bedroom. After a shower and a shave, he packed the remaining clean clothes into the bag he'd brought from Texas. A commotion outside drew his attention. He opened the door and found Jana and Bonita loaded down with shopping bags and struggling to get through the door.

"Is there anything left in the store?" he asked.

"Not much," Jana replied. "We had to buy everything we thought we might need in Cartagena. Dresses, shorts, tops, shoes, and a few accessories."

"We couldn't go without accessories," Alexander said with a sarcastic eye roll.

Jana added, "We would have bought more, but Bon said as tourists, we'll have to go shopping there. You know, to keep up appearances."

"How long will it take you two to pack all that...stuff?"

"Not long," Jana replied. "Bon, there are suitcases in the closet in your room. The medium-sized one should work for you."

"Medium?" Alexander said, again with a touch of sarcasm.

"Don't be an ass, Alex. Are you ready?"

"I am."

"We've got about two hours before the plane is ready. We have plenty of time to pack, swing by Dick's, and get to the airport."

Jana and Bonita shuffled their shopping bags into their rooms and closed the doors. Alexander sat and opened his laptop. He thought about how Jana had called Bonita, "Bon." That was what he called her, but he hadn't called her that since she left. He wondered why Jana was now calling her Bon. They must have bonded on the shopping trip.

Alexander emailed Bat to give him an update on their plans to go to South America and asked if there had been any more pings from the cell phones he'd been monitoring. He also asked Bat to monitor Jana's, Bonita's, and his phones. In a worst-case scenario, it might be handy to have their last locations.

He closed the laptop and put it and the charger in a canvas laptop bag. As soon as he did, he wished he'd checked to see if Colombia used one-ten-volt or two-forty-volt power. The power adaptor for the computer would work on either, but the plug might not fit. It would be fine. Most modern hotels had dual plugs, and if their hotel didn't, they likely sold adaptors. He let out a sigh. He was overthinking things. The power voltage was the least of his worries.

Jana was the first to join him in the living room. She wore a navy-blue floral print midi dress with pink, green, and white flowers, a dipping sweetheart neckline with spaghetti straps, and a gathered waist. She looked stunning.

A short time later, Bonita came out of her room. She too wore a midi dress. A woven satin dress with a red, pink, and green floral print, spaghetti straps, and a surplice neckline. Her long black hair lay gently on her bare shoulders. She, too, was stunning.

Alexander looked at the two beautiful women standing before him. He wanted to call off the trip. Too dangerous. But he'd committed, so he put on a brave face. "Wow, you two look gorgeous, but aren't you a bit fancy for the flight?"

"While we were trying on clothes, we thought we should look like jet-setting tourists when we checked into the hotel."

"Well, you nailed it. Do you all have everything? Passports?"

"I do," Jana said. "What about you?"

"Everything but my gun, which I'd like to have."

Both women gave him an odd look that he couldn't interpret. Without a great deal of enthusiasm, he said, "We better go."

Jana drove Rey's pickup truck. Alexander sat in the front seat. Bonita and the luggage were in the back. When they reached Dick's Sporting Goods, the women waited in the truck while Alexander went inside. He grabbed a pair of small, lightweight Bushnell ten by twenty-five binoculars and checked out.

When Alexander returned, Jana drove them to the QuickJet Aviation terminal. "I usually use Uber when I fly," she said. "I hate leaving my Alfa sitting outside. Driving the truck and having it here when we return is much more convenient."

Alexander didn't respond. He stared out the window, wondering if they would return.

19

The Embraer Praetor 500 touched down at Rafael Núñez International Airport and taxied to the ramp leading to QuickJet's private terminal in the northeast corner. An employee escorted Alexander, Jana, and Bonita to the office for customs and immigration processing.

QuickJet Aviation staff had all the customs and immigration clearance forms prefilled. The arriving passengers only had to sign them. The process was much easier and quicker than Jana had expected. She didn't need the three one-hundred-dollar bills she had ready to hand out.

A private SUV picked up the group and drove them along the coast toward their hotel. "¿Hablas inglés?" Bonita asked the driver.

"Yes, a little," the driver replied.

She had hoped he didn't speak English. She wanted to talk to Alexander without their driver understanding. Though he spoke a little English, she didn't want to take the chance so she tried some small talk with him. "Are you from Cartagena?"

"Sí," he replied but offered no details. Bonita decided that was enough small talk. During the remaining ten minutes of the drive to the hotel, she politely discussed the view of the Caribbean with Jana and Alexander.

"Nosotras estamos aquí," the driver said as he pulled into the hotel entrance.

"We're here," Bonita translated, although everyone in the SUV could see for themselves.

Jana handed the driver a hundred-dollar bill. He thanked her profusely in Spanish and broken English.

A hotel porter met the SUV and loaded the luggage onto a cart. He followed the group into the hotel and waited while they checked in. The desk clerk spoke English well. Jana's request for three keys to each room garnered an odd look but was granted without question.

While Jana was checking in, Alexander checked out the hotel and the staff. Other than one couple coming through the large glass doors into the lobby, no other guests were in sight. Three counters separated by a few feet were against one side of the lobby. Opposite the counters were four oversized white chairs with small tables between them.

The clerk handed Jana the keys and shouted the room numbers to the porter. "Elevators are around the corner. A porter will bring your bags to your rooms shortly," she said to Jana in English. Jana thanked her, then motioned Alexander and Bonita toward the elevators.

As requested, the hotel rooms were adjoining. Both rooms had two double beds and a view of the bay, which is what Alexander wanted but had forgotten to request. He went into the second room and looked at the view. It was the same as the other.

"Alex, do you have a preference?" Jana asked.

"No, either room is fine with me."

"Then Bon and I will take this one," she said.

"But you two must share a room," Bonita protested. "You must look like a couple."

"We will," Jana said. "But I'll sleep in here." She turned to Alexander. "It's not that I don't trust you, but it would be a little weird."

"Understood. No one will know where you're sleeping."

"The maids will," Bonita said. "If anyone is curious about us, the maids are who they will ask."

"Hmm. Good point. If only one bed in my room looked slept in, the maids would assume we slept together. We'd have to make the second bed in the other room ourselves before the maids come."

"Is that a big deal?" Jana asked.

"It could be," Bonita replied. "It's a large city with many tourists. But most tourists won't be asking the questions we are going to be asking. I bet word travels fast in this town. We are going to draw attention."

"Fuck it," Jana snapped. "I'll sleep with Alex. We've got separate beds."

"My, Jana, you certainly know how to charm a guy," Alexander said.

Jana laughed. "I guess that didn't come out right. How about—"

A knock on the door interrupted her. Bonita opened the door, and the porter carried in the luggage. In Spanish, she instructed him to put her suitcase in the adjoining room and leave Alexander and Jana's bags in the current room. When he finished, Jana handed him a hundred-dollar bill and said, "Gracias."

When the door closed behind the porter, Bonita said, "Jana, I'm not sure you should give everyone a hundred dollar tip. In Colombia, people appreciate tips, of course, but they don't, um, expect them. I mean, tipping is not required."

Alexander added, "I was wondering about that. I mean, it's nice, but does it add an extra layer of attention we don't need or want?" He paused for a moment. "Or does it buy loyalty? If someone asked that porter about us, will he answer their questions?"

"Hundreds are all I have," Jana said. "I need to get some local currency. What's the currency here?"

"Colombian Pesos." Bonita tapped on her phone. "A dollar is worth about three thousand eight hundred pesos." She tapped a few more times. "You gave the driver and the porter each a three hundred eighty-six thousand peso tip."

"That should buy loyalty," Alexander said.

"Or he will spread the word that Jana has money," Bonita added. "Speaking of money, I don't have any. Um...could I borrow a few bucks? I can also exchange dollars for pesos while I'm out tonight if you'd like."

"Oh my gosh, absolutely you can have some cash. You're working for me. I need to pay you anyway. Alex, what's the going rate for a PI? A thousand a day?"

Surprised by the question, he didn't reply.

"Whether it is or not, that's what I'm paying." Jana opened her purse and pulled out a wad of bills. She counted out forty one-hundred-dollar bills and handed them to Bonita. "Let's call that two days' pay, money for expenses if you have any. Bring me a couple of thousand dollars' worth of pesos."

"Be careful where you exchange it," Alexander said. "That's a lot of cash to be carrying around. Try not to flash it."

"Don't worry," Bonita said. She disappeared into the adjoining room and closed the door.

"Don't worry?" Alexander said. "Letting a substance abuser loose on the streets of Cartagena with four-grand cash. What can go wrong?"

"Shit," said Jana. "I shouldn't have given her so much."

"Too late now. It would be awkward to ask for it back." Alexander sighed and said, "I could use a drink. I'm also getting a bit hungry. How 'bout you?"

"I could use a drink. We should ask the man at the counter for a recommendation. I didn't see a concierge. A hotel like this should have one."

"Maybe we missed him. We can check when we go down."

Jana glanced around the moderately furnished hotel room. She found a local restaurant guide on the small desk against the wall. One side of the guide was in Spanish, the other in English. "According to this, there's a McDonald's close by," she said.

"There's always a McDonald's close by, no matter where you are."

"So true," Jana said without looking up from the brochure. "7 Cielos looks good."

Alexander typed the restaurant into his phone. "It's close," he said. "It's a three-minute drive. Or about an eight-minute walk."

"Is it safe to walk around here?"

"During the day, it's probably fine. We should ask about walking at night."

She looked back at the list of restaurants on the brochure. "There's one in the hotel that looks good. It's already getting dark, maybe tonight we should stay in."

"I like that idea. But—"

"But..."

"I'd like to get out and see a bit of the city. Let's ask in the lobby for a nice place and have a good dinner."

"Sounds good. I hope we aren't pointed to a local's uncle's restaurant that's an overpriced tourist trap."

"Are you worried about the price?"

Jana grinned, "No. I'm worried about terrible food and how we might feel in a day or two."

"Good point. The food and water here are safe to eat and drink. Whether it agrees with you is a different story."

"Now I want to go to McDonald's," Jana said.

"We may end up there. For now, let's get out and be adventurous. Remember, we're a couple on vacation."

"I forgot about that." Jana grabbed her purse and put her arm through Alex's. "Let's go, sweetie."

The restaurant the hotel staff recommended was excellent. To continue the ruse of a couple, Alexander and Jana tried to keep their conversations light. They told only the fun stories of their past. They didn't dwell on missing exes or missing boyfriends. When the wine flowed, they became flirtier, but only to keep up appearances, they told themselves.

The flirtation continued throughout dinner, during the taxi ride back to the hotel, through the lobby to the elevators, and into their hotel room. Once inside the room, Jana hugged Alexander. "This was a nice evening. Thank you. I needed it. But now I need a shower and a bed. Are you going to shower? Do you want to go first?"

Alexander was lost in thought.

"Alex?"

"Huh? I'm sorry, what'd you say?"

"I asked if you wanted to shower first. What's wrong?"

"I was thinking about Bonita. It's still early, so I don't imagine she's back."

"Text her."

"I thought about it, but damn, I don't want her to think I'm checking up on her."

"Honestly, whatever she's into we can't help her tonight. Give her space, and we'll worry about it tomorrow."

"You're right. This was a great evening. I'm sure she's fine."

Alexander wasn't convinced, but Jana was correct, Bonita needed her space. "Go ahead. I'll shower in the morning."

Jana grabbed an extra-large T-shirt from her suitcase and went into the bathroom. Alexander was asleep when she came out twenty minutes later. She stared at him for several seconds, then turned out the light and crawled into the empty bed.

Not long after, Alexander woke and looked toward the other bed. The room was too dark to see anything other than the outline of Jana. She was on her side, facing him. A clump of hair fell across her neck. He lay there watching her sleep, listening to the slight wheeze she made as she exhaled. He smiled slightly and fell back into a deep slumber.

The next time he woke, soft rays of sunlight were gently filtering into the room through the crack in the curtains. He looked over at Jana who was still lying on her side, facing him, but her eyes were open.

"Good morning," she said.

"Good morning. How are you?"

"I feel pretty good. How much wine did we drink last night?"

"Three bottles?"

"Three? I guess I feel great, considering."

"It must have been a decent wine. Had it been rot-gut, we'd be feeling it this morning."

Jana laughed. "But I do need to pee." She climbed out of bed and disappeared into the bathroom. When she returned, Alexander had gotten dressed in the same shorts and shirt he'd worn the night before.

"My turn," Alexander said. "I'm going to shower and shave. It won't take long."

"I'll order breakfast from room service. Would you like anything special?"

"Surprise me. You might see if Bonita is awake and if she wants anything." He pulled a set of fresh clothes and his shaving kit from his suitcase and went into the bathroom.

After his shower and shave, Alexander found Jana sitting on the bed, her face scrunched up with worry. "What's wrong?"

"Bonita's not in her room and the bed's made. She didn't come back last night."

20

"Shit!" Alexander went into Bonita's room and looked for any evidence she'd returned during the night and left again but there was none. He went back into the adjoining room. Jana was still sitting on the bed, her hands clasped in her lap.

"This is all my fault," she said. "I gave her the money. I can imagine what happened. What should we do?"

Alexander picked up his phone and called Bonita. No answer. He sent a text. No reply. He sent a text to Bat asking him to ping her phone. A few minutes later, Bat replied that her phone was not active.

"Her phone must be off...or dead," Alexander said to Jana.

"I hope only her phone is dead," she said, her voice cracking.

"Bon's streetwise. She may have relapsed, but I'm sure...I hope she's okay. If she got drugs, we may never find her."

"Once again, we both have missing exes."

"Exes?"

"I guess not technically, but that's where Rey and I were headed," Jana said, her face flushing. "I shouldn't call him an ex. Our relationship is a lot like you and Bon's. I care for Rey, a lot, but it wasn't working."

"I'm sorry to hear that. But for now, we need to find—"

The knock on the door interrupted him. Both he and Jana jumped toward the door, hoping it was Bonita.

"Room service," the voice from outside the door called.

Jana opened the door and a young man wheeled a cart in. He placed the contents of the cart onto a small table near the window. "Do you need anything else?" he asked in Spanish.

Neither Jana nor Alexander understood him. They could only stare at the man. He held out the receipt and Jana took it. She signed it, added a tip, and handed it back. The man said, "Gracias," and pushed the cart out of the room.

"I'm not as hungry as I was when I ordered," Jana said. "I assumed Bon was in her room, so I ordered for three."

"My stomach is in knots too, but we need to eat. After breakfast, we'll look for the *Miss Jana*. Hopefully, Bon will show up."

"Maybe when she runs out of money?"

"You gave her four thousand US. That could last a long time in Colombia."

"Jeez, Alex. What'd I do? I shouldn't have given her that much."

"It's not your fault. Don't beat yourself up over it."

There was another knock on the door. No one moved. They both assumed either the man who brought breakfast forgot something or housekeeping was already checking to see if they could clean the room. Alexander casually went and opened the door.

"Hi," Bonita said. She wore a broad smile. "The key to my room is at the bottom of my purse. I was hoping y'all were up."

"Where have you been?" Alexander asked, sounding like an angry father whose daughter had been out all night.

Bonita walked past him with a bounce in her step. "Good morning. Nice to see you too."

"I'm sorry," Alexander said. "We were worried." He wanted to ask where she'd been all night but decided to wait and see if she would volunteer the information.

"I'm sorry too. I should have called or texted, but my phone died. I didn't charge it before we left Florida. I'm not used to using my phone. It's usually dead."

"You're back, and you're safe. That's the main thing."

Bonita pulled out a large stack of bills from her purse. "Here's two thousand dollars' worth of pesos. It's like seven million pesos. That's crazy. They're mostly one-hundred-thousand and fifty-thousand peso notes. I got a few twenty-thousand notes, but they're only worth about five bucks."

"Thank you," Jana said, taking the cash from her.

"I got something for you too, Alex." Bonita removed a matte black Taurus 856 six-shot thirty-eight special revolver with a two-inch barrel and handed it to him. "You said you wished you had a gun."

"Damn! Where'd you get this?"

"I asked around. I was told that Taurus is made in Brazil and they smuggle them into Colombia by the truckload. It was only two hundred dollars. Oh, and I got these. I could only get ten. I hope that's enough." Bonita handed him ten Magtech thirty-eight special, full metal jacket rounds.

Alexander inspected the bullets. "More than enough. If it takes more than ten, I'm in deep shit and it won't matter. Hopefully, I won't need one round." He clicked the cylinder open, spun it, and closed it. He squeezed the trigger. The hammer dropped onto an empty chamber. "That doesn't feel too bad. Taurus guns are cheap and plentiful in the States. They're...decent guns. Not great, but good enough. A Taurus is the weapon of choice for most crimes in the US. It's usually a semi-automatic. This gun is similar to the one Angel had. I appreciate you getting it, but for now, I won't carry it. When it's necessary, I will. I sure as hell don't want to get caught with it."

"Should I have not bought it?" Bonita cupped her forehead with her palms and looked down.

"No, I'm glad you did. It's nice to know it's here." Alexander hesitated before he asked, "We were worried. Can I ask where you were all night?"

"Again, I'm sorry. I went to where I was kept many years ago. I wanted to look around. There was a guy who helped me when I was kept here. I went into a few bars, let some guys buy me tequila, and asked a few questions. After a few shots, those guys would tell me anything. Especially since they thought I was a local. I guess I haven't lost much of my cachacos accent."

Bonita sat on the chair next to the bed. "I asked about drug smuggling. They said it's pretty tight. The Mexican cartels have moved in and control it. No one messes with them. The head guys mostly stay in Mexico and send people here to run the operation. They pay well but if they fuck up, they end up dead. Dead in a most gruesome manner.

Cartageneros are afraid of them and stay clear. They won't work for them. They recruit from the poor and desperate. Those people hope to make quick money and then go back to their families. What they don't know is, once they're in, they don't get out. Not alive."

Alexander sat, his lips pursed. "It doesn't sound like something a small group from Fort Lauderdale would get involved with. It would be way too dangerous to move in on a cartel's turf."

Bonita leaned back in her chair, her voice low and cautious. "Deadly dangerous."

"So, what the hell is Rey doing here? What are they into?" Alexander asked, his brow furrowed with concern.

Jana sat next to Bonita and crossed her arms. "I know nothing about drug smuggling, but aren't they–the smugglers–always looking for ways to move the drugs to the US? Maybe they're recruiting small-time smuggler wannabes to move their drugs. They could load the *Miss Jana* with a few hundred pounds of drugs and sail north. If it makes it, fine. If not, fine. It's worth the gamble. If only half of those they send out get through, it's a win."

"Good point," Alexander said. "There would be no ties to the cartel if they don't make it. A few years in prison would be a lot better than what they'd get if they snitched on the cartel. What would they be smuggling? Heroin, meth, cocaine?"

"All of the above," Bonita said. "Plus fentanyl. I heard the word fentanyl a lot last night. The authorities seized a huge shipment of pills at the US border, over five hundred thousand pills with a street value of eleven million US dollars. He said it was only like fifty-five or sixty kilos."

"That's only about a hundred and twenty-five or thirty pounds. Less than the weight of a person–not an issue at all for the boat. But how big is the footprint? Do five hundred thousand fentanyl pills fit into a large garbage bag? Or does it take ten garbage bags? Weight is not a problem. Size might be. Where would you hide that on a boat? Even a boat the size of the *Miss Jana*."

Bonita shrugged. "I'll try to find out tonight. Oh, can I get a picture of Rey too? I'll charge my phone so I can show his picture around and see if anyone has seen him. I didn't want to ask too many questions last night."

"Do you really want to go back?" Jana asked.

"It's fine. I'll be okay."

"Try to keep your phone charged and on. If you're gone too long, we can get Bat to track you."

"Please don't," Bonita asked in a calm, collected manner. "Don't come looking for me, even if I'm not back by tomorrow. Even if Bat gave you a general location, you'd never find me. If I'm gone for more than a few days, I'm probably dead and you couldn't help me, anyway."

"Bonita!" Jana said. "Don't talk like that."

"No, don't talk like that," Alexander reiterated. "The first hint of danger, get the hell out of there and come back to the hotel."

"Don't worry about me. I'll keep in touch when I can. What did y'all do last night? Do you have plans for today?"

"We had a nice dinner and went to bed," Jana said.

"Oh?" Bonita glanced at Alexander with a sly grin.

Alexander ignored her insinuating smile. "I thought the three of us could drive around the marinas and look for the *Miss Jana*. There's surprisingly few marinas in this city. But I imagine you're tired and want to sleep. Jana and I can get a driver and go by ourselves. If we have a driver who speaks English, we'll tell him we're thinking about chartering a boat for a tour or fishing."

"That's a good story," said Bonita. "Jana, stop at the first market and buy a wide-brimmed straw hat. One that will hide your face. Alex, you and Rey never met, right?"

"Right."

"If Rey sees you, he won't recognize you. You should be okay. More importantly, none of the guys he's with should recognize you. Jana, if they were following you in Florida, they might know what you look like, or they have a picture of you. Keep the hat on and wear dark glasses. Pull your hair back into a ponytail, too. If you find Rey or the boat, call me and I'll meet you. Rey doesn't know me. I could try to contact him. If he's alone, I'll tell him who I am. If he's not alone, I could...I don't know...maybe proposition him to get him alone. Would he come?"

Jana thought for a moment. "I'd like to say no, but he's Latino. Hot blooded. And Bonita, you are gorgeous. The bastard would go with you."

"That would be awkward. I suppose he'd be pissed when I didn't give it up."

Alexander threw his hands in the air. "Whoa, we are getting off track, and let's not go down that road."

"I agree," Jana said.

"Bon, you rest. We'll call if we need you. Jana, are you ready for a bit of an adventure?"

Jana nodded, but her mind raced as she tried to reconcile the fact Rey would go with Bonita if she propositioned him. Would he go with her while they were still together? Were they still together? Other than the occasional tryst on the boat, their relationship had become stagnant. The sex was still great, but conversation and compassion were lacking. At that moment, she realized why Rey accepting Bonita's proposition bothered her–she still enjoyed the sex with him. The mixed emotions gnawed at her, leaving her confused.

"Jana?" Alexander said.

"Oh, I'm sorry. I'm ready."

Bonita went into the adjoining room and closed the door behind her.

Jana looked at herself in the full-length mirror hanging on the outside of the bathroom door. She wore mid-rise denim shorts with a white pintuck top. She'd noticed on the drive to dinner the previous night, most women wore casual, conservative clothing. Mid-thigh shorts and a loose top would be inconspicuous. The combo would not attract any undue attention.

Alexander handed her a small black case containing the binoculars he'd purchased from Dick's Sporting Goods in Fort Lauderdale. "Will these fit in your purse?"

"Without the case," Jana said. She removed the binoculars and put them in her purse. "I'm ready."

Alexander still didn't like the idea of taking Jana–or Bonita–onto the streets of Cartagena, looking for what could likely be ruthless drug smugglers, but decided the danger element today would be low. They were going sightseeing. No one should know they were in Colombia, and no one other than Rey or Cole should be able to recognize Jana. He remembered what JP had said–Jana may have been followed. If she was, it could have been by one of the other two men in the picture getting on the boat, and they might recognize her.

"The first thing we need to do is go to a shop that sells hats," Alexander said. "It's hot out. We'll tell the driver you need a hat."

Jana nodded. "I'm sure there are lots of souvenir shops that sell hats. But I want a classy hat, not some cheap straw thing."

Alexander wanted to mention that Cartagena had high-end stores, like the ones on Rodeo Drive in Beverly Hills or Fifth Avenue in New York, but he drew a blank on a store name. He shrugged. "I have no doubt you will find one you like."

They approached the hotel front desk. A small man in dark slacks, a white shirt, and a thin red tie greeted the couple with a toothy smile. "Buenos días, Señor. You would like a car and driver?"

"Uh, yes, we would," Alexander said, his expression one of confusion.

"Your friend, the tall girl, she told me you would ask about a car. One is ready for you. The driver speaks good English."

"Oh, okay."

"Sí. The tall girl said you wanted to visit our marinas. You're looking for a sightseeing charter."

Jana didn't know if he was asking, or if that was what Bonita had told him. "Yes, we thought that would be fun. We thought we'd check out the boats and get the prices and maybe take a tour in a couple of days."

"Your driver is young, but knows all the spots."

"I also need a hat. A nice hat. Not a cheap touristy hat."

"No problem. Just tell your driver. Your car is waiting for you in front of the hotel."

"Gracias," Jana said. She opened her purse and thumbed through the wad of Colombian notes Bonita had given her. The banknotes were a mix of ten, twenty, fifty, and one hundred MIL PESOS. Most of the notes were of the fifty and one hundred variety. Jana studied the notes, trying to remember what the exchange rate was. She knew it was high, but it would have to be crazy high for one hundred million pesos not to be a lot in US dollars. Since many of the bills in her purse had "100 MIL PESOS" in the upper left corner, she handed one to the smiling man, who was speaking Spanish into a small microphone that hung from his neck.

"Gracias, señorita. Your driver is waiting for you."

Jana nodded and turned to Alexander. She took him by the arm and they walked across the lobby toward the front door. When they were out of hearing range of the concierge, she leaned in and whispered, "Do you remember what the exchange rate for the peso is?"

After a brief hesitation, Alexander said, "No. Why?"

"I gave the guy a hundred mil peso bill."

"A hundred million pesos? That can't be right?"

Jana opened her purse and produced a bill for his inspection. "Damn. How many of these do you have?"

"A bunch."

"They can't be worth that much. We need to Google it when we get in the car."

They walked through the front doors and saw a white Mazda CX-5 parked under the hotel's porte-cochère. An attractive young girl who had been leaning on the fender stepped forward to greet them.

"Hola," she said, sticking her hand out. "My name is Gabriela. Call me Gabby."

"Hi, Gabby, I'm Alex and this is Jana." They all shook hands.

Gabby eyed Alexander, then opened the rear door to the small SUV and motioned for Jana to get inside. "You'll need to sit in the front seat, señor Alex. There's not much room in the backseat."

Gabby was in her mid-twenties, short compared to Alexander, but at five foot five, she was average for a Colombian woman. Her face and body were well above average—above average for a Colombian, which had an above-average number of above-average-looking women. She wore a satin pleated skort. Jana told Gabby that her skort was the perfect combination of style and functionality, combining the comfort and freedom of shorts with the elegance of a skirt. The two formed an immediate bond.

"I understand you wish to see charter boats," Gabby said.

"Yes," Alexander replied. "We like boats, and we want to look at the marinas and maybe look into chartering a boat in a couple of days."

"But we plan to do some sightseeing, too. The sun here is brutal. I need a hat, but not any straw hat, a nice hat. One with a wide brim."

"I know the place, Señorita Jana."

"Please, call me Jana. He's Alex."

"Um...okay, Jana," Gabby said timidly. She started the SUV and pulled onto Carrera 1. "I know you don't want a touristy hat, but there are shops in the historic center of Cartagena that sell nothing but hats. I know you will find the perfect hat, and it won't be too expensive. If you don't find one you like there, I know a few other shops on the way to the marinas."

"That sounds good," Jana said. She thought about adding that price wasn't an issue, but decided against it. "Do you know the exchange rate from US dollars to pesos?"

Gabby thought for a moment. "It's about three thousand eight hundred pesos to a dollar. It fluctuates, so give or take a hundred pesos."

Jana's face contorted. "Geez, that's too many zeros. I'm having trouble grasping the exchange rate."

"Sí, it can get confusing. Foreigners have trouble with our currency at first. In Spanish, the word for thousand is 'mil.' Our banknotes have the number, then 'mil,' for thousand. The common notes are ten, twenty, fifty, and one hundred mil. Tourists think mil stands for millions and they have twenty million pesos, but they only have twenty thousand." Gabby laughed.

Jana blushed slightly. "I could see that happening."

Gabby turned the SUV onto Avenida Santander, then onto a small street that went through a gap in the original masonry limestone wall that protected the city. The modern paved avenues turned into streets paved with bricks, streets so narrow only one car could pass at a time. She navigated the narrow lanes, pulling onto the curb more than once to pass a delivery truck or car parked on the side of the street.

After a short but adventurous trek into the heart of Old Town, Gabby stopped the Mazda on the side of the street. "I can't park here. Down that alley are several nice shops. One sells nothing but hats." She pointed at the alley and then handed a business card to Alexander. "Here's my number. Text me when you've finished shopping and I'll pick you up. Take a picture of the buildings and the street names. If you get lost, call me."

21

Jana chose a dark-colored felt fedora. The gray hat perched on her head like a relic from a bygone era, transporting her back to the film noir movies of the 1940s. Its wide brim cascaded downward, creating a dramatic shadow that concealed Jana's features, giving her an air of mystery and intrigue, and making her unrecognizable to the casual observer.

She and Alexander walked through Old Town, the sound of bustling street vendors and the aroma of exotic street food filled the air. They casually made their way back to the pickup location where Gabby was waiting for them.

"I love the new hat," Gabby said as Jana approached. "It's not a typical Panama hat like most tourists buy. It will get attention."

Alexander gave Jana a wide-eyed look that said what she was thinking: *That's not the look we were going for.* Jana shrugged and climbed into the SUV.

"To the marinas?" Gabby asked after her passengers were buckled in.

"Yes, please," Alexander answered.

Once the SUV had made its way out of Old Town and onto a main road, Jana said, "That was an amazing area. We didn't see much of it. We need to go back one day and explore it."

Alexander wondered if Jana was making small talk as part of their cover, or if she meant it.

"It's a cool place," Gabby said. "You should go back and spend the day. The night too. It's magical after dark."

"We will. Changing the subject, Gabby, your English is good. I've noticed most people here don't speak English, and those who do speak it don't speak it well."

"Thank you. My father is American. He was working for Chevron in Bogota when he met my mother. They were married, and I came along soon after. His Spanish and her English were okay, but not great. My mother spoke Spanish to me and my father spoke English to me. I went to a private school where we were taught both Spanish and English. I also spent summers with my grandparents in Pennsylvania."

"What part of Pennsylvania?" Alexander asked.

"Near Reading. It's close to Philly. Maybe an hour, I guess."

"I'm curious, why you didn't stay in Reading?"

"My mother hated it there. She thought it was cold in the summer and after we spent one Christmas there, she said never again. My parents split when I was ten. I love my dad, but he's odd. He's an engineer and good at it, which is why he was in Bogota, but..." Gabby hesitated, "he's odd. He's awkward and I feel bad for saying it, but he's not an attractive man. My mother is beautiful. She's never said it, but I think she married him for money. To her credit, she stuck with him for a long time. He was transferred to Midland, Texas and Mom said no. Dad took it hard, but he still supported me...and my mother. I don't blame Mom, but I feel sorry for my dad."

"So, both your mother and father are doing okay?" Jana asked.

"Yeah. I mean, I guess. I text both almost every day. Mom's still in Bogota–she has lots of family there–and Dad's in Texas. He's in Houston now."

Jana said, "Can I ask, why are you in Cartagena?"

"I was going to school at Universidad de Antioquia in Medellín and came here with my boyfriend. That didn't last, but I liked the area and stayed. I've been here for about a year. Eventually, I'll have to get a big girl job, but for now, I enjoy doing what I'm doing."

"How nice for you. Doing a job you like is important." Jana wanted to get the tea on Gabby's boyfriend but didn't pry.

Gabby slowed the SUV and pointed at a row of boats tied to a long concrete pier that ran parallel to the street. "This is the first area. It's not exactly a marina, but most of the boats are for charter." She drove slowly down the street. The first boat was a large yacht, close to two hundred feet long. The second boat was a large try-masted schooner named *The Galeon Phantom*, a replica of a nineteenth-century pirate ship.

They drove past several small sailboats and center cockpit runabouts. Nothing came close to the *Miss Jana*. "These aren't what you were looking for?"

"Right," Alex said. "We're looking for either a mid-size motor yacht, maybe around fifty feet, or a sport fisher around that size."

"Fifty feet?" Gabby asked. "I wasn't in the States long enough to grasp feet and inches." With one eye on the road and the other on her phone, she Googled the length in meters. "That's about fifteen meters. I know where to go next."

She drove down a narrow road lined by old buildings. After a few turns, the road widened, and they were driving along a large bay. Across the bay were the modern high-rise hotels and buildings of New Cartagena. After a few minutes, they crossed a long bridge. From the middle of the bridge, they could see more boats. It was an eclectic mix of large and small sailboats and power boats tied to long piers.

Once they crossed the bridge, Gabby followed the shoreline road toward the marina. When they were close, Alexander asked her to pull over. A concrete sidewalk divided the road and the bay. Alexander and Jana walked to the sidewalk to get a look at the boats in the marina.

"See anything that looks like the *Miss Jana*?" Alexander asked.

Jana shook her head.

Alexander asked her for the binoculars and then checked out the boats anchored in the bay and those docked in the marina. "I don't see her. You look." He handed the binoculars back to her.

"Nothing. But we can only see about half the boats...maybe less. We need to look from the other side." Jana dropped the glasses and looked at him. "Does this look suspicious? Does it look like we're looking for something, or someone, in particular?"

"It probably does," Alexander agreed.

"What should we say if Gabby asks?" Jana had a worried look.

"As little as we need to. Maybe, 'we have a specific type of boat in mind and there's no need to spend hours walking around a marina when we can see from here if what we want is there.'"

"Sounds plausible. Will she buy it?"

"She seems like a smart girl. Not a chance. But she'll pretend to," Alexander said with a wink.

Jana laughed. "And then she'll go tell the authorities we were spying on boats in the harbor."

"Not if you tip her a hundred mil pesos."

"True. Let's go."

They climbed back into the SUV. Alexander told Gabby they didn't see what they had in mind and asked her to go past the marina and stop. Gabby did as asked. At each marina, Alexander and Jana checked out the boats, got back in the vehicle, and Gabby drove to the next one. From the SUV, it was obvious none of the boats anchored in the bay were what they were looking for. Most were sailboats.

"This is the last of the marinas in this area," Gabby said when she pulled up to a small marina. "Over there it's industrial. The cruise ships dock there. Beyond that, there are a few marinas, but they're small. That area is sketchy too. I mean scary sketchy."

Alexander looked back at Jana, who gave him a slight nod. He turned to Gabby. "That sounds interesting. Would you mind taking us there?"

"It's only about five kilometers, no problem." Gabby tapped the steering wheel a few times. "If you tell me what you're really looking for, maybe I can help. If you don't want me to know, just say so."

Again, Alexander looked back at Jana and got another nod. She put her hand on Gabby's shoulder. Gabby jumped.

"I'm sorry," Jana said, "I didn't mean to startle you. You're right. We are looking for a specific boat. My boat. Well, my boyfriend's boat."

Gabby looked at her in the rearview mirror, then at Alexander. Her eyes narrowed in confusion.

"I'm not her boyfriend," Alexander said. "I'm a private detective. She hired me to help find her boyfriend. We believe he's here in Cartagena but we don't know why. I'm guessing it's a drug deal, but, again, we're only speculating. If it is, he may be working with the cartels. We'd rather they didn't know we were looking for someone who could be involved with them. Does that make sense?"

"Perfectly. Even in the heyday of the drug wars, from what I heard, Cartagena wasn't that bad. Unless you were trying to move in on their territory, they didn't bother you. I've most likely bumped into members here and there, but I wouldn't know it. It's not like they wear signs that say, 'Drug Cartel Member' around their neck. But if your friend is mixed up with them, and you try to interfere, I've heard they can be ruthless."

"Which is why we didn't tell you what we were looking for and why we are acting as a couple at the hotel," Jana said.

"It may not be necessary, but it's better to be safe than sorry. Just an FYI, most Colombians don't like the cartels or the drug trade. It gives us a bad name, and it doesn't help us at all. It's not like they employ lots of people and pay good wages. Fact is, those they hire often disappear."

"That's interesting," Alexander said. "I assumed the cartel had informants all over the city and would pay well for any information about strangers who asked too many questions."

Gabby thought for a bit. "There might be a few informants, but if you take money from the cartel and the info doesn't pan out...well, you can guess what happens. Like I said, most people don't want to get involved."

"I can see why," Jana said. She was looking out the window at boats anchored in the bay. Still, none resembled the *Miss Jana*.

Gabby maneuvered through the streets of Cartagena, attempting to parallel the waterfront. Traffic was light, but she maintained a slow, even pace, slowing and easing through the intersections without stop signs.

For a while, they lost sight of the bay. Then they hit a dead end. Gabby used her phone to look at a map. After a few zigs and zags, they were on a street lined by high-rise hotels. Another turn put the group on a four-lane-divided street. "That's the port and the cruise terminal to the right," Gabby said, pointing to the tops of large cranes poking above a line of trees.

Alexander drummed his fingers on the dash, rubbed his chin, then pulled out his cell phone. "I have a friend in Texas who helps me a lot. He's a tech savant. He hasn't gotten a signal from Rey's phone–Rey is Jana's boyfriend–since it left Fort Lauderdale, but he found two other phones that hit off the same towers at the same time as Rey's. The other phones went dark until a couple of days ago when they pinged off towers in Cartagena. For the past thirty-six hours, they've been pinging off three towers near a little island. That's…" He used his thumb and index finger to zoom and expand the screen on his phone. "Close to where we are. There's a small marina near the island."

Gabby checked the rearview mirror and saw no one behind her. She pulled to the side of the road when Alexander showed her the map on his phone. "That's close. Can you get directions to the marina?"

While Alexander fiddled with the phone, Gabby noticed a car coming up behind them. She put the Mazda in gear and sped away. She had a good idea how to find the area they were looking for. She drove in the general direction while Alexander worked on the map app.

They crossed a low bridge, then merged onto a winding four-lane one-way road with no side roads. There were no right-hand turns that led to the waterfront.

"Got it," Alexander said. "This road is going to curve to the left. Don't take it, go straight."

Gabby followed the instructions. She eased around several eighteen-wheelers parked on the side of the road and continued along the rough concrete road past many people, mostly men, hanging out under thin palm trees.

The street was narrow. Unlike the first road, which was lined with trash and discarded tires, this one was clean. Ramshackle houses looked as if they would fall at any time. The iron bars on the doors and windows may have been the only thing holding up the houses. People sat on small porches and watched as the white Mazda SUV eased past.

"Alex, can you slink in your seat? Maybe hide your face a little? Jana, the back windows are heavily tinted. No one can see in. Tilt your head so you can't be seen from the front." Gabby was whispering, as if she feared the people sitting on their porches could hear her.

"What's up?" Alexander asked.

"You kinda stand out. I'd rather people not notice us. Crap! This is a dead-end."

Alexander checked the map on his phone. "I'm sorry, we should've taken the first right as soon as we got off the main road."

Gabby had no choice but to back down the narrow street to the first intersection. Instead of backing into the side street, she passed it, then drove forward and turned on it. "Where does this road go, Alex? I don't want to go back on the road we came in on."

He studied his phone for several seconds. "It's a dead-end. All the side roads are too. You'll have to go back the way you came."

Gabby tightened her grip on the steering wheel and fidgeted in her seat. "Okay. You all stay down. I'll drive like I know what I'm doing. Hopefully, no one will pay any attention to us." At the next intersection, she made a U-turn.

"That's it, take a left," Alexander said when they were almost back on the main road.

Gabby eyed the main road. She wanted to keep driving straight – straight onto the main road and straight back to the hotel where she could drop off her passengers. She was in an area of town most locals avoided. The area frightened her, despite it being broad daylight.

The street was wider than the other streets they'd been on. Large trucks lined both sides, most of them were parked in front of one-story concrete buildings. At the first intersection, there were more trucks, and the road deteriorated. Gabby maneuvered around a couple of large potholes. The road turned to gravel. "Are we going the right way?"

"Yes. Keep going straight."

A man leaning on the fender of an old Jeep-like vehicle watched as the Mazda slowly drove by. When they passed, he took out his cell phone.

The road got worse; a mixture of gravel, ground concrete, and dirt. Gabby maneuvered over the uneven terrain. A blue gate with "Manzanillo Marina Club" painted on it stood at the end of the road. Gabby turned left and rolled slowly along the front of the building. "Can you see anything?" she asked.

Alexander and Jana were craning their necks to get a better look at the boats on the other side of the chain link fence.

"Duck," Gabby yelled. She slammed the SUV into reverse. Gravel flew from the tires when she accelerated backward and again when she sped back onto the road she'd just come down. "Get down."

Without asking questions, Gabby's passengers did as they were told. Once she was on the main road, she said, "Okay, you can sit up." Her voice cracked with fear.

"What happened?" Jana shouted.

Gabby didn't answer. She held the wheel in a death grip and stared at the street. When she eased her grip, Alexander could see her hands shaking.

"Gabby, what'd you see?" Alexander asked, his voice calmer than Jana's had been.

"Did you see the people?" Gabby asked, her voice trembling.

"No. What people?" Jana replied.

"One couple down the road and another looking out the window of the marina. They were staring at us, then they pointed their phones at us. It looked like they were taking pictures." Gabby took a deep breath and exhaled slowly. She bit her lower lip to keep her chin from quivering. After several seconds of silence, she took another deep breath and said, "You know what I said about people not cooperating with the cartels?"

"Yes," Alexander and Jana said together.

"That's in the city. We just drove into a hornet's nest. These people are dirt-poor and would do anything for a few pesos. As soon as we turned into the neighborhood, people were looking at us. It didn't register until we were a few blocks in. People were pulling out their cell phones. Some looked like they may have been taking pictures of us and others looked like they were texting. They're likely paid to let the cartels know whenever a strange car comes through. I doubt anything would have happened had we kept driving, but they'd have pictures of the car and us. Hopefully, we got out before anyone got a good photo of us."

"Are all the poorer neighborhoods like that?" Jana asked.

"No, not at all. There's always people out on the street, but they might wave or ignore you. Everybody back there took notice. That's how I knew something was up. You hear about it, but this is the first time I've experienced it. I'm sorry, but it scared the hell out of me. If your friend is involved with them, and they link you to him, they'll link me to you."

"I get it," Alexander said trying to speak in a soothing voice. "And I understand. If you want to go back to the hotel, that's fine. It's getting a little late. Can you recommend a place for lunch...in the city, not out here?"

"I know several places I can drop you."

"Can you have lunch with us?" Jana asked.

"Yes, I'd love to. You don't mind?"

"Not at all. I hope we haven't dragged you into this, but we still haven't found the boat. Alex is the investigator, but I have a feeling it's docked at that marina or close by. How do we get back in there?"

"You don't," Gabby replied matter-of-factly. "The only taxis that will go back in there will be ones that would let the cartel know. Most drivers would refuse you when you gave the address."

"There wasn't a decent road to water in the area," Alexander said. "You had no choice but to go through the side streets. Even then, it wasn't a straight shot. I suggest going at night when they can't see in the car, but I have a feeling the area is more dangerous after dark."

"It's a little more risky," Gabby agreed. "Plus, you wouldn't be able to see the boats well. Would you like my suggestion?"

"Yes, definitely," Alexander said.

"Rent a boat. Like you said you wanted to do. You could check out the whole harbor in half a day. No traffic, no neighborhood spies watching you."

"I love that idea," Jana exclaimed from the backseat. "We should have rented a boat to begin with."

"Yeah," Gabby said, "But what would your cover story have been? You couldn't say you were looking for a boat to charter."

"True," Jana said.

"After lunch, I'll make a few calls. I'll see if I can find us a boat with a captain who won't ask questions. But just in case, can either of you drive a boat?"

"I can. Alex?"

"I can handle your basic runabout with an outboard engine. As long as it's not too big."

"Cool," Gabby said. "I say you should go in the morning. Would you like me to come along?"

"We'd love to have you," Jana replied. "We should get Bonita to come with us, too."

"Who's Bonita?"

"My ex-girlfriend."

Gabby glanced at Alexander, then into the mirror at Jana, a confused smirk on her face.

22

Bonita joined Alexander, Jana, and Gabby at a cozy Italian-Mediterranean restaurant close to the hotel where they were staying. It was early afternoon, but Gabby assured the group that she had safely tucked away her Mazda for the night. She would Uber home. The hotel was within walking distance. They ordered wine.

By the second bottle of Chardonnay, the women were discussing clothing, pedicures, shoes, and shopping. Alexander lost interest and studied the room. He was sitting with three stunning young ladies and assumed most of the men who were sneaking peeks envied him. If they only knew...

"Alex," Jana said. "Alex?"

"What? I'm sorry. You were saying?"

"Gabby said we can rent a twenty-foot Sun Tracker Party Barge tomorrow. We can rent it without a skipper. Any of us can drive it. How's that sound?"

"Perfect. We'll definitely look like tourists out for a joy ride. Gabby, will you be joining us?"

"Yes! It'll be fun. I can pick you up in the morning and take you to the boat. I'm not too familiar with the bay, but with GPS, it shouldn't be hard to get around. From the hotel to the marina that we tried to go to today was about nine kilometers. By water, it's maybe half that. Maybe even less."

Jana turned to Bonita. "Bon, did you bring a swimsuit?"

"No, I didn't. Alex, I don't suppose you brought one my size from your collection?"

Alexander blushed slightly. "No, I didn't. Gabby, I can tell that you have questions. I live on the beach in Texas. Well, one row off the beach. In the mornings, I walk along the beach and gather discarded clothing. I sort it and donate most of it, but anything nice I keep because I often have guests come by and they'll end up a little too tipsy to drive home. Having a wide selection of clothing comes in handy."

"It's mostly women who are too tipsy to go home?" Gabby asked.

The women laughed. The pink in Alexander's cheeks deepened.

"Well, Alex, are you going to answer Gabby's question?" Jana asked, still smirking.

"Sometimes females. Occasionally male friends with their dates. Okay, usually females. Honestly, not many in recent years. There was Mayte, Briana, and then Bonita. Jana stayed, but she had her clothes."

Bonita whipped her head toward him, then to Jana. She wiped her mouth with a cloth napkin to cover her smile.

"Except for Jana, those sound like Hispanic names. Do you like Hispanic girls, Alex?"

"It's a long—"

"I got this," Bonita said, then spoke to Gabby for several minutes in Spanish. While she was telling the story, Gabby would glance at Alexander and grin. Bonita finished and said, "I'm sorry guys, it was easier for me to tell in Spanish."

Gabby leaned forward. "Oh, Alex, you're a knight in shining armor. Saving all the girls?"

Uncertain of what she meant, Alexander simply nodded.

Their server came and interrupted the awkward silence. "Would you like anything else? Dessert? Coffee?"

"Just the check," Jana said.

When the server returned with the check, Jana grabbed it. "Gabby, do they include the tip in the bill?"

"Usually, they add ten percent. It's not mandatory so you don't have to pay it but you can add more if the service was exceptional."

"That makes it easy. I'll add a little extra. Speaking of bills, we need to pay you for today."

"The hotel booked me. They'll charge you and pay me. We're good."

"We are not good," Jana retorted. She dug into her purse and looked through the stack of Colombian banknotes. Once again, the conversion rate eluded her. She couldn't remember if a hundred thousand pesos was a lot. It sounded like a lot, but she had it in her mind that it wasn't. Instead of Pesos, Jana pulled out five one-hundred-dollar bills and handed them to Gabby.

Gabby's face lit up. "Oh, no, I can't accept that. It's way too much."

Jana pushed the bills into her hand. "You offered the perfect amount of resistance. You deserve every penny. I have one more request."

"Anything," Gabby said, gripping the US currency in her hand like it was a freshly caught trout about to slip from her grasp.

"Take Bon shopping. Get her a skimpy bikini. When we're on the boat tomorrow, I want all eyes to be on you two. Are you comfortable with that?" Jana looked at Bonita. "How 'bout you, Bon, are you okay with it?"

"Yes, no problem," Bonita replied. She was looking forward to being on a boat in the sun. It had been a long time.

"Me too," Gabby said. "Most of my swimsuits are skimpy. That's what we wear here. Most people shouldn't wear them, but they do. Nobody gets offended or says anything."

"If you want to," Jana said, "you all can leave and go shopping. We'll wait for the check."

"Okay," Gabby replied. "But what are you all going to do the rest of the afternoon?"

"I don't know. Any ideas, Alex?"

"I want to check in with Bat and see if there's been any movement of the cell phones or if they're still pinging from the same location. That won't take long. Jana and I will find a way to amuse ourselves."

"Jana, would you like to come with us?" Bonita asked.

"No, thank you. I'll keep Alex company." Jana handed the check and a credit card to the server.

Gabby and Bonita left the table and walked out the door. Alexander watched a man get up from the bar and walk out behind them. He was in his early forties and wore dark shorts, a navy blue polo shirt, and black tennis shoes.

"Did you see that guy?" Alexander asked Jana.

"Uh, no. What guy?"

"He just left. I was people-watching while you all were chatting. He came in right after us and sat at the bar. It looked like he was drinking cocktails, but he drank too much for that to be true. I think he was drinking club soda or tonic water. He followed the girls out."

"One way to find out." Jana walked over to the bar and leaned in toward the bartender. His gaze naturally looked at her top as it drooped open. The two talked for a few seconds, then she put several folded peso notes in his hand and returned to the table. "He was drinking club soda, just as you suspected."

"Damn. He didn't come in for lunch or drinks. He was watching us. Now he's following Bon and Gabby."

The server brought the receipt and credit card back to the table. She thanked Jana, picked up the empty wine glasses from the table, and left.

"Let's go," Alexander said, pulling Jana by the hand. When they got to the door, he opened it slowly and peeked outside. Gabby and Bonita were standing by the curb in front of the restaurant. A dark Renault pulled next to them and stopped.

"Wait," Alexander yelled and rushed to the car to warn the girls they were being followed. The man from the bar was sitting behind the wheel. The driver's side door was locked but the window was down. With a slight uppercut, he slammed his fist into the driver's jaw. The driver fell forward, then sluggishly leaned back, shaking the cobwebs from his brain.

"Oh my God," Gabby cried. "You hit that poor man!"

"Yes, ma'am, just as hard as I could."

"But why?"

Alexander reached inside and grabbed the man by the throat. The man struggled, but in his dazed state, he was no match for Alexander's grip.

"Unlock the door," Alexander ordered. The man didn't understand what he said but had a good idea what the man gripping his throat wanted. He pressed the button to unlock the door. Alexander released the man's throat long enough to open the door, then grabbed him by his navy blue shirt and pulled him from the seat.

"What's going on?" Gabby asked.

"Is this your Uber driver?" Alexander asked her.

Gabby checked the app on her phone. "Oh, no, it's not. We were talking and not paying attention when he pulled up and stopped." She put her hand over her mouth when she realized what might have happened had she and Bonita gotten in the car.

Alexander slammed the man against the rear door. "What was your plan?"

Pinned against the door by a man who stood nearly a foot taller and weighed a hundred pounds more, the man looked up defiantly and grinned. Alexander took half a step back and hit the man with a right hook. The man's knees buckled. Alexander caught him as he fell.

"Gabby, can you drive a stick?"

"No problem." Shock crossed her face and the color drained from her cheeks.

"Bon, get in the front. Jana, get in the back and slide over. We need to get out of here." Once Jana was in the backseat against the far door, he slid the limp man in next to her and got in. "Go," he shouted.

Gabby put the car in gear and eased away from the curb. "Where to?"

"Anywhere," Alexander replied. "We need to move."

"What are we going to do with him?" Jana asked, leaning as far from the man as she could get.

"I don't know."

"I do," Bonita said coolly. She turned to Gabby, whose color was returning to her face. "Head toward Carrera Eleven and Calle Thirty."

Gabby shot her a glance. "That's on the edge of the Walled City."

"Sí. It's okay."

Gabby wore the same nervous look she'd worn earlier in the day when she found herself in a dubious section of Cartagena. Her instinct was to pull the car over, get out, and order an Uber to take her home. It was either the five glasses of wine she drank at lunch or the five one-hundred US dollar bills Jana had given her, but she ignored her instinct.

The shortest route to where Bonita had told her to go was through the Walled City, but she didn't like the route. Police often patrolled the entrances to the popular tourist location, and she was driving a car with an unconscious man in the back seat. Avenida Blas de Lezo to Avenida Venezuela was the quickest, but it was also the most populated. Gabby decided the prudent route would be to take the coast road around the Walled City and come in from the backside. Bonita had said Carrera Eleven and Calle Thirty. It was only one kilometer further.

While Gabby drove, Alexander checked the man's pockets. He found a cell phone and tossed it out the window. In the man's other pocket was a wad of banknotes that added up to a hundred and twenty thousand pesos—just over thirty US dollars.

Only a few minutes into the ride, the man opened his eyes and mumbled a few words in Spanish. When he realized where he was, he looked at Alexander, then at Jana. He leaned over Jana and reached for the door handle, but she grabbed him by the wrist and twisted, preventing him from opening the door. When she twisted his arm, he sat up in the seat where the left side of his head met the full force of Alexander's right fist. The man's head pitched, and he fell back into the seat.

"Nice move, Jana. If you hadn't grabbed him, he may have gotten the door open and pushed you out with him."

"Another move I learned at Miggie's. This one worked."

Bonita, in the seat in front of Jana, was oblivious to what had happened. Gabby had witnessed the punch in the rearview mirror. Her mouth dropped open.

"Gabby!" Bonita shouted.

Gabby refocused and slammed on the brakes, stopping inches from the car in front of her. Her passengers lurched forward, restrained by the seatbelts they'd buckled out of habit. Not buckled in, the unconscious man flew forward, hitting his knees on the console. Alexander grabbed him by his shirt and pulled him back into the seat.

"Sorry, guys," Gabby said. "I guess I'm a little freaked out right now."

"It's okay," Alexander said. "Do you have a spatula in the glove box?"

Jana burst out laughing. Gabby and Bonita looked confused and neither replied to his question.

"Turn here, then go a block past the white building and circle the block," Bonita said, then pulled out her phone and sent a text.

Gabby made the block and drove slowly up the narrow street lined with colorful concrete and plaster walls.

"Stop at the brown doors," Bonita said.

When they stopped, a short, muscular man with long, gray hair met them. Bonita jumped out and ran around the car. In Spanish, the gray-haired man said, "Good to see you, Bonita. Quickly, come inside. Back the car to the intersection, park, and leave the keys in it."

The gray-haired man helped Alexander lug the unconscious man through the large wooden doors. "Bonita, you wait here for your friend. We'll be in the back room."

They went into a small room off the bar area and dropped the unconscious man into a chair. He slumped forward, his head landing on the table in front of him. The gray-haired man said something Alexander didn't understand. His grasp of Spanish was extremely limited.

After a few minutes, Bonita and Gabby entered the bar and made their way to the back room. Bonita hugged the gray-haired man. In English, she said, "Everyone, this is Juan Cabrera. It's a long story, but I've known him since I was first brought to Cartagena. I texted him and told him we had a person and a car we needed to get rid of. We can trust him."

Juan spoke briefly to Gabby, then shook Alexander's and Jana's hands. "What do you want to do with the man?" Juan asked in Spanish. Bonita translated everything he said.

"I'd like to know what he was up to," Alexander said. "Either he was following Gabby, or Gabby and Bonita. He didn't seem too interested in me or Jana. We need to know if he was on his own or if he was working with anyone."

"We will find out," Juan said. "Then what?"

"It depends on his answers," Alexander said, "but I don't see a bright future for him, no matter what he says. If he's working for a cartel, we need to get rid of him. If he was planning on kidnapping one or both of the girls and using or selling them, I'd say get rid of him."

Gabby gasped. Her stomach was churning. "Where's the toilet?"

Juan told her it was in the bar, to the left, in the corner.

"Bon, ask your friend if he has a rope or something we can tie this guy up with," Alexander said. "If he wakes up and takes off, I'd have to knock him out again. I want to talk to him."

Bonita relayed the message. Juan then went into a storage room behind the bar and returned with a coil of three-eighth-inch diamond braid rope. He handed the rope to Alexander, but Jana grabbed it.

"Do you know how to tie a handcuff knot?" she asked.

Alexander hesitated. "I guess not, since I didn't know there was such a thing."

"There is. I learned it from a knot book when I was learning the basic sailing knots." Jana formed two identical loops with the rope and overlapped them as though she were tying a clove hitch. She threaded each loop through the original loop, put the man's hands into the loops, tightened, and knotted the loose end around the coil. "That's a handcuff knot. What should we tie him to?"

Juan didn't understand, but he had an idea of what they wanted. "Un minuto, por favor." He went back into the room he'd gotten the rope from and came out again with a heavy-duty C-clamp and an adjustable wrench. He clamped the clamp to the table and tightened it with his hand. When it was hand-tight, he put the hole at the end of the wrench through the tightening pin and rotated the screw several more times until the pad at the end of the screw indented into the table. He lifted the C-clamp to prove it wouldn't come off.

Jana nodded her approval, folded a section of the rope, and ran it through the clamp. She secured the loop with two half-hitches. "He won't go anywhere," Jana said proudly.

The man came to and immediately struggled against the rope binding his hands. His head cleared quickly, and he tried to stand, but the rope stopped him. "What the fuck! Untie me!" the man yelled in Spanish.

Gabby returned from the restroom feeling better but stopped and recoiled when she saw the man tied to the table.

"Tell him we have a few questions. Tell him his life depends on the answers."

Gabby told the man what Alexander said. He looked up and sneered at them. Juan walked to the table and slammed the side of the crescent wrench onto the man's knuckles. The man jerked and cried out in pain, but couldn't move his hand.

In Spanish, Juan said, "That was nothing. Answer the questions or I'll cut your fingers off at the knuckles. One by one. One for each question you don't answer truthfully."

Gabby turned and ran toward the bathroom.

The man's sneer disappeared. Genuine fear replaced it. He nodded.

Juan asked Alexander what he'd like to know. Bonita translated.

"Ask him what he planned to do with the girls."

Juan asked the question. Bonita translated. "He said he saw her park and get out of her car near the restaurant. He thought she was hot and was going to grab her and take her and rape her. He used more graphic terms."

Gabby returned from the bathroom just as Alexander said, "Tell Juan to cut off a finger."

Gabby made a U-turn.

The man struggled against the rope and vehemently protested.

"He says he's telling the truth."

"I gathered that. Gabby is cute as the dickens, but that's a lot of trouble for a quickie. Prostitution is legal here. If he wanted to get laid, he didn't need to kidnap and rape. He didn't have a lot of money in his pocket, but enough to buy a woman off the street."

Bonita told the man what Alexander said. Juan walked into the back and returned with a large meat cleaver.

Gabby returned right after Juan. She looked at the cleaver and groaned.

"Think before you answer," Juan said, running his finger over the sharp end of the blade.

"I told you. I planned to rape her. When I was finished, I would sell her to traffickers. When the two of them came out of the restaurant, I wanted both of them. I guessed that they were waiting for an Uber, so I stopped to pick them up. It would have worked too, if the big guy hadn't come out."

Bonita translated. Her voice was gravelly, filled with fear and rage at the thought of being trafficked again.

"Ask him who helps him, and who he sells the girls to," Alexander said. "Did he have help waiting? He didn't have a weapon. He'd have a tough time kidnapping both of them."

Gabby moved closer to the table. Her light brown complexion glowed deep red with anger. She asked the man the question. He replied he was alone and had no help. He would have figured out how to subdue the girls without help. He didn't know any traffickers, but they weren't hard to find in Cartagena.

Gabby translated. "Do you believe him?" she asked.

Alexander scratched his head. "Mostly. This wasn't his first rodeo. He's kidnapped girls and sold them before. I'd bet on it. Show him the pictures of Rey and the *Miss Jana*. Ask him if he's seen either of them."

The man shook his head when shown the pictures.

"You're positive you've not seen them?" Bonita asked in Spanish.

"Sí."

"I think he's telling the truth about not having seen Rey or the boat. He's lying about not knowing traffickers. As you said, Alex, this wasn't his first time," Bonita said.

Gabby took the cleaver from Juan and stepped next to the man tied to the chair. He made fists to protect his fingers. She spoke to him in Spanish. The man's face went pale. Juan and Bonita laughed. Alexander and Jana looked at each other blankly.

Bonita, still grinning, said, "Gabby told him not to worry. She would not cut off his finger. Because he was going to traffic her, she's going to cut off his penis."

23

When Alexander, Jana, and Bonita came out the front door of the hotel the next morning, Gabby was leaning on the fender of the white Mazda CX-5. She wore loose-fitting cargo shorts and a white tank top. Under the tank top, the outline of a bikini top was visible. Her face was melancholic. She gave the three a half-hearted grin, then opened the rear passenger door for Jana. The others got into the Mazda, and Gabby drove away. She jumped slightly when Jana touched her shoulder.

"I guess I should stop doing that," she said. "I wanted to know if you were okay. Do you want to talk about last night?"

Her comment made Gabby smile. "No, it's fine. I mean, I'm fine. I'd rather not talk about the man. Maybe later. I didn't sleep well last night. Thinking about how close I came to being taken kept me awake. First, I was angry at him. Then I was mad at myself for being stupid. I almost got into that man's car without checking the app."

"It's not your fault, Gabby," Bonita said. "We were talking and not paying attention...I guess it was our fault, but luckily, and thanks to Alex, we learned a valuable lesson."

"That's so true. I won't make that mistake again. I can't stop thinking about what would have happened if Alex hadn't stopped us from getting in the car. Where would we be now?"

"I could give you a good idea," Bonita said, "but you don't want to know."

Gabby glanced at her in the rearview mirror. "Do you mind if I ask, how do you know Juan?"

Bonita leaned back into the seat. "My parents made a deal with a man, Sebastián, to get me to the US when I was fourteen. My mother had relatives there and wanted me to have a better life than what we had in Bogota. She paid him, but when we got to Cartagena, he said it wasn't enough and I'd have to work to pay the rest of the fee. He kept me in a room above the bar we were at last night. Juan was like an all-around helper. He did whatever Sebastián asked. He bartended, cleaned the toilets, washed the dishes, and took me to the square to prostitute."

"What? He pimped you out?" Gabby asked.

"You could say that. He would apologize every time and said he wished he could help me, but he had no choice. He never tried to have sex with me. I don't know if Sebastián told him not to or if he didn't want to."

"Oh my God, how long did this go on?" Gabby glanced in the mirror again. Bonita's expression was distant. "I'm sorry, Bon, if you don't want to talk about it—"

"It's fine. People should know. I should back up. I just turned fourteen when Sebastián took me. He told me what I was going to have to do, and he proceeded to 'train' me. I remember when he'd come into the room, I'd cry. He'd laugh and rape me."

Gabby gasped. Alexander stared out the window, unsure if he wanted to hear the story.

"Sebastián molested me for a week or two. It seemed like forever. It got to where I wouldn't cry–I couldn't cry–it didn't make any difference. I just laid there and let him do what he wanted to me. I guess he either tired of me or figured I was 'trained.' That's when Juan took me to the streets. I got pregnant right away and when Sebastián realized it, he brought in a hack to fix it. They gave me a pill to knock me out. Juan said the guy almost killed me. That was my first in-home abortion. It wasn't the last."

Gabby glanced back at her in horror. She bit her bottom lip, fought back tears, and wondered how Bonita could tell the story with no emotion. "That's awful. I'm sorry..."

Bonita forced a slight smile. "Thanks. That bastard took my virginity, my dignity, my childhood, my innocence. That's why I went looking for him when we got to Cartagena. I planned to kill him. When

I find him, I still plan to kill him. But first, thanks to you, I'm going to castrate him before I kill him."

"We were wondering where you disappeared to," Jana said, trying to change the subject.

"When I got to the bar, I was surprised it and Juan were still there. Sebastián wasn't. Juan told me Sebastián started dealing drugs from the bar. I guess that was more lucrative than trafficking underage girls. Juan said Sebastián misplaced a hundred and twenty-five thousand US dollars. When he couldn't pay the dealer, they came looking for him. He disappeared. Juan waited a few months and bought the bar. He said he 'happened to find a hundred and twenty-five thousand dollars about the time Sebastián lost it.' Juan winked at me, but he didn't need to. I got it. Juan was so happy to see me, he cried. I didn't. I haven't cried since I was fourteen."

"So, Juan bought the bar and has been running it ever since?" Gabby asked.

"Yes. We had a long talk, and he said he makes enough from the bar to pay the bills, and he's happy with that. Because the bar's been there so long, it's become a local hangout for old-timers. Everyone knows Juan and trusts him. He knows what's going on in the city and the black market. That's where I got the gun for Alex. I told him about Rey and the boat and he said he'd discreetly inquire, but he didn't come up with anything."

"That's odd," said Alexander, perking up when the conversation moved away from her being abused. "He sounds like someone who could find Rey."

"Cartagena's a big city. Lots of players. It would be hard for Juan to know everything. But if he asks around, he'll probably hear something," Gabby said.

"But do we want him to? Loose lips sink ships," Alexander said.

The mood inside the SUV turned somber. The rest of the drive to the marina where Gabby had chartered the pontoon boat was strangely quiet.

"Here we are," Gabby said, pulling the Mazda into a parking spot next to the marina office. The mood improved when they all got out of the SUV and looked at the boat, the crystal-clear water, and the cloudless sky. A slight breeze blew from the north. "It's a perfect day for boating," Gabby said. She smiled for the first time that morning. "Alex, I got a tote bag with water and a mixed fruit platter from the hotel, and a bag with a swimsuit for Bon, towels, and sunscreen. They're in the back. Will you grab them?"

Alexander grabbed the bags from the back of the SUV and waited outside with Bonita while Jana and Gabby went inside the marina to complete the boat rental. They came out five minutes later with paperwork, boat keys, and a rudimentary map of the bay in hand.

"We're ready," Gabby said. "Since our shopping trip got nixed yesterday, I grabbed a bikini for you, Bon. The bottom might fit. The top will be small. It's got long ties. You can tie it to size, but you'll...uh...hang out a little." She chuckled.

"Isn't that the look we're going for?" Bonita asked when they climbed onto the twenty-foot party barge.

"It is," Alexander said with a lascivious grin.

"Maybe we should leave Alex here," Jana said. "Make it a girl's trip. We could gather a lot more info without him than we can with him."

The other two girls nodded in agreement and laughed at the idea.

"Information like what it's like to be shanghaied on a big yacht, never to be seen again."

The smiles disappeared. It had only been a joke, but Alexander's retort was sobering. They'd had a close call the day before. They didn't want to tempt fate again.

"Sorry, y'all. I didn't mean to be a downer."

"That's okay, Alex, you're right," Jana said. "Three half-naked women on a boat alone is inviting trouble."

"Especially where we're going," Gabby added.

Even with a man on board, three beautiful, half-naked young women are inviting trouble. Alexander was glad he'd slipped the revolver in his pocket.

Two men in their early twenties emerged from the back door of the marina. They hurried to the boat and, in Spanish, offered to show Gabby how to operate it. When she told them she had it under control and thanked them, they turned and dejectedly walked back to the office. She started the sixty-hp Mercury outboard, asked Alexander to untie the dock lines, and then eased the boat out of the slip. Alexander, Jana, and Bonita sat on the aft L-lounge couch. At slow speed, the outboard motor was quiet enough to talk over. Gabby held up the map she'd gotten from the office and pointed at their current location.

"We're here," she said, then moved her finger to the lower half of the map. "This is where we were yesterday, and where your boat might be."

Alexander took a closer look at the map. He pulled out his phone, opened a map app, and entered the coordinates. "It looks like it's a little over three miles, about five and a half kilometers. Let's take it easy like we're sightseeing. It'll take less than an hour to get there."

"Sounds good to me," Gabby said. "The guys at the marina said to cruise at around ten kilometers per hour. They said we could push it, get the boat on plane, and make over twice that, but they didn't recommend it. So, we'll definitely take it easy."

"Gabby, you said you had a suit for me?" Bonita asked.

"I do. It's in the bag."

Bonita dug through the bag and found the two-piece swimsuit. She held it and looked at it. "This is tiny," she said.

"I'm sorry, it's the largest I had."

Bonita scanned the water around the boat, then unbuttoned her light blue beach cover-up, removed it, and set it on the seat beside her. She didn't seem to mind that Alexander was sitting close by. She tied the strings of the pink bra around her back, letting the cups hang below her breasts. Once tied, she pulled the remaining ties around her neck, adjusted them for the correct size, and tied them.

Alexander couldn't keep from staring. He'd not seen Bonita topless in almost a year. He could tell she'd lost weight. Her once-firm breasts sagged noticeably, an unfortunate consequence of a poor diet and illicit drugs.

Bonita's exhibitionism surprised Jana and Gabby, but it didn't shock them. Both glanced at Alexander, then back at each other, and gave a 'figured he would look' nod. They both wondered, as did

Alexander, if Bonita would don the lower half of the bikini with the same phlegmatic attitude she had when putting on the bra.

Bonita wore a blue jean mini skirt that hugged her hips. Peeking out above her belt, the peacock feather tattoo glistened in the sunshine. She held up the thong-style bikini panty. "This is a little small. How 'bout I just wear the skirt and the top?"

"You should at least try it on," Alexander said.

"Ha, ha," Bonita said, flashing him a go-to-hell look.

"You look great," Jana said, removing the floral print sundress covering the bikini she wore underneath. Gabby followed suit, removing her top and dropping her cargo shorts. Jana's bikini was conservative compared to Gabby's white Brazilian cut swimsuit.

Alexander's heart raced when he looked at the three women on the boat. He was fine for the moment, but he was glad he wore an extra-large Hawaiian shirt that would hide any involuntary arousal, should it arise.

Jana seemed to be the only female onboard who noticed his awkwardness. "Alex, would you like a cold water?"

"I would. Thank you."

She pulled out a plastic water bottle from the cooler. She slid next to him, handed him the bottle, and whispered, "Are you okay?"

He couldn't help but take a peek at her body. She had ten years on the other girls but was as fit and perhaps more beautiful. His heart jumped when he looked into her deep blue eyes. He let out a long breath and said, "Absolutely."

Bonita looked at the gauges on the instrument panel while Gabby goosed the outboard. The hum of the motor increased and kept them from hearing the conversation going on in the back of the boat.

"Was that awkward for you?" Jana asked Alexander.

"What?"

"Seeing Bon topless. Your expression changed dramatically."

"It usually does when a girl takes her top off in front of me."

Jana chuckled, "Like that happens all the time." She paused. "You miss her, don't you?"

Alexander twisted the top off the water bottle, took a sip, and shrugged. "Honestly, no. Pardon the pun, but that ship has sailed."

"But you were aroused when she removed her top?"

"Without a doubt. I'd get aroused if any of you took your tops off. There's a big difference between lust and love."

Something in front of the boat caught his attention. Jana found herself slightly disappointed that while she was talking to him, he seemed to be fixated on Gabby or Bonita. "Alex." When he didn't respond, she repeated his name.

"Hand me the binoculars from your bag."

"Why don't you walk up and take a closer look at her?" Jana snipped in an insolent tone.

"What? Look at that boat coming this way. Just off the port bow. Get the binoculars."

Jana looked down the bay and saw a large, white motor yacht coming toward them. "Fuck!" She yelled as she reached for the binoculars. Gabby and Bonita looked back when they heard her. She looked through the binoculars, focused, looked up, then through the glasses again. She handed them to Alexander. "That's the *Miss Jana*. I can't see the bridge. We need to veer off."

"No, they've probably seen us, but we don't want to do anything odd. Stay the course," he told Gabby. "We need to get out of sight."

"It's a fucking party barge," Jana exclaimed. "There's no place to hide."

Bonita grabbed her by the arm and gave her a slight nudge toward the aft L-couch. "Lie down." She said. "Alex, get on top of Jana."

"What?"

"Lie on top of Jana and hide your faces."

Alexander looked bewildered. Jana extended her arm, inviting him to join her.

"Hurry," Gabby shouted from the driver's console.

Alexander eased himself on top of Jana, putting one leg between her legs, supporting his weight on his left side. He put his arms to the side of her head. She wrapped her arms around his shoulders. He rested his head above hers.

Bonita nuzzled Alexander's head until he and Jana's lips touched.

"Make it look real!" she said and went to the starboard bow console couch and stretched out, making herself visible to the oncoming boat.

Gabby stepped to the side of the console, steering with her right hand. She wasn't as well-endowed as Bonita, but she showed more skin, especially from the rear. She positioned herself so if there were men on the *Miss Jana*, and they were looking, they'd be looking at her backside.

"Like she said, make it look real," Jana said. She kissed Alexander gently on the lips, hiding her face from the approaching yacht. She rested her cheek against his cheek and whispered in his ear, "Hey, Alex, you're making this a little too real."

"I'm sorry, I can't control that."

"Oh? Is it lust or love?"

24

When the *Miss Jana* was within a hundred yards of the party barge, the man on the bridge slowed her speed from eight to four knots. A casual observer would have thought the big cruiser had slowed so her wake wouldn't swamp the smaller party boat. Everyone on both boats knew it slowed so the men on the *Miss Jana* could gawk at the girls on the barge.

The man on the aft deck of the boat pointed his cell phone camera at the girls. Gabby waved, grabbed her phone, and snapped several pictures. She thumbed the screen to activate the optical zoom and rapidly snapped as many photos as she dared. She lowered the camera, smiled, and waved as the big yacht separated from the party barge, then she turned toward the bow. She wanted to confirm the barge had not veered too far off course while she was flirting with the men on the yacht. The turn was also to give the guys one last shot at her ass, just in case they were watching with binoculars or had a camera with a telephoto lens.

Bonita moved aft and pulled a water bottle from the cooler. She opened it, took a sip, and watched the trawler slowly fade from view. "They're a ways off, but if they look, they might still see you. Y'all should stay down for a bit. I gotta say, you made it look real."

Alexander rolled onto his back and flipped Jana on top of him. She slid off, half on the seat, half on him, then brought her leg up. Her knee was covering his crotch. "We had to. If Rey was onboard, we couldn't risk him seeing me."

"No chance of that. Alex certainly had you covered," Bonita said.

Jana couldn't tell if her tone contained a hint of jealousy or sarcasm.

"What now?" she asked, her head still resting on Alexander's chest.

Bonita used the binoculars to look at the yacht. "They're out of sight. You can get off of him now."

Alexander looked aft toward the boat that had passed. "We need to follow them, but how? They'll notice us for sure. Gabby, let me see that map."

He spread it out on the table next to the L-couch. The girls gathered around him. Gabby slowed the boat to a crawl and kept checking that no other boats were approaching. Alexander glanced around the bay to get his bearings, then put his finger on the map. "We're here, hugging Isla Manznillo. We think, or thought, the *Miss Jana* was moored or anchored on the back side of the island about here." He pointed at the marina they'd visited the day before. "The bay is deep for the most part, but there's a shallow area that extends off the island. A boat the size of the *Miss Jana* would have to swing way around, make a U-turn, and come back this way. That's assuming they came from behind the island." He grabbed the binoculars and scanned Cartagena Bay. "There's a lot of coastline, but it's mostly industrial. Not many marinas and there's no protected anchorage. I still say they were behind that island." He poked the map with his finger to make a point.

"What were they doing heading into the bay?" Gabby asked. "That part of the bay is landlocked."

"Good question," Alexander replied. "Do you know if there are any fuel docks on the backside of the bay? It seems most of the marinas are in this area. Maybe those are the only places to get fuel."

"That's possible. Or provisions. You saw what was near that marina–nothing."

"They would need fuel and provisions if they were planning to head back to Florida soon. Or they could be picking up whatever they came for and will turn around and head out to sea, in which case we won't see them again until they get to Florida...or wherever they may be going." Alexander opened the map app on his phone and zoomed in on their location, then slowly zoomed out. He looked back at the island they were next to. "There," he said, "Casa de something."

Gabby looked at his phone. "Casa de Huéspedes Ilustres. In English, the House of Illustrious Guests. It's where important guests of the state stay when visiting."

"Hmm, I was hoping it was a restaurant. I guess they wouldn't appreciate us tying to their dock."

"They might shoot us."

"That's no bueno. What about this place, the Oasis?"

"That's a restaurant."

"There's a little pier close to it. Let's try to dock there and walk to the Oasis. From there, we can see any boat that passes through that section of the bay. If the *Miss Jana* comes out, she will have to go through that straight."

"It's worth a shot," Gabby said. She climbed back into the console seat and throttled up the outboard motor. The boat crept along the coast and all four passengers kept an eye out for the big Cheoy Lee trawler.

The pier was in front of a large building that had a sign that read, "Centro de Investigaciones Oceanograficas e Hidrograficas DIMAR". Alexander assumed it was an oceanographic institute of some kind. He didn't ask. Three fiberglass boats and one inflatable were tied to the pier.

"We should dock between the two boats to remain hidden from the bay," Alexander suggested. "We'll sit for a minute to see if anyone chases us off. If not, we'll walk to the restaurant. You all might wait a few minutes before covering up. If we aren't allowed to dock here, you might change their minds."

"Alexander Christian, you're such a sexist," Jana said, only half-jokingly.

"Would we have a better chance of getting permission to dock here if I took my shirt off? I'd be happy to."

"This is Colombia," Gabby said. "You may have a better chance with the locals."

"Plus," Jana added, "if anyone comes out, it could be a woman. You'd have a better chance than we would."

"It doesn't look like anyone's coming at all. Cover up and we'll go to the restaurant. Bring the binoculars so we can watch the boat and keep a lookout for the *Miss Jana*."

The girls dressed–Jana in her short floral print sundress, Gabby in a tight tank top, and Bonita in a blue cover-up– and Alexander thought they looked sexier than they did in the bikinis. *Hell, maybe I am a sexist.*

They walked along a grassy area to a deserted paved road, then along the road to the restaurant. Alexander looked back at the pier where they'd docked the boat. No one was in sight. He checked out the boats in the bay. The *Miss Jana* was nowhere to be seen.

The Oasis was a tight two-story space that barely sat twenty people. The narrow entrance only allowed a single person at a time to squeeze between a small restroom on the right and a work counter on the left. Inside, a bar-like table sat against a mirrored wall. The mirror gave the illusion the room was twice its size. There were no tacky souvenirs or other tourist trappings on display. A young woman told them in Spanish to sit wherever they liked. Since they were the only people in the restaurant, they chose a table by a window with a view of the bay and a view of the end of the pier where they had tied the little party boat. The menus were in Spanish and had no pictures. This was not Tex-Mex.

"I can translate the menu. What are you hungry for?" Gabby asked.

Out of habit, Jana glanced at the menu. She recognized a few items but wished there were pictures. "I'm still kinda full from breakfast."

"We have to order," Alexander said. "Maybe an appetizer. Isn't that 'tapas' in Spanish? Are tapas on the menu?"

"It doesn't say it, but it looks like the entrees are more like appetizers. We can order a couple of them and share. We can keep ordering if we have to while we wait for your boat to come back," Gabby said.

"Sounds good to me," Alexander said. "I can always eat." He scanned the menu but couldn't translate any of the items. "When Bon and I were together, I spent a few minutes every day on Duolingo, trying to learn Spanish. I didn't get far. It's spoken way too fast for my ear and brain to get. But I learned gato–cat and perro–dog. On the menu, I see Trillogia Cabeza de Gato. Please tell me that's not cat."

Bonita stifled a smile. "You're right, gato means cat. Translated, it means cat's head trilogy."

"Are you fucking kidding me? They serve cat?" Jana dropped the menu and pushed it away.

Gabby and Bonita laughed at her reaction. "No, it's not cat. That's just what it's called. It's usually green plantains mixed in a tomato, onion, and pork rind sauce."

Jana turned up her nose at the description. "Sounds yummy. What else do they have?"

Gabby looked at the menu again. "They have a couple of kinds of shrimp. Camarones Búfalo is like your Buffalo Wings but with shrimp instead of chicken." She let out a loud laugh and it took several seconds before she could speak without giggling. She held up her hand, as to say "Give me a minute," and took several deep breaths. "Bon, you're going to love this one. Coquillas de Camarones."

Bonita laughed.

Jana said, "Okay, what's so funny?"

"Coquilla, in English, means groin cup. Coquillas de Camarones, in English, would be Groin Cup Shrimp."

Jana made a sour face. "What the—"

"She's messing with you, Jana," Bonita interrupted. "Yes, coquillas does mean groin cup, but it has a lot of other meanings too. On a menu, it means shells. Shrimp in shells."

"Like peel and eat shrimp? That sounds a lot better."

"I guess so. Garlic mushrooms are on the menu. We'd be safe with those, too."

Alexander put his menu on the corner of the table. "Let's start with those two. We can order more if we need to."

The server, a heavy-set woman with an attractive face and a genuine smile, approached the table. Gabby pointed at the items on the menu while she ordered. She said something and the server replied, then she and the server looked at Jana and chuckled.

"Very funny," Jana said. "You might want to remind her who's paying and who'll be leaving a tip."

Gabby put her hand on Jana's. "I'm sorry. I told her what we told you, and she thought it was funny you thought they would serve cat. She also said, 'She is muy beautiful.' I couldn't agree more."

Jana patted Gabby's hand. "Awe, you're such a sweet suck-up."

"I try."

Bonita had been looking at her phone and texting. "Jana, how much fuel does the *Miss Jana* hold?"

"What?"

"How much fuel does your boat take when you get fuel?"

"The max capacity is twenty-five hundred gallons. Rey rarely filled it. Only when we were taking a long cruise and knew we'd need it. He usually kept it about a quarter full, so the fuel wouldn't go bad. Why?"

"You said they might be going for fuel. I asked Juan about fuel. He said most of the industrial docks sell what he called 'dirty diesel.' He said a boat like yours wouldn't use it."

"No. Rey would never use dirty diesel unless there was absolutely no other choice."

"That's what Juan thought. He said there's only a couple of places in the bay that sell high-grade diesel and enough to fill a big boat. He guessed it would take four thousand liters." Bonita tapped her phone several times to convert liters to gallons. "A little over a thousand gallons. He was way off if they were low on fuel."

Alexander leaned forward in his chair. "So that means there's a good chance they're at one of only a couple of marinas right now."

"That's correct," Bonita said, still looking at her phone. "Either the Cartagena Yacht Club, Club de Pesca, or Club Nautico Marina. From Pargue Lineal Getsemani, that's the park on Calle 24, right before you turn onto 25 to go over the bay bridge. Juan said he could see all three marinas. He's on his way there to see if he can spot them."

"It'll be nice to know if Rey's there, or at least if the boat is there, but then what?" Jana asked.

"Juan will come get me and take me to the marina. I'll get close and see if I can spot Rey. I can watch them and let you know what they're doing."

"I don't like you going alone," Alexander said.

"Isn't that why you brought me? I'm the only one Rey doesn't know. Maybe he wouldn't recognize you, Alex, but you stand out."

"He doesn't know me," Gabby said.

"You're our guide, Gabby. You shouldn't get mixed up in this."

"After last night, I'm already mixed up in it."

"About last night. We need to talk about that. But first, Bon, as long as you don't get too close. It would be nice to know if Rey's on the boat and get a heads-up when they're headed back this way. If I remember correctly, when I was trying to find the *Miss Jana* in Texas, I figured it would take a couple of hours to fuel up. Is that about right?"

"It could," Jana said. "It depends on how empty she is and how many gallons per hour their pump can pump."

"Gabby, let me see the pictures you took earlier."

Gabby opened the photo app and handed her phone to Alexander. He scrolled through the images and found one Gabby had snapped as the *Miss Jana* passed. Her waterline was clearly visible. He handed the phone to Jana. "Look at this. Can you tell if she's riding high or low in the water?"

Jana looked at the picture and zoomed in and out several times. "She's riding high. She's low on fuel, fresh water, or both."

"So, if they're going for fuel, it'll take them a while?" Bonita asked.

"It will. A couple of hours, at least," Jana said.

"Then I should go to the marina. No one knows me. I can see if Rey is on the boat."

Alexander leaned back in the chair and rubbed his forehead. "Like I said, I'm not thrilled about you going alone, Bon, but it's a good idea. You have time to get there, check them out, and get back here before they leave. When they pass, we'll follow at a safe distance to see where they're docking."

Bonita looked up from her phone. "I'll do that. Juan spotted the boat at the Club de Pesca fuel dock. He's on his way to get me."

The server brought the appetizers and set them in the middle of the table. She then put small plates in front of her guests, continuing to smile, but it seemed disingenuous. It was obvious she hoped her only customers would have ordered the more expensive entrees.

"I know this isn't dinner conversation, but what happened to the man from last night?" Gabby asked.

Bonita grinned. "You mean the guy you made piss his pants when you threatened to cut his dick off?"

"Yeah, him. I was so pissed, but I could have never done it."

"You were extremely convincing," Jana added.

"I wasn't acting. The thought of being taken and sold scared the hell out of me."

Gabby gently placed her hand on Bonita's arm, her voice filled with disbelief. "Bon, the things you shared with us are unbelievable. You're one of the strongest women I've ever met."

Bonita glanced around the table, staring at Alexander a little longer than she did at the others. "No, I'm not, but thanks, Gabby. I had no choice. I wanted to survive. Until I didn't."

"Huh?"

"I'm going to wait for Juan outside. Alex will tell you my story, if you want to hear it."

"Wait, but what happened to the man? Did Juan kill him?"

"He wanted to. He hates human traffickers more than anything. But he's not a cold-blooded killer. He's got a great rapport with the local cops. This morning, Juan called his buds and told them what the guy tried to do. They came and got him. The law here isn't like the United States. He will have a trial, be found guilty, and will disappear into the depths of a Colombian prison for the rest of his life, which may not be long."

"That makes me feel better. He's gone, but we didn't do it to him. I'll sleep better knowing that."

"Me too," Bonita said. "There's only one man I want to kill. And when I find him, I will." She glanced at her phone. "Juan's almost here. I'll keep in touch."

"Be careful," all three said to her.

Bonita nodded and disappeared out the front door.

"Alex, should you have let her go?" Jana asked. "What if she's recognized by the men from the boat? They took pictures."

"Hopefully, she won't get too close. She said she'd watch and report."

"And that's what she'll do? Just watch and report?"

"I doubt it."

"What?"

"I know her pretty well. She's liable to do anything."

"You know Bonita well, Alex?" Gabby asked.

"We lived together for several months. We were doing great until she lost the baby and went down a slippery slope."

"I'm sorry."

"Thank you. The doctor said she lost the baby because of the botched abortions she'd had. He said she shouldn't get pregnant again because she would never carry a child to term and it could kill her."

"Oh my God," Gabby gasped.

"We tried to make it work, but she became distant. I didn't help. She left and went back to the life she'd known before me and started using again. I believe we found her just in time. This trip has helped her considerably. I didn't know she also came here to find the man who trafficked her and kill him. I'm not saying anything to her one way or the other about that, but I hope when it comes time to leave, she'll come with us."

"I think you could convince her to come with you. She seems like she's still into you. I got the impression she wasn't too pleased with you and Jana making it look real on the boat. Funny, it was her idea. If you'll excuse me, I need to go to the toilet."

When Gabby left, Jana said, "I noticed Bon was a little testy after our couch episode. Was she a bit jealous?"

"Maybe, but I wouldn't read much into it. Had it been her and some guy going after it on the couch and I was watching, I would've been a little testy as well. But I can assure you, there's nothing there anymore."

"Nothing? I'm curious. Why did you feel the need to assure me?" Jana locked her blue eyes on his.

"No reason, it's just a phrase."

"It is? You never answered my question from the boat. Was what I felt in your pants love or lust?"

Alexander laughed. "My dear, it was neither. What you felt was the barrel of the gun I have in my pocket."

Jana grinned. "Your gun is a Taurus thirty-eight special revolver with a two-inch barrel. What I felt was NOT a two-inch barrel."

25

The drive from the Oasis to Club de Pesca was slow. Honking cars and impatient drivers congested the narrow, winding road. Bonita was antsy. She kept checking the time on her phone. Jana said it took up to two hours to fuel the boat, but that was when the tanks were empty. Fifteen minutes had elapsed since Juan picked her up. It felt like it took an hour to make the six-kilometer drive.

A rough brick wall adorned with vibrant graffiti bordered the Club de Pesca. The closed chain-link gate, secured with a large lock, blocked the first opening in the wall. The graffiti stopped, but the wall continued until it connected with a small building that looked like the marina office. Past the building, the brick wall turned into a wrought-iron fence. The surrounding area featured meticulous manicuring with vibrant flowerbeds, flawlessly trimmed hedges and a majestic Banyan tree. An imposing iron gate blocked the entrance. The gate connected to an old stone wall that was part of Fort of San Sebastián del Pastelillo, an eighteenth-century fort designed to protect the city from attacks by pirates and to prevent the smuggling of goods. A heavy-set man wearing a blue security guard uniform stood outside a narrow, arched entrance to the fort.

Juan inched past the entrance and the security guard. "Will the guard let us in?"

"Why not?"

"It's a fancy place. The guard will know I'm not going to the restaurant."

Bonita took a long look at Juan. His peppered hair was long and stringy, and he looked like he hadn't shaved in several days. He wore an oversized t-shirt with the logo of an American basketball team and well-faded off-brand jeans. "Yes, Juan, you didn't dress for success today."

"And you are funny today. It's good to see you laugh. I would've worn a suit, but you didn't give me much time."

"You're right. My fault. The next time I need to spy on a boat, I'll give you more notice."

"You do that. For now, what do you want to do?"

Bonita leaned forward in the seat and untied the top string of the bikini bra. She untied the back strap and pulled the bra out from underneath the coverup. After tossing the top to Juan she said, "The top's not mine. Take care of it for me. Around the corner there's a sign for a tourist bus stop. Drop me off at the sign."

Juan made the block, which took him to the main street before he could turn back onto the same road they'd come in on. He pulled to the tourist bus sign and stopped. "Do you want me to wait for you?"

"If you don't mind, wait fifteen minutes. If I'm not back by then or I haven't texted you, leave. When I need to go back to the Oasis, I can call an Uber."

"Are you sure? I can wait a while."

"Yes. I may just sit and watch until the boat leaves, and that could be hours. Don't you need to get back to the bar?"

"I do, but I shouldn't leave you alone."

"I'll be fine."

"Just confirm the car you get into is your Uber ride."

"I will. Thank you, Juan. Remember, fifteen minutes."

Juan slouched in the car at the bus stop and watched Bonita as she walked to the opening of the fort. Once she was through the opening in the wall, he drove past the fort and backed his car into an open spot in front of a beach area. He lowered the windows, turned the motor off, and checked the time on his watch.

The security guard noticed Bonita when she appeared from the corner where Juan had dropped her. He fixated on her breasts, which jiggled unencumbered beneath the blue cover-up. Her graceful legs propelled her forward. With each confident stride, the sound of her heels clicking against the pavement echoed against the ancient walls of the fort.

Bonita could tell the guard wanted her to stop, maybe to ask her what her business was inside the fort or to have her sign the register that sat on a tall wooden stool in front of him. His mouth hung open as he gazed at her. She smiled, waved politely, and walked through the entrance, not breaking stride. She waited for him to collect his wits and call out for her to come back, but he never did. She had a feeling the uniformed guard was too busy watching her walk away. His brain had likely turned to mush, as most men's brains tend to do in the presence of a beautiful woman.

Restaurante Fuerte de San Sebastián was straight ahead on Bonita's path. Several cars were parked in front. She looked around, then headed toward what she thought was the fuel dock. If the *Miss Jana* was there, that's where she'd be. She slowed her pace and strolled toward the marina. Passing the restaurant, she realized she needed to use the bathroom. She entered the building and walked to the maître d'. Unlike the security guard, his mouth was not agape, and he eyed her with contempt, not desire.

"Can I use your restroom?" she asked in English. She thought if she played the part of an American tourist, she would be treated better than a local.

"The toilet is for customers only," the man said in Spanish.

She understood him but pretended not to. "I'm sorry. I don't understand," she said in English. "Um, dónde el baño?" she said, purposely omitting "está" so that her question became, "Where the bathroom?"

The man scoffed, possibly offended by her butchering of the language. "The toilet is for customers only," he repeated, again in Spanish.

Bonita gave him a confused look, as though she still didn't understand why she couldn't use the restroom.

"He said the toilet is for customers only."

Bonita turned quickly to see who had translated for her. A man not much older than her and about the same height stood behind her. "Oh, thank you. I guess I need to order something."

"I'm sorry, we're booked. Do you have a reservation?" In the presence of a translator, the maître d' suddenly spoke English.

Bonita looked around the dining room. There was a smattering of customers among the mostly empty tables. "The place is empty," she said snarkily.

"The tables are reserved," he said in English. Then he turned to the man behind Bonita and addressed him in Spanish. "We don't allow whores to hang around the restaurant and harass the customers."

Bonita bit her lip to keep from lashing out at the man. She forced a grin and looked at the man behind her.

In Spanish, he said to the maître d', "She's not a prostitute. She doesn't even speak Spanish. She's a tourist who would like to use the toilet."

"Look at her. She's not wearing a bra, letting her tits flop around, advertising. And the tattoo that disappears into her short pants. I'll bet the feather goes all the way between her legs. Another advertisement. You must pay to see the rest of the feather."

The man's words were so loathsome that Bonita wanted to claw his eyes out. Instead, she faked a laugh she hoped hid her anger. She didn't want either man to know she understood.

"He said it's policy. He can't let you use the toilet."

"Oh?" Bonita smiled.

The maître d' grunted and started to speak, but the man cut him off. In Spanish, with a harsh tone, he said, "You've said enough."

Bonita thanked the maître d' in her sweetest southern voice then turned to the man behind her. "Do you know if there's a bathroom nearby that I can use?"

"Believe it or not, there isn't. I think there are public toilets over by the beach, but that's quite a walk from here."

"I don't have a lot of choice." She turned to leave. The man followed her out the door.

"My boat's at the end of the dock. It has a nice toilet if you'd like to use it."

Bonita studied the man. He wasn't tall, but he was remarkably well-built. His hair was reddish brown and cropped on the sides. Despite his tanned complexion, his face revealed a multitude of freckles. He had a pleasant smile with perfect teeth.

"I don't know if climbing on a boat with a strange man in Cartagena would be considered a great idea."

The man laughed. He had a good laugh. "I totally understand. I guess it sounded a little odd."

"Actually, considering the circumstances, it wasn't all that strange. Unless you and that maître d' are in cahoots and this is how you lure women onto your boat."

He laughed again. "It wasn't. But if it works, I may go back and make a deal with him." He smiled and continued, "Seriously, if you need to use the toilet, my boat's at the end of the pier at the fuel dock. There's lots of other boats and people around. You'll be safe."

Bonita's heart raced as she studied the man's face. He resembled the picture she'd seen of Rey, but she couldn't be sure. "I'd ask you to promise me I'd be safe, but that's exactly what a kidnapper would say. Maybe if you tell me your name."

"I'm Rey," he said, extending his hand to her.

Bonita took his hand and shook it, squeezing firmly to mask the nervousness that overwhelmed her when Rey confirmed his identity.

"Nice to meet you. I'm Bon...Bonnie." She used her bar name because she didn't know if Rey had ever heard of her and she didn't want to take any chances.

"It's nice to meet you, Bonnie. The boat's this way." He led her down the concrete sidewalk toward the fuel dock. They walked slowly and exchanged pleasantries. He mentioned he thought she looked Hispanic and was surprised she didn't speak Spanish. She gave him what she thought was a reasonable explanation. By the time she was close enough to read the Cheoy Lee's transom, her heart was in her throat.

"There she is," Rey said when they approached the boat.

"Miss Jana. Who's Jana?"

"She's my...the lady I bought the boat from."

"It's a beautiful boat. You're from Fort Lauderdale?"

"I am," he said, without elaborating. "Watch your step."

Bonita carefully crossed the boarding plank that connected the pier with the *Miss Jana*'s swim platform. She climbed the ladder from the swim platform to the aft deck and could feel Rey's eyes on the back of her legs as he followed her up the ladder.

"The head's on the other side of the main salon."

"The head?"

"That's what they call the bathroom on a boat."

"Oh, okay. Thanks."

Bonita walked through the spacious salon, admiring the woodwork. She found the head but the door didn't have a lock. While she peed, she sent a text to Jana and Alexander:

Found the boat and found Rey. He's fine.

She pursed her lips, back-spaced over 'fine,' and typed, 'okay.'
The first reply came from Jana:

THANK YOU!

Alexander's reply came a few seconds later:

Good news. Is Juan still with you? Get back here as soon as you can.

Bonita murmured, "Oh, shit," and looked at her watch. It had been fifteen minutes since she left Juan. He'd likely be gone. She didn't want to tell Alexander and Jana that she was on the boat. She thought for a few seconds, then sent:

Juan is gone. I'm going to hang around a bit and see if the boat leaves soon.

Alexander replied:

OK. B Careful!!!

Bonita followed the instructions on the wall to flush the marine head. She washed her hands and cautiously opened the door, hoping Rey wasn't waiting on her with a rope or handcuffs. With no sign of him, she walked to the aft deck.

"No trouble?" Rey asked.

"No, I figured out how to flush the toilet. Thank you so much. I didn't realize how badly I needed to go."

"Any time. Would you like a beer?"

Bonita looked into his large green eyes, which looked sad and lonely to her. "I'd like that. Thanks."

"Sit. I'll be right back." He hurried into the galley and returned with two cold beers. He sat in the deck chair beside her, twisted the top off one bottle, and handed it to her.

"Cheers," she said after he opened his bottle.

Rey tapped his bottle against hers, then took a long drink. "Where are you from, Bonnie?"

She realized she hadn't thought this through. Sitting on the boat with Rey, drinking beer, and having a conversation was not what she planned. She had no backstory. She'd always heard the easiest way to keep a lie straight was to tell the truth but color it as necessary.

"I'm from Houston. I have a friend from Cartagena and she was coming back for a vacation. She asked me and another friend to come with her. I thought, 'Why not? I've never been there.' They wanted to go shopping today, and I was tired of the stores, so I came to see the fort. It looked better in the brochures."

Rey let out a laugh that she found very appealing.

"What about you? Why are you here?"

Rey scratched his unshaven cheek. It was his turn to concoct a story. He hadn't planned ahead when he asked her to stay for a beer and not being as smooth as Bonita, he tripped over his words. "Uh...no reason. I was sitting around with friends and we talked about taking a cruise. We just went."

"Wow, a spur-of-the-moment cruise. Did you plan to come all the way to South America? Aren't there lots of beautiful islands in the Caribbean you could have gone to?"

"There are. And we stopped at a few. We kept going south until we hit Colombia."

"Where are your friends now?"

"It takes a while to fill this boat with fuel, especially with the slow pumps they have here. I plan to be here for a while. My friends went into the Walled City."

Bonita jerked, pretending like there was a buzz from her phone. "Excuse me a sec." She pulled the phone from her pocket, pretended to read a text, chuckled softly, and sent a group text to Alexander and Jana.

Took a chance. Met Rey. On boat now. His friends went to town. He said it'll take a while.

"I'm sorry. It's my friends," she told Rey.

Her phone buzzed for real. It was from Alexander.

WTF! Great info, but get off the boat now!

Bonita stuck the phone in her pocket. She gulped the beer and looked into Rey's eyes. Even had she not known he was lying, she could tell it by his eyes. She could also tell he didn't enjoy lying to her. After a quick scan of the pier and finding no one in sight, she leaned close to him, put her hand on his wrist, and said, "Rey, have you ever hurt a girl?"

"What?"

"Have you ever, or would you ever, hurt a girl?"

"That's a crazy question. Are you asking if I'd hurt you?"

"Maybe."

"Because you're in a foreign country on a yacht with a guy you just met? I thought we covered that earlier."

"We did. And I think you're a nice guy. That's why I'm here. But most serial killers are 'nice guys.'"

"Thanks, Bonnie. I like to think I'm a decent guy and I guarantee you I'm not a serial killer. I've made some bad choices, but I've never purposely hurt a woman."

Bonita faked a gasp. "Purposely? You have hurt women?"

"No, that's not what I meant." Rey didn't want to share the details of how he smuggled girls into the US from Cuba and delivered them to sex traffickers. "I did something I'm not proud of and some girls may have gotten hurt because of it. At the time, I felt I had no choice."

"Geez, Rey, what'd you do?"

He squirmed in his seat and scratched at the label on the beer bottle. "I got into trouble with some sex traffickers and was forced to deliver some girls for them."

"What the fuck?" Bonita jumped to her feet. "You're a sex trafficker?"

"Bonnie, no, I'm not. Please sit down and let me explain."

"Explain how you trafficked girls? I think I should leave."

"I'm not a trafficker. I was coerced. It's a long story, but believe me, I didn't want to. As it turned out, all the girls were rescued."

Bonita sat. "Okay, I'm listening."

"Call it a poor execution of a bad idea and leave it at that. But I reached out to a private detective who helped find the girls, free them, and bust the traffickers. He conveniently forgot about me when he gave the information to the police."

"That's quite a story. Earlier, I thought you were lying to me. You couldn't make up that story."

"Bonnie, I did lie to you. Jana, as in the woman for whom this boat is named, was my girlfriend...is my girlfriend. Honestly, I'm not sure. We've been drifting apart for the past few months. I haven't spoken to her since we left Fort Lauderdale."

Bonita wanted to trust him, but she distrusted men in general. She was about to ask him a question but she was afraid of how he'd react. If it went badly, she wanted to be able to get off the boat in a hurry. She walked aft to the stern and looked over the edge. The swim platform was seven feet below the top of the stern rail. To jump from the rail, she'd break an ankle, if not her leg. The distance from the deck to the platform was only about four feet, but the walkway door was closed. She didn't know if there was a trick to opening it. She decided if she had to escape, she would climb over the stern rail, lower herself as far as she could, and drop the rest of the way. It would only be a foot or two. She would survive the fall.

She hopped on the railing and got into a position where she thought she could easily swing her legs over and lower herself to the swim platform if she needed to. "Rey, are you in trouble?"

26

Rey ambled toward Bonita. He put his hands on the rail, leaned forward slightly, and gazed across the marina. Seeing no one, he turned to her. "I'm in such deep shit," he said, his voice melancholic, his eyes were distant and cold.

Instinctively, Bonita rested her hand on his chest. His warmth radiated through his shirt, and she felt the steady beat of his heart against her palm. His expression was as flat as Cartagena Bay. She had seen similar looks on men's faces when she worked the bars. Men dejected because of their job, or lack of a job, or because of a problem with their spouse, or not having a spouse. Often, a hug would help, but in the bars where she worked, most men came for sex.

As she would do in the bars, Bonita slid her hand up Rey's muscular chest and around his neck. She gently pulled him close and squeezed. He put his arms around her and gripped her in return. Their embrace was brief but seemed much longer to Bonita. She leaned back and saw that his expression hadn't changed. She gave him a gentle kiss on the cheek.

A slight smile came to Rey. "What was that for?"

"It seemed like you needed it and I wanted to."

Rey pulled her close and passionately kissed her. She kissed him back then abruptly pushed him away. "I'm sorry Rey, I can't."

"I'm sorry too, Bonnie. I shouldn't have—"

"Don't be sorry. It was nice, but we just met and...I'm...just not ready."

Other than Alexander and Juan, men had abused Bonita for most of her life. She'd become wary of all men. Rey seemed nice, but she knew he was in a relationship with Jana–a relationship on rocky ground, but a relationship nonetheless.

Telling Rey she wasn't ready seemed like a good out. It could mean anything: She wasn't ready for a quickie on a boat with a man she just met, or she wasn't ready for a relationship. What it didn't tell him was she wasn't interested in either. What she was interested in was information.

In her entire life, Bonita had only had sex with one man where money or rape wasn't involved, and that was Alexander. In her heart, she knew the truth, but a persistent feeling told her that Alexander's intentions on the night they met might not have been as honorable as they seemed. Rey was no different. She'd known him less than half an hour, and he'd already kissed her. Granted, she had pecked him on the cheek first. She was positive that if she hinted at it, he would invite her to his cabin for a brief boff. It would mean nothing. Just one more in a countless string of sleazeballs who wanted to play hide the salami with her.

Rey seemed like a nice guy and, from how Jana described him, he was. But Bonita didn't know if it would be a wham bam thank you ma'am and adios. He was, after all, a man. If that happened, she wouldn't get the information she wanted. Her best option was to play it cool. Go slow. Seem interested. But she had never gone slow with a man in her life. She didn't know what she was getting herself into.

"Rey, I'm going to be honest with you. Well, kind of honest. We just met, but I like you. Tell me what deep shit you're into. I need to know if I should walk away and not look back."

"Since we are being honest, you should run, not walk away from me. I seem to invite trouble."

"Oh, Rey." Bonita grabbed him and held him close to her. She was glad he didn't seem to pick up on her being "kind of honest" statement. She gently pushed him back and said, "Tell me what's going on."

Rey pulled her close and kissed her intensely. She wrapped her arms around him and squeezed as tightly as she could. They shared a lingering kiss. A passionate kiss. Slowly, the two separated. Both of them were smiling, but only one was genuine.

"I'm not complaining, but that was a surprise," Bonita said between deep breaths.

"I like you, Bonnie. Maybe more than I should, considering we just met. I'm going to tell you what's happening, but I wanted one more kiss before I did. It may be our last."

Bonita stared out at the boats anchored in the bay. Rey wasn't a sleazeball. Well, maybe a bit of one. He seemed to have become infatuated with her in a brief amount of time. It wasn't the first time a man became obsessed with her, but she had never cared before. Rey seemed vulnerable, and she didn't want to hurt him. She finished her drink. "How 'bout another beer first?"

"My pleasure. I knew I liked you." He went into the galley to get fresh beers.

Bonita faced a dilemma. Tell Rey who she was and what she was doing before he told her what he was involved in, or wait and tell him afterward. Should she tell him at all? He would find out eventually. The longer she waited, the angrier he would be. Did she care? She did. She also cared about Jana. But Jana said she and Rey were growing apart, and she didn't seem too worried about him when she and Alexander were 'making it look real' on the party barge earlier that morning.

Rey returned with two beers. He handed Bonita one and sat on the rail beside her.

"Thanks," she said.

Rey took a long slug of the beer. "I told you I got messed up with human traffickers."

Bonita nodded.

"That was more or less my fault. I got involved in things I shouldn't have. The mess I'm in now was just bad luck. A friend brought a couple of guys to my boat and before I knew it, they were pointing guns at me. They told me to take the boat out, which I did. I knew I was in trouble when they tossed my phone overboard..." Rey looked past her at the fuel dock. "Crap! They're back early. You need to go."

"Who? Why?"

"You need to leave now. Do you have a phone?"

"Of course."

"What's the number?"

Rey typed her number into his phone, added a text message, and pressed send. "You've got my number. I want to see you again, but I understand if you don't reply. You probably shouldn't and I shouldn't ask, but—"

Bonita interrupted Rey by kissing him. "I'll text you," she said. She gave him a quick hug and descended the steps to the swim platform.

"It's better if they don't see you. The way they're coming is the only way out. Go to the next pier and walk up it. Walk normally. The sailboats will hide you. When those guys get on the boat, leave. I'll distract them so they aren't looking your way."

"Rey?"

"Go. I'll text you later."

Rey watched her walk to the pier. He'd seen her walk across the parking lot toward the restaurant earlier when he'd been out walking and decided he wanted to get a closer look. He had no plans to talk to her, but when the maître d' turned into a dick, he felt obliged to assist. Now, he wondered if it was good luck or bad luck that he bumped into her.

He downed his beer and picked up the bottle Bonita had left. He took a small sip, sat, and waited for the men to reach the boat.

Bonita kept her back to the main walkway leading to the fuel dock. She glanced over her shoulder and when she saw the men board the *Miss Jana*, she waited a few minutes, then hurried back down the pier and toward the parking lot. The vibrant flowers lining the path offered a cheerful facade, which masked the anxiety that gripped her stomach.

The beer had worked its way through her system, and she needed to pee. She considered going inside the restaurant and telling the maître d' in perfect Colombian Spanish that she was not a prostitute, that she'd flown in on a private jet, and there was no fucking way she'd pee in his restaurant, let alone eat there, but a better thought struck her. One day, after Rey and the boat were gone, she would bring Jana, Alexander, and Gabby to eat at the restaurant. Alexander and Jana would go in first and get a table for four. No way the asshole at the door would turn them away. She and Gabby would join them a little later and she'd wear the sluttiest outfit she could find.

Lost in thought, Bonita passed through the gate without realizing she was. Rey mentioned that a beach park beyond the fort had bathrooms. She checked her phone while she walked and found one new text.

> *Bonnie, sorry I rushed you off the boat. Best you not meet the other men. I want to see you again. Moving the boat back to Manzanillo later. Can we meet tomorrow?*

Bonita read the text message several times. She knew what she was going to reply but wondered if she should.

> *YES! I want to see you too. Let me know when and where.*

> *I'll text you in the morning.*

Bonita typed a red heart emoji as a reply but deleted it before sending the text. Too soon. She sent a thumbs-up emoji instead. When she got to the park, she saw playground equipment and two water fountains, but no toilets. She crossed from the street to the park and followed a gravel path along the bay. She'd walked a hundred yards when she reached the end of the park. No toilets.

A building with two large decks on the roof was just past the park. A pointed thatched roof covered one deck. The sign said Mabare Restaurante-Bar. It didn't look as hoity-toity as the restaurant-bar inside the fort. Bonita wanted another beer...or something stronger.

She climbed the steps and a middle-aged man wearing black slacks, a white shirt, and a bow tie greeted her. He gave her the once-over. She was impressed his gaze didn't linger on any part of her anatomy other than the feather.

"Hola. ¿Quieres una mesa o sentarte en la barra?"

"Hola. El bar. Dónde está el baño?" She preferred sitting at the bar versus a table, and she still needed a bathroom.

Bonita used the bathroom, then went back to the bar. She chose a worn-out barstool at the far end of the bar, away from the three separate groups of men sitting there. All of them checked her out as she walked by. As much as she wanted a shot of fine tequila, she ordered a beer instead.

When the bartender set the beer in front of her, she opened her purse to pay. The bartender stopped her and, in Spanish, said, "No, compliments of the man at the bar."

Bonita looked across the bar at the man who'd bought her the beer. She gave him a half smile and extended her glass toward him in thanks. As she expected, the man slid off his barstool and walked over to her. He smelled of cigarette smoke and stale beer.

"Hola." He hesitated, then asked in Spanish. "Are you a prostitute?"

Bonita's expression turned to anger. She exclaimed loudly in English, "Why the fuck do people keep calling me a prostitute?"

The man recoiled. He only understood 'fuck' and 'prostitute.' The words often go together, but from her tone, he realized she wasn't a prostitute...not anymore.

"I'm sorry. Usually, pretty girls who are alone at the bar are prostitutes. You're pretty. Too pretty, maybe. Again, I'm sorry."

"No, I'm sorry. I shouldn't have snapped at you. I'm having a bad day. Thank you for the beer."

"You're welcome." He turned to the bartender. "All her drinks, put on my tab." He began to walk away, but Bonita grabbed him by the elbow.

"Thank you. I need to send some texts. When I finish, you're welcome to join me."

The man nodded and walked back to his seat. Bonita pulled out her phone. No new messages. She opened the joint conversation with Alexander and Jana and typed a new text:

Hello?

A few seconds later, she received a reply from Alexander.

Bon! Are you OK?

Yes. Fine. I'm at a bar near the marina.

Has the boat left?

No. It will soon. They're going back to Manzanillo.

Good info. We don't need to wait and follow them.

The bar I'm at is the first building after the beach. They have a dock. Can you pick me up?

Yes. Will leave soon. Send us a picture of the dock.

Bonita walked to the end of the bar and took several pictures of the dock, the bay, and the surrounding area. She sent them to the joint thread and walked back to the bar.

Pictures sent

She'd left the glass of beer on the bar when she went to take the pictures. About a third of the beer remained. All of the men at the bar were nonchalantly looking at her. She picked up the glass, swirled it around, and set it back on the bar.

"Uno más, por favor," she said to the bartender. She spoke to the man whose tab she was using. "It got warm. I hate warm beer. I hope you don't mind that I ordered a new one."

The bartender poured the beer and carried it over to her. She thanked the man and took a sip. She made a fist and gently struck the bar. It was the second time in as many days she'd nearly fucked up. She'd committed a cardinal sin by leaving her beer on the bar unattended. She picked up the two glasses of beer and walked around the bar to the man who'd paid for them. She sat beside him and put the original beer in front of him. "I hate to waste beer. You can have it."

"Gracias." He picked up the glass and chugged the beer. "It wasn't that warm. I'm Pedro."

The bartender saw Bonita's confusion and said, "You thought he slipped you a drug. It happens a lot in Cartagena. But I don't allow it in my bar."

Bonita's face reddened. "I'm so sorry. I...The way you guys were looking at me when I returned..." she said loud enough for the others to hear.

The man next to her said, "Dear, Colombia has many beautiful women. Few are as beautiful as you. Even less as beautiful as you come here and sit at the bar. You're wearing a sheer top and you're not wearing a bra. We are men. We are going to look." He took a long pull on his beer.

Bonita put her arm on the man's back and kissed him on the cheek. "You're sweet. If I were a prostitute, I'd give you a freebie."

Beer shot from the man's mouth into his lap. Bonita reached for a handful of napkins. As tempted as she was to wipe the man's crotch for him, she instead handed him the wad of napkins.

<h1 style="text-align:center">27</h1>

Gabby slowed the barge and put the outboard into neutral. The boat nudged against the dock. Alexander wrapped a line around a cleat and secured it. Gabby cut the engine.

"Should we join Bon for a cocktail?" Jana asked.

"We should pick her up, get the boat back, and then go for drinks," Alexander answered.

"Probably the wiser choice."

Alexander texted Bonita to let her know they were at the dock. She came bounding down the steps a few minutes later with a newfound energy that had been absent for months.

"Hola," she said when she got to the boat.

"You seem to be in a cheerful mood," Gabby said.

"I am. A man at the bar bought me several beers. When I left, I hugged him. He had his arm around me and when I turned, my boob went into his hand." Bonita laughed. "I even slowed my turn so he could hold it for a split second. He was noticeably shaking when I walked away." She dropped onto the L-couch on the back of the pontoon barge. "Whew. That's the most walking I've done since I left the beach house. I'm totally out of shape."

Jana, her face lit with excitement, ignored Bonita's comment. "You met Rey? How is he? How did he look?"

"He's okay. He could use a shave. I could tell he wasn't happy. I'm pretty sure he's...um...what do you call it...being forced to do whatever he is doing."

"Coerced, maybe?" Alexander said.

"That's it. Coerced. He said he was in 'deep shit.'"

"Deep shit?" Jana said. "That's what he said?"

"Yes. He was going to tell me but then he saw the guys coming back to the boat. He spotted them long before they saw us. They were still a ways off, so they didn't see me leave."

"Which means we still don't know what they're doing here," Alexander said.

"We don't. But Rey gave me his cell number and asked if I'd meet him tomorrow near Manzanillo."

"Manzanillo? That's where we were yesterday. You were right when you figured that's where they'd be," Gabby said. "Bonita, exactly where are Rey and the boat right now?"

"They're on the far side of the marina, almost to the bridge that goes over the bay."

Gabby looked at the chart of Cartagena Bay, then scanned the bay. The entrance to the bay between the end of the pier at the marina and the Navy hospital dock was less than a hundred and thirty meters wide. The channel the *Miss Jana* would have to use was narrower.

"We need to get through the gap before they come through it," Gabby said. "They've seen us once, and they'd probably recognize us if we passed again. Ordinarily, that wouldn't be a problem, but it would look odd if Alex and Jana were still humping on the couch, and now they, or at least Rey, know what Bonita looks like."

"Let's untie and get the hell out of here," Jana said.

Gabby started the engine, and Alexander released the lines. Gabby took off slowly, weaving her way through the array of anchored boats. When she passed the last boat, she eased the throttle up. The pontoons plowed through the water, gradually gaining momentum. She pushed the throttle to full speed. When the pontoons got on plane, and the boat picked up speed, she eased back on the throttle, giving it just enough power to keep the pontoons on top of the water. As soon as they reached the far side of the bay, they could see the *Miss Jana*, still moored alongside the fuel dock. After another half kilometer, Gabby pulled back the throttle, and the party barge's pontoons settled back to their floating depth. The *Miss Jana* had become a mere speck in the distance.

"We're good now," Gabby said. "There's no way they're going to see us." Fifteen minutes later, she pulled the party barge up to the dock. One of the young men from the morning saw them coming and was waiting for them.

"Have fun?" he asked in Spanish.

"Sì, muy bueno," Gabby answered.

Once the girls were off the boat, Alexander picked up the tote and stepped off. He glanced one last time to ensure he didn't leave anything behind. He walked to the Mazda and dropped the tote in the back. "Does anyone want water?"

When no one did, Alexander closed the hatch and got into the front passenger seat. The girls were already seated. Bonita's eyelids were getting heavy. The beer and sun had taken a toll on her. A light to medium pinkness appeared on Jana's face and body. It didn't show through Gabby's natural medium-tan skin color, but she had burned as well. She couldn't see it, but she would feel it. The tube of sunscreen had never left the bag.

"Back to the hotel?" Gabby asked.

"Yes," Alexander replied. "We talked about going to a bar, but we all need to clean up. Afterward, we'll meet at the hotel bar. You're welcome to join us, Gabby, if you'd like."

"Thank you. I'll drop you off and go home. We weren't on the water long, but I can feel it. I'll go home and get some rest. Will you need me tomorrow?"

"We might. Jana, Bon, and I need to talk. Right now, all I know is Rey and the boat will be at Manzanillo Marina tomorrow."

"I'm sorry. If it's all the same to you, I'd rather not go back over there. I can see if I can find you another driver."

Bonita opened her eyes. "No need for a driver. Not unless Alex and Jana want to go out. I'll get Juan to take me to Manzanillo."

"Okay, that's much appreciated," Gabby said.

"Bonita, we can discuss this later," Alexander said, his jaw clenched. He had never wanted her to come to Colombia, but he brought her along, in hopes of pulling her out of the depths of her depression. And it was working—she was smiling again for the first time since her miscarriage. But she had gone to the fuel dock to find the boat and find out if Rey was alive and onboard. She had found the boat, and she had boarded it and talked to Rey. She proved herself to be invaluable, but going back to the marina and meeting Rey, surrounded by his associates, was too dangerous. Alexander wouldn't let her go. Couldn't let her go. But her mind seemed to be made up. His gut twisted with fear as he wondered how he would stop her.

Gabby turned into the drop-off area in front of the hotel. She put the Mazda in park but left the motor running. She slid out and opened the door for Jana, who'd been sitting behind her.

Jana handed her five one-hundred-dollar bills. "Thank you again, Gabby. You've been wonderful." Gabby looked at the bills and started to protest, but Jana shushed her. "That tote's full of water and fruit. We didn't touch the fruit. Would you like to take it home?"

"My icebox is tiny. I'll keep a little and give the rest to my neighbors."

"Oh, that'd be nice." Jana wondered if Gabby had an icebox—a cooler that used ice to keep things cold—or if she called a refrigerator an icebox. Icebox was such an antiquated term. She couldn't imagine anyone who was born in the twenty-first century using the term "icebox." Perhaps the translation was to blame, she thought. Then she remembered Gabby spent time with her grandparents in Pennsylvania, which is where she likely learned the term.

Alexander held the front door of the hotel open, then followed Jana and Bonita to the elevator. They entered the elevator and punched the button for their floor. "How do you all feel?" he asked, more concerned with Bonita than Jana.

"A little tired," Bonita replied. "But after a shower, I'll be fine. I'm starving."

"That's right. You left before the food came. You should have eaten some fruit on the way back," Jana said.

"I didn't even think about it."

The elevator stopped, and the doors opened. Alexander and Jana went to one room, and Bonita went to the adjoining room. Inside, Jana turned to Alexander, "If you don't mind, I'd like to shower first. I need to wash my hair and I can dry it while you shower."

"Fine with me. I may have a beer from the minibar while I wait." Alexander pulled the little Taurus .38 Special from his pocket and put it in the nightstand drawer next to the bed. "I don't drink and play with guns."

"Not even one beer?"

"Not even one."

"Enjoy your beer. I'll try to be quick."

Alexander pulled out a Bogota Brewing Company Lager. The other option was a Heineken. He opted for the local beer, his first of the trip. After several attempts to unscrew the top and only managing to inflict pain on his hand, he realized it was not a twist-top. He used the magnetic bottle opener stuck to the side of the minibar to pry the cap off. He lifted the bottle to his lips, swished the beer around his mouth, and swallowed. He let out a contented sigh and took another long sip. A bitterness hit the back of his tongue that was quickly followed by a watery aftertaste. The beer was on the lighter side, almost like a Corona. Overall, it was palatable.

He walked to the window. The fourteenth floor of the hotel offered a breathtaking view of Cartagena Bay. The sun was just beginning its descent to the west. He realized they'd crammed a full day into only five brief hours. He leaned against the windowsill and peered through binoculars, making a mental note to rinse off any salt spray that may have landed on the lenses. He could see several large navy ships lashed together in the marina, their sleek gray hulls reflecting the sunlight. Turning his focus to the opposite side of the bay, he spotted a bustling marina filled with sailboats and yachts.

The marina was Club Nautico de Cartagena. Not the marina he was looking for. He scanned to the north along the coast and spotted the walls of the old fort next to Club de Pesca Marina. Club de Pesca was smaller than Club Nautico. Most of the boats were in the forty-five to seventy-five-foot range and mostly white.

Bonita said the *Miss Jana* was at the fuel dock near the end of the marina. Alexander panned along the pier, studying each boat as best he could. He estimated the distance to the marina to be about a mile as the crow flies. He pulled up Google Maps on his phone, found the hotel, and used the 'measure distance' feature to get a more accurate distance. Three thousand two hundred feet–just over six-tenths of a mile. Almost one kilometer. Under the power of the binocular's 10X magnification, looking at the marina was like looking the length of a football field with the naked eye. When he focused on the far end of the marina, it didn't take long to spot the boat. She was backed into the long pier, presumably in front of the fueling station. His view was limited to the front and three-quarters of the port side, but there was no doubt the boat was the *Miss Jana*.

Jana crept up behind him and whispered in his ear, causing him to startle. She stood there with a towel wrapped snugly around her body, catching him off guard.

"I didn't realize you were a peeping Tom," she teased. "You should be more careful."

Alexander blushed.

"I'm sorry. I didn't mean to startle you. I forgot my robe and when I saw you looking through those binoculars, I had to comment. I didn't mean to sneak up on you."

Alexander playfully patted his chest. "You didn't. I wasn't paying attention. I spotted the boat. It's still at the fuel dock."

"You're kidding, let me see." Jana held the towel with one hand and tried to focus the binoculars with the other. "Where?" she asked.

"Look straight across. Do you see that marina with all the boats?"

"Yes."

"Now follow the shoreline to the left." Alexander put his hand on her bare shoulder and gently turned her. "It's just a little way up. You'll see the next marina."

"I see it."

"Look straight at the boats, but look over them. The fuel dock is at the far end. If you see the bridge over the bay, you've passed it."

"Lots of boats look like her. How can you be sure...wait...I see her. That's the *Miss Jana*. I'd know that big trawler anywhere. It's cool we can see her from here. Too bad we didn't know that this morning." Jana's voice brimmed with excitement. "Can we see that other place?

Where they're going to later?"

"I doubt it. It's further that direction." Alexander pointed in the general direction of where he thought Manzanillo to be. He'd pointed with his left hand, his right hand remained on her shoulder.

Jana put her hand on top of his, using her forearm to hold the towel up. She leaned back into his chest and stared out the window. He gently caressed her bare shoulder.

"Alex?"

"Hmm."

"You took your gun out of your pocket, didn't you?"

"I did."

"You should take a cold shower."

28

Alexander sported a year-round tan. In winter, it would fade slightly, but the Texas Gulf Coast had plenty of sunny days to maintain some color. By May, he was darker, but liberal amounts of sunscreen kept him from looking like a pot of gumbo roux ready for the holy trinity. His base tan protected him from getting burned even worse during the boat trip on Cartagena Bay.

He adjusted the water in the shower to lukewarm and stepped in. After he washed, he gradually turned the hot water knob down and allowed the cold water to cool his skin, still radiating from the morning sun. The cold water helped but didn't eliminate the desires Jana had stirred in him. He stepped out of the glass shower enclosure, toweled off, shaved, and dressed. When he opened the bathroom door, he saw Jana standing at the window, gazing out through the binoculars.

"Are they still there?" he asked.

"They are. Haven't moved. These are good binocs, but I still can't make out faces. One guy is bigger and has lighter hair than the others. I think that's Rey, but I'm not positive." Jana put the binoculars down. "Bon just texted and asked if we were ready."

"Let me get my shoes and I'm ready."

Jana knocked on the adjoining door.

Bonita quickly opened it. "Your hair is wet."

"It'll dry," Jana said. "I got preoccupied."

The trio took the elevator to the restaurant on the top floor of the hotel. Both of the women wore sleeveless floral-patterned sundresses that were low cut, tight around the waist, and short—so short that they rendered the effects of Alexander's cold shower useless. But the cold water had helped ease the sting of the sunburn.

The hostess seated them at a table by a window with a view of the bay. Without the binoculars, the *Miss Jana* was an indistinguishable speck in the distance. Alexander and Jana still glanced toward the marina, hoping to catch the boat moving.

A server came and took drink orders. Bonita ordered an appetizer and requested they come out as soon as possible. Jana and Alexander followed suit. The appetizers they'd had at the Oasis were a distant memory.

When the server left, Bonita said, "I guess you're curious about what happened today?"

"You could say that," Jana said sarcastically, but nicely.

Bonita couldn't remember what she'd told them after they picked her up from the bar. She started at the beginning when she first saw him and didn't recognize him. His hair was longer than it was in his picture, and he had several days of facial hair growth.

The server brought the drinks and assured them the appetizers would be out soon. She took their entrée orders and left.

Bonita took a loud slurp of her premium margarita, then another. "I thought speaking English to the maître d' at the restaurant would help, but it didn't. When Rey stepped up, he assumed I didn't speak Spanish. I saw no reason to tell him I did."

"That's when he invited you back to the boat?" Jana asked.

"Yes, to use the bathroom. Again, I didn't know it was Rey and was hesitant to go with him. Genuinely hesitant. But I needed to pee, so I thought, why not? He said his boat was at the fuel dock. That's when I realized he could be Rey. When we got to the boat, I saw the name and knew it. I can't remember if he introduced himself before or after we got to the boat. Either way, I knew it was him.

"After I peed, he asked me if I wanted a beer. Again, why not? This whole time, he never smiled. I could tell something was bothering him. I came right out and asked him. He was about to tell me what they were up to when he saw the guys coming back. That's when he ran me off."

Bonita mentioned hugging Rey but left out any mention of him kissing her. From the way Jana looked at Alexander, and the act they had put on earlier on the pontoon boat, Bonita guessed Jana had moved on from Rey. If she told Jana that her boyfriend, or soon-to-be ex-boyfriend, had kissed her, it might only stir up feelings that were best left undisturbed. Bonita knew the feeling.

"And that's when he gave you his phone number?"

Alexander noticed a hint of jealousy in Jana's voice. He studied the lines that had formed on her forehead.

"Kinda. I gave him my number, and he texted me so we'd have each other's numbers. He told me the guys threw his phone overboard and gave him a burner phone."

"That's interesting," Alexander said. "They obviously didn't want him receiving any calls. They probably assumed he didn't know any phone numbers, and he couldn't make any calls or send texts. Jana, did he know your phone number?"

"I doubt it. He hardly knew his number. Whenever someone asked for his number, he'd pull out his phone and read it to them."

"Maybe that's why he asked for my number and sent me the text. He didn't know his number to just give it to me. Clearly, he was in a hurry to get me off the boat, so maybe he thought that was the quickest way."

Alexander leaned back and took a sip of his dubious-quality blended scotch. He grimaced at the taste—somewhere between peaty asphalt and creosote. "If they threw his phone overboard, it's a good bet he's not here of his own free will."

"There was no doubt about that," Bonita added. "I got the impression he doesn't plan to go through with whatever they're planning to do. Tomorrow, I hope to find out what that is and maybe how he plans to stop it."

"That sounds like Rey," Jana said. "When he was smuggling those girls into the States, he only did it because they were holding me. He came up with a plan to get me away from the guys who were holding me and to save the girls. All thanks to Alex, to be honest."

"It was a joint effort." Alexander took another sip of his drink and motioned for the server. When she came to the table, he handed her his glass. "Please take this and pour it down the drain. Bring me a Glenlivet or Glenmorangie, if you have it."

When the server left, Alexander said, "Where was I? Oh, without Rey giving those girls tracking devices, I may have never found them. That was ingenious."

"I know Rey would be happy to hear you say that. Would they help now? If we can find a little tracking device in Cartagena, we could give it to him," Jana said.

"We have a tracking device for him," Alexander said.

"We do?"

"Yes. Bonita. It seems she made quite the impression on young Mr. Cruz. Unless his friends figure it out and put a stop to it, I think he may keep her in the loop."

"I don't think we should call those guys his friends, considering the circumstances," Jana added.

"You're right. What should we call them? 'Partners' isn't right. 'Abductors' is appropriate, but for simplicity, we'll say friends."

Jana turned to Bonita and said, "As Alex said, you must have made quite an impression on Rey for him to give you his phone number. How long were you with him?"

"Maybe twenty or thirty minutes. I—"

"Wait, never mind," Jana interrupted. "I'd known Rey less than fifteen minutes and we were in a berth having sex."

"What?" The revelation surprised Bonita, but she was more surprised by the fact Jana mentioned it.

"When I was getting divorced, my ex told me he'd sell the *Miss Jana* and give me the proceeds. He'd bought the boat for me, so it was technically mine, but he didn't want to give me anything. One day, I showed up at the boat and Rey was sitting there having a beer. He said he had bought the boat that afternoon. I knew my ex was going to sell her, but it was still a surprise. I asked Rey how much he paid for the boat and when he told me, I went ballistic. I yelled and cussed at him, even though it wasn't his fault. When I finished my tirade, he asked me if I wanted a beer. I couldn't help but laugh. Then I got the idea that I'd fuck him and tell my ex that he fucked me over, so I fucked the guy he sold the boat to."

"Oh my God, Jana. What'd your ex do?"

"Nothing. I liked Rey, so I never told him."

"And you've been together ever since?" Bonita asked.

"Not from day one. I told Rey to call me and he never did. A couple of weeks later, I'd been out drinking with a friend and afterward, I went back to the boat. I still had a key. I let myself in, went to his cabin, and crawled into bed with him. We've been together since. Our adventures in trafficking brought us closer together. In the last couple of months, we've grown apart. I hope we'll always be friends, but we have different ideas about the future."

"I'm sorry to hear that, but I get it," Bonita said, glancing at Alexander.

"So, Bon, are you interested in Rey?" Jana asked.

"What? Why would you ask that?"

"Rey is a trusting soul, but for him to give you his number and trust you enough not to tell anyone what he was doing, something else must have happened. I know you didn't have time to fuck him, not that you would. That's my gig."

Bonita laughed. "Well, he was looking dejected. Sad, maybe. I positioned myself on the back railing of the boat so I could spin off and drop to the swim platform if I had to. Then I asked him if he was in trouble. He walked over to me. He moved slowly and was non-threatening. That's when he said he was in deep shit. I hugged him. He held me so tight I had trouble breathing."

The server brought a fresh drink, set it on the table, and waited for Alexander to take a sip. He gave her a thumbs up. "Much better," he said. "I'm sorry, Bon, continue."

"And that was it, just a hug?" Jana asked.

"Until he kissed me."

"A peck on the cheek or a serious kiss?"

"It didn't last long, not like you and Alex on the boat, but, um, yeah, it was serious."

Jana was impressed. "Touché. But we were only acting."

"To be honest, I was too. When you hustle drinks in bars for a living, you learn how to gain a man's trust. I made almost as much money listening to sad stories as I did giving..."

"Bon, I know. I've been there. It's the same in strip joints. Couch dances paid well, but having the guy buy you overpriced drinks after overpriced drinks is easy money. Back to Rey. You've only known him for, what, twenty minutes? Do you like him?"

Bonita took a sip of her margarita and ran her finger over the rim of the glass. "A little. But not romantically. I have mixed feelings right now."

The server brought the appetizers and Bonita dug in. While she was eating, Jana said, "If you do like Rey, it's okay. As I told you, we've drifted apart. We haven't fuc...uh, slept together in a few months."

Bonita covered her mouth to keep food from flying out. "Alex, your sunburn is showing."

"I'm sorry, Alex. Are we embarrassing you?" Jana said, laughing.

"Funny, he's not a prude at all. I can't imagine why that made him turn red."

"He's not?"

"No, not at all. In fact, of all the men I've been with, he was the best. Then again, most men I've been with only wanted me to do things their wives wouldn't do."

"Excuse me, ladies, I'm right here."

Jana ignored him. "Been there too, sister."

"I'm glad you two are having such a good time. It looks like you're bonding at my expense."

"We are bonding. It's the first time we've really had a chance to talk. We aren't that different, Bon and I."

"Maybe that's why I like you both," Alexander said.

"You have a thing for prostitutes?" Jana asked.

"Ex-prostitutes," he clarified.

"Jana," Bonita said. Her voice had turned glum. "You were a dancer, right?"

"Yes. In strip joints."

"Do you consider yourself a prostitute? Not now, of course. Back then."

Jana thought for a few seconds. "I never called myself one until just now. But I had sex for money a few times, so I guess you could say I was. Why?"

"Except for the time I was with Alex, that's what I was. Forced at first, but then willingly. I want to get past it, but I don't know if I ever will."

"I was fortunate," Jana said. "But you'll be fine. You'll need to find a real job and that'll be a big change. You'll most likely be doing something you don't like for eight hours a day and making less than you made in an hour turning...um, being in your old line of work. But you'll make it."

"Thanks, Jana. I hope so. Part of the problem is I'd like to have a family. Kids. And that won't happen." Bonita stared at her drink. She couldn't bring herself to look at Alexander.

"Adopt. Or find a guy who has a young kid or kids, who's divorced or maybe his wife has died, and raise those kids. If they're young enough, you'll bond and they'll be like your own kids. Or here's an idea. You stay clean, get a job, find a guy...or not, and when you're ready for a baby, I'll pay for a surrogate."

"Jana, please don't play with me. That would be amazing. I promise, no more drugs for me. Never." Bonita's chin quivered, but she didn't tear up.

"I'm serious. All you have to do is produce an egg...and find a sperm donor."

Both ladies looked at Alexander. His eyebrows rose in fear of what might be said next. Bonita's phone dinged and vibrated. All eyes went to Bonita and her phone.

"It's a text," she said. "Rey wants to meet me in the morning."

29

Alexander was sitting on the loveseat, sipping coffee, and admiring the view of Cartagena Bay when Bonita eased open the door from the adjoining room. She walked past a sleeping Jana to him. "I got another text this morning from Rey," she whispered.

"What'd he say?"

"He wants me to meet him this morning near Manzanillo. He asked if I could buy a burner phone and not bring my phone."

"Did he say why?"

"I asked that question. All he said was, 'It would be safer.'"

"Are you going to the boat?"

"No. He wants to meet at a little hotel called Hotel El Palma. He gave me the address and asked if I could be there by ten this morning. I texted Juan earlier. He said he'd drive me."

"Bon, I appreciate that you want to help, but I don't like it. If Rey doesn't want you to bring your phone, he thinks his 'friends' may want to look at your phone. In order to look at your phone, they have to meet you. If they meet you, they may not let you leave."

"Why wouldn't they?"

"Let's back up. You're meeting him at a hotel. Rey has to get away from the boat. They seem to keep him on a tight leash. To get away, he must lie. My money is on him telling them he's hired an escort for an hour and she's meeting him at the hotel. The other guys probably wouldn't blame him."

"An escort would be a good reason to want to be alone for a while. It's legal in Colombia to hire escorts, and it's easy. Pick one from a website and make a call."

"Exactly. So, you two meet, spend an hour together, and then he leaves. They might watch. Maybe just to see if he was meeting an escort and not a cop. If they think you're a cop, they might ask to see your phone. He'll likely tell you to delete any texts that aren't related to him hiring you as an escort."

"If they check my phone, all good. They wouldn't have a problem with me."

"No, but they might want to hire you for a few more hours. That would be a problem."

Jana stirred in the queen-size bed against the far wall. She rolled over and squinted at the bright light coming in through the window. "Hey, did I hear you say you were still meeting Rey this morning?"

"Yes, in a couple of hours."

"And you might run into the other guys?"

"Maybe. Look, if Rey could talk, he'd call me. For some reason, he can't, which is why he wants to meet. Me meeting him is the only way we can find out what's going on, and we need to know. Isn't that right, Alex? We have to know what they're doing before we even think about how to help him."

"Unfortunately, you're right, Bon. But there has to be another way to find out. He can text you. Can't he explain it via text?"

"His texts are brief." Bonita scrolled through her phone to confirm. "Yeah, they're all short, like he doesn't want to get caught texting me."

Alexander nodded. "And explaining what he's doing would take more than a few brief texts."

"I need to go meet him."

Alexander looked down and pinched the bridge of his nose. "If he can get away for a couple of hours to meet you, why can't he get away long enough to call you?"

"Because he wants to see her again," Jana said. "He wants to see her again in a hotel room. You don't have to slap me in the face with a wet mop. I know what he's after."

"No, Jana, you have it wrong. He wants to talk to someone, but in person. Like going to a shrink. You tell them your troubles in person, not over the phone."

Jana shrugged. "Okay, I'll give him the benefit of the doubt."

Alexander leaned back and crossed his arms. "Yes, let's give him the benefit of the doubt. But let's also say he's telling the other guys he's meeting an escort. They follow him. They see Bon. They like. They want her too."

Bonita gasped and put her hand to her mouth. "Oh, my God."

Jana stared at her. "Are you willing to fuck Rey and maybe one or more of the other guys for info?"

"No!" Bonita buried her head in her hands. Her body was shaking. "No. I won't fuck Rey or his friends. I said I'm done with that, and I meant it. It makes me sick to think of having one more man slobber over me while he pounds my...and then, you know, Jana, what they want to do. I refuse to let another man get his nut on my face. I'd rather die first. Sorry for being so graphic, Alex. That's the way I feel."

Jana jumped from the bed and hurried to Bonita. She gave her a long hug. "I know exactly what you mean," she said. "We'll figure out another way."

"Thanks, Jana." Bonita took several deep cleansing breaths. "I got this. I still have mood swings from the meth, but they don't last and they don't come as often. Something about having to have sex with those guys got to me."

Jana rubbed Bonita's shoulder. "Until now, I hadn't noticed any of your mood changes. You're doing great."

Bonita forced a smile. "You said Rey was a nice guy. I don't think he'll force himself on me. I'm not worried about him. If I have to string him along to get him to talk to me, I will. I won't like it, but I will. As far as the other guys go, maybe I won't even see them. If I do, hopefully, I can convince them I'm not that kind of girl. If all else fails, I'll run."

Alexander spoke but didn't look at Bonita. "These guys are not fine, upstanding, law-abiding citizens. Except for Rey, and I'm having doubts about him. If you run, they'll assume Rey told you about their plan and they will shoot you."

"Right now, I'd rather get shot in the face with a bullet than with a man's—"

Jana put her hand over Bonita's mouth. "Shush. No, you wouldn't.

You can't wash off a bullet."

Alexander gave Bonita a long, tender hug. "Jana's right. You've turned the corner on a new life. Don't risk it. Do what you must do to survive. But, whatever you do, take solace from the fact it'll be the last time."

Bonita took a deep breath and nodded. "If it comes to that, I'll decide what to do then."

Jana said, "You'll need to leave soon, but I thought of another potential problem."

"What is it?" Alexander asked.

"A couple of guys on the boat took pictures of us when they went past yesterday. There's no way of knowing how clear the pictures were, but if the images were sharp, and they zoomed in on them, they might recognize Bonita."

"Good point. Bon, do you remember where you were on the boat when they went past us?"

"I was in the front seat. No, wait, I got up and stood next to Gabby. When the boat got close to us, Gabby stood up. She was wearing the skimpiest bikini and wanted them looking at her. I was facing forward, and she was facing them when she said they were taking pictures. That's when she pulled out her phone and took pictures. I don't think I ever turned around. They couldn't have gotten photos of my face."

"Your hair was in a ponytail yesterday, wasn't it?"

"It was. Today, I'll wear it down...or maybe in a bun. I guess I'll go heavy on the makeup this morning too. Make myself look like an escort, in case that's who he told the other guys he was meeting."

"You know," Jana said, "all this escort talk is just speculation. It's possible Rey told his friends he met a girl at the marina and asked her to meet him."

"Maybe," Alexander said. "But if it were a 'date,' wouldn't he ask her to meet him at a restaurant or coffee shop instead of a hotel in a sketchy part of Cartagena?"

"Rey would. Unless he thought he was going to get lucky. Even then, he's not the type to rent a room in advance."

Alexander sat, put his hands behind his head, and stared out the window. He shook his head, and said, "Something's not adding up. Rey's been texting you in English, right?"

"Yes, he doesn't know I speak Spanish. That's how we met. He was translating at the restaurant when I wanted to use the bathroom."

"How could he tell the others you're an escort if you don't speak Spanish?"

Jana said, "Bon, your English is great, but you have a bit of an accent on certain words. Maybe Rey knew you were pretending to not know English."

"I forgot to tell you. When we were walking from the restaurant to the boat, he said I looked Hispanic and asked why I didn't speak Spanish. I told him I was a third-generation Mexican-American. I said my grandparents couldn't speak English but my parents grew up speaking both, but mostly English. By the time I came around, we only spoke English, but I picked up a bit of an accent from my grandparents. He seemed to buy the story."

"He wouldn't say she was an escort," Jana said.

"He could say he was meeting an escort and not mention the fact she didn't speak Spanish. Maybe he told the guys the truth. Or a variation of it. He met this hot American girl in the marina and he made a date with her." Alexander stared out the window and thought a little more. "And he's meeting her at the hotel because it was her idea. He'll say they had an instant physical attraction, but she didn't want to do it on the boat with other people around."

"That makes a lot of sense, Alex," Bonita said. "But why the burner phone?"

"In case his friends are suspicious and want to make sure you're not an undercover cop or DEA type," Alexander said.

"What does a burner phone with no info on it say?" Jana asked.

"Undercover cop."

Bonita shrugged. "We are trying to cover every scenario and we don't have a clue. I'm going to go meet him and whatever happens, happens. I can take care of myself. It doesn't matter if they think I'm an escort, an undercover cop, or a horny American tourist. I'll be fine."

"She's right," Jana said, "We're guessing and wasting time."

"No, we're not. Considering all the various scenarios and having a plan is called preparation. And we don't have a plan for any of them. We're counting on Bon to get in, get information, and get out. If she gets in trouble, we don't have a backup."

"Yes, we do. Juan is taking me. He'll drop me off a few blocks away. Then he'll move where he can watch me. If there's trouble, I trust he'll bail me out."

"Juan's a good guy to know," Jana said.

"He is. It's getting late. I should get ready."

"Wait, one more thing. Don't let Rey know you speak Spanish. If you slip and he finds out, tell him that because of what the maître d' at the restaurant said, you thought it would be better if he didn't know you understood him. And now, you thought it would embarrass him if you told him that you knew what the man said."

"Okay. If he finds out I speak Spanish, I'll go with something along those lines."

"Lastly, he doesn't know about us. Especially Jana. That's good. At least for now."

"I agree," Jana said.

"I almost said something yesterday, then thought maybe it's better if he doesn't know."

"I guess that's it. Did you want breakfast before you go?" Alexander asked.

"No, I don't think I could eat anything."

Bonita's comment surprised them because, except for a minor meltdown, she seemed calm and composed. Inside, she was anything but.

"Okay," Alexander said. "Put our numbers in the burner phone but use the names Fred and Wilma. There's not much Jana and I can do except wait, and I'm not good at waiting. Please keep in touch. Let us know what's going on."

"You got it. I'll see you soon." Bonita went through the adjoining door and closed it behind her.

"What do you think, Alex?"

"She's clueless about what she's getting herself into, and I'm an idiot for getting her into it."

30

Bonita slumped down in the passenger seat while Juan drove past the Hotel El Palma. Rey had asked her to meet him at ten. It was only fifteen minutes past nine. Juan had wanted to arrive early. He was unfamiliar with the area and needed to check it out before he dropped her off.

The hotel was two blocks off a major street, down a narrow road that had an eight-foot-high concrete wall topped with broken glass on one side. On the other side were small houses with wrought iron fences. El Palma's parking lot was on the other side of the concrete wall. The building was a three-story white brick with black accents. The office was on the far side of the parking lot. Potted palm trees lined a walkway that led to a pair of red, rustic French doors.

Juan eased past the hotel's office, keeping an eye out for anyone who looked suspicious. Parked cars filled the sidewalk, leaving just enough room on the street for cars to get by. Two men sat in plastic chairs outside a used appliance store.

The narrow street dead-ended into a right-turn-only one-way street. Juan made a note of the street name and turned. The road was decent. Well-kept houses and businesses lined both sides. One block further, the area deteriorated. Potholes littered the road, many of them filled with water, making them invisible until a car's tire bottomed out in one. Trash littered the sides of the road. A two-story market stood on the corner. Iron bars protected the front doors. Several people, mostly men, sat in chairs under a tin awning.

Juan and Bonita spent the next twenty minutes driving slowly up and down every road near the hotel. Nothing seemed out of place, and no one took notice of Juan's old beater.

"It's about time to drop you off. Here's the phone you asked for. I wiped it and put my number in it. I'm John." Juan tried hard to say 'John' in English, but it came out 'Juan.'

"I got it. I'll put my friends' numbers in the phone too, along with Rey's."

Juan made the block back to the main street. He crept past the narrow road to the hotel. A hundred yards past the narrow road, he pulled over. "I'm going to go around the corner and park. I'll move every five minutes or so, but I'll never be too far away. If you need me, text or call. Calling will be faster."

"Thank you. It's nice knowing you're close." Bonita got out of the car and watched him drive down the street and turn. She wore skinny jeans with cuffs and a V-neck t-shirt tucked into the front. Her hair was in a bun. She wore a matching pink bra and panty set she hoped no one would see.

She checked the time on her phone. Ten to ten. Still early. She walked slowly, but she was at the hotel's office door in two minutes. She sat in one of the white chairs on the porch.

"¿Hola, puedo ayudarle?" An older man wearing khaki pants and a white shirt asked if he could help her.

Bonita thought about answering the man in Spanish but knew Rey could walk up at any moment. "Hola," she replied and held up her hand as if to say, "Just a minute." She typed into her phone, looked up at the man, and read in very poor Spanish, "No, thank you. I'm waiting for someone."

The man replied, but Bonita only smiled and shrugged.

The man tried several more times to communicate with her. He didn't want to leave. Women as attractive as Bonita rarely visited his hotel. When all she did was smile and shrug, he relented and went inside.

A couple of minutes later, Bonita was thinking about texting Rey to let him know she was at the hotel when she heard footsteps behind her. She ignored them, assuming the man from earlier had returned. "Hi Bonnie."

She jumped up and embraced Rey, feeling a mix of surprise and relief.

"Have you been here long?" he asked.

"No, I just got here. A man from inside said 'Hi,' and something else. I didn't understand him."

"That was the manager. He's a nice guy. Come on, I have a room."

"Wait, Rey." She put her hand against his chest and pushed away. "I hope I didn't give you the wrong impression yesterday, but—"

"Oh my God, Bonnie, I'm sorry. I wasn't thinking. I...I just wanted to hang out with you. Hang out in private."

"Don't worry about it, I get it. We're on the same page."

Rey took her by the elbow and gently led her inside the hotel. "This place is less than half a mile from the boat. I'd seen it before, so I called them. The room was seventy-five thousand pesos. Around nineteen US dollars."

"You're kidding?"

"No, but to get them to let me have the room before noon, I had to give them another twenty-five grand."

"Another...um..."

"Around six bucks."

"Twenty-five US for this room?"

"Yep."

"I guess I should be more afraid of the room than you."

"Are you afraid of me?"

"Should I be?"

"Not of me, no. Of what might happen to you if you hang around me, maybe."

"Is that why you had me get a burner phone?"

"It is. But we're okay. I told the guys I needed to take a walk every day, especially after being on the boat for such a long time. At first, they followed me, but after a couple of days, they got tired. I guess they figured out I wouldn't leave my boat. They haven't checked my phone in a while either. I wanted to be safe, not sorry."

They reached the door of the room, and Rey unlocked it. The key was a Kwik-Set door key connected to a diamond-shaped piece of gray plastic with the room number stamped on it. He pushed the door open and stood aside for Bonita to enter.

"This isn't so bad," she said. "It's air-conditioned, that's a surprise. It looks like a king-size bed, but no chairs."

"Should I ask for a couple of chairs?"

"It's okay." She hopped on the bed and bounced. "This is comfy." She adjusted the pillow against the headboard and leaned against it. She patted the bed next to her, signaling him to sit beside her. He obliged. She twisted to face him, but he was staring straight ahead, lips pursed.

"Rey?"

He looked at her.

"Talk to me. Isn't that why we're here?"

"It is. It's weird. I want, no, I need someone to talk to, and all I thought about last night was you, and now, I don't know if I should."

"Why not, Rey?"

"I have a bad feeling. I almost got my last girlfriend killed."

"Jana?"

"Uh-huh. I got into a predicament, and I told her about it. She said she'd help me out, and that was a disaster."

"How 'bout I promise to just listen and not offer to help you?"

Rey smiled a little. "Promise you won't try to help?"

"I won't promise, but odds are, I won't. I'm not very adventurous. Meeting you here this morning is the craziest thing I've done in years."

"Crazy or stupid?"

"I guess that chapter hasn't been written, has it?"

"I guess it hasn't. But I hope the stupid ship has sailed."

"I hope so too. Now, tell me, what's this deep shit you're in?" Bonita scooted to the middle of the bed, sat cross-legged, and looked at him.

Rey put his hands together and interlocked his fingers. Bonita could tell he was in deep thought, but found it interesting that he was studying her. Suddenly, he looked her in the eyes.

"A few weeks ago, I was hanging out on my boat. A guy I know, Cole, he's a friend of my brother, came by with a couple of guys. He said the guys were interested in buying the *Miss Jana*. I'd mentioned I was going to sell her because I wanted to buy a sport fisher and do fishing charters. I let these guys come on board, and they pull out guns. Cole looked more shocked than I was. They said they had people watching my girlfriend and my brother. If I didn't cooperate, they'd kill them. They didn't say what they wanted or anything, just that we needed to get underway. I did what they said. When we got into the Atlantic, that's when they threw my phone overboard."

"The Atlantic? Where were you? Wait, Fort Lauderdale? It's on the back of your boat."

"Yes. Fort Lauderdale. We got about a mile out and they told me to turn south. Then they asked how much fuel was onboard. I told them. They seemed to know how many gallons per hour the *Miss Jana* used at various speeds. They didn't say where we were going, only that we didn't have enough fuel to get there. I was told to chart a course to Matthew Town on Inagua Island."

"Inagua Island? Where's that?" Bonita hoped he would get to the point, but felt she should ask questions.

"It's a small island close to Turks and Caicos. It's tiny, but they have a fuel dock. It's popular with people cruising the Caribbean. We got there and put about a thousand gallons of fuel in the tanks. We took off, and that's when they told me where we were going. I drove at night and during the day I'd put it on cruise control and sleep. In the open ocean, anyone can drive a boat. One of the other guys had the day watch. All they had to do was pay attention and not hit anything. It took about five days to get here."

"When was that?"

"A couple of days ago."

"Cole and I got a chance to talk. He apologized and said he had no idea what was going down. He said he'd gotten into debt with them, and they asked if he knew anyone with a big boat they could charter for a couple of days. Cole told them about me, and they said they'd like to meet me. I think they had it all planned from the get-go."

"You said Cole was surprised when they hijacked you. He wasn't on the boat yesterday. Did he go to town with them?"

"No. Cole said he was worried they wouldn't need him since they had me. He was right. They need me to drive the boat. They needed him to get to me, and now he was expendable. When he asked me if I minded if he took off, I told him if he got the chance, go. I guess they weren't expecting either of us to leave. I mean, neither of us had our passports. Cole doesn't speak Spanish. Where would he go? The next night, when they were asleep, he took off. The guys were pissed but got over it pretty quickly. I think Cole leaving kept them from having to kill him."

"Any idea where he went?"

"Nope. He just disappeared into the Cartagena night. He was in the army. Special Forces. He's a survivor, he'll be fine."

"Special Forces? Why didn't he just kill the guys?"

"We talked about it. When they first came onboard, they said they had people watching Jana, and they'd kill her if we didn't cooperate. We had no reason to doubt them." Rey blinked hard several times to clear his watery eyes. His voice choked with emotion. "Oh, I need some water. I brought water, beer, and soda," he said, his voice quivering. "Can I get you anything?"

"I'd love a water. It's a little early for a beer."

Rey got two bottles of water from the mini fridge and handed one to her. He sat back on the bed, closer to her than he had been. He opened the water, took a sip, and continued. "I had no way of knowing if they'd hurt Jana. I do what they tell me."

"You two are still close?"

"Not really. But I wouldn't let anyone hurt her. The day after Cole lit out, another guy showed up. He's been staying on the boat. People have been coming around working on the boat. They added scuba tank racks around the aft deck. There weren't any tanks in the racks yesterday, so you probably didn't notice them."

"I didn't."

"They're bringing in tanks this morning and at noon we are going diving. At least that's what they said."

"Diving? They hijacked you and threatened to kill your girlfriend to go scuba diving?"

"It's a ruse. They aren't telling me much, but I can hear them sometimes and they don't seem too concerned about it. I know they plan to smuggle something out of the country. It has to be drugs. They plan to go out to the dive site every day and hope the Colombian drug enforcement, whatever they're called, stops us and checks us out. Everything on board will be legit, except me."

"What do you mean, 'except you'?"

"I'm in the country illegally. No passport."

"If stopped, they could arrest you?"

"I guess. I mentioned that. They said not to worry about it. They may have a fake ID for me. I doubt it's a very good ID, but good enough to pass a quick inspection. Anyway, here's what I gathered from them. They have identical scuba tanks that are in two pieces. They'll fill the bottom part with drugs and the top part with air, screw the two pieces together, Bondo the seam, and paint them. The tanks will look exactly like real tanks. They'll even hold air and you could dive with them if you wanted to. The only difference is they hold half the air as a regular tank...and they're full of drugs."

"Any idea what drugs they're going to fill them with?"

"I've heard them mention heroin and fentanyl. Both in pure form. I've never done drugs, but I'd guess the street value has to be in the millions."

"Tens of millions, maybe," Bonita said, realizing afterward what she was saying. Rey didn't question her.

"Plus, I heard them talking about smuggling contraband gold, too. It's illegally mined in Colombia or Brazil, maybe both. They can't legally export it, so it has to be smuggled out. I haven't heard where they plan to put it, but a hundred pounds of gold, sixteen hundred ounces, is worth over three and a half million. It shouldn't be hard to hide a hundred pounds of gold on a fifty-five-foot trawler."

Bonita got a faraway look in her eyes. "Wow, so they've thought this out. Drugs, gold. I'm surprised they aren't taking a few teenage Venezuelan girls, too."

"Christ! Don't give 'em any ideas." Rey had flashbacks to the time he smuggled the young Cuban girls into the US.

"When are you going back to the States?"

"I get the impression it'll be three, maybe four days. We're going to make dive trips for the next couple of days. We'll leave at the same time every day and take the same route. One day, we'll keep going."

"What are you going to do? Do you have a plan?"

Rey rested his chin on his chest. He leaned back against the headboard and closed his eyes. His voice was bleak. "I can't let those drugs reach the states. There's only three of them. When I'm on night watch, I could take them out pretty easily."

"Take them out? As in—"

"Kill them. They wouldn't be expecting it. Sneak in while they're sleeping. It'd be easy."

"Have you killed a man before?"

"Once. It was more of an accident, not intentional."

"You've never killed anyone in cold blood?"

"No, I haven't."

Bonita sighed and put her head in her hands. "But you could?"

"Yes. Does that bother you?"

"Uh, yeah. You're talking about murder."

"It's them or me. Me, and who knows how many people if the amount of drugs they're talking about hits the streets."

Bonita forced a slight grin. "I said it bothered me. I should be proud of you. Most people in your situation would make a deal. Become part of it. You want to stop them. That's impressive. What would you do after you kill them?"

"I'll toss the bodies and the drugs overboard, take the boat home, and park it in the slip. Sooner or later, their partners–I'm working on the assumption they have partners in Florida–would pay me a visit. I'll tell them the drugs were delivered to the boat late one evening. The next morning, everyone was gone and so were the drugs."

"Will they buy it?"

"Maybe. I'll also be armed when they come."

"That sounds like it could get messy. What if you motored around the Caribbean for a few months? They'd never find you."

"They wouldn't. But they'd suspect me. They wouldn't stop looking for me. Plus, they said they're watching Jana and my brother. No, I need to get the boat back before they know anything is wrong so I can blame it on the other guys. I hope they simply leave and look for them."

"It's not a bad plan—if they believe you," Bonita said optimistically.

"That's why I have to show up in Lauderdale like I did nothing wrong. There are a few flaws in my plan."

"Flaws?"

"The biggest being as soon as we clear Cartagena Bay, one of those guys puts a bullet in the back of my head."

Bonita gasped. "That's a flaw all right."

"Also, I said I could take them out. They have guns. If one stays awake all night with me and keeps his distance, he wouldn't be so easy."

"Damn, Rey, I thought you had a good plan."

"It's still good. But I have to act before they do—and beat them."

Bonita wrapped her arms around him. He held her close, leaned off the headboard, and slid flat onto the bed, pulling her with him. She rolled slightly, ending up half on the bed and half on Rey.

"I wish I knew what to say to help you."

"Say nothing. Just let me hold you for a while. You don't know how much I've missed holding someone."

Bonita ran her fingers through his reddish-brown hair. He kissed her softly on the lips. She put her hand between them. "I'm sorry, Rey. I—"

"Don't be sorry. I'm moving way too fast. I think you're amazing."

"That's sweet. I like you. I really do. But—"

"There's always a 'but.'"

"There is. But I'm conflicted. There's someone I like, maybe like too much." Bonita sat up and faced him. "I shouldn't say this, but a roll in the hay with you would be nice."

"Another but?"

"But I can't."

He tried not to show his disappointment. "I understand. I have the room for the night. We're going diving in a little while. I should be back by five or six at the latest. If you change your mind..."

"No, I shouldn't." She cocked her head. "Rey?"

"Yep."

"What you told me. Was any of it true?"

"What the fuck? How could you ask that?"

"Maybe you wanted me to feel sorry for you, so I'd sleep with you."

Anger appeared on Rey's face. He had a few choice words for Bonita but bit his tongue. Instead, he said, "Every word was true."

"Then why me?"

"Huh?"

"Why did you tell me?"

The ire in Rey was fading. "I needed to tell someone and..." He smiled slightly, "You're the only person I know. Maybe I wanted someone to know the story. There's a good chance I'm going to die. Maybe you could tell my story."

"Don't say that, Rey. I don't want to get involved with a man who's about to die."

His brow furrowed. "Involved?"

"I shouldn't and I may regret it, but if you want to..." Bonita didn't know why she said what she said. She knew everything Rey knew, or thought she did. The truth was, her heart yearned for someone else, and she had no desire to become involved with Rey. The look in his eyes told her he wanted her. It was clear he wanted to be involved with her. She swore she wouldn't, but now she'd made her bed.

Rey put his hand behind her head and gently pulled her close. "There's no question I want—"

The knock on the door interrupted him.

31

"Damn," Rey said when the knocking persisted. "That can't be good."

"Maybe it's housekeeping, checking to see if we need anything," Bonita suggested.

"At what I'm paying for the room? I doubt it."

A louder, firmer knock.

Rey walked to the door. With no peephole to peer out, he cracked the door open. José and Carlos pushed their way inside. José was older, in his mid-forties. He was short, heavy set, and wore a goatee that stood out from the stubble on his cheeks. Carlos was thin with long hair and a full beard. Both men were Hispanic.

Rey knew he could've easily stopped both of them from entering the room, but he stepped aside and let them enter. This was not the time nor place to make a stand. Inside, both men immediately saw Bonita on the bed.

In Spanish, one said, "Ah, we knew something was up this morning. You were much happier than you normally are. Carlos followed you, and when he saw you go into the hotel, he called me. What's going on?" He checked out Bonita again and let out a creepy laugh. "As though I need to ask."

Rey didn't like the look on José's face. If he said she was an escort and he'd hired her for the morning, he knew they would want their turn. Bonita was leaning against the headboard and looked confused. Rey remembered she didn't speak Spanish.

"This is Bonnie. She's American. I met her yesterday at the marina. She agreed to meet me here this morning. She doesn't speak Spanish."

"Have you already nailed her?" José asked in Spanish.

"Have a little respect. To answer your question, no. We were just talking. If you leave, maybe…"

"No time. We need to head out for our first dive run. Bring the girl with you."

"I thought we were heading out at noon." Rey glanced at Bonita. "I don't think she'll want to come."

"Most of the dive boats leave early. We decided we should head out with them. We finished loading the tanks. Bring the girl. It's not a request. I don't know what you talked about with her and she's seen us. I want to keep an eye on her."

Rey wiped his mouth with the back of his hand. "I didn't tell her anything. We talked about getting together when we get back to the States. She's beautiful and seems sweet. I like her." He smiled at Bonita and she returned the smile, pretending she didn't understand what was they were saying.

"Which is why she met you at a hotel. Uh-huh. Until we can figure out who she is, she's coming with us."

"That isn't necessary," Rey protested.

"Yes, it is," José said sternly. "Ask her if she'd like to go boating with us. If she says no, tell her we insist."

They had never spoken English, but Rey had a feeling José, and maybe Carlos, understood at least a little English. He didn't want to take a chance. He asked Bonita if she'd like to go for a boat ride.

She looked at the time on her phone. "That sounds like fun, but I'm supposed to meet my friends this afternoon for lunch. In fact, I should be going."

Rey relayed the conversation to José. For a second, it seemed he might allow Bonita to leave.

"No," José said after more thought. "She comes with us…or I shoot her now." He studied Bonita for any sign she might have understood him, but her expression never changed.

"Rey, tell her she's going with us," José said. "If she tries to run when we get outside, I'll shoot her."

Rey's face flushed. He clenched his fist and glared at the two men.

"You try anything and I'll shoot you and then the girl. Do you understand?"

Rey nodded.

"Say it."

"I understand."

"Good. I wanted to make sure we were clear. Now, explain to your friend that she's coming with us."

Rey held out his hand toward Bonita. He still had a feeling either José or Carlos could understand what he was saying, so he continued the ruse. "Bonnie, I'm sorry. My friends don't like that I was talking to you. They want...insist...you come with us. You'll be okay, I promise. But if you don't come with me...um...well, I don't know what they may do."

Having understood what the men had said, Bonita knew she would go, but she played along. "What the fuck? Rey, are you kidnapping me?"

"No. Well, I guess we are. They're concerned that I told you something you shouldn't know."

"You did tell me shit I shouldn't know, but tell them you didn't."

"I did. They didn't believe me."

Bonita was animated and almost yelling at Rey. "How the hell am I going to convince them? I didn't record our conversation. Do they plan to torture me to get the truth? What happens if I refuse? As soon as we get out the door, I could take off."

"Bonnie, if you run, they will know that I told you something. They will shoot you."

"Oh, Rey—"

He scratched his head. "Look, I'm sorry I got you into this. We're going to motor out to a popular dive spot, drop anchor, sit for a while, and then come back. By the time we get back, I'll have convinced them you don't know anything. You'll be fine, I promise. You might even enjoy the ride."

Bonita grabbed his still outstretched hand and allowed him to pull her off the bed. "You're saying they don't trust me, but I'm supposed to trust you all? Right. I have a feeling I know what's going to happen on the boat. Is it just going to be you, or are all of you going to take a turn?"

"Take turns? What? No. That won't happen. I won't let it."

"Damn. Rey, you're sweet, but bullshit. Look at 'em. They're already trying to figure out who goes first and who gets sloppy seconds." She tried to force a tear, but none would come. "Let's get this over with. Is there any alcohol on board? Get me drunk and I might not fight much."

"Bonnie, please. I know you're scared, but they won't touch you."

She wanted to say she wasn't frightened. Getting gang raped was nothing new to her. But when she tried to walk, it felt like her feet were encased in concrete. She leaned on his arm and forced one foot in front of the other to get to the door.

Outside the hotel, Carlos led the way, followed by Rey and Bonita. José stayed a couple of feet behind. His hand rested on a small semi-automatic pistol in his waistband, a pistol he was ready to draw and fire if Bonita tried to run. They walked down the narrow street outside the hotel to the main street, the same one-way street Juan had driven earlier. They turned and walked against the flow of traffic. One block down, they passed another side street.

Juan, now slumped in the front seat of his old car, watched as they walked by. He knew he couldn't follow in the car. He'd have to turn right on the road they were walking along and in the time it would take him to make the block, they might be gone. He got out of the car and followed on foot.

Five minutes later, Bonita, Rey, and the two men walked through the gate leading into the marina. Juan moved far enough to one side to see the boat through the chain-link fence. Several men who were working on the dock stopped what they were doing when they walked by. Juan couldn't hear them, but their gestures toward Bonita were offensive and sexually suggestive. Bonita seemed to take it in stride.

Four of the men from the dock who'd been ogling Bonita climbed into a truck and left the marina. Rey, Carlos, José and Bonita boarded the boat and were greeted by a fourth man, Alberto, who was the youngest of the group. He was also the tallest and best built, with the exception of Rey. He was in his early thirties, dark skin, and black hair with a prematurely receding hairline.

Juan continued to watch the boat, and when Rey went to the

wheelhouse to start the engines, he pulled out his phone and texted Alexander in Spanish.

> *This is Juan. Bonita got on that big boat with three men. She didn't look happy. They started the engines.*

Juan received a reply from Alexander:

> *No bueno. Gracias.*

The text conversation was slow. Each man used a translator to read the texts.

> *No, it's not. They untied the boat and it's leaving. What should I do?*

> *Nothing. We'll discuss here and figure out what to do. I'll text if I need you.*

> *Yes. Let me know. I should have stopped them.*

> *Not your fault.*

Juan didn't read the last text from Alexander. He was watching the *Miss Jana* ease out of the slip and motor down the channel toward the bay. He put his fingers through the links of the fence and shook it violently. After he kicked the fence several times, he cussed at the fence, the boat, and the men who took Bonita. Reluctantly, he went back to where he'd left his car, wondering what he could have done, what he should have done.

Bonita sat in the wheelhouse while Rey maneuvered the big trawler through the channel. She felt safe next to him. He promised nothing would happen to her, and she believed him. The channel was wide and boat traffic was light, but he was concentrating on the bay.

"Rey?" Bonita said softly, not knowing where the other three men were.

"Yes?" He replied without looking away from the channel.

"Tell me the truth. What are you guys going to do to me?"

Rey's head snapped around. "I'm not going to do anything to you. If any of those three try anything, I'll stop them."

"If they try, how will you stop them?"

"Bonnie, I don't know. I'm so pissed right now I can hardly think straight. You want the truth? Yes, they'll try something. Will they rape you? Maybe torture you to find out what you know? Maybe they'll kill you...and me."

"Rey, I'm a big girl. You don't need to sugar-coat it. Tell me what you really think they're going to do to me."

He grinned at her. "Thanks, I needed that." He pulled her close and kissed her. She didn't stop him this time. "Here's my issue," he said after the kiss. "I could take out those three guys without too much trouble. I'd have the element of surprise. We've got a full load of fuel. I could head north and not look back."

"Why do I think there's a but coming?"

"Yep. If they are watching Jana, they may harm her when they don't hear from these guys. If we don't return from this dive trip this evening, the guys at the dock will call Florida. I won't let anything happen to you, but I can't risk anything happening to Jana."

Bonita thought about telling him the truth. Jana was safe, and she was here in Cartagena. With Jana safe, he'd have no reason not to kill the guys on the boat and head home. But that would mean she'd have to come clean with Rey, tell him who she was and why she was there. That might be just enough to piss him off to the point he and his friends would take turns with her and then kill her. She felt she knew him well enough that he wouldn't throw her to the wolves, but there was a slight chance he was lying and in this of his own free will. She decided to see how things went. Telling him the truth would be the last resort.

Carlos walked into the wheelhouse and spoke to Rey in Spanish. "Tell your little Chiquita to go put on a bikini that's in your stateroom. The smallest one she can find. We want her on the aft deck so any patrol boats can see her."

Bonita acted like she didn't understand and waited for Rey to translate. He then replied to Carlos in Spanish. "She doesn't know where the stateroom is. You'll have to show her. I can't leave the wheelhouse right now. Show her where it is, then leave. Don't mess with her."

Carlos gave him a sneer but said nothing. He led Bonita out of the wheelhouse and down the stairs to the cabins. In a small closet, she found several two-piece bathing suits hanging on wire hangers. She selected an aqua bikini set with a triangle top and cheeky bottom. It seemed to be the largest of the bunch.

"Excuse me," Bonita said when Carlos didn't leave. He understood enough of what she'd said to back out of the stateroom. She closed the door behind him. Judging by the size, the bikini must have belonged to Jana. The bottom fit snug but worked. The bra was adjustable. She let it out to the max but it was still a tight fit. Tight, but not uncomfortable. The alternative was a skimpy string bikini set. As a string set, it was fully adjustable, but the bra lacked cups, leaving only small triangles of light polyester which revealed too much skin.

When she was about to leave the cabin, she realized her purse was on the bed with her clothes. She opened her purse to get her phone. Her hand trembled as she hurriedly pulled it out and checked for service. She couldn't believe they didn't check her for a phone. She saw there was service and quickly created a group text with 'Fred' and 'Wilma.'

> *I'm on Miss Jana. Rey and 3 other men onboard. Heard we are going to a popular dive spot. A dry run. Not sure of their plans for me. Don't reply. I won't be near the phone.*

She pressed the send button, then deleted the message and turned the phone off. She scanned the small teak-walled cabin for a hiding spot. Drawers lined the base of the walls with cabinets above them. There were more drawers under the bed. She checked them all. They were not full enough to hide the phone if they searched the room. She saw the master's head, which was through a small door in the corner.

There she found a sink, marine toilet, and more small cabinets. She checked the cabinet under the sink. An extra roll of toilet paper, a plunger, and cleaning supplies. The cabinet above the sink contained the usual toiletries: toothbrush, toothpaste, shaving cream, and razor. She noticed a half-empty box of tampons next to the razor. She slid her phone into the box, which fit perfectly and blended in seamlessly. It was the perfect hiding spot. Satisfied, she placed the box back in the cabinet where it had been before. Returning to the cabin, she covered her purse with the skinny jeans and a top she had taken off earlier. When she opened the cabin door, Carlos was waiting for her. His eyebrows rose as he inspected her.

"You can look, but you'll never touch me, you prick," She said to him, checking his expression to see if he understood. Unless he was too busy checking her out, he didn't seem to understand English. She motioned for him to go up the steps, but he pulled her by the arm and made her go up first. On the first step, she looked over her shoulder at him. He was already studying her ass.

"Take a good look, prick. That's as close as you'll ever get."

She hurried up the steps and into the main salon. José and Alberto were less subtle than Carlos. Each let out a yelp and a crude comment. She ignored their lecherous looks and pretended not to understand their comments. "What now?" she asked.

Carlos motioned her toward the aft deck. When outside, he told her in Spanish to dance and pretend like she was partying and having a good time. Dance. She ignored his instructions and repositioned a deck chair into a shaded area in the corner of the deck. It was also an area that couldn't be seen from the main salon. She sat and propped her feet on the railing.

Carlos protested in Spanish, but Bonita said, "No...uh...entiendo." She mangled the word. "Una cerveza por favor." Her pronunciation was better, but still horrible.

He stormed inside and returned with a beer. He handed it to Bonita, who was still sitting in the shade. "Grassy ass," she said.

Carlos went back inside the boat and closed the sliding glass door. She could hear him yelling, but couldn't make out what he was saying over the drone of the twin diesels. She leaned back in the chair and breathed in the salt air. It felt invigorating. She took a few sips of beer and thought about how she could get used to this kind of life. Maybe being with Rey wouldn't be so bad.

Rey came onto the aft deck alone. "You've got Carlos all worked up. He said he told you to look like you were partying back here. To dance, and you sat. Plus, you told him to get you a beer." He couldn't hide his grin.

"Is that what he said? Well, I'd look pretty stupid out dancing by myself. Tell him to go—"

"Whoa, Bonnie. Let's not rile them up. I don't know exactly what they're planning, but for now, they're happy to have you out here. It looks like we're a legit dive boat. They came into the wheelhouse and ran me out. Before that, they asked about you. How'd we meet? How'd you get to the hotel? Why did you come to the hotel? I told them how we met and that you came to the hotel because I asked you. I couldn't answer the last question truthfully, so I told them I thought you might be a gold-digger."

"A gold-digger? Okay, I get it. Girl sees guy on big yacht. Girl assumes guy has big bucks. Girl agrees to meet guy at hotel. It's a tale as old as time itself."

Rey chuckled softly. "Was that the real reason you came this morning?"

"No, of course not. I came because you said you were in trouble. I hoped I could help you. It looks like I've made things worse."

"Things were already bad. You didn't make them worse. For the record, I'm glad you're here. They came into the wheelhouse for privacy. I think they're calling someone to ask what they should do with you. I think I convinced them you're what you say you are–a tourist I met at the marina. Since you have friends in Cartagena, if you turn up missing, your friends will contact the police. Maybe even the US Embassy and the news. When your picture is flashed all over the media, your Uber driver and the hotel manager will recognize you. The hotel was too close to the marina for comfort. The last thing José and his compadres want is a bunch of cops and newspeople swarming around the marina."

"So, you're saying they won't kill me?"

"Not likely."

"What about rape?"

"If they raped you, they'd kill you."

32

When Alexander and Jana received the last text from Bonita, letting them know she was on the *Miss Jana*, they immediately called Gabby and asked if she was available. She was. It took her fifteen minutes to get to the hotel.

"Where to?" She asked after Alexander and Jana got into the white Mazda.

"Can you take us to the end of the peninsula? We want to watch the boats going in and out of the bay."

"Oh, shit! Is Bon on the boat?"

"I believe she is."

"Oh my God. Is she okay?"

"Don't know. I'm hoping we can get eyes on her. Or at least on the boat."

"I know a perfect spot. It's less than ten minutes from here."

Gabby pulled out of the hotel driveway and onto Carrera 1. Modern high-rise buildings, mostly hotels, lined the left side of the street. On the right was the Caribbean. The street followed the sea until it turned south, becoming Calle 1B. Alexander figured out Carrera streets run north and south, and Calle streets run east and west. After a few blocks, Gabby slowed and turned onto a small street lined with parked cars. She found a gap, pulled in, and parked.

"The beach is down there, maybe fifty meters. From the beach to the other side of the bay is maybe two kilometers. This is where the bay is the narrowest."

They locked the Mazda and walked the fifty meters to the beach. A small, tin-roofed combination bar and restaurant was to the right. Four wooden tables with chairs and umbrellas were around the building. A few scattered coconut palms provided a smidgen of shade.

"You said you wanted to watch for the *Miss Jana*. I thought this little bar and grill would be perfect. The table closest to the water will give you a view of the boats that go by."

"This is perfect," Jana said. "But I'm not entirely sure why we are here."

"In her text, Bon said they were on the boat heading to a popular dive spot," Alexander said. "She said it was a 'dry run.' I think what they're doing is taking the boat out to see if the local authorities stop and board them. They're hoping they get stopped. If they get stopped and boarded, and the authorities don't find anything, they're less likely to stop them again in the future."

"When they're actually smuggling shit out," Jana added.

"Exactamundo."

"Why is Bon on the boat?" Gabby asked. Her tone lay somewhere between worry and fear.

"My guess is Rey's friends, as we call them, found them together and took her. We had a feeling they might."

"Or Rey invited her, and she went," Jana added. Compared to Gabby, her tone was a touch belligerent.

"I doubt that, Jana. Rey didn't want the others to see Bon yesterday. He wouldn't want them to see her today."

"Is Bon safe?" Gabby's voice cracked.

A server brought menus to the table and asked about drinks. Gabby translated, then translated the drink order: Beer for Alexander, water for Jana, and she ordered herself a Coke.

Alexander asked Jana for the binoculars. She pulled them from her purse and handed them across the table. He scanned the water, looking at every boat coming up the bay.

"You didn't answer my question," Gabby asked sternly.

He lowered the binoculars and looked at her. "I didn't. I wanted to get eyes on the boat. See if Bon was still on it."

"Still on it? Like, she was on the boat when it left, but she might not be now?" Gabby asked, her voice showing signs of concern.

"Calm down. Take a breath. Unless Rey told her what they're up to and they know he told her, she'll be fine."

"But what if they know what Rey told her? Fuck! What can we do?"

"First off, we don't know if Rey told her the plans, and if he did, he wouldn't tell those guys he told her. She'll be okay."

"I hope so. She's cool. I really like her." Gabby's intensity tapered.

"Look," Jana said. "Is that the *Miss Jana*?" She pointed at a white boat with blue trim coming up the bay.

"It is." Alexander jumped from his chair and hurried to the water's edge. Jana and Gabby followed.

The *Miss Jana* had followed the channel from the marina around Isla Manzanillo and cruised straight across the bay toward the Caribbean. Their course put them on the far side of the bay, a little over a sixth of a mile–exactly one kilometer–from where Alexander was standing.

Alexander watched through the binoculars as the trawler trudged its way from the bay to the sea. The boat was still south of them. Only the starboard bow quarter was visible. No one was in the lounge area forward. He handed the glasses to Jana, then turned to Gabby. "The two skiffs beached over there. What are they for?"

"They're rentals. Charters, actually. They take people on rides in the bay," She said, studying him.

Jana lowered the binoculars. "You have a plan?"

"I was kicking around the idea of us jumping in one of those boats and having the skipper run us over to the *Miss Jana*. We could yell at Bon and Rey to jump and we'd pick them up."

"Would that work?" Jana asked, the excitement in her voice unmistakable.

"Probably not...it would likely get us shot."

The *Miss Jana* was now perpendicular to the group on the beach. Jana looked through the binoculars. "Bon and Rey are on the aft deck. It looks like they're alone. If we got on a boat now, maybe we could make it to them, have them jump, and get out before the others knew they were gone."

"It's worth a try," Alexander said. "Gabby, go ask the skipper if he'll take us out to—"

"Wait," Jana interrupted. "Rey went inside and there's another guy on the aft deck with Bon."

"Damn. Jana, watch them. Gabby, ask the skipper of the little boat if he goes into the ocean or if he stays in the bay."

Gabby went to speak to the owner of the small skiff. After a brief conversation with him, she returned and told Alexander that he said the sea was too rough today. He would not leave the bay.

"Too bad," Alexander said. "If we could have followed them long enough, we might have gotten Bon and Rey alone again. Those two alone, on the aft deck, would be our only chance of safely getting them off the boat."

"What now?" Jana asked, still watching the boat through the binoculars.

"Gabby, how far is it to the most popular dive sites?"

"That would be the Isla del Rosario–the Rosario Islands. They're about forty to forty-five kilometers from most of the marinas. From where we stand, maybe two or three less. There are other good sites, but Rosario is the best. I've been there a few times."

He pulled out his phone and googled the conversion. "About twenty-three nautical miles. Jana, what's the cruising speed of your boat?"

"Eight to nine knots."

"Around three hours. My guess is they'll anchor for an hour or so, then head back. Another three hours. Plus an hour or two to the marina where they're docked. That's at least eight hours. We have time."

"Time for what?" Jana asked.

"May I see the binoculars?" Gabby asked. Jana handed them to her. She focused on the back of the boat where Bonita was. "Wow, she looks hot."

"What?" Jana asked.

"Uh, she looks…mad. She was pacing around the deck, dropped into a chair, and crossed her arms. She didn't look happy. It doesn't look like she wants to be on the boat, if it was ever in question."

"We weren't sure, but I agree with Gabby," Jana said. "Alex, you said we have time. Time for what?"

"Time to come up with a plan. Gabby, call Juan and tell him what's happening. Ask him if he'd be willing to help me get Bonita off the boat tonight."

She pulled out her phone and called Juan.

"You plan to rescue Bon tonight? How?" Jana said.

"Yes. And I'm working on it. I hope they let her walk off the boat. I doubt it. Hopefully, Juan can help. It would be nice if he'd bring a little muscle, too. I don't want to storm the boat and get into a shootout. That could get messy."

Jana chuckled.

"What's funny?"

"Nothing's funny. It just hit me. This will be, what, the third time you've saved your ex? It's getting to be a routine. While you're at it, would you mind saving mine?"

"Your ex?"

"If he wasn't an ex, Bon wouldn't be on the boat as we speak."

"Jana, I'm sorry."

"Don't be. Haven't I said that before? We've been growing apart. I know I shouldn't call him my ex...not yet, not without talking to him. Maybe I should have gone to the hotel room this morning instead of Bon. That would have been a shock."

Gabby rejoined the group. "I talked to Juan. He said he'd do anything to help. Just let him know."

"Thank you. Um...Gabby, I'm going to need your help on this one. If you don't want to do it, I'll understand."

"What do you need?"

"I don't speak Spanish. Juan doesn't speak English. We need a translator."

"I'm in."

"It might get dangerous."

"I said, I'm in."

"Great. You're the only person I know and trust. Let's go back to the table and get a drink. I'm hungry too."

From the table, all three watched the *Miss Jana* until she turned south toward the Rosario Islands and disappeared. The only sounds were from a lone seagull chirping at a group of sunbathers, hoping for a handout, and faint salsa music, which drifted from the café along with the aroma of Colombian coffee. The gentle breeze coming from the bay couldn't cool the air that was heavy with unspoken tension.

"I feel so helpless," Jana said, breaking the silence. "We don't know what's happening on the boat. They might be headed to the dive site, as Bon said in her text. Or they could be on their way to Florida. Or to another island. Maybe they're heading out to sea to toss Bon overboard."

"Oh my God, Jan, don't say that," Gabby said.

"I'm sorry. Please don't call me Jan. I hate that name. It reminds me of *The Brady Bunch*."

Alexander's belly laugh broke the tension at the table. "*The Brady Bunch*? How in the hell do you even know that show? They were off the air long before you were even a gleam in your father's eye."

"Reruns. They were popular when I was in sixth or seventh grade. The Brady's and *Full House*."

"I never watched the show, but what was wrong with Jan?"

"People teased me about my name. They called me Jan. Marcia was the beautiful, mature, and popular girl. Jan was always jealous of her. Since then, I've hated the name."

"I get it. I bet you haven't told that to anyone in a long time."

Jana leaned back in her chair, glanced up at the cloudless blue sky, then back at Alexander. "I don't think I've ever told anyone that."

"I'm sorry. I won't call you Jan again. I didn't know. I've heard of the show, but I've never seen it."

"Gabby, you're fine. I'm sorry if I snapped at you. I guess I'm a little on edge right now."

"We all are," Alexander added.

Jana and Alexander jumped when their phones buzzed. Both quickly pulled out their phones and checked the message.

"It's from Bon," Jana said.

"Yep. A group text."

"What'd she say?" Gabby asked anxiously.

Alexander read the message aloud, "'I'm in the head. Not much time. I'm okay. Rey says I'll be fine. We are going to an island, will return later. Don't know if they'll let me off the boat tonight. Rey says maybe. Don't reply. Turning off phone. Will text when I can.'"

"What now?" Gabby asked, "Are we still going to get Juan and go to the boat tonight?"

"We should plan on it. We need to check with Juan, but we should plan on meeting him at his bar around seventeen-thirty or eighteen hundred."

"What time?" Gabby asked.

"Sorry. Five thirty or six this evening. If we haven't heard from Bon by eight-ish, we go stake out the boat and hope we get lucky."

33

Bonita was asleep on the long couch in the main salon when the *Miss Jana* made her way back into Cartagena Bay. The combination of sun, salt, and beer had exhausted her. Rey took over driving the boat when it entered the bay. Carlos, José, and Alberto hung around the main salon, admiring Bonita's long, slender, tan legs.

In Spanish, Carlos said, "What do we do with the girl?"

"I'd like to take her to the cabin and—" José said.

"You touch her, and Rey will break your neck," Alberto interrupted.

"He'd have to get past Señor Smith and Wesson first," José said, patting the lump of steel and polymer in his waistband.

"José, you ass, you carry a Glock. You need to watch out for Rey. He's not a trained fighter, but he's been training in martial arts for years. I have a feeling he'd take Señor Glock away from you and shove it up your ass before you knew what hit you."

Bonita woke but didn't move. She laid still, listening to the men. She rolled from her side to her back and pulled one leg under the other, spreading her legs. Having the men study the peacock feather, its lower tip hidden by only a small swatch of white cloth, would keep them from noticing that her breathing changed when she woke.

"Damn. If I could drive this boat in and out of the marina, I'd put a bullet in Rey's head right now, then check out the rest of her feather."

Alberto thought José sounded too serious. "Forget about her. Cartagena is full of beautiful women. Go to the Walled City tonight and get one."

"Those girls cost money. This one is free for the taking."

"This one could cost you your life. I'm telling you, don't fuck with her."

José stared at Bonita. He wiped a bead of sweat that rolled down his cheek. "Ha! When the time is right, I'll more than fuck with her." His voice resonated throughout the main salon.

José's comments terrified Bonita. She kept her breathing steady and slowly opened her eyes. "Hey," she said in English. "I must have fallen asleep. Where are we?" She sat up on the sofa. "I need to use the restroom." When neither man replied, she stood and said, "El baño?"

José pointed to the bathroom off the main salon. She ignored him and went toward the stairs leading to the master cabin. José followed her into the cabin. He gave up trying to tell her there was a toilet on the main deck, and watched her disappear into the master's head.

Inside the head, Bonita retrieved her hidden cell phone. She raised the toilet seat lid, allowing it to clank against the teak cabinet behind it. While she was waiting for the phone to boot up, she realized she needed to pee. She eased the bikini bottom to her knees and urinated.

The phone seemed to take forever to boot. When it did, it made a beep that echoed throughout the head. Bonita sat quietly on the toilet, wondering if Carlos was still on the other side of the door and if he was, did he hear the beep? She stayed silent for a few more seconds. When she heard nothing from the other side of the door, she sent a group text to "Fred and Wilma."

> *Just about back to the marina. One guy wants to kill Rey and fuck me. Others told him no. Rey thinks they're smuggling heroin and fentanyl. Maybe contraband gold. All I know now. Don't know if they'll let me leave the boat. Will let you know when I know.*

She checked the power status of the phone. It was at seventy-eight percent. She left the phone on but set it to Low-Power Mode, put it back in the tampon box, and put the box back on the shelf. She flushed the toilet and opened the door to the master cabin. José was sitting on the bed, waiting. He stood and motioned toward the cabin door.

"No," Bonita said, "I want to get dressed." She picked up her clothes from the bed and pointed to them, then to her body.

"Sí, Sí," José said. He moved to the door leading into the head, leaned against it, and crossed his arms. "Go ahead," he said in Spanish. His wide grin exposed tobacco-stained teeth.

Bonita sat on the bed and gradually spread her legs, slid her hand down her stomach and over the thin material of the bikini bottom, gently nuzzling her pubic area. Moving slowly and deliberately, she untied the string that was holding the two pieces of the bottom together.

José's breathing intensified. His eyes widened, his mouth dropped open, and a swell formed in his shorts. With trembling hands, he reached for the Glock in his waistband, his finger wrapping around the trigger. As he jerked the gun from his waist, a round discharged.

The tremendous blast from the Glock was deafening in the small cabin. Bonita jumped and covered her ears, hoping to silence the ringing. Knowing the other guys would come soon, she hurriedly put on her jeans. She zipped the zipper, then pulled her legs up against her chest and rested her head on her knees. With the ringing in her ears, she couldn't hear the cries of pain coming from José, now writhing on the floor in a pool of blood.

The door to the cabin burst open. Carlos and Alberto stepped in, froze, and stared at José. A few seconds later, Rey ran in and also froze when he saw José. "What the hell happened?"

Bonita took a deep breath. "I wanted to change clothes and he wouldn't leave."

"You shot him?"

"God no."

Carlos bent over José, who'd stopped moving. In Spanish, he said, "It looks like he was reaching for his gun and shot himself. Must have blown his dick off. He's dead."

Bonita bit her lip to stifle a laugh. She covered her mouth with her hand.

Alberto didn't seem angry, but clearly, he wasn't happy. "What happened?"

After Rey translated Alberto's question, Bonita said, "Like I said, he wouldn't leave, so I thought I'd change clothes in front of him. You know, give him a little show. Crank him up a little. I figured if he tried anything, I'd scream like a banshee and then all you guys would come running and stop him before he did anything to me. He grabbed for his gun, maybe to remove it so he could drop his pants. It went off."

Rey translated for Carlos and Alberto.

Carlos couldn't suppress his laugh. He didn't try. "Glocks are notorious for that. The safety's on the trigger. When you pull it out of your waistband, or even a holster, you can accidentally pull the trigger and discharge a round. Not only did he shoot himself in the dick, it looks like the bullet pierced the big artery in his leg."

"What do we do with him?" Alberto asked.

"Tomorrow, when we go to the dive site, we'll dump him overboard," Carlos replied.

"What if a patrol boat stops us on the way out?"

"We'll tell them the truth. He shot himself."

"And we left him there for a day?" Rey said. "They wouldn't like that. Plus, we'll be headed out, not in. They could impound the boat as a crime scene. We need to get rid of the body now. Wrap him in a sheet and bring him topside. I need to go check our course. I turned on the autopilot and slowed the boat to a crawl, but I need to see where we are." He turned to leave, stopped, and looked at Bonita. "Finish getting dressed, then come to the wheelhouse." He then told Carlos and Alberto what he had said.

Before Rey left the cabin, Bonita threw her shirt on over the bikini bra and followed him out. When they arrived in the wheelhouse, Rey took the boat off autopilot and made a slow swing to starboard, toward the widest section of Cartagena Bay. Bonita sat on the high sofa behind the helm and wrapped her arms around her legs.

Carlos came into the wheelhouse, followed by Alberto. "José's in the main salon. Do you have a plan?"

Rey checked the GPS and the depth chart. "We're about a mile from land in any direction, and the water's seventy-five feet deep here. Strap a couple of dive belts full of weights to José and ease him off the stern. Then clean up all the blood in my cabin."

"We'll dump José, but you can clean the blood. Or have the girl clean it."

Switching to English, Rey said, "Bonnie, any chance I can get you to clean the floor of my cabin?"

"Eck. All that blood? Are you kidding?"

"How 'bout if I help? I have vinyl gloves in the engine room."

"If you help, okay, I will."

"Thanks." Switching to Spanish, he said, "Carlos, after you dump the body, come back here. You'll need to take the wheel. José was the only person who knew how to drive the boat. Now you'll have to learn."

Carlos and Alberto left the wheelhouse. Bonita slid off the sofa and wrapped her arms around Rey's barrel chest. "What happens to me? Are they going to let me leave after what happened?"

"They should. If you go to the police, you're the one they'd question since you were in the room when it happened. I'll tell the guys. They'll let you go back to your hotel tonight."

"Then what?"

"What do you mean?"

"Should I come back? I still want to help you. Just because José is dead, that doesn't mean they won't finish what they're doing, does it?"

"Unfortunately, no." Rey swung the boat around and pointed it toward the marina. He kept the speed at dead slow.

Carlos returned to the wheelhouse. "José is gone."

"Take the wheel. Keep us on this heading. We're going slow. I should be back before we get close to the channel to the marina. Send Alberto if you have any problems."

Carlos nervously took the helm. Rey and Bonita went to the engine room where Rey grabbed a bucket, mop, bleach, and several pairs of vinyl gloves. He and Bonita mopped up the blood covering the cabin floor and flushed it down the toilet.

"That was awful," Bonita said, peeling the gloves off and tossing them in the wastebasket. "I hope I never have to do that again."

Rey removed his gloves and washed his hands. The master head was barely large enough for one so they were standing toe to toe. He pushed a few strands of Bonita's long brown hair behind her ear. The bun from earlier in the day was long gone. "I guess this is neither the time nor the place to get romantic," he said.

"No, it's not. I need some air. The bleach is making me dizzy."

"Me too. Let's go topside."

When they reached the main salon, Rey checked in on Carlos at the helm. The boat was still heading toward the channel. "I'm going to give it a little more speed. You're doing good. We're going to get some air."

Rey took Bonita by the arm and led her to the aft deck. He leaned on the railing and looked at the trail of white froth bubbling in the boat's wake. "I'm beginning to think this boat is jinxed. José's the second body I've rolled off the swim platform."

"Beginning to?"

Rey laughed. "Okay, it's jinxed...or cursed. As soon as I get back to Fort Lauderdale, it's going on the market."

Alberto stepped onto the deck with three bottles of water. He handed one to Rey and Bonita. "I thought you might need water."

"Gracias," Bonita said in perfect Spanish. Neither man noticed.

"I'm sorry about your friend," Rey said.

"Thanks. He wasn't my friend. I didn't care much for him. He came with Carlos. Since he's dead, there's one less to get a cut."

Rey leaned against the aft rail. "What is the cut? What are you planning to haul? Isn't it time you told me?"

Alberto looked at Bonita, who was intentionally staring blankly at the bay.

"She doesn't speak Spanish. Tell me what's up."

Alberto looked back over his shoulder. Carlos was in the wheelhouse, both hands tightly gripping the helm. "Drugs and gold. Heroin and fentanyl. Contraband gold is mined in illegal mines in Colombia and Brazil. I was told the street value is over twenty million US dollars. A Colombian National living in Florida and a guy I haven't met set it all up. They're paying me a hundred K plus a percentage. I doubt I'll see the cut, but that's okay."

"A hundred thousand US dollars isn't bad for a few weeks' work."

"No, it's not. I've been in the US for about a year. I've worked for the Colombian a few times."

"Who's the Colombian?"

"I've said too much already. Don't tell Carlos I told you."

"Don't worry. I won't say anything. But I have to ask. Does it bother you that a lot of people might die from the drugs you're smuggling in? Maybe even kids?"

"Nah. If we don't bring the stuff in, someone else will."

Rey saw they were nearing the channel. "I need to drive the boat in." In English, he said, "Bonnie, you want to come with me?"

"Sure."

Carlos was happy to relinquish the helm. As he was leaving the wheelhouse, Rey said, "Get the lines ready. We should be at the dock in about half an hour."

Carlos nodded and left.

"I kinda liked Alberto," Rey said to Bonita. "But he has no remorse about how kids could die of a fentanyl overdose. How can people be so fucking cold?"

Bonita remembered what Jana said about Rey not being a cusser. Carlos' comments must have touched a nerve. She lightly caressed his jaw. "You're not letting those drugs enter the US."

"That obvious, huh? I could walk away from the boat right now, get a hold of Jana and my brother, and tell them to disappear for a while...did I tell you they threatened to kill them if I didn't cooperate? They may have been bluffing, but I couldn't take the chance."

"You could take off and notify the feds that a boatload of drugs was coming in."

"If I took off, they'd get a new boat, figuring I'd rat them out. If they didn't get a new boat, who's to say they'd go to Florida? The *Miss Jana* has a long range. They could go anywhere. My guess is they'd have satellite boats meet them offshore and pick up the drugs, so when they arrive in Florida, there'd be nothing on board."

"How are we stopping them?"

"We?"

"Why not?"

"I thought the stupid ship had sailed."

<h1 style="text-align:center">34</h1>

Rey maneuvered the eighty-thousand-pound boat into the slip and watched Carlos and Alberto secure the dock lines. He cut the engines and double-checked the lines. They couldn't drive the boat, but they were becoming decent deckhands.

Bonita was waiting on the aft deck when Rey finished checking the lines. "I told them that you were going back to your hotel and you'd be back in the morning. They seemed okay with it. I think José was in charge. The other two seem a little lost without him."

"That could be a good thing, couldn't it?"

"I think they'll call their boss and get guidance. I don't think it changes anything."

"Oh. That's too bad. I was hoping they'd call this whole thing off."

"Not a chance. They're committed. Look, you better take off before they make the call and decide you shouldn't leave. Are you still coming back in the morning?"

"I am. Can I use your phone?"

"Sure."

Rey handed her his phone and watched while she typed a text. After it was sent, she deleted the message. She kissed him on the cheek and hurried off the boat, down the pier, and out the main gate of the marina.

It took Juan twenty minutes to reach her. When Bonita got into his car, she spoke to him in Spanish. "Thank you for picking me up. I hid my phone in the head. I couldn't call an Uber. I knew your number and used Rey's phone to text you."

"You know I'm more than happy to come get you. I'm glad you're okay. When I saw those men take you this morning and there was nothing I could do, I texted your friend Alex and told him what happened. They saw you on the boat too. He texted me, and we were planning to rescue you tonight."

"You're kidding! What was the plan?"

"He didn't say. But we should text Alex and tell him you're safe."

"We're only ten minutes away. I'll surprise them. Oh, can you get me another phone?"

"No problem."

"And a ride back to the boat in the morning?"

Juan's head snapped. "You're going back to the boat tomorrow?"

"I am. Rey needs me. I want to help him."

Juan stared at the road ahead. "How can you help him?" His face turned serious. "You had sex with him, didn't you?"

"No, I didn't. Why would you ask?"

"You have the same look you had years ago when I brought you back from the square after you had sex. But with those men, you had no choice. Why do you have that look?"

"What look are you talking about? Is it a look? Maybe it's because I saw a man die on the boat."

"What? A man died? Who? How?"

Bonita told the story to Juan, who couldn't help but laugh when she said he shot his dick off.

When he stopped laughing, Juan said, "I guess there's worse ways to die, but I can't think of one." He shivered when he pictured José's demise. "What'd they do with him?"

"Strapped dive weights to him and dropped him in the middle of the bay."

"He'll never be seen again. Fish and crabs will make quick work of the body."

Bonita squeezed her eyes shut. "Please, Juan..."

"I'm sorry. Look, we're at the hotel. I don't like you going back to the boat, but I'll take you. I'll get you a phone, too. What time do you want me to pick you up?"

"I want to talk to Alex about it. I left the phone you gave me hidden on the boat. I'll text you later from my phone." She leaned over and kissed him on the cheek. "Thanks again. See you tomorrow."

Bonita rode the elevator to her floor, walked past her room, and tapped on the door to Alexander's room. Jana opened the door and held it.

"Bon, oh my God! What...how..." Jana threw her arms around Bonita and hugged her. "I'm so happy to see you. We've been worried. Juan texted—"

"I know. He picked me up from the boat and told me he texted you."

Jana pulled Bonita into the room. Alexander was waiting and gave her a bear hug. "We were planning to come get you tonight—"

"Juan told me that, too."

"Come in. Sit. Tell us what happened," Jana said.

"I've got a lot to tell you, but I'm starving. Can we go for dinner? They didn't have much food on the boat."

"We had a late lunch," Jana said. "We can order room service."

"That'd be fantastic."

Jana pulled the room service menu from the desk drawer and handed it to her. She opened it and scanned the limited options. "Ooh, they have Hawaiian pizza. I'll have that."

"Can I see the menu?" Alexander asked. Bonita handed it to him. He read the description of the pizza. "I'm not really hungry, but that sounds good. I'll have one too."

Bonita called room service. After she'd ordered the two Hawaiian pizzas, she whispered to Jana, "Do you want anything?"

Jana glanced at the menu. "Get me the Volcano."

"What's a Volcano?" Alexander asked after Bonita hung up the phone.

"I'll read you the description: Arequipe lava cake, vanilla ice cream, and garrapiñada of almonds." Jana butchered two of the words in the description. Bonita corrected her. "Okay, but what are they?"

"Arequipe is a sweet sauce made with sugar and milk," Bonita said. "Garrapiñada is peanuts, sugar, and vanilla, cooked until caramelized."

"I should have asked before I ordered."

"If you don't like it, I'd like to try it. I've heard of it, but never tried it. When I was living in Cartagena, all I ate was rice and potatoes. Sometimes Juan would bring me a hamburger."

Alexander noticed Jana was fighting back tears. "I'd love to sit here and listen to y'all talk about desserts, but I want to hear about today."

Bonita settled in the large upholstered lounge chair near the window. Alexander and Jana sat on the small couch catty-corner to her. Alexander leaned forward, his forearms resting on his thighs. Jana, on the edge of the seat, was leaning on the arm toward Bonita.

"Do you mind if I have a beer?" Bonita asked. She was uncomfortable with Alexander and Jana leaning in, staring at her.

"Of course not." Alexander pulled a bottle from the minibar fridge, popped the top off, and handed it to her. She took a drink and relayed the story Rey had told her, what she heard from Alberto on the boat, and about José shooting himself. It was the same story she told Juan on the way back to the hotel, but this time, she included the details of refueling in Mathew Town. Jana was familiar with the place. Bonita was interrupted when room service knocked on the door.

Jana hopped up and let the porter in. He pushed a cart with plates of food covered by aluminum tops. He placed the plates on the small table between the lounge chair and sofa. Jana signed the receipt and closed the door behind the porter.

"This looks so good, thank you," Bonita said, picking up a slice of pizza and devouring it in four bites. She washed the slice down with a swig of beer and grabbed another slice. She ate the second slice more slowly. "Rey said Cole knew nothing about what was going down. He said a couple of guys in Florida set it all up."

"A couple? Two?" Alexander asked.

"Yes. Carlos said one is a Colombian National living in Florida."

"That's encouraging. If there are only two."

"Two of them set it up," Jana added. "They could have an army working for them."

"Good point. We don't know a lot more than we knew last week."

"We know what they're smuggling in, and we know Rey is going to try to stop them," Bonita said between bites of pizza.

"I'm bothered by that, too. We're talking about a lot of money. They aren't going to give it up easily."

Jana's phone buzzed. It was a text from Gabby. She asked if they still needed her later to translate for Juan when they go look for Bonita. "Shit. I forgot about Gabby. She doesn't know Bon's here." Jana replied with an update. Gabby immediately replied. Jana read the text to the Bonita and Alexander.

"Gabby says it's great you're back and safe. She also said you and her talked about going clubbing one night. She wants to show you the Cartagena nightlife. Did you want to go tonight?"

Bonita's eyes lit up. "I took a long nap on the boat this afternoon, so I feel good. I'd love to go out. Do you all mind?"

"Not at all," Jana said. "I'll tell Gabby you're on. How much time do you need to get ready?"

Alexander butted in. "I'd like to hear about today before you go."

"There's not much more to the story. Tell Gabby an hour."

Jana exchanged texts with Gabby, then said, "She'll pick you up in an hour. Go ahead with the story."

"Where was I? Oh, Rey said he talked with Cole and he was convinced the guys didn't need him and would kill him, so he wanted to take off. Rey gave him his blessing. That night, Cole disappeared."

"Did Rey have any idea where Cole went?" Alexander asked.

"No. He said Cole had little or no money, no passport, and didn't speak Spanish. But he said Cole had been in Special Forces in the Army and thought he'd be okay."

Alexander held up his hand. "It's a hell of a long shot but ask your friend Juan to put the word out. See if anyone's seen a big, tattooed, white guy who can't speak Spanish around. He might be living on the streets of Cartagena."

"Or long gone," Jana added. "If it were me, and I found a way, I'd be long gone."

"If you could find a way. Sorry, Bon. Go ahead."

Bonita ate another slice of pizza, finished the beer, and asked for another while she repeated Rey's theory of how they were going to use scuba tanks to smuggle in the drugs.

"Wow," Alexander said when Bonita paused for a drink of beer. "If they make it back to the US, they could make millions. With that kind of money, why the hell didn't they buy a boat?"

"The boat wasn't the issue," Jana said. "They needed a captain. Let me rephrase. You need a boat with the range to get here, but it's the Caribbean. You don't have to make the entire trip without stopping. Once you're in the open ocean, driving a boat isn't difficult. With modern navigation, anyone could get from Florida to Colombia without a problem. Where it gets dicey is maneuvering a big boat like the *Miss Jana* through narrow channels, around anchored boats–like Cartagena Bay is full of–and docking. You need an experienced captain to be safe."

Alexander nodded. "Which is why Rey is still alive. They need him to drive the boat. I know why they need the *Miss Jana* too. You said there were plenty of places to get fuel in the Caribbean, but not if you're carrying several million dollars' worth of illegal drugs and contraband gold. When they leave Cartagena, they don't want to stop until they reach Fort Lauderdale." He interlocked his fingers behind his head and leaned back. "We need to stop them."

"Exactly what Rey intends to do," Bonita said.

Alexander remained seated, hands behind his head. "Did he say how?"

"When they leave for Florida, he plans to kill them and toss the drugs overboard. Then he'll take the boat back and wait for someone to show up. He's going to tell them the guys on the boat took off with the drugs."

Alexander grimaced. "And when they do show up, he's going to tell them that right before they kill him."

"No. He thinks they'll believe him because he brought the boat back and docked it like nothing happened. He said he'd be armed too, if things go bad."

"Things will. Dumb idea."

"It might be, but I plan on helping him."

"What?" Jana exclaimed. "Are you crazy?"

"Maybe. But for the first time in my life, I feel needed. Needed in a real way. Not just needed by some creep who wants me to swallow his nut."

"I know the feeling, Bon," Jana said. "You won't get an argument from me. I think I know the answer, but I need to ask. Did you tell Rey about us?"

"No, why?"

"No reason. I was wondering if he'd leave the boat if he knew we were here in Cartagena."

"I doubt it. He was pissed about the drugs getting into the US and determined to stop it."

"Alex," Jana said, "what if you notified the FBI of a shipment coming in and they, the DEA, and border patrol were there to pick them up?"

"Rey said if he took off, they'd either go somewhere else instead of Florida or have smaller boats meet them offshore and take everything off the *Miss Jana*," Bonita said.

"Exactly what they'd do," Alexander agreed. "I'm surprised they let you off the boat with what you know."

"They don't know I know anything. I pretended not to speak Spanish, and they don't speak English. Rey told them he didn't tell me anything about what they were doing here."

"And when she goes back to the boat tomorrow, it will reinforce their opinion that she is unaware of anything nefarious going on. But I have to ask, why would you do that? I'm playing devil's advocate here. You just met him. Why would you risk your life to save him?"

"Because I fell madly in love with him?" Bonita said nonchalantly.

"Did you?"

"No."

"Did you fuck him?" Jana asked.

"Jana! How could you ask that?"

"You did, didn't you?"

Bonita gave a half smile. "I didn't. I think he wanted to, but there was never an opportunity. Even if there had been, I wouldn't have."

"You wouldn't have fucked him? Why?"

"Well, there's you, which is a big reason. You guys are...were...still kinda together. I had other reasons too...in my heart, I...uh...never mind. Rey's a good-looking guy, but...I can't explain it. I've had more dicks in me than a urinal at the Super Bowl game and...I guess I've had enough, at least for a while. Poor Rey. When we were in the hotel room, on the bed, I knew he wanted to have sex. I thought he had to be the unluckiest guy in the world to be with me the day I decided to stop having sex."

Jana chuckled. "I'm sorry. I didn't mean to laugh, but you're right, he is unlucky. He was in bed with a gorgeous woman who has been around–I won't be as graphic as you–and he doesn't get laid."

"I felt a little sorry for him. To be honest, I almost gave in after we finished cleaning the blood from the main cabin. He's got such cute puppy dog eyes. But the smell of bleach was so strong we had to leave the room."

Alexander had been staring out the window. Jana put her hand on top of his and said, "Alex, are you okay? I'm sorry, Bonita and I should have had this conversation in private."

"I'm fine. Nothing happened. If something had happened, it seems like it would bother you more than me. I kind of tuned Bon out. My mind is on how to keep those drugs off the street and Rey alive...and out of prison."

35

"Alex, are you awake?" Jana asked from the queen bed next to his.

"Yes. Good morning. Did you just wake up?"

"Good morning. No. I've been laying here thinking about Bonita."

"Hmm. I was hoping you were going to say you were lying there thinking about me."

Jana laughed. "Oh, Alex, I do think about you, but she was on my mind. She seems to be doing well. She's eating and I've seen no ill effects from withdrawal. But she went out partying last night and I have a feeling drugs, especially cocaine, are rampant in the clubs of Cartagena. It would be easy for her to relapse."

"You're right. It could be a test for her. Considering what she is planning to do, she might want something to escape reality for a little while."

"Gabby seems to have a good head on her shoulders. Maybe she'll talk some sense into her."

"Maybe. But what Bonita said last night, about feeling needed, I understand. Her whole life, she's been used and abused. Now, for the first time, she feels useful. It doesn't matter if she is or not. She may end up hindering more than helping. Rey will have to take care of her as well as himself."

Jana sat up in the bed and sighed. "I never thought about that. Maybe we should stop her from going to the boat."

"I considered it. Then I thought about how it would destroy her self-esteem. I can't do that to her."

"Even if it means she gets herself killed? Gets Rey killed in the process?"

Alexander stared out the window in deep thought for several seconds, then leaned forward. "Then again, maybe she'll be enough of a distraction that she'll help. She's already got one of them to shoot himself."

"Excellent point. Beautiful women make men do strange things."

"So we don't try to stop her?"

"Nope. And we'll have to live with the decision."

"Jesus, Alex. I don't like the way you said that. If something were to happen to Rey, that'd be horrible, but Bonita? Unforgivable."

"Maybe we should have her tell Rey we're here and that he should leave with her. I know he hopes he can prevent those drugs from reaching the US, but if I notify the FBI, they have ways to track the boat. They'd stop them at some point."

"What about the guys that set it all up?"

"They'd likely get away."

"And come after Rey–and me and you."

"Yep."

Jana's face turned red with anger. "This is so fucked up."

"It is. Let's let Bon go to the boat as planned. She said they were going to make a couple more dry runs to the dive site hoping to get noticed by the border patrol so they look like a legit dive boat heading out when they have the drugs onboard."

"Okay..."

"Bon goes on those dry runs. They might not let her go to Florida with them when they leave, but I have a feeling they will. She said she stashed her cell on the boat, in the head. When they get close to Florida, or another island, if they decide to go elsewhere to unload the drugs, she can text us and let us know when and where the drop will be. I guarantee the two principals will be there to ensure it goes smoothly. I'll have every agency available on standby, and when it goes down, they'll bust them all."

"That's brilliant. But what about Rey and Bonita?"

"They're informants. They'll be arrested and hauled away, same as the rest of them. The others won't suspect a thing. I can contact a friend in the Bureau, and we can have it established that Rey and Bon are working for us."

"It sounds like a great plan, Alex. What can go wrong?"

"As soon as they're a few miles into the Caribbean, they could tie dive weights to Rey and Bon and toss them off the swim platform."

"Fuck! Alex! Why'd you have to tell me that?"

"You asked."

"What are the odds they'd do that?"

"Bon is eye candy to get them out of Colombian waters. After that, she's a liability. I'd put her odds at about fifty-fifty. Rey's the only one who can drive the boat. He'll make it to the drop-off point."

"If she's a liability, why fifty-fifty? Seems like one hundred percent they'd get rid of her."

"Jana, you've seen her. There's an old joke about being on a boat with a woman. I can't remember how it goes, but the punchline is something like, are you going to fuck or swim? If push comes to shove, Bon will do what she has to do to survive. In fact, I'm counting on it. Rey might protect her as well. He's a chivalrous man. They'd have to go through him to get to her and they wouldn't want to do that."

"That's Rey. So, her odds are better than fifty-fifty?"

Alexander shrugged. "Meh."

"Alex, you can be such a dick. But I love you."

"What?"

Shock crossed Jana's face. She put her hand over her mouth. "Oh shit. I didn't want to tell you."

"Want to or mean to?"

Jana put her arm over her eyes. "Don't put me on the spot. I didn't mean to say it, but I've wanted to. I'm so confused."

"I love you too, Jana. And I'm just as confused."

Jana moved to Alexander's bed. She laid on top of him and kissed him.

He rolled her off to the side. "This is going to sound absurd, but let's keep it professional...for now. When this is all over—"

Jana stopped him with a deep kiss. "Whatever you say." She jumped off the bed and disappeared into the bathroom. She came out a minute later, grabbed clothes, said she was taking a shower, and went back into the bathroom.

Alexander took several deep breaths. His racing heart slowed. *When will I learn to keep my damn mouth shut?* He got out of bed and walked to the window. Using the binoculars, he scanned the bay for any boats that resembled the *Miss Jana*. He watched for a few uneventful minutes, then called room service for coffee.

Jana came out of the bathroom a while later. "Are you looking at boats?" She laughed.

He turned around and gave her a smirk. "Wow," he said, studying her black Lululemon high-rise pants that looked painted on, and white T-strap tank top. "There's nothing out the window that would look any better than you."

"Aw, that's sweet. Thank you. Seriously, did you see anything worthwhile?"

"Nope. Just the usual small boat traffic and a few ships coming and going. I was killing time until you got out of the shower."

"Should I wake Bonita?"

"It's time," Alexander said and gave her a half grin. "You know, you were calling her Bon from almost the day you met her until last night. When you heard about her and Rey getting a little cozy, you called her Bonita again."

"Did I? Maybe her saying Rey wanted to...or would have...bothered me a little. It didn't bother you? I wonder how Bonita feels about us."

"It's hard to say how she feels. She and I haven't been together for months, and there's no telling how many guys she was with after she left. Her and Rey almost doing it shouldn't bother me at all. But you and Rey haven't technically split, it should bother you. Regarding how she feels about us, I doubt she cares."

"When she told us about almost sleeping with Rey, she said something like, 'Someone was in her heart.' I assumed she was referring to you."

"She hasn't acted like it. I got the impression she's been trying to put us together since we landed in Cartagena."

"Maybe we should ask her."

"I think we should let that sleeping dog lie."

"Agreed." Jana tapped lightly on the adjoining door, then cracked it open. They'd agreed when they arrived that they'd leave the door unlocked. She poked her head in. Bonita and Gabby were sleeping back-to-back in one of the queen beds.

"Boni...Bon," Jana said in a voice slightly louder than a whisper. When neither girl stirred, she repeated herself with a bit more volume.

Bonita's eyes popped open. She looked around the room darkened by the closed curtains as though she didn't know where she was. When she got her bearings, she said, "Oh, hi Jana. Good morning."

"Good morning. How are you feeling?"

"Tired. We stayed out kinda late last night. Gabby stayed with me. She's going to take me to Juan's this morning."

"When you get up, come see us. We need to talk."

"Okay. Give me a few minutes."

Jana turned and closed the door behind her. "Bonita will be here in a minute. Gabby's with her."

"Gabby?" Alexander said, surprised.

"She said they got in late and Gabby's going to take her to Juan's this morning. I guess she decided to stay instead of going home and coming back this morning."

"Makes sense. The coffee I ordered while you were in the shower came. Want some?"

"Please."

Alexander poured two cups of coffee. He searched his brain but couldn't remember how Jana took her coffee. Better safe than sorry, he asked.

"One cream, two sugars," Jana said. Alexander was happy she didn't chastise him for not knowing.

They sat on the long couch in front of the window that looked out at Cartagena Bay. Jana took a sip of coffee. "It's perfect."

Bonita entered the room alone. "I smell coffee. Is there more?"

"It's by the ice bucket. Help yourself."

Bonita poured a cup and joined them near the window. She sat in the oversized chair next to the couch.

"Did you have fun last night?" Jana asked.

"We did! It was a blast. We went to several popular bars. It was crazy. So many people. The last bar we went to closed at three in the morning. Gabby said there was another bar nearby that closed at four. By then, I was exhausted."

"Oh, to be young again," Alexander said.

"Speak for yourself, Alex," Jana said. "I could still party until four."

Bonita chuckled. "Could you? Before we leave, Gabby and I'll take you to the bars. We'll see how long you last."

"I'm game," Jana said. "I see why you're tired. You're not hungover?"

"Not at all. I had maybe two or three drinks all night. Guys kept offering us shots, but it was usually cheap tequila. I'd take a sip and sit the glass down. Alex spoiled me with his tequila. All his liquor. He only had top-shelf stuff."

"I had cheap stuff too. You only drank the good stuff." Alexander laughed, then turned serious. "You're still planning to go to the boat this morning?"

"I am. Gabby tried to talk me out of it last night. This is something I have to do. For me, as much as for Rey."

Alexander leaned in, his dark blue eyes locking onto hers with an intensity that made her heart race. "I understand," he said softly, his hand reaching out to gently grasp hers. "But is this really worth risking your life for?"

Bonita gazed out the window for a few seconds then turned to Alexander. "Truthfully? No. But if I don't go, if I don't at least try to help...I...I know I'd hate myself. I'd hate myself as much or even more than I hated myself when I was giving head for a ten-dollar rock or a speedball."

"Bon, don't say that. We all want to help Rey, but we don't want anything to happen to you either. Alex and I have talked about it. They need Rey to drive the boat. Once they get out of the bay, they may not need you. If you know what I mean..."

"I know. You think I'm stupid for doing this."

"Not at all, Bon. We understand. But you need to understand, you may not be able to help Rey–" Alexander stopped in mid-sentence. He looked into Bonita's large, dark eyes. He couldn't tell her that her presence could be detrimental to Rey's chances of survival. Instead, he said, "I have a bad feeling, but I won't try to stop you. Promise me this. From what we know, they're making trial runs to the dive sites. You said Rey mentioned doing three of them. While you're on the boat today, get with Rey and ask him if he wants you on the boat. He'll feel like he's responsible for you, and if the shit hits the fan, he'll likely react differently if you're there. Ask him if he wants you onboard. If he says no, don't go back tomorrow."

"Agreed. I want to help, but if I'm just in the way, I'm not going to be of any help to him." Bonita stared dejectedly into her coffee cup.

"Bon, you've already helped him tremendously. Because of you, we know what they're transporting and have a good idea of when. We CAN stop the shipment. You've already done more than I expected when I brought you."

Her face lit up. "You aren't just saying that?"

"Absolutely not. And I need you to do one more thing."

"Sure."

"You hid a phone in the head, right?"

"Right."

"Does Rey know about it?"

Bonita thought about the question. "Uh, no, I didn't tell him I hid it in the head."

"You need to tell him about the phone. Tell him your friends' numbers are in it. Ask him to keep them posted whenever he can. As soon as he learns when and where they're unloading the drugs, he needs to text that info to them so they can contact the authorities. That's your mission today. Give him the message, then you've done more for him than you could imagine. But, be careful! You've done fantastic so far. Give Rey the message and get through the day without the others finding out. That's the key. If they find out about the phone, or that you're not some random chick who was hanging around the marina..."

"I get the picture, Alex. I'll be careful. You're right. If I'm on the boat, Rey will try to take care of me first. I wouldn't want that. After I deliver the message, I won't go back. Should I tell him I'm not coming back? Should I tell him who I am?"

Alexander pressed his fingers together in front of his face. "Good questions, Bon. I'm inclined to say don't tell him who you are. Tell him your friends are going back to the States tomorrow and you're going with them. When you get home, you'll contact the FBI, ICE, Homeland Security, the Coast Guard, and the local cops in Florida, and tell them you have information on a huge shipment of drugs coming into the US. Then you'll wait for his text and pass the information on to the authorities."

"I like it," Bonita said. "What about the phone numbers in the phone?"

"Those are your friend's phone numbers. You lost your phone and got a burner phone, which is the one he'll be using. Tell him you'll text him your number when you get a new one."

"Okay. I got it. Gabby should be awake by now. I'm going to get ready. She's driving me to Juan's, and he'll drive me to the boat. She's still a little freaked out over that area of town. She doesn't want to go there alone."

When Bonita left the room, Jana scooted next to Alexander. "That was good. You gave her a way to help so she can feel good about herself, and you convinced her not to go with the boat when they leave. And you did it without coming right out and telling her she'd be more of a hindrance than a help. I'm quite impressed, Mr. Christian."

"Thank you. It played out a little better in real life than it did in my head. Now she just needs to pull it off."

36

According to Rey, every day for three straight days, the *Miss Jana* would leave the Manzanillo Marina and motor twenty-three nautical miles to Isla del Rosario–the Rosario Islands–where she would anchor. There was no hurry. He would cruise at seven knots, making the trip to the anchorage in three hours.

The *Miss Jana* carried three complete sets of dive gear: a buoyancy compensator, scuba regulator, fins, mask, belt, weights, and a wetsuit. Rey was the only certified diver on the boat. Carlos didn't know how to swim. Alberto could swim but was deathly afraid of sharks. José had been swimming with the fish for the past twelve hours. The scuba equipment was only for the illusion.

The Rosario Islands were one of many natural national parks in Colombia, established to protect the coral reefs along the Colombian Caribbean coast. The area was one of the most popular diving spots in the Caribbean. Boats of all sizes and shapes anchored in the shallow reefs while their occupants dove the pristine waters. Many spent the night at anchorage or left Cartagena for the islands at first light.

Juan dropped Bonita off in front of the large blue gate at the entrance to the marina. The docks buzzed with a larger crowd than the previous day. She thanked him for the ride and walked through the gate. When she walked down the pier towards the boat, she realized the increased activity was centered around the big trawler. She looked back and watched Juan drive away. It didn't matter. She had committed to helping Rey and nothing would stop her. When she approached the stern of the *Miss Jana*, a woman was standing on the aft deck. She had medium-dark skin, stood maybe five feet two, and was heavyset. She wasn't an attractive woman.

"Can I help you?" she asked in English with only a slight accent.

"I'm looking for Rey. He invited me to go to Rosario with him."

The woman studied Bonita, who wore stonewashed denim shorts with a frayed hem that rode low on her hips and high on her legs, and a brown mesh patchwork V-neck lace camisole top. "You must be Bonnie."

"That's me," Bonita replied smiling.

"Rey is in the engine room. Come aboard."

Bonita cautiously stepped onto the swim platform and climbed the ladder to the aft deck.

"Come with me. I'll take you to Rey. Let me see your purse."

"My purse? Why?"

"It wasn't a request." The woman snatched the small blue, double-zippered purse from Bonita's hand, checked the contents, and removed her phone. Bonita offered some resistance but wasn't surprised. She expected them to search her and take her phone when she boarded the boat the last time.

"You won't be needing this," the woman said before stuffing the phone in the pocket of her baggy cargo shorts and handing the purse back. "This way." She led Bonita through the main salon and down the steps to a narrow hallway which took them to the engine room. "Rey, you have company."

Rey came out of the engine room, wiping his hand with a red shop towel. "Bonnie! It's good to see you. I wasn't sure you'd come."

"I wouldn't miss it. The water is so beautiful. I've done a little diving, and I was hoping we could dive when we get to the islands." Bonita wondered if the woman, whoever she was, bought her ruse.

After taking another long look at Bonita, paying close attention to the feather protruding from her cutoff shorts, the woman said, "I'll be on deck. When you're finished in the engine room, stay in your cabin. I'll let you know when we're ready to leave."

"Will do," Rey replied.

When the woman was out of sight, Bonita asked, "Who's she? What's going on?"

"That's Daniela Diego. Goes by Dani. She put this thing together. She was born in the US, but her mother was Colombian, so she has dual citizenship. Carlos called her yesterday after José shot himself and told her what had happened. She didn't like it and jumped on a red-eye out of Miami. Got here this morning."

"There were a lot more people around the boat today. Do you know what they're doing?"

"No. It's Dani's doing. She told me to go below and she'd let me know when we're shoving off. She said it might be later than usual. I told her I might have a girl coming onboard this morning. She wasn't happy with it but agreed to let you come."

Bonita checked out the hall. She saw no one. "Rey, we need to talk. Is it safe here?"

Rey took her into the engine room and closed the door. "This is a heavily insulated room to muffle the noise from the engines. No one can hear us in here. What's wrong?"

"Nothing's wrong. I've got a plan. Me and my friends are leaving for the States tomorrow. When I get home, I'll call the FBI and other authorities and tell them about the boat and the drugs. When you know where the stuff is going to be delivered, you text me the location, and I'll forward the info to the cops."

"I like the idea, but Dani took my phone. I may be able to use one of their phones to text you the location, but not likely."

"No worries. I stashed my phone in the tampon box in the cabinet inside your cabin bathroom. I left it on. You'll need to charge it. The only numbers on the phone are my friends. You can text them and they'll let me know. When I get home, I'll get a new phone and text the number to that phone. Text me, but text the others too."

"That could work. Since Dani is here, most likely her partner will be at the drop-off location. I'll end up in jail too, but that's okay if I can keep those drugs off the street."

"Maybe you won't. My friend called his lawyer last night and if I tell the feds you're an informant, they'll arrest you, so it looks like you didn't know, but they won't charge you." Bonita thought adding the lawyer was a nice touch.

Rey leaned against one of the big Detroit diesel engines. "That's amazing. You may have saved my ass."

"One more thing. I'm worried they might not need you once you get out of the bay. Watch yourself."

"I appreciate the concern, but they'll need me. Not only am I the only one who can drive the boat, I'm the only one who can maintain the engines. The last thing you want is to be floundering around the ocean with no power."

"Good to know...but watch your back."

"I will. Don't worry about me. Now I'm wondering if we should get you off this boat."

"Wouldn't that be suspicious?"

"There's nothing to be suspicious about. They think you're a gold-digger and I want to sleep with you."

"Then I guess we should go back to your cabin. You get what you want, or maybe you don't, and you throw me off the boat."

Rey pulled the dipstick from the tube, checked the level, wiped it clean, and reinserted it. He fiddled with the eye of the dipstick. "Except I'm afraid they'd still want you on the boat as eye candy. That would make the rest of the day awkward between us."

"Would that be a bad thing?"

Rey shook his head. "Bonnie, if you're on the boat, it might be better if we are together...so to speak. Otherwise—"

"They want a piece?"

"Exactly."

"This Dani woman is in charge? Would she stop the guys? So there wouldn't be another José moment?"

"She might want a piece of you for herself. She's a nasty bitch."

Bonita cringed. "She wouldn't be any worse than the guys, but I'd rather not."

"I'll do my best to keep that from happening." Rey wiped the side of his face with the shop rag. "Anything else I need to know about your plan? I assume we're going to Florida. What if we go to Texas, or Mexico, or a Caribbean island?"

"My friend, who's not an expert, said they'd get the most money for the drugs in the US. That's where they'll go. You've got Fort Lauderdale painted on the back of the boat. It would be the inconspicuous place to go, too."

Rey nodded. "It's the most logical. If it's not Lauderdale, it would likely be Miami or maybe the Keys, but somewhere in the US."

"Yep. I'm glad we talked it out. As for me, I should stay, and we should be an item. It'll make for a nice day, too. Isn't that why I'm here? Let's enjoy it. Act like that's the only reason I'm here." Bonita paused, looked around the engine room, and turned up her nose. "It kinda stinks in here. Can we go to your cabin?"

"That smell could be me. Let's go to my cabin. I'll take a shower."

When they got to Rey's cabin, Bonita laid on the bed. "My friend took me bar hopping last night. I'm beat. Do you mind if I take a nap while you shower?"

"Not at all."

Bonita may have heard the answer, but she didn't react to it. Her eyes were closed. By the time Rey stepped into the shower, she was asleep. Rey showered and put on clean shorts and a t-shirt. He laid next to Bonita and fell asleep.

Dani pushed the cabin door open. She saw Rey spread out on his back. Bonita was on her stomach, half on Rey, with her leg angled over and between his leg. Her arm draped across his chest.

"Hey, Rey," Dani said in a low, husky voice.

Rey opened his eyes and blinked a few times to clear the fog of sleep.

"Time to head out. You can let your girlfriend sleep for a while."

"I'll be up in a sec. Let me hit the head."

"Don't be long."

Rey eased himself out from under Bonita. She stirred but didn't awaken. He walked around the bed and into the head. After he peed and washed his hands, he checked the cabinet for the box of tampons where she had hidden the phone. The box was where she said it would be and the phone was inside. Dead. But he was relieved, knowing he had a spare cable that would fit. He kept a supply of cords in the engine room. He put the phone back in the box, and the box on the shelf. He left the head, glanced at Bonita, and tiptoed out of the cabin, closing the door behind him. Dani was waiting for him when he reached the top of the steps.

"About time. I thought you were going to tap that tall drink of water one more time before you came up."

Rey ignored her and headed for the wheelhouse. He started both engines—port engine first. Dani had followed him and was leaning against the sofa behind him.

"That's interesting," she said after he had both engines idling.

"What's that?"

"You got a hot blonde in Fort Lauderdale that we got people watching, and here you are pokin' that sweet young thing. I can't say I blame you. She's a hottie."

Once again, he ignored the crude woman's comments. "We're ready. Tell the guys to cast off. Starboard first."

"Huh?"

"Jesus Christ! Tell them to cast off–never mind." Rey stepped out of the wheelhouse. Alberto and Carlos were leaning against the stern rail. The door to the aft deck was open. "Prepare to cast off. Starboard first," he yelled.

Back inside, Rey eased the engines into gear and signaled for the guys to release the lines. The big boat chugged forward. He spun the wheel hard to port and revved the port engine to force the boat to starboard. After the boat had made a slight turn, he reversed the procedure, exaggerating each move.

The *Miss Jana* was a nimble boat for her size. Rey could have eased the throttles up slightly and easily steered the boat out of the slip and into the channel. His exhibition was purely for Dani's amusement. His maneuvers on the bridge would have frightened even the most seasoned of skippers. He could tell by her expression that she would never attempt to drive the boat. He had made his point.

"We have to follow the channel out, swing around the shallow area at the southern tip of the island, and then we're in the bay, we can make a straight shot into the Caribbean. It'll take an hour and a half or so."

"I'm going to wake your girlfriend and have her get on the back of the boat. Isn't that why she's here?" Dani let out a belly laugh as if to let him know she knew the real reason Bonita was there. He gave her a slight grin and went back to steering the boat. She left the wheelhouse and went down the steps to the cabin where Bonita was sleeping. She pushed the door open and whispered in Spanish, "Hey, Bonnie, time to get up. Change into your bikini and come upstairs."

Coming out of a deep sleep, Bonita almost replied in Spanish. She also realized whoever was waking her called her "Bonnie." This iteration of Bonnie didn't speak Spanish. She caught herself and said nothing. She peered through half-open eyes and looked at Dani. "Oh. Hi. I must have been sleeping hard. What'd you say?"

In English, Dani said, "Time to wake up. Put on your..." She paused. "Just put on the top. The shorts look good. Sexy. Hurry. We'll be at the back of the boat."

Bonita got up, went to the bathroom, and changed her top. When she got to the aft deck, Dani was pacing. "Damn, girl. You're slower than Christmas. What took you so long?"

"I needed to pee. What's the hurry?"

Dani stomped over to her, stood as tall as she could on her tiptoes, and pointed her finger in her face. "When I say do something, you do it. Your long legs and big boobs don't mean shit to me, comprende?"

"Fuck. Who died and made you captain?"

Dani's face turned red. She took a step closer to Bonita, but Carlos grabbed her and pulled her away. He spoke to her in Spanish.

"Boss, she's not part of this. She thinks she's going diving. She knows we want her out here looking sexy, but she doesn't know we want her out here to make it look like we're a legit charter."

"Is she necessary? I'd like to wrap a dive belt around her tattooed waist and toss her ass overboard. Right now."

"First, those dive weights are three kilos of solid gold, dipped in a black plastic coating. I wouldn't use even one to weigh her down. Second, don't piss Rey off. He's a martial arts expert. He could kill us all if we're not careful. Third, I wouldn't mind spending a little time with your new best friend before we kill her."

"You assholes are all alike. Wanting a little piece of her is what killed José. When the time comes, we'll see if you get any. If you do, you will need to take care of Rey first. Thanks for reminding me about the weights. How many are there?"

"We've got six belts. Five weights on each belt. Each weight weighs three kilos."

Dani pulled out her phone and used the calculator to do the multiplications. "Ninety kilos. Gold is around seventy-seven thousand a kilo...that's almost seven million in gold."

"Seven million?" Carlos' eyebrows rose with excitement.

"I've seen that look. Don't get any ideas. Seven million's the retail value of gold. Legit gold. We're paying a lot less for it, and we'll sell it for a lot less."

Bonita took advantage of a break in the conversation. She looked Dani in the eye and said, "I'm going to get a bottle of water, unless you'd like to get it for me."

Dani took a step toward her. Carlos stepped between them.

Bonita went into the galley and got a bottle from the fridge. She glanced toward the back of the boat where Dani, Carlos, and Alberto were talking. She stepped into the wheelhouse.

"Hey," Rey said. "You're up."

"We got a problem. I pissed Dani off, and when she was talking in Spanish to the other guys, she said they plan to kill us. She didn't say when or anything. I was trying to pretend like I didn't understand them."

"I was afraid of that," Rey said. "No loose ends—" He did a double-take and then stared at Bonita. "You pretended you don't speak Spanish? You speak Spanish? And well enough to understand what they were saying?"

"Oh shit. Yes, I do."

"But—"

"You were so cute the day we met, fighting with the maître d' so he'd let me use the bathroom. I didn't want to tell you I knew what he said, then I thought it would be better if you didn't know I knew what you were saying about me to the other guys."

Rey laughed out loud. "That was smart. And extremely helpful. But it means we have a new problem. Why did Dani say she was going to kill you? There's no reason to do anything to you today. Maybe she thought you were going to be going with us when we leave. You said you pissed her off. Maybe she was just letting off a little steam."

"Carlos said he wanted me before they killed me. That sounded definite to me."

Rey slammed his fist onto the console. "Fuck! Can you swim?"

"What?"

"Can you swim?"

"I can. Not well. I mostly dog paddle. Why?"

"I can't imagine they'd do anything today, but I can swing the boat over toward the city. It's pretty deep, so I can get within fifty yards of the shore. If you jumped, could you make it?"

"With a life jacket. Is that the only option?"

"The other option is to stay on the boat, stay clear of Dani, and when we get back tonight, you take off."

"I prefer option two."

<h1 style="text-align:center">37</h1>

When the *Miss Jana* cleared Cartagena Bay and entered the Caribbean, Rey checked the clock on the wall in the wheelhouse. It read 1545: Three-forty-five in the afternoon. He did a double-take, slid off the seat, and checked the time on the GPS. 1547. The wall clock was two minutes slow.

Rey didn't take naps. Falling asleep with Bonita had thrown off his internal clock. When Dani woke him and said it was time to leave, he assumed it was noon. Maybe a little after. If it took them an hour and a half to get out of the bay, they left the dock around 1400–two o'clock. *Way too late to be heading to the islands.*

Dani stepped into the wheelhouse, closed the door, and leaned against it.

"I was coming to see you," Rey said. "It's later than I thought. There's no point in going to Rosário. As soon as we get there, we'll need to turn around and head back."

"I agree."

Dani's reply surprised Rey. "Should I U-turn? Head back? We can take it slow and cruise the bay."

"How much fuel do you have?"

Rey checked the gauges. "Mostly full. We filled both tanks a couple of days ago. Capacity is over twenty-five hundred gallons. Since then, including today, we've used maybe seventy gallons."

"Good. Set your course for Miami."

"What?"

"You deaf? Miami. Is that a problem?"

"It could be. I haven't checked the weather. I should double-check the engines and generator. Bonnie's on board too. We should've let her off."

"Not a chance. She's my insurance. If you don't do what I say, I'll toss her skinny ass overboard. Then we'll take care of your other girl-friend, the one in Florida."

Rey took a step toward her.

"Uh-uh, big fella. Don't even think about it." She put her hand on a bulge in her waistband.

He stopped, his eyes narrowed. "I'll take the boat to Florida. But I guarantee you, if anything happens to Bonnie, you won't be on it when it arrives."

Dani raised her shirt and put her hand on the grip of a semi-auto-matic pistol.

"If that's José's Glock, I'd be careful how you pull it out. Glocks have a trigger safety. You pull it out of your waist and accidentally pull the trigger, you'll shoot yourself. Like José did. When you do remove it, do it slow and easy, and keep your finger off the trigger."

"Don't tell me how to handle a gun. I know what I'm doing. You drive the boat."

"Send Bonnie in here. There's no need for her to be out on the deck."

"Why?"

"I need the company. I'll be here all night. In the morning, someone else needs to take over so I can get some sleep. Maybe Carlos. He's steered before."

Dani left in a huff. Rey smirked. He'd neglected to tell her in the time it would take her to remove the Glock from her waist, he could–and would–break her neck. He also didn't mention the cruise control. Driving the boat is nothing more than not running into a large com-mercial vessel.

Rey checked the *Miss Jana*'s electronics. A sea crossing required more data than a three-hour tour to the Rosário Islands. The laptop mounted on the helm booted up and connected to NOAA weather via satellite. He downloaded the latest data for the Eastern-Caribbean and did a double-take.

TS Bonnie developed from a tropical wave that left the coast of Africa on May 25. After forming on May 28 in the Main Development Region, it began rapidly intensifying as it moved west through the central tropical Atlantic. The storm intensified further as it entered the Caribbean Sea, with winds of seventy-five mph. This was the farthest east a hurricane has formed in June. In the following 24 hours, Bonnie is expected to rapidly intensify and become an extremely dangerous Category 3 hurricane.

"Shit!" Rey said. "Hurricane Bonnie. How appropriate. Where is she?" He waited for the current data to download from the satellite. He drummed on the ship's wheel, waiting for the images. The data speed of the satellite system was similar to an old dial-up modem, a piece of computer technology he had never experienced. The current location and the expected track of the storm appeared on the screen. The current position was approximately a hundred and twenty miles north of Curaçao, moving west-northwest at twenty-two miles per hour. In twenty-four hours, the forecasted track put the eye of Bonnie two hundred and forty miles north of Cartagena.

After a rudimentary calculation, Rey determined if he cruised at nine knots on his intended path for twenty-five hours, he would be in the eye of a cat two or cat three hurricane. He grinned. *I wonder how Dani would like that?*

The wheelhouse door opened suddenly. He quickly cleared the computer screen before realizing it was Bonita. "You startled me."

"You thought I was Miss Congeniality coming back?"

"I did." He laughed.

"It wasn't that funny."

"No. Well, kinda. She is a charmer, isn't she? What made me laugh is a tropical storm has formed, and it's moving westerly at twenty-two miles an hour. If it stays on course, and we stay on course, we'll run straight into the eye about this time tomorrow."

"We'll be in the eye? What's so funny about that?" Bonita's face turned to panic. Having lived on the Gulf Coast, she knew there was nothing funny about hurricanes.

"It's Hurricane Bonnie."

"Bullshit."

"I'm serious." Rey turned the computer screen on. "Look."

Bonita studied the screen and saw the name of the storm. "What the hell? That is funny." Her head twisted, and she looked at Rey. "You said if we stay on course. Won't we be back at the marina? Can't we wait for the storm to pass before we leave again?"

"I guess she didn't tell you. Change of plans. We're headed to Florida."

"What the...are you kidding? Straight into a hurricane? Is she nuts?"

"She doesn't know about the storm. I just downloaded the information."

"Well, tell her, and let's turn this boat around."

Rey pulled her close and kissed her on the lips. "That's for appearances. We must look like a couple, remember? Don't worry. I can slow the boat and the storm will be long gone before we get anywhere near it. I can also turn east and go around it."

"Which are you going to do?"

"I haven't decided."

"Jeez, Rey. Isn't it about time to decide?"

Rey sat on the high sofa behind the wheel and motioned for her to sit beside him. She sat sideways, facing him.

"Is this safe? Shouldn't you be steering?"

"It's on autopilot. All I have to do is watch that we aren't on a collision course with a tanker or cruise ship."

"That would be bad, but a collision course with a hurricane is okay?"

"It could be."

"How?"

"Hear me out. It could have been José shooting himself or another reason Dani jumped on a plane and flew here and escalated the timeline. From when she arrived until we left the dock, she had the real scuba tanks switched out with the tanks filled with drugs, and the gold weights loaded. I had the impression it was going to be at least two more days until they were ready. I'm not concerned about the gold, but I don't want the drugs to hit the streets. Your plan was brilliant. But now, you aren't going home. You can't contact the cops, so they won't be waiting for a location. You said your friend's phone numbers were in the phone you hid. When we get close, we could call them, but I doubt they'd have enough time to notify anyone. The drugs would be off the boat long before any type of law enforcement could get to us."

"My friends know a little about what's going on."

"How much did you tell them?"

"Not a lot. I didn't know too much until today. I knew it was drugs, and you were taking them to Florida."

"When you don't make it back to the hotel tonight, will they do anything?"

Bonita thought about what Alex would do. She knew he wouldn't contact the local authorities. He'd have Gabby text Juan and ask if he'd seen her. "I mentioned I might stay on the boat with you tonight. No, they wouldn't do anything. After a couple of days, they'd probably go to the cops. I don't know if they'd leave Cartagena without me. There's no way to get a message to them?"

"Not now. Our only chance would be if I'd swing close enough to Jamaica to get a cell signal. That's not likely. After that, we wouldn't be in range of a cell tower until we got to the Keys. By then, it would be too late."

"What are we going to do? You mentioned killing them, dumping the drugs, and going back to Florida. Is that an option?"

"Not anymore. Dani's been in contact with someone. I'm sure she's told them we're on our way. I can't say they disappeared with the drugs."

"Tell them Dani lied and took off."

"Too risky."

"Fuck! Do you have another plan?"

"Maybe. I need you to do something for me. Go to the galley. In the cabinet above the stove there's a bottle of Dramamine." Rey looked over her attire. "I don't know how you're going to do it with what you're wearing, but you need to sneak that bottle to the head in my cabin. In the cabinet, next to the tampon box, is a bottle of pills. It's a green bottle labeled Zinc. Switch out the pills. Put the tablets from the zinc bottle in the Dramamine bottle and the Dramamine pills in the zinc bottle. Then sneak the Dramamine bottle back here."

"Ah, so when the others get seasick and take a pill, they're only getting a zinc tablet. They'll still get sick."

"Not exactly. The pills in the zinc bottle are Rohypnol."

"Rohypnol! What the hell are you doing with a date rape drug?"

"Dramamine won't cure seasickness. It only prevents it. If we're on a cruise and we hit rough seas and someone becomes violently seasick, we give them a Rohypnol. It knocks them out. We only use it in the worst cases, but when it's needed, it's needed."

"I get it. The others will take Rohypnol thinking it's Dramamine. They'll be out in fifteen or twenty minutes and out for twelve hours or more."

"You know your drugs."

"I know roofies. I've been in places where they used it for other reasons."

"Do I want to know?"

"You don't."

"Fair enough." Rey looked through the window on the wheelhouse door. "They're all on the aft deck. Go now. If they should catch you either coming or going, tell them you're bringing the pills to me. Oh, leave a few of the Dramamine in the real bottle. The pills are similar, but if you look closely, you can tell the difference. We may need to take one to convince the others to take one."

"Got it." Bonita scampered out of the wheelhouse and disappeared into the galley. Rey checked the radar. There were no surface targets, meaning no boats were following them. He switched to weather radar. The Garmin Fantom Open Array Radar displayed weather images on the chartplotter map up to seventy miles out. The circular outer bands of Hurricane Bonnie were forty-five miles to the northeast.

Bonita returned with the bottle of Dramamine.

"Any problems?" Rey asked.

"None. They're all still on the aft deck. I just glanced, but it looked like they were having a heated discussion."

"They'll be coming in soon. We'll be in the crosshairs of the outer bands of the hurricane in a couple of hours. The sea is a little rough now. It won't be long and it's going to get nasty. When they come in, I want you to go get us a couple of bottles of water. When you get back, I'll have the two Dramamine out. Dani will be right behind you, asking about the rough seas. Before I answer, you and I'll take a pill. Then I'll tell her about the storm and how she ain't seen nothin' yet."

Bonita smiled. "And she'll demand pills for herself and the other guys."

"I'd bet my life on it."

"Then what? Do we turn around and head back to Cartagena?"

"Only to do this all over again when they wake up? Or have the guys who supplied the drugs waiting for us when we get to the dock? They wouldn't be happy. That's the best-case scenario. The other is that a patrol boat picks us up, and I spend the rest of my life in a Colombian prison. No thanks."

"We could be gone before they wake up. Leave the boat. Forget about it."

"They'd hire a new captain and take the boat and the drugs without me. I wouldn't know when or where the drop was going to be. I told you, I'm going to stop those drugs from getting to the US."

"You have a plan?"

Rey cringed. "I do. Maybe not a good plan, but a plan."

<h1 style="text-align:center">38</h1>

The sun set, casting a deep red glow over the Caribbean. Rey stared at the sky. "It's said, 'Red sky at night, sailor's delight.' Not tonight. It's going to be a mother out there before long."

"How long?" Bonita asked.

Rey could see the worry on her face. He eased the throttles back slightly, the same as he'd done every ten minutes for the past hour. The *Miss Jana* was now inching along at five knots instead of her cruising speed of nine. He decreased the speed slowly, so the others on board wouldn't notice the change in the engine's sound or the reduced speed.

"Not long. I've slowed us as much as I dare. Any slower and we'll bounce around more than I want. You should go get the water. I have a feeling Dani will waddle in here soon, complaining about the ride."

Bonita went to the galley for water. As Rey expected, Dani entered a few minutes later.

"What the hell is going on?" she demanded.

Rey handed Bonita a pill, then took one himself, making sure Dani could see what they were doing. "There's a storm ahead. It's going to get rough. We're taking Dramamine."

"Those are for seasickness, right?"

"Yep."

"Give me one. We all should take one."

Rey looked in the small jar and gently shook it. "There aren't many left. I should save them. Maybe Carlos can have one. He'll have to drive the boat while I sleep."

Dani snatched the pill container from Rey's hand. He offered minor resistance. At the same time, the boat breached the side of a wave, leaned heavily to port, then to starboard. Dani braced herself against the wall, then staggered out of the wheelhouse. Rey watched her wave Carlos and Alberto over.

"Just like taking candy from a baby. Except she's the baby, and they just ate the candy." Rey made eye contact with Bonita and smiled.

"Now what? You haven't told me your plan."

"I'm going to scuttle the boat."

"What? Scuttle. Doesn't that mean sink?"

"It does."

"Rey, what the fuck. If I wanted to swim, I would've jumped off the boat in Cartagena."

"You won't have to swim. You and I will get in the life raft."

"In a life raft? Are you shitting me? You want me to get into a life raft in the middle of the ocean?"

"That's the plan."

"Fuck that. It's a dumb idea to begin with, but in the middle of a hurricane. Uh-huh. At least turn the boat around and get us close to land."

"You'll be fine. It'll be like a SeaWorld ride for a while, but you'll be okay."

Bonita stared at him. "You're serious, aren't you?"

"Yes, ma'am."

"Why? I mean, why here? Let's head toward an island and sink the boat when we get close. In daylight."

"I want her to sink in the deepest part of the Caribbean. That's where we are. We could try to get close to an island, but what if we're boarded by the local coast guard? If they find the drugs, we end up in a hole-in-the-wall prison. No thanks."

Bonita wiped her sweaty palms on her denim shorts. "How long will we be in the raft?"

"Less than a day. When I'm confident the boat has sunk, I'll activate the EPIRB. We are still close to Colombia. It shouldn't take long for the Coast Guard to find us."

"What's an EPIRB?"

"It's an Emergency Position Indicating Radio Beacon. When I

activate it, it'll transmit a signal that'll notify search and rescue teams of our exact location. We should be found in a matter of hours."

"Rey…I'm scared."

"You need to trust me." He slid off the seat and looked out the door toward the main salon. "I'm going to check on the others. Stay here. Keep an eye out for any lights in front of us. There's nothing on the radar but keep watch."

Rey went into the main salon where Dani, Carlos, and Alberto were sitting. They all looked a little green around the gills. "You guys all right?"

"I'm not feeling well. Tired too," Carlos replied.

"Dramamine can make you drowsy. You should get some rest. I'll wake you when I need you to take over. All of you should go to a cabin and try to sleep. There's usually less roll below decks."

"I'm not sure…I should…okay, maybe I'll go below," Dani said. Her eyelids were heavy.

The trio made their way down the steps. When the boat rolled, Rey expected them to end up in a pile at the bottom of the steps. It didn't happen. He went back to the wheelhouse. "In about fifteen minutes, they'll be out."

"Rey," Bonita said solemnly. "Are you going to kill them?"

"Not exactly."

"You're going to sink the boat and let them die. Same thing."

"Dani has José's Glock in her belt and threatened to use it. Carlos is more than happy to put thousands of Fentanyl tablets on the street, endangering the lives of everyone who gets one, including kids. Didn't Alberto say he planned to fuck you before they killed you?"

"He did."

Rey sat on the sofa next to her. "Bonnie, what would you do with them?"

She looked deep into his eyes and brushed a few strands of his reddish-blonde hair to the side. "Couldn't we tie them up and go to Miami? When we get in cell range, call the feds and set up a bust, like the original plan."

"Except in the original plan, Dani didn't know who set them up. I was going to get hauled away too, then quietly released. Dani has contacts. When they find out what we did, we're as good as dead. If we let them go down with the boat, everyone will assume the boat sunk in the hurricane, and the crew lost."

"If they think you're dead, no one comes after you."

"Bingo."

"What about the other partner Dani mentioned? Does he know you? If so, eventually you're going to run into him."

"Remember, there's a money flow issue too. There are cartel people who expect payment once delivery is made. When they don't get it, they'll come looking for it. They're going to be looking for Dani and her partner. The partner will either skip town, if he's lucky, or they'll find him. I'm betting nobody knows me. It's Dani and the partner they'll be after. When I get back, I'll lie low for a few days. I'll get ahold of my brother and explain what happened. Maybe JP or my brother knows who the partner is. If they do, they can watch him. When he disappears—"

"What about your girlfriend?"

Rey's gaze dropped. "I'm going to have to talk to her. She won't be happy, but she'll get it. Technically, we're still together. That's because we haven't been around each other for the past few months to break up. When we officially split, it'll be hard. We are very different, but she's...enough about her. We need to get off the boat."

His sudden change in direction surprised Bonita. "What should I do?"

"Right now. Nothing."

Rey left the wheelhouse and went to the guest cabins. He found Dani lying half on the bed, snoring. He removed the Glock from her waist, then moved to the next cabin. Carlos was able to put his gun on the nightstand next to the bed before he passed out. He took the gun and went to find Alberto. He didn't find a gun and couldn't remember Alberto having one. He hoped it wouldn't matter.

He went to the aft deck, tossed the guns overboard, opened the storage locker, and removed a large orange zippered valise that contained a six-person life raft. An outer band from Hurricane Bonnie pelted the boat with wind and rain. The wind-driven rain stung his face as he lashed the bag to a cleat with a dock line. Once the raft bag was secure, he hurried back inside the main salon.

"Bonnie," he yelled over the increasing roar of the storm. She came out of the wheelhouse when she heard him. "Go get your phone. There are Ziplock bags in the galley. Wrap the phone tight. Grab a shirt and your purse too. Under the bed, there's a large orange duffle bag. Bring it up and put in several bottles of water and any food you can find. Food that's easy to eat. Nuts, chips, cookies, whatever you can find. Meet me in the main salon. I'm going below to open the seacocks and turn off the bilge pumps."

The boat rode up a rogue wave and dropped off the backside with a resounding thud. The wind howled through the cabin.

"Rey, are you sure about this? There's no other way? You're losing the boat, too."

Rey glanced at the interior of the boat. "I wish there was another way. I've got a lot of memories in here. We gotta do this. Oh, the life jackets are under the settee. Get one out and put it on. Leave one for me and put the rest on the aft deck."

"Anything else?"

"No. I'll be right back." Rey scurried down the steps. Bonita lifted the settee. She found twelve fluorescent orange life jackets with reflective panels, all neatly stowed in two rows of six. The jackets seemed to be the same size. She undid the clip, loosened the nylon belt, and slipped the jacket on. The back of the jacket pushed her head forward. She frowned at the flimsiness of the fittings. "This is going to save my life?" she whispered.

With the strap clipped and the belt tightened, she tossed one jacket on the settee for Rey. She carried the others, five at a time, and tossed them onto the aft deck. A gust of wind swirled the bright orange floatation devices around the deck. The boat rocked side to side. Bonita sat quivering on the sofa inside the salon. The boat pitched. She held the arms of the sofa in a death grip. The boat settled. She put the canvas bag with food, water, and a Ziplock-protected phone between her legs and waited for Rey. She attempted to swallow, but her mouth was dry.

Rey came up from below, grabbed a life jacket, and put it on. "You ready?" He pulled on her arm until she stood, then she wrapped her arms around him.

"Don't worry. I gotcha." He led her to the aft deck and sat her in a lounge chair. She sat but held on to Rey's arms. The wind was still howling, but the rain had eased. "Hang on. I need to do a few more things. I won't be long." He twisted his arm from her grasp, ran to the wheelhouse, put the engines in neutral, and sprinted back to the aft deck. He opened the new storage locker Dani's crew had installed and removed two dive belts, each with five black dive weights attached. After he untied the raft from the cleat, he pushed the bag toward the opening to the swim platform. The boat rolled in the heavy seas, and the bag slid through the opening, landing on the platform.

Bonita screamed.

Rey followed the bag to the swim platform. Waves crashed over the platform, pushing the bag toward the edge. He wiped the saltwater from his eyes and removed a flap on the small end of the valise. He pulled the painter line out, wrapped it around a cleat, and let a wave push the bag into the water.

"Rey! The raft!" Bonita screamed from the deck above him.

"It's okay. That's how it inflates." He pulled the painter line until taut. The uninflated raft drifted fifty feet behind the boat.

From her position on the deck, Bonita couldn't see the long black strap that attached the raft to the boat. "Rey! It's floating away," she yelled in an abrupt, disjointed, staccato voice, easily heard over the storm.

Rey ignored her. When he'd pulled out all the painter line, he gave it a fast, sharp pull. Nothing happened. He yanked the line again. The raft inflated and burst from the valise. A small locator light activated. He tugged the line, pulling the raft back to the boat. Once back at the boat, he slid it onto the swim platform and secured it. He went back up the steps to Bonita.

"Can you make it?" he asked her.

"I don't know." She was still shaking and breathing heavily.

Rey helped her down the steps and into the raft. "I'll be right back.

Don't go anywhere." He looked at her, hoping his attempt at humor would ease her fear. It didn't. He ran back up the steps and grabbed the orange duffle bag. On the aft deck, he put the two dive belts over his shoulder and headed back to the raft. Bonita was in the fetal position near the back. He tossed the duffle bag beside her, then laid the weight belts off to the side.

"One more thing." He disappeared out the door, ran to the wheelhouse, and checked the cruise control to confirm their current heading would put the *Miss Jana* on a collision course with Hurricane Bonnie. The boat and the storm would meet in ten hours–if she stayed afloat. Under the helm, he grabbed the bright yellow waterproof ditch bag. He pushed the throttles to three-quarters, then sprinted across the main salon, over the aft deck, and down the steps. He pushed on the raft, but the combination of the raft's weight, Bonita, and the dive weights made it too heavy. It wouldn't budge. He positioned himself between the stern and the raft and used his legs to push. "Fuck!" He stuck his head inside the door. "Bonnie, you need to come out." He extended his hand to her.

Bonita crawled to the opening. With a shaking hand, she grabbed his hand and stepped out. Rey pushed on the raft. It inched closer to the edge of the swim platform. He kept pushing until the raft was half off the platform, and then he told her to get back in. The raft tipped, throwing her against the side. Another gust of wind battered the raft, blowing more sea spray inside.

A wave crashed over the swim platform. Rey gave the raft another hard shove. It slid into the water and quickly separated from the boat, which was cruising north at nine knots. He dove and swam toward the door to the raft. Waves pounded the raft, filling the inside with seawater. He climbed the boarding ramp, slid inside, grabbed the knife from the pocket on the side of the raft, and cut the painter line. He took one last look at his boat and zipped the canopy door closed. The inside of the raft was dimly lit by the locator light glowing through the top of the raft. Rey turned to Bonita, who was curled into a ball, soaked and shivering. Damp hair stuck to the sides of her face. He crawled to her and wrapped his arms around her. She snuggled against his warm body.

The small raft lurched violently, throwing the water inside the raft against them. Rey put his hand under Bonita's chin and propped her head up. He wiped her hair from her face and kissed her. "Are you okay?"

She nodded. "I...I should have gone to the bathroom. I need to pee."

"There's water in the raft. Go ahead. I'll bail it all out when you're finished."

"Pee in the raft?"

"There's no bathroom. You don't have a lot of choice. Unless you want to hang out the door. Or you can pee in the bailing bucket and I'll dump it."

"The bucket sounds okay. This is embarrassing." Bonita stifled a laugh. She hoped Rey couldn't see her in the dim light. She thought about the many men who had paid her to urinate on them. It seemed silly to be embarrassed to pee in a bucket in front of him.

The raft rode up a wave, dropped, spun, and rocked. It was more violent than the steady rocking they'd been experiencing. "This is what a SeaWorld ride is like?" Bonita asked, her voice sounding calmer over the howling wind.

"I don't know. Never been."

"If it is, I'm never going. Where's the bucket?"

Rey opened the survival equipment pouch attached to the side of the raft. He found the fabric-bailing bucket and handed it to her.

"That's cute. It's not what I was expecting. Is there any toilet paper in there?"

"No, but you're soaked. Toilet paper wouldn't be much good anyway. There are a couple of terrycloth towels. After I bail out the raft and get it as dry as I can with the sponges, you can use one to dry yourself. You shouldn't sit in wet clothes all night."

Bonita unzipped her shorts and wiggled out of them, then removed her panties. She got to her knees, faced Rey, and straddled the bucket. The raft rocked. Rey grabbed the edges of the life jacket to steady her. When she finished peeing, she unzipped the door and dumped the contents of the bucket into the Caribbean. She zipped the door up. A wave slammed against the raft, causing it to list sharply to one side. She dropped the bucket and fell into the water covering the floor of the raft. Before she could get up, another wave crashed onto the top of the raft, partially collapsing it. The raft spun, bobbed, and rocked in the turbulent surf and gusting wind. "Rey?"

"Yeah?"

"Are we going to make it through the night?"

39

Neither Jana nor Alexander were in the mood to go out. The lunch from room service had been excellent so they decided to use it again and order dinner along with a good bottle of wine, not the cheap stuff in the mini-fridge. After dinner, Jana refilled their wine glasses and turned off the room lights to kill the reflection in the big window. She sat on the couch and snuggled next to Alexander to admire the lights of Cartagena.

"Bonita's on the boat with Rey. What do we do?"

"We wait. Bon said they were going to make three trips to the dive site before actually loading the drugs and heading for Florida."

"Ugh, waiting. I have no problem hanging around and not doing anything at home, but here, now, jeez. The stuff on television that's in English sucks. We've walked around the Walled City. I'm a little sunburnt from the boat ride yesterday. I don't want to go outside. I'm worried about Rey. It's going to be a long three days."

"We'll find something to do."

"I have an idea, but you haven't been too receptive so far." Jana put her arm around Alexander's neck and kissed him. He momentarily returned the kiss, then pushed her away.

"You really don't want to make love with me, do you?"

"Oh, I do, in the worst way."

"Why do you keep pushing me away?"

"Jana, another time, and another place, you couldn't keep me off you. But this isn't right. I'm not attached, but, technically, you are. I know you and Rey have been drifting apart, but you're still together. We need to see what happens over the next few days...."

"You're saying you don't want to sleep with me? Even after what happened between Rey and Bonita?"

"Nothing happened between them."

"No, but Bonita said it almost did. Rey wanted to. That's almost the same as doing it."

"Almost, but not the same. They didn't. Even if they did, we shouldn't. When we make love, it won't be for revenge, pity, loneliness, or any other reason. It'll be because it's the right time."

Jana leaned over and kissed him again. He wasn't so quick to push her away this time.

"I understand," she said. "A lot's happening right now."

"A lot. If I'm honest, had you dropped the towel last night, I'd have carried you to the bed. You suggested I take a cold shower. Tonight, you seem to want to hop in bed. Is it because of Rey and Bon?"

"Maybe. Maybe I'm bored...or horny."

"You're such a romantic. How can I resist?"

Jana slid one leg up his thigh, exposing the entirety of her long, slender leg from beneath the soft mini-skirt. "Very funny. I do like that you said, 'When,' not 'if.'"

"I have to see how this plays out with Rey. If you guys officially split after you've seen him again, and you're still interested in me when all this is over, I'll be ready, willing, and able. If you guys don't split, I'll regret not carrying you to the bed right now, but I won't regret not taking advantage of you."

"Awe. You know, that's so romantic. Would it help if I said I'm ninety-nine percent sure Rey and I are through? I had a strong feeling before, but after what Bonita said, I know it."

"Bon is pretty. She was there. Rey thinks he's going to be killed any day. It's hard to blame him for his desire. You need to give him credit for what he didn't do."

Jana buried her head in Alexander's chest. "Except the credit goes to Bonita...and lack of opportunity."

"No argument from me. But his life is in danger."

"I know. I know. She is beautiful. He may die. I'm scared. I'm pissed. I'm jealous. Rey, hold me like you'll never let me go."

"Uh, I'm Alex," he said nonchalantly, knowing Rey was on her mind. There was no need to read anything more into it or make a fuss over it.

"Oh, shit! I'm so sorry, Alex." Jana jerked away and stared at him, red from embarrassment.

He pulled her close, and she nestled her head against his chest. He felt the warmth of her breath seeping through his shirt. He wrapped his arms around her and sat in silence, letting her find comfort in him. Slowly, their breathing fell into a synchronized rhythm, bringing a sense of peace and calm to both of them.

Jana whispered, "I know I just called you by the wrong name. Please forgive me. But I need you. YOU, Alex. Don't make me beg."

He didn't.

***

Colombia doesn't observe Daylight Savings Time. In early June in Cartagena, the sun rises at 5:40 a.m. By six a.m. the sun was blasting through the large window in Alexander and Jana's hotel room. A ding and buzz from a cell phone woke her. She opened her eyes, moaned loudly, and squeezed them shut.

Her moan woke Alexander. He opened his eyes, squinted, and looked at the window. "We forgot to close the curtain last night."

"Oh my God, that's so bright. I'm glad I'm not hungover." Her phone dinged again. Then his. "Geez," Jana said, "it's six in the fucking morning. Who's sending us messages?" She grabbed her phone from the nightstand between the beds. "It's Gabby."

Alexander sat up in bed. "What does she want?"

"She's asking if we've heard from Bon. They were planning to go out again last night, but she never heard from her."

Alexander closed his eyes for a few seconds to clear his head. "Ask her if she's heard from Juan. Maybe she's with him."

Jana typed the message and waited. Her phone buzzed, and she read the message. "She has. He hasn't heard from her since he dropped her off at the marina yesterday morning."

"It might be nothing to worry about. Maybe she spent the night on the boat with Rey." After he said it, Alexander wished he hadn't. Jana didn't need a reminder.

"Maybe," Jana said, rolling her eyes. Her phone buzzed again. "Gabby says Juan went to the marina as soon as she texted him. The boat's not there."

Alexander leaned forward. "That's not good."

"What does it mean?"

"They could have spent the night at the islands. But I have a feeling they may have left."

"Left?"

"For Florida. Or wherever they're going."

"Does that affect the plan to have the feds intercept them?"

"If they left? No. It moves the timeline up a few days."

"Will it still work?"

"No reason it wouldn't. They need Rey to drive the boat. As long as he lets us know when and where the drop is, I can get the feds there. My only concern is they make the drop offshore. The others switch boats and they no longer need Rey or the *Miss Jana*."

When Jana's hands began to shake, Alexander wrapped his arms around her. He could feel her heart racing. "Are you okay?"

"Alex, I'm scared. Terrified. I'm burning up. Will you turn the AC down?"

He felt her forehead. It felt warm, but not hot. She didn't have a fever. He turned the air conditioner down several degrees. "Can you shower? It might make you feel better."

"It would, but I don't know. I feel nauseous and weak, like I'm going to faint."

"Do you want me to help you?"

"You better."

Naked from the night before, Alexander helped her off the bed and led her to the bathroom. He turned on the shower and adjusted the water temperature, then helped her into the shower stall and stepped in with her.

"Let me lean against you," Jana said. "Hold me." She used a

washcloth to soap her body, then scooted forward to let the water rinse her. Her breathing steadied. "I'm feeling better. Thanks, Alex. I don't know what happened."

"Panic attack." Alexander turned off the water and grabbed two towels hanging next to the shower. He patted her dry, then himself. She took a towel and wrapped it around herself. She held onto his arm as they stepped out of the shower enclosure. "Can you walk?" he asked.

"I think so. Maybe. I need to brush my teeth."

Alexander finished drying himself while Jana brushed her teeth. He slipped on a pair of briefs and waited for her to finish.

"Help me to bed," she said after spitting out the toothpaste residue. "I need to lie down a minute."

Alexander held her arm while she warily walked to the bed. She laid down and covered herself with a sheet. "The worst seems to be over," he said.

"That was strange. Nothing like that has ever happened to me."

"Your emotions did a Wile E. Coyote."

"Huh?"

"Ran straight into a brick wall. It's been a tough couple of days."

Jana scrunched up her face. "Okay…With tougher days to follow. If they go straight to Florida, it'll take them five or six days, depending on how hard Rey pushes her."

"The first thing we have to do is confirm they actually left. I'd say we give them another twenty-four hours, maybe forty-eight, then go back to the States and wait for Rey or Bon to text us and let us know where they are."

"If they're in the islands, maybe they have service and they'll let us know what's going on."

Alexander didn't think she sounded very convincing. "I'll text Bat and see if those other two phones that were with Rey are still hitting off towers in Cartagena. If they are, it means they're still in the area. Maybe they went to get more fuel."

Jana frowned. "Which means we wait. I wish we could do something other than wait."

"We should call Gabby and have her take us sightseeing."

"Sightseeing? Seriously?"

"You have a better idea? If we just sit in the hotel for two days, we'll go crazy. Besides, if we hear from Juan, Gabby can translate."

Jana sat up and took deep breaths until she felt steadier. "Text Gabby. I'll get dressed."

40

By midnight, the worst of the storm was well north of Rey and Bonita. An occasional steep-sided wave and gale force gust would slam and rock the small raft, but the gusts became fewer and fewer. By the time Rey had the floor inflated and dry, the wind had all but died. Bonita fell asleep first. Exhaustion and Dramamine won out over adrenaline. She slept on her side, her back against him, her legs touching his. She pushed the life jacket up and formed a pillow out of the collar.

Rey had one arm under his head, and the other draped over Bonita. The thick life jackets kept their torsos separated. He could feel the warmth and smoothness of her legs on his. It reminded him of the night Jana snuck onto the boat, crept down the steps, and crawled into bed with him. Her legs were soft and warm.

He and Jana had been inseparable for over a year before they began drifting apart. It started slowly. He'd be restless and would spend the night on the boat. First, only a couple of nights here and there. Then it became most nights. Their communication was mostly via text messages. How he longed to be sitting in her condo, looking at the ocean, bored. He drifted off, thinking about her. In a deep sleep, he dreamed of the girl he was holding, the girl he knew as Bonnie.

Hurricane Bonnie continued northwest, pulling her outer bands with her. By morning, the eye of the storm was three hundred miles northwest of the small raft floating sixty miles north of the Colombian border. What little breeze that remained came from the west. The sea was calm, with small, slow-rolling waves.

Rey woke to the gentle sway of the raft and smiled. They had survived the night. The six-person life raft fit two comfortably. He had dried and inflated the floor with the manual air pump from the life raft's survival kit. During the night, Bonita had rolled over and was now facing him. The thickness of the life jackets still separated them, her leg entrenched between his. Her head rested on his arm. From the orange glow emanating from the east side of the top of the raft, he knew morning had dawned. After the torrid night, it would have been easy to sleep late into the day.

Rey enjoyed holding the half-naked woman who slept next to him. He knew any movement on his part would wake her, and he knew she needed her sleep. But, he needed to take care of a full bladder. He slowly slid his arm out from under Bonita's head, rotated, and eased her leg off his. The force caused her to roll onto her back. He crawled over her and gingerly unzipped the door of the raft, hoping the sound of the zipper wouldn't wake her. The seas were calm, and the sky was clear. A slight breeze cooled the air. He stepped out of the raft and onto the boarding ramp, held onto the lifeline, and relieved himself. When he finished, he sat on the upper buoyancy tube and stared at the ocean.

He pictured the *Miss Jana* motoring off, slowly filling with seawater from the open seacocks. She would ride lower and lower in the water as she headed into the storm. The wind and waves would get stronger as she sailed north. The boat would be buffeted until a large wave crashed over the aft deck and filled the main salon with water. With the added weight, the boat would heel over, allowing more water to rush in. She would disappear below the surface and sink to the bottom of the Caribbean.

Rey thought about Dani, Carlos, and Alberto. More than likely, the Rohypnol had worked, and they never woke up. When the water reached them, it may have awakened them but they would have been in the dark and disoriented. Without the roofie, they might have been able to find their way up the steps and off the boat. Without life jackets and near the eye of a hurricane, they wouldn't have lasted long. Rey closed his eyes and tried to imagine what they would have gone through.

A hand wrapped around his neck. He jumped, screamed, twisted, lost his balance, and fell backward into the water. Bonita screamed and reached for him. She grabbed his life jacket and pulled him back to the boarding ramp.

"I'm so sorry, Rey."

Rey wiped the saltwater from his eyes. "Jesus! I was sitting there thinking about the people we left on the boat when I felt your hand. It scared the hell out of me."

Bonita disappeared inside the raft and returned with a terrycloth towel which she handed to him. She bit her lip to suppress her smile. "I'm sorry. I didn't mean to scare you. The zipper woke me, and I guessed what you were doing. At least I waited until you finished."

"That was ladylike of you." Rey's breathing and heartbeat returned to normal.

"It was." Bonita smiled. "Except I need to pee too. I guess I should do what you did. It isn't very ladylike. More so than the bucket."

Rey crawled into the raft. "There's a boarding ramp just under the surface. Stand on it, face me, I'll hold you, and you can squat into the water. It'll be as ladylike as possible on a ten-foot raft."

Bonita laughed. She eased herself out the door and turned around. Rey held her outstretched hands as she lowered her bottom into the sea. "Nothing's going to bite me?"

"Not likely. The only thing out this far are sharks."

Bonita jerked her butt out of the water, causing a large splash. "Sharks?"

"Relax. The chances of a shark attacking as you're peeing are slim." He neglected to tell her sharks attacking life rafts, deflating them, and eating the occupants wasn't all that uncommon.

Bonita finished her business and climbed back inside the raft. After she dried herself off, she checked her shorts that had been sitting on top of the survival equipment pack. They were dry enough. She put her panties and shorts on. "You know, there's not much to these shorts, but I feel much better with them on."

"You felt naked without them?"

"Funny. But I did. Did you look at me?"

Rey flashed a sly grin. "I did. Reluctantly."

"I figured you would. That's okay. But you didn't touch. I appreciate it."

"Not exactly. When I woke up this morning, my hand was resting on your ass. As far as I know, that's all I touched. That's all I remember, anyway."

"Rey, you are the sweetest guy." She leaned over and pecked him on the lips.

"Now you want to get romantic after you've put your shorts on. Just my luck."

"Oh. Sorry about that. Bad timing, I guess."

"Tell me, Bonnie, who's the other guy?"

"Uh?"

"When we first met, you said your heart belonged to someone else."

"If it's all the same, Rey, I'd rather not talk about it."

"That's fine. He must be special."

"Why do you say that?"

"I like you. A lot. I have from the moment we met. You seem to like me, but you're in love with someone, which is why we haven't...you know. Here we are, stuck out in the middle of the Caribbean, you half-naked. It seems logical we'd—"

"You've watched too many James Bond movies, Rey."

"True. I am a Bond fan. For the record, I would like to get up close and personal with your feather."

"Believe it or not, Rey, I'd love that. But not now. How 'bout this? If it doesn't work out with the other person, I'll call you and you can check out my feather as long as you'd like."

"Sounds good to me. I almost wish you hadn't said that, though. My heart's racing."

"Oops, sorry. Let's change the subject. Have you done the plerb thing?"

He blushed, assuming plerb was slang for something sexual. "I...uh...don't know what that is?"

"The thing you said you had, so we can get rescued."

Rey laughed. "Oh, the EPIRB. I haven't. It's time." He opened the green ditch bag he brought from the wheelhouse, pulled out an odd-shaped tubular device, and attached it to the lanyard from the bag. He flipped the red flap and pressed the button. A green LED on the top of the unit flashed. He tossed the unit into the sea.

"Rey!" Bonita yelled.

"Don't worry. It floats. It has to be vertical and have a clear view of the sky. It'll float along with us."

Bonita sat at the door, watching the EPIRB bob in the water. "How's that little thing going to get us rescued?"

"It may sound like I'm mansplaining, but it sends a signal to satellites. The satellites calculate our position and send it to local users who send out the alert with our position to rescue services like the Coast Guard. Any ships in the area may get the alerts, too."

"So, it shouldn't take long for us to be found?"

"It shouldn't. Which reminds me. We need a story."

"What do you mean, a story?"

"When we're picked up, most likely by the Colombian Coast Guard, they're going to ask what happened. We need to have a story and be consistent. They may talk to us separately. We need to have the same story."

"Oh shit. You're right. We can't tell them what actually happened."

"No, we can't. Our story needs to be easy to remember. We tell them what happened but change a few facts. Here's what we should say. You and I are friends. We met a guy in Fort Lauderdale who was cruising the Caribbean on his yacht, and he offered to take us for a token fee. It was cheap. We said it sounded like an adventure. Say his name was Carlos. You couldn't leave Florida at the time, so I came with him. We went to The Bahamas, Turks and Caicos, Jamaica, and then Cartagena. You flew in and met us. We've been here for four days. Did a little diving at Rosario and sightseeing in Cartagena. Yesterday, we were heading back to Florida. With me so far?"

"Yes. Just curious. Why didn't I come on the boat with you from Florida?"

"You flew in, right?"

"Yes."

"Which means there's a record of you entering the country. We never cleared customs. I was told where to take the boat and customs never came looking for us. If anyone asks, that's what I'll tell them too. That's why there's no record of me entering Colombia."

"It sounds plausible."

"Yesterday, around noon, we started back to Florida. We'd been underway for several hours. It was getting dark. The boat lost all power. Carlos didn't know what the problem was, but water was coming in. He wasn't too worried about it and said he could fix it. But he deployed the life raft, put us and a bunch of stuff in it. It was windy, and the sea was rough. We were getting bounced around, so we zipped the door and huddled together until we fell asleep. When we woke up this morning, Carlos and the boat were gone. The seas had calmed. We sat for a while, wondering what to do. I looked through the stuff in the raft and found the EPIRB and turned it on."

"That's a good story, Rey. I'd believe it."

"It's simple, with enough detail to be believable. Don't say it exactly as I said it. It will sound rehearsed. But don't add too much more."

"What about the name of the boat, if they ask? Do we say it was the *Miss Jana*?"

Rey stared out the door at the empty sea. "No, we shouldn't. Let's call it, 'Missing Exes.'"

"Missing Exes? What an odd name for a boat."

"I knew a guy in Miami who would get involved with a woman, she'd leave him, and he'd miss her. To fill the void, he'd go boat shopping and buy a bigger boat. After the third boat, he was trying to come up with a name and a friend suggested 'Missing My Exes.' He shortened it to 'Missing Exes.'"

"That's funny. Still, it's a strange name."

"We could say the name was 'Wet Dream.' Every guy with a big boat and a small dick names his boat 'Wet Dream.'"

"Missing Exes, it is. Oh, by the way, in case you're asked, my real name is Bonita. I go by Bonnie. My last name is Alvarez."

"I'm Reymundo Cruz. It's nice to meet you, Bonita Alvarez."

"The pleasure is mine, Mr. Cruz."

Rey smiled. "One more thing. Are we boyfriend and girlfriend?"

"Uh...Rey...I—"

"Bonnie, for our story. Are we a couple?"

Bonita blushed. "Oh. Yes, of course. Uh...we've known each other for a year. This was kind of an anniversary trip. Next time, sweetie, we're taking a Disney cruise, like I wanted to."

"Yes, dear."

The sound of an approaching helicopter interrupted the playful banter. Rey and Bonita squeezed through the opening in the raft and scanned the sky. The chopper made a wide circle around the raft. When the pilot saw Bonita frantically waving, he maneuvered closer and lower. When the helicopter was twenty yards from the raft and ten yards above the water, a man in a black wetsuit dropped from the side of the craft.

He swam to the raft. "Are you all right?" he asked in Spanish.

"Sí, sí," Rey and Bonita yelled over the sound of the helicopter's rotors.

"The closest patrol boat is two hours away. We are going to airlift you out."

"What?" Bonita exclaimed, her eyes wide with fear. "You mean lift us to the helicopter?"

"Yes, ma'am."

"Shit. I'm afraid of heights. Can we wait for a boat?"

"Sorry. We can't leave you out here. You'll be fine. It's not scary."

The diver signaled the crew on the helicopter to lower the harness. Once Bonita was strapped in, he signaled again, and she ascended. Inside the raft, Rey slid the weights off the belt and stuck one in each in the deep pockets of his cargo shorts. He pulled Bonita's purse from the duffle bag and stuck it in a pocket with the weight.

"What about the raft and the stuff in it?" Rey asked the diver.

"A boat will pick it up and take it to Cartagena. You can claim it there."

The cable came back down, and Rey was lifted into the helicopter. When he was safely aboard, they brought the diver up. After the diver was unbuckled from the long line, Rey shouted toward Bonita. "That wasn't so bad, was it?"

Bonita glared at him, furious. "The next time I say we're taking a Disney cruise, we take a fucking cruise."

41

There's a fine line between being angry and being scared. Anger stems from frustration, injury, or a perceived injustice. Fear is triggered by the perception of an imminent threat. Bonita had a genuine fear of heights. Even though the doors were closed, and she was buckled in, she was just as afraid in the helicopter as she was in the raft. Her expression did not hide her fear. The crew of the Colombian Coast Guard's Airbus AS365N3+ Dauphin rescue helicopter mistook her expression for anger.

The ride from where they were plucked out of the sea took thirty minutes. When the helicopter landed at Base Naval ARC "Bolivar" in Cartagena, Bonita was relieved but decided to continue to look angry at Rey. It was easy to do.

An ambulance greeted the helicopter. The EMT waited for the rescued couple and despite their insistence they were fine, he took their vital signs. An officer and two enlisted men watched. The EMT finally proclaimed that, yes, their vitals were indeed fine.

The officer was tall, slender, and young. Not much older than Rey. Bonita gave him a slight smile. He flashed a grin, then looked at Rey, who was several inches shorter but twice as big. In Spanish, he politely asked both to accompany him to the office.

It may have sounded like a request, but they knew resistance was not an option. The three followed the two enlisted men to an SUV parked at the edge of the heliport. Rey, Bonita, and the officer got in the back seat, Bonita in the middle. The officer tried not to look, but the allure of her long legs and the peacock feather rising from her shorts was too much of a temptation. He held his phone, pretending to be reading messages, but his focus was on Bonita.

The base offices were a two-minute ride away. The officer led them to the building and into a small conference room. "Please have a seat. Can I get you anything?"

"Water would be great," Bonita said. She offered him a half-smile and puppy-dog eyes, then glared at Rey in an effort to keep up her anger ruse.

The officer left the room and returned a few minutes later with two water bottles and another officer. He passed out the bottles and sat across from Bonita. The other officer sat at the end of the table.

"Whenever we do a rescue, we have to do a report," the first officer said. "I'll need some basic information and a statement about what happened."

"I'll tell you what happened," Bonita said gruffly. "My cheap-ass boyfriend wouldn't take me on a Disney cruise like I wanted. He said going on a yacht would be more fun. An adventure. Cheaper, too." She glared at Rey.

The officers couldn't contain their laughter. "Please. We need to start at the beginning. What are your names?"

"Bonita Alvarez."

"Reymundo Cruz."

The officer filled in the form on the desk in front of him. "Where are you from?"

"We're both from Fort Lauderdale, Florida," Bonita said.

He looked up from the form and stared at her. "You're American?"

"Yes."

"Your Spanish is excellent."

"Rey is from Puerto Rico. I was born in Bogota."

The officer's face lit up. "You're Colombian?"

"Yes. I left when I was young and became a US citizen."

Rey glanced at her but said nothing.

"Do you have any identification?"

"Uh, no, it was on the boat."

"Wait, I have your purse." Rey pulled the small bag from his pocket and handed it to her. She fumbled through it until she found her Texas driver's license. She handed it to the officer.

"Texas?"

"That's where I was living when I moved to Lauderdale. I haven't gotten a Florida license yet. Oh, my phone. Do you have a charger?"

The officer looked at the phone, then handed it to the other officer. "See if you can find a charger that fits," he told him, then he copied Bonita's information onto the form. "What's your current address?"

"2911 Biscayne Drive." Bonita didn't know if the address existed. The numbers were from the address of the bar in Houston. Biscayne Drive sounded Floridian.

"That's my address as well," Rey said.

"Neither of you have a passport?"

"No, they're in our bag on the boat," Bonita said.

"I'll need your social security numbers and dates of birth. Before you leave, we'll photograph you. You need to let us know where you're staying. The US embassy will help you get the documents you need to return to the States."

Rey and Bonita gave the officer the information. He entered the data on a form and made notes on a legal pad then leaned back in the chair. "Okay. Tell me what you two were doing in a life raft in the Caribbean."

Because he was looking at Bonita, she answered. Rey listened intently so he could repeat her version of the incident if necessary. He was proud of her. She kept to the script they'd discussed while in the raft, with little ad-lib or deviation.

"...And when we woke up this morning, the boat was gone." Bonita took a long drink of water.

The officer finished writing and looked at her. "You don't know what might have happened to the boat?"

Bonita forced a frown and made her lower lip quiver. She looked at Rey, then back at the officer. "No. When we realized the boat was gone and there was no sign of Carlos, we hoped he fixed whatever was wrong with the boat and then couldn't find us in the storm. But...we both have a feeling...um..."

"You think the boat sunk with him on it?"

Bonita lowered her head and nodded.

"We'll issue a lookout for the boat, but an early-season hurricane went through last night. It was north of where they found you. The seas were rough, as you mentioned in your statement. If the boat was floundering and got hit by high winds, it wouldn't have had a chance. What did you say the name of the boat was?"

"I didn't. Sorry. It's 'Missing Exes.'" Bonita said "missing" and "exes" in English. She repeated the story of the name.

"Odd name. I guess he's the missing ex now," the officer said in decent English.

"You speak English," Bonita said, her smile returning.

"I do. I trained at the US Coast Guard Academy in Connecticut. It was a joint operation between us and the US." The officer paused and looked at the form in front of him. "I have all I need. I'm glad you're okay, and we'll keep looking for your friend. Do you have any place to go or someone to help you?"

"Thank you very much," Bonita said. "I have an uncle in Cartagena. My phone?"

Before he could ask, the other officer left the room to retrieve the phone. He returned and handed it to the first officer who glanced at the screen and said, "It got to about forty percent. Is that enough?" He handed Bonita the phone.

"Yes, thanks. I just need to send a text."

"I'm sorry for your loss. If there's anything else you need, please don't hesitate to call," the officer said to her.

"It might be petty, considering, but I had a duffle bag and a weight belt we used for ballast in the raft," Rey said. "Is there any way I can get those? They're kinda sentimental. The raft and all the survival gear inside are worth a lot more, but those items belonged to Carlos."

"A patrol boat will pick up the raft and bring it in. Call me in a few days and you can come get anything you want."

"Thanks, I appreciate it."

The officer escorted Bonita and Rey to the front door and directed them off the naval grounds. He stood for a few seconds, along with a few passing seamen, and watched Bonita walk away.

The walk from the office to the street outside the concrete barricades was short. When they were next to the street, Bonita said, "Let's walk to the beach. I want to get away from here before I call Juan."

"You have an uncle in Cartagena? I thought you made that up."

"He's an old friend. He'll help us." When they reached the main road that ran along the beach, Bonita looked in both directions. "Let's go that way." She pointed to the left. They walked a couple of minutes, then sat on steps under a large tree. Holding the phone close, she sent a text to Juan.

> *This is Bonita. I'm on Carrera One at Calle Fifteen. Can you come get me? Don't tell anyone. Rey is with me. Need to figure out what to do.*

> *Are you okay? REY IS WITH YOU???*

> *Yes. Long story. Will tell you when I see you. Rey speaks Spanish. Don't mention Alex or Jana.*

> *No problem. Be there in ten.*

> *heart emoji   heart emoji   heart emoji*

It took Juan eight minutes to reach Bonita and Rey. Bonita introduced him to Rey but didn't offer any details on how they knew each other. During the drive back to his bar, she told Juan the short version of the past twenty-four hours. When she finished, Juan glanced at Rey in the rearview mirror. "You're positive the boat sank?"

"As much as I can be without seeing it go down," Rey said. "I turned off the bilge pumps and opened a couple of seacocks. The boat was on a course into the eye of a hurricane. I left the door to the aft deck open. Even if I hadn't sabotaged her, the storm would likely sink her."

Juan nodded. "You shouldn't have to worry about the three you left onboard. It would be nice to know if the boat did sink."

"Maybe. I'm more worried about what I'm going to do now. I have no money, no place to stay, and no identification."

Juan turned onto the side street next to his bar, then pulled onto the curb and parked. "We can talk about it inside."

When they went into the bar, there was a young girl behind the bar.

She was pretty, with short black hair and braces on her teeth. Bonita looked from her to Juan, horrified. "Juan, you aren't—"

"No. Oh no. She's my niece. They live a few streets over. She helps in the bar. You know I'd never do that."

Bonita felt relieved. "I know you wouldn't, Juan. But when I saw her...she reminded me of me."

"You worked in the bar?" Rey asked.

"You could say that," she replied.

Juan rested his hand on her shoulder. "She does kinda remind me of you." He stared at the young girl a second, then asked, "Who'd like a beer?"

"I would," Rey answered quickly.

"Me too," Bonita said. "Juan, can we get food too? We haven't eaten all day."

Juan signaled, and the young girl brought three beers to the table. She was tall and thin, just as Bonita was at her age. Watching the girl brought back memories of when she worked the bar, but in a much different capacity. Bonita shuddered and took a large drink of beer.

"There's a restaurant at the end of the block. I'll have Ariel get food. A couple of combo platters should be plenty."

"Thank you," Bonita said, opening her purse.

He raised his hand to stop her. "No need. I got it. Rey, if you don't mind, I'd like to speak to Bonita in private. Will you excuse us a minute?"

"Sure." Rey watched Juan and Bonita walk through a door in the back of the bar and wondered why Juan didn't call her Bonnie. She said Bonnie was the name she went by. The thought didn't last. He drank his beer, glanced around the small room, and smiled at the girl behind the bar.

When the door closed behind them, Juan hugged Bonita. "When the boat didn't return, I was worried. You haven't contacted your friends?"

"No, I haven't. No chance. I don't know how to tell Rey. I can't just show up at the hotel with Rey and say, 'Surprise.'"

"I'll go to the table. You stay here and call your friends and tell them what happened. We'll tell Rey he can stay here. I have rooms above the bar. Tell him he can't go with you because you're sharing a room with your friends. See if Gabby can come get you. When you get to the hotel, you all figure out what you want to do."

"That's a great idea, Juan. Thanks. I'll let Jana and Alex figure out how to deal with Rey."

Juan left the room. Bonita called Gabby. She answered on the first ring.

"Bon, are you all right? Where are you? I'm with Jana and Alex. You're on speaker."

Jana yelled from the backseat. "Bonita?"

"Yes, I'm okay. I'm at Juan's."

"We'll come and get you," Gabby said.

"No, don't. Rey's with me."

"What?" Jana yelled again.

"It's a long story. I'm going to tell Rey I need to go to the hotel and stay with my friends. Juan said he could stay here. You shouldn't just walk in and surprise Rey."

"Where's the boat?" Alexander asked.

"Alex, the *Miss Jana*'s gone," Bonita said. "I'll tell you about it later. Gabby, we haven't eaten all day, so Juan is ordering us food. Can you drop Alex and Jana off and come get me? We'll have finished eating by the time you get here."

"Of course," Jana said for Gabby. "Tell Rey she's the friend you're staying with. When you get here, we'll figure out how to deal with him."

42

When Gabby returned to the hotel with Bonita an hour later, Jana and Alexander had finished off the better part of a bottle of Chardonnay. When the obligatory hugs were out of the way, they all sat near the window that overlooked Cartagena Bay. Alexander filled two new glasses with wine and handed them to Gabby and Bonita.

They all listened intently while Bonita described the *Miss Jana*'s final voyage. She began when she met Dani. She omitted a few of the minor details, such as peeing in a bucket and spending the night half-naked. When she finished, her audience sat silent. Jana was relieved Rey was safe but sad their boat was gone. Gabby sat next to Bonita, her hand resting softly on her thigh. She tried to suppress her happiness about Bonita being back but couldn't.

Alexander sat next to Jana, his hands behind his head with his fingers interlocked. "That was quite an adventure. It must have been harrowing," he said when Bonita had finished her story.

"When Rey told me to get in the raft and he pushed it into the water, I was so scared I could hardly move. But once he was in with me, even though the raft was rocking like crazy, I felt safe."

"Rey has that effect on people," Jana said.

"I think it's safe to assume that the three you left on the boat are dead. What about the other partner? He wasn't there?"

"No, he wasn't. Just Dani. Rey thinks when the boat doesn't make it, there're going to be a lot of pissed-off people. Maybe Dani had the money upfront to pay for the stuff here in Colombia, but most likely, they only gave them a down payment, with a promise to pay the rest after they sold the stuff. When they don't get paid, they'll go looking for the other guy."

"And if they don't, the motherfucker gets away scot-free?" Jana asked.

"Not if I have anything to do with it," Alexander said. "I still think JP knows more than he's told us. I bet he knows the other guy. I'll find him...if the drug guys don't find him first." He glanced at Jana, who smiled for the first time since Bonita began her story. "But first things first," he said. "What about Rey? Do we all go over to Juan's and say, 'Hi, Rey, we've been here the whole time, and Bonita's with us?' Jana, you know him better than anyone. Will he be pissed, happy, indifferent?"

Jana pondered the question. "At first, he'll be confused. I would be. Then, as everything sinks in, he'll be upset with Bonita for leading him on, or at us for putting her up to it. He'll be glad I'm okay, maybe embarrassed because I know he had desires for her. He'll be shocked when he sees us. Then, when he realizes that his boat is gone, his girlfriend is in love with another guy, and Bonita is in love with another woman, he'll be very depressed."

Alexander's head whipped toward her. "What'd you say?"

"Which part?"

"The last two."

"Alex, I told you I loved you. You didn't believe me? I do love you. You couldn't tell that Bon is in love with Gabby? Look at them. I've seen the signs. The way they look at each other. Okay, maybe I didn't know they were in love, if they are, but I noticed a connection."

Bonita squeezed Gabby's hand and said, "You're very perceptive, Jana. We might not be in love...yet. But we're going to see how things go."

Alexander sunk into the couch. "Well, you could've knocked me over with a peacock feather. I didn't see that coming."

"Are you okay, Alex?" Bonita asked.

Jana answered for him. "No doubt, he isn't. Do you know what he is doing right now? He's picturing you and Gabby together. It's killing him. Isn't that right Alex?"

"What? No. Absolutely not. I'd never—"

"Bullshit," Jana said, laughing. The other two women joined her.

Alexander blushed. He knew a little light-hearted banter was needed, even at his expense. "Okay. You've had your laugh. Seriously, girls, I'm happy for you. But, Gabby, you said you had a boyfriend when you moved to Cartagena."

Gabby had been questioning her sexual orientation for years. She had been attracted to girls since she was in high school, but she had had sex with both girls and boys–mostly boys. She thought she preferred girls, but how could she be a lesbian when she had also slept with boys? Her friends told her she was bisexual, but she didn't like to be labeled.

She didn't feel it was the time or place to discuss her feelings, but she wanted to answer Alexander's question. "I dated boys in high school and college, but I was attracted to girls. It wasn't long after we moved here that I knew I preferred girls."

Alexander got the answer to the question he wished he didn't ask. He didn't know how to respond. He already said he was happy for them, what else could he add?

The room went quiet. Bonita's ringing phone broke the silence. She looked at the number but didn't recognize it. She reluctantly answered, thinking Juan had given Rey a new burner phone. "Hello?"

"Is this Bonita?"

"Yes."

"This is Captain Muñoz of the Colombian Coast Guard."

"Hi, Captain."

"I wanted to let you know we found debris floating in the water about fifty miles north of where they picked you up. Several life jackets, boat cushions, that type of stuff. We found a life ring, but the name stenciled on it said 'Miss Jana.' That wasn't the name of the boat you were on, was it?"

"No. It was Missing Exes."

"It's possible there was another boat in the area that sunk. Or it could have been a previous name of the boat. They didn't find any survivors, and they're calling off the search. I thought you'd want to know."

"Yes, I did. Thank you for calling."

"You're welcome. Oh, one other thing. A patrol boat picked up the raft. If you all want to claim it and its contents, let me know and we'll schedule a time."

"I will. Thanks again." Bonita hung up the phone and relayed the conversation to the others. "I guess the *Miss Jana* sank. I'm sorry Jana."

"It's sad. I loved that boat. Rey wanted to sell it, but it was originally my boat. The end of an era, I guess."

"That confirms the fate of Dani, Carlos, and Alberto. Now we have to break the news to Rey."

"I think I should tell him," Jana said. "I mean, I definitely should, but alone. Tomorrow, I'll go see him at Juan's and tell him everything." She sunk deeper into the couch. "Man, I'm not looking forward to this."

"Maybe I should go with you," Bonita said. "Gabby will drive us. I should be the one to tell him about me."

Jana nodded. "It might be better if we both went. I could use a little moral support."

"It's settled then. We both go," Bonita said.

"Bon, can you text Juan and ask how Rey's doing, and let him know we'll come by in the morning?"

"I'll do it as soon as we're done here. Which, I gotta tell you, I'm exhausted. I still need a shower and I'll be ready for bed." She looked at Gabby. "Okay with you?"

"Yes. I could use a shower, too." Gabby smiled and kissed her. They got up and went through the adjoining door to their room.

Jana looked at Alexander and burst out laughing. "You had no idea?"

"None. I guess I'm a little naïve. However, a shower and bed sound wonderful right now."

"It does, but I'll warn you, I may not be able to sleep, worrying about seeing Rey tomorrow. I may keep you up."

"I feel good. I'll be up for it."

Jana wrapped her arms around him and said, "Promise me one thing."

"Anything."

"Tonight, you won't think about what those two might be doing in the other room."

"Not tonight, sweetheart. Not with you beside me." He led her to one of the queen-sized beds. The image of the two beautiful young women in the room next door never entered his head as he gently made love to the woman beside him.

Afterward, sleep came easy to Jana. Once Alexander heard her rhythmic breathing, he fell into a deep sleep.

***

Alexander woke up alone in the bed and squinted at the bright light beaming through the window. They'd forgotten to close the blackout curtains...again. He could make out the silhouette of Jana sitting on the couch.

"Good morning."

She turned and looked over the back of the couch. "Hi. Morning. Coffee?"

"Love some. You're up early."

Jana walked to the small bar near the bathroom and poured a cup of coffee. She handed it to him and said, "I woke up and couldn't go back to sleep. I'm glad I didn't wake you."

"Are you worried about Rey?"

She sat on the bed next to him. "I am. In a way, on top of everything else, I'm breaking up with him too. Bon mentioned he told her we had drifted apart. He may have said that to get her in bed, or he meant it. Either way, it means the same."

"Have you thought about what you're going to do after you tell him? What we're going to do?"

Jana shrugged. "I guess we'll go back to Fort Lauderdale."

"Will Rey stay with you? Should I go back to Texas?"

"Oh, shit. I haven't thought that far out. Rey could stay with his brother. Or at a hotel. It would be weird if he stayed with us. He would've been staying on the boat, but it's gone."

Alexander shook his head. "He shouldn't stay with his brother. He shouldn't contact him either. Hopefully, he hasn't already."

Jana got up and refilled her coffee cup. Alexander studied her intently as she added sugar and cream to the cup. She wore silver short satin pajamas with pink trim that she must have put on when she woke up. She was a vision.

"Why not?" Jana asked when she returned to the bed with her coffee.

"What? Oh, I'm sorry, I was distracted. Because Miggie might tell JP he's alive. I don't like JP. I still think he knows more than he's told us. I'd just as soon have him thinking Rey is still on the boat. If he knows what has happened with the boat, and he happens to run into the other partner, he might tell him what happened. Maybe on purpose, maybe not. Like I said before, JP's not the sharpest tool in the shed."

"I agree with that. Until this all blows over, Rey should remain out of sight?"

"Yes. Fort Lauderdale isn't safe for him. When we get back, I want to have a little chat with JP. See if he's found anything. I'm betting he hasn't."

"I doubt it. He probably hasn't tried all that hard." Jana looked at her phone. "It's seven. I'm going to wake Bon and Gabby so we can see Rey early. I don't want him calling his brother."

"He's going to be in shock. Once he's past it, he'll need a passport. There's bound to be a US Embassy in Cartagena. Gabby or Juan should know what to do. Ask them."

"I will." Jana hopped off the bed, tapped on the door connecting the two rooms, and slowly opened it. The room was dark. Bonita and Gabby were asleep. "Bon..."

Bonita opened her eyes. "Hey," she said, still groggy.

"Sorry to wake you, but I'd like to go see Rey as soon as possible. Can you all get up?"

"Yeah, give us a few minutes."

Jana closed the door, dressed, put on makeup, and combed her hair. She walked to the bed, leaned over, and kissed Alexander on the lips. "I'm going to Bon's room to wait in there for them to get ready. Wish me luck."

"Good luck. I'll be here. Call if you need me."

43

The three women sat in the white Mazda outside Juan's bar. Bonita had texted Juan and given him a heads-up they were on their way. He said he would unlock the door for them.

"Now that we're here," Bonita said, "how are we going to do this?"

"Bon should go in first," Gabby said. "She's a familiar face. He'll be happy to see her. Then say something like, Rey, we need to talk, and you may not like it. That'll prepare him, kinda. Then tell him Jana is here. He'll be confused. Bring him down while he's still confused. He'll see her, see you, he won't know what to say. Then introduce him to me, and you and I will leave and let Jana talk to him."

"I like all of it except the last part," Jana said.

Gabby laughed. "Okay, we'll hang around a little while. But you two have a lot to talk about. You'll want a little privacy."

"I guess we should get this over with," Bonita said.

Juan was wiping the bar when the three women walked in. He tossed his rag on the bar and greeted them, bear-hugging Bonita. "Rey told me the story. You don't do that again."

She kissed him on the cheek. "Don't worry, Juan. Never again. Where's Rey?"

"He's upstairs, first door on the right."

Bonita took a deep breath and exhaled slowly. "Wish me luck." She walked up the steps, found the first door on the right, and knocked.

"Come in," Rey said.

Bonita eased the door open. He was lying on the bed and jumped up when he saw her. He opened his arms to hug her, but she pushed him away.

"I'm sorry, Rey," she said.

"That's not exactly the reception I was expecting."

"I know. I'm so sorry. This is hard for me. We need to talk. I have something I need to tell you."

"Let me guess. The other person you mentioned."

"That's part of it. She's downstairs."

"She?"

"Yeah, She. I wasn't certain about our relationship, but last night confirmed it."

Rey walked back to the bed and sat down. "I guess I can't compete with that. There's more?"

Bonita paced around the room. "There is."

"I'm not ashamed to say it. You just broke my heart. Whatever you have to say, just spit it out. It can't be any worse."

"Okay. Jana's downstairs."

Rey sat quietly for several seconds, dumbfounded. "What?"

"Jana's here. Downstairs."

"My Jana? Jana Wilson?" He stared at Bonita, trying to reconcile what she was saying. *How does she know Jana, and why is she downstairs?*

"Yes. And considering you said I broke your heart, I guess it'll be okay to let you know she's no longer 'your' Jana."

Rey shook his head as if trying to shake himself out of a horrible dream. "How do you know? Do you know her? Did you tell her about us?"

"I thought you'd have questions. Yes, I know Jana. No, I didn't tell her about us. Well, sort of, but there was nothing to tell. We didn't do anything. Anyway, she hired my ex-boyfriend, Alex, to find you once you went missing. Because I'm from Colombia, he asked for my help to find you. They've been here the entire time."

"They've been here the whole time? How long?"

"We got here the day before I met you at the restaurant."

Rey glared at her. "You were being paid for what you did?"

"No. When we met, I was just trying to find out if you were on the boat. After we met, I liked you, and I wanted to help. That's why I kept coming back."

"Even though you had a girlfriend?"

"She didn't actually become my 'girlfriend' until last night. I was hoping..."

"I guess you told Jana I hit on you?"

"Not exactly. I told her that you seemed to have feelings for me. But that wasn't it. You said you and her were drifting apart. She said the same thing. I've said too much already. She's waiting. You need to talk to her."

"I do. If I sounded like I was blaming you, I'm sorry. Jana and I were growing apart. Then I met you, and I was okay with it. Please don't tell her, but right now, losing you hurts more than her."

"I won't tell her. Maybe under different circumstances, you and I, maybe..."

"I'm confused. Do you prefer men or women? You said Jana hired your ex to find me. Your ex is a guy?"

"He is. You know him. He helped you when you brought the girls in from Cuba."

"Alex? Alex is your ex?"

"He is. He found me at the bar when he rescued Briana."

"Bonita. I thought the name rang a bell, but I would've never linked the name to you."

"Alex and I were in a relationship. I got pregnant, lost the baby, and went off the deep end. I started using and then hooking to pay for it. When he tried to get me to come with him, I tried to kill myself. But then suddenly, I realized that I had a purpose in life–saving you. Then I met Gabby, and it was special."

"Bonnie—"

"It's Bonita."

"Sorry. Bonita, I'm happy for you. I mean that. But if it doesn't work out, and you want to try a guy again, let me know."

She chuckled and kissed him on the cheek. "I will. Ready to go see Jana?"

"Not really."

Bonita led him out of the room and down the stairs. Halfway down, he saw Jana. She met him in the middle of the bar, wrapped her arms around his neck, and held him. He held her but couldn't speak. After what he had just been told, he didn't know what to say to her.

"I'm so glad you're okay, Rey. Too bad about the *Miss Jana*. We had a lot of memories on her."

"We did. Some I'd rather not remember."

"There were a few of those," she said. "Come, let's sit."

The two walked back to the table where Jana had been sitting. Gabby stood. Bonita took her by the arm and said, "Rey, this is Gabby."

He gave Gabby the once-over then shook his head. "I never had a chance, did I?" A murmur of laughter lifted the tension from the room.

"You told him?" Jana asked.

"I did. I...also...kinda—"

"She told me we were no longer together...officially."

Jana cleared her throat delicately. Her forehead creased. "Rey...I don't—"

Rey slapped his hand on the table. It was a loud, violent slap that got her attention. "No, Jana. Let me." He exhaled noisily. "We were drifting apart. Would it be fair to say we love each other, but we aren't in love?"

Jana nodded, still a little shaken from his emotional outburst. "I didn't want to hurt you, and you didn't want to hurt me, so we didn't talk about it. You did your thing, and I did mine. You were the best thing that ever happened to me, and I should be on my knees begging for forgiveness. But even if you took me back, it wouldn't last. Maybe it's for the best. I'm sorry if I hurt you."

She hesitated, trying to read him. Was he hurt, angry, jealous, all of the above? It was hard to tell.

"You're right, Rey. I still love you, but I'm not in love with you. If I'm being honest, thinking about you and Bon may have bothered me a bit, but it's okay. I didn't want to tell you, but since we are all coming clean, I should, too. I've fallen for Alex."

"Alex, the PI? Bonita's ex?"

"One and the same."

Rey looked around the table. "So, Bonita has a new girlfriend. You have a new boyfriend. I'm the odd man out."

"Maybe not," Gabby said. "I have several hot friends if you're interested. Just to get your mind off Jana and Bon."

Rey grinned as if to say, "Okay."

Jana saw it. "Let's worry about your love life later, Rey. We need to get you home. You need a passport."

"I have no home. The boat's gone, and I'm not ready to shack up with you and your new guy."

"Rey, we weren't married, but I'll take care of you. The boat was insured. You'll get a settlement out of it. We have a joint account. I'll transfer more money than you'll need to get you on your feet."

Rey lowered his head and squeezed the bridge of his nose. He was hurting inside, but getting angry or voicing pain wouldn't change a thing. If anything, he might talk himself out of Jana's generous offer. He also had the gold bars disguised as dive weights he pocketed before being lifted into the helicopter, gold bars he didn't want to be seen flashing around town. He laughed and said, "Wow. This has got to be the strangest day of my life. I should be mad that my girlfriend has a new boyfriend, or that she has offered to buy me out—"

"Damn it, Rey, that's not—"

He raised his hand but caught himself before he banged the table again. "Please, don't interrupt me," he said in a calm voice. "The woman I thought I was falling for has a girlfriend. I should be mad or hurt or embarrassed. I'm none of the above. I'm grateful I have all of you in my life. Gabby, you too. You said you have a friend. I'm interested."

Gabby showed him a hint of a smile and picked up her phone.

Jana's mouth dropped. "Rey, I'm glad to see you're taking it so well. I was worried..."

"Honestly, my head is spinning. But what's done is done, and I need to move on. I may feel differently later when I'm alone and I've processed everything. But for now. I'm good."

"There's one more thing," Jana said.

Rey waited for the other shoe to drop.

"Alex doesn't want JP to know you're alive. You haven't contacted your brother, have you?"

"No. His number was on my phone. I had a business card with his number on it, but it went down with the boat."

"Good. We're afraid Miggie might slip and tell JP about the boat. Alex thinks JP knows more than he's telling us. It's just a hunch, but it's better if JP doesn't know what happened to the boat."

"I get it. I'd like to let Miggie know I'm okay. When are you going back to Florida? Maybe you can talk to him and let him know."

"You mean when are we going back?"

"Not necessarily. I have a feeling Bonita is staying for a while. I thought I might too. Meet Gabby's friend. Cartagena is a nice place to lie low." Rey looked at Gabby, then at Bonita. "If you all don't mind."

Gabby smiled. "Not at all. There's a cheap hotel around the corner from me where you can stay. It's nice. My family stays there when they visit from Bogota."

"When I get home, I can send you your passport," Jana said. "You'll have to figure out a way to leave when you're ready since you're in the country illegally."

"Couldn't I go to the embassy and get a new passport? It'll take a while, but I have time."

"I guess. Gabby, do you know where the US Embassy is?"

"It's in Bogota."

"There's not one in Cartagena?"

"Nope, Bogota. About a thousand kilometers from here." Gabby spoke to Juan in Spanish and then translated for Jana. "Juan said Barranquilla has an embassy office, but to get a passport, Rey would have to go to Bogota. He must apply in person. But Juan said he has a source for passports. He can get Rey one that's good enough to get him out of Colombia. Since you're flying private, it might even get him into the US."

"It might?" Jana asked. "What happens if it doesn't?"

Rey shook his head. "I end up in a detention center until I can prove who I am. That's risky. I can hang out here in Colombia for a while."

"Are you sure you don't want to go with us?" Jana asked.

"Damn," Rey said. "I'm torn. Part of me says go. The other part says stay, hang out here, and lie low."

"Meanwhile, Rey, you have a date tonight." Gabby handed her

phone to Rey. There was a picture of a young Latina girl with long, jet-black hair, big dark eyes, and an enormous smile full of straight white teeth. "While you all were talking, I texted her, and she agreed to meet you."

Rey looked at the picture and smiled like a lunatic. "She's incredible."

"She is. And she's so much fun. The four of us will go out tonight." Gabby now gave him the once-over. "Do you have any other clothes?"

"I don't."

"We need to go shopping."

Rey was still admiring the picture. "I may need a lot of clothes. Jana, I'll be staying in Cartagena for a while."

"Let me see the picture." She took the phone from him and looked at the photo of the girl. "Hmm, I guess you will. Unless your date with her tonight goes horribly bad." She opened her purse and fumbled through the stack of peso notes. "Here's...uh...two million pesos. Is that enough to get Rey decent clothes?"

"More than enough."

"Good. And here's five hundred US for you, Gabby. Take me back to the hotel, then you guys go shopping. Bonita, ask Juan if Rey can stay here tonight."

Once Juan assured them Rey could stay as long as he wanted, he went into the back room and returned with a key. "In case you come back late," he said and handed the key to Rey.

"Bonita..." Jana paused. "You're staying in Colombia?"

"Yes. No doubt." She smiled at Gabby.

"Do you remember my promise to you?"

Bonita got a puzzled look on her face.

"I told you that if you stay off drugs, I'll pay for a surrogate and IVF so you can have a child. So far, you've held up your end of the bargain. When you're ready and have a surrogate in mind, let me know." Jana glanced at Gabby. "Make certain she's someone you want carrying your baby."

Bonita's chin began to quiver. Her eyes filled with tears. It was the first time she'd cried since she was fourteen. She tried to speak but couldn't.

Gabby leaned over and held her. "Jana, that's amazing."

Jana cleared her throat to stop from becoming emotional. "One more thing, Bon. Set up a bank account and send me the details. I want to fund it so you don't have to worry about finding a job for a while."

Between sobs, Bonita uttered what Jana thought was a thank you. She couldn't help but smile. She'd only known Bonita a week, but it filled her heart with joy to be able to help her.

"Gabby..." Jana said. "Give me your address. It'll be best if I send Rey's passport to you."

"Yes, by all means. I'll text it to you."

Jana looked around the table. "Have I forgotten anything? Rey, since you and Bon are staying in Cartagena, if I can get a plane, Alex and I may leave tonight. Oh, I almost forgot. Juan. He was a lifesaver. I want to reward him."

Bonita still struggled to speak, so Gabby translated. Juan held up his hands in protest and spoke in Spanish. The only thing Jana understood was, "No, no, no."

"He said he's happy Bonita is back," Gabby said. "He doesn't want money."

Jana dug through her purse, counting how much money she had left in pesos and dollars. She found an envelope at the bottom of her purse. Inside was a banded stack of one-hundred-dollar bills totaling ten thousand dollars. She counted out twenty of the bills and handed them to Juan.

"No. No," Juan waved his hands.

"Gabby, tell him to take it and save it for a rainy day. If he doesn't need it, have him save it and use it to help pay for the education of that little girl Bonita said was at the bar last night."

Gabby translated. Juan smiled and took the money from Jana. He said something, but Jana waved off the translation. She heard 'gracias' several times. It was all she needed. The room fell silent except for an occasional sniffle from Bonita.

"We've been here a while. You guys need to go shopping, and I need to see about getting an airplane. Alex and I will leave this afternoon or in the morning, whenever we can get a plane. Rey, are you certain you don't want to come with us?"

Rey nodded. "I appreciate it, but I don't think I want to try one of Juan's fake passports. Plus, I'd like to meet Gabby's friend." He didn't know how much money Jana would give him, but he had a feeling it would be enough to live like a king in Colombia. "Even if it doesn't work out with her, there's no shortage of beautiful women here."

"Then we should leave," Jana said. She hugged Juan and whispered 'Gracias' in his ear several times. Bonita hugged him and told him she'd see him again soon.

The ten-minute ride from Juan's bar to the hotel was muted. At the hotel, Jana got out of the Mazda and waved as Gabby, Bonita, and Rey drove off. She let out an enormous sigh of relief. The conversation she'd been dreading was over. It had gone better than expected, thanks to Gabby's introduction of her cute friend into the conversation. She walked into the hotel and straight to the elevators. When the door closed, she leaned against the back wall, closed her eyes, and took another deep breath. The elevator opened, and she walked to her room, pressed the card key against the lock pad, opened the door, and froze.

The white sheets on the bed closest to the door were red with blood. Splattered blood decorated the walls and ceiling. Blood pooled on the floor. Her instinct was to turn and run, but she couldn't move. A man lay face down on the blood-covered bed. She struggled to breathe and tried to scream, but had no air.

44

The door to the adjoining room opened. Jana screamed, then yelled, "Alex!"

When he came around the corner, she jumped into his arms. He let out a painful shriek. She could see the strain and discomfort etched on his face as he held a blood-stained towel against a gash above his rapidly swelling eye. Blood trickled down his cheek and stained the corner of his mouth.

She pulled away and looked at him, visibly shaken. "What the fuck happened Alex?"

"Your friend JP came looking for you."

"JP? Are you sure? How the hell…"

Alexander nodded toward the bed. "Take a look."

Jana cautiously stepped around the crimson pools of blood, her heart racing in her chest. Approaching the bed, she saw JP lying still, his eyes open, gazing into the unknown. She clenched her arms tightly across her stomach, trying to quell the growing feeling of dread in her gut. "What the fuck is he doing here?"

"I have no idea. I was just lying here when there was a loud knock at the door. I thought it might be you, having forgotten your key. When I opened the door, there was JP. He barged in and demanded to know where you were, then asked about Rey and the boat."

"He knew about the boat?" Jana's mind was reeling. "And he knew it was missing?" The realization hit her like a ton of bricks–JP must have been involved in Rey's disappearance. Her breath caught in her throat as she struggled to process this new information.

"He did. Evidently, JP was the other partner."

Jana backed away from the body, her knees buckling. She leaned against the wall to steady herself. "No fucking way!"

"I went through his phone. There was a long text conversation between him and Dani until they sailed. Dani said she was switching to the Iridium phone and would update him on the hour. I couldn't find any other message threads. The boat must have sunk before she could send another message. It's speculation, but when JP didn't hear from her, he must have gotten worried she was cutting him out. He came here looking for her."

"Jesus!" Jana said. "How did he end up here, asking about Rey?"

"That may remain a mystery. When I told him I knew nothing about the boat, he took a swing at me. I tried to duck, but he hit me on the side of the head. I staggered, and he kicked me in the chest. I never saw it coming. I fell over the bed, hit my head on the corner of the nightstand, and landed in the space between the beds. I pulled the revolver out of the nightstand, and he lept at me. I got one round off. He hit me above the eye before collapsing on the bed."

"Dead?"

"Not quite. He tried to come at me, but I scooted away. He squirmed and tried to talk before he bled out. I couldn't make out what he was trying to say. It's just as well."

"Shit, Alex, what are we going to do?"

"I was about to call Bonita and tell her what happened, have her ask Juan if he could help. He took care of the molester for us. I hope he can take care of JP."

"Great idea. He'll help." She stared at JP's lifeless body. "That motherfucker. He was in on it the whole time. No wonder he said he couldn't find anyone who knew anything." She turned to the body and shouted, "You son of a bitch!" Taking a seat in one of the chairs, she turned back to Alexander. "Do you think anyone else knows about Rey...or us?"

"Nothing on JP's phone leads me to believe so. It looks like JP arranged the boat and Dani did most of the dealing here in Colombia. They were probably going to split the profit, which is why JP was antsy when he didn't hear from Dani."

"We shouldn't wait around to find out or wait for the police to ask questions. Put the Do Not Disturb sign on the door. I'll call Bonita and ask her to call Juan. Then I'm calling QuickJet to see how quickly we can get a plane out of here."

A light tapping came from outside the room door.

"Fuck," Jana said. "Could it be friends of JP? It's too soon for Bon and Gabby."

Another knock echoed through the room, this time louder than before. The metallic click of a card key unlocking the door followed. The porter entered cautiously, then he noticed the body lying on the bed, and his expression turned to one of concern.

"Are you alright?" he asked in heavily accented English, his gaze shifting between Alexander and Jana. "I heard a loud noise. It sounded like a gunshot. I would have come sooner, but I wanted to wait and see if anyone left the room." He gestured toward Jana. "Then I saw you go into the room and I thought I should check on you."

The room filled with an eerie stillness as the three of them stood frozen, unsure of what to say or do next in this gruesome scene. The only sound was the faint hum of the air conditioning unit, a stark contrast to the chaos that had occurred earlier.

The porter walked to the bed and studied the body. He seemed unphased by it. "He is not your friend?"

"No, why do you ask?"

"He checked in this morning. He only had one small bag. He didn't need me, but when he saw your lady leave with two other ladies, he said the blonde one—you, he called you Jana—was a friend and asked me for her room number. It's against the rules, but I gave it to him. I'm very sorry."

"That's okay," Jana said. It wasn't okay; he almost got Alexander killed, but Jana didn't want to anger the man who, with one phone call, could put her and Alexander in prison for life. "It wasn't your fault. But we do have a problem. Can you help us?"

"Sí, sí. You tipped me very well when I brought your bags up. Don't worry, I can help you. I know a person who can bring a laundry hamper and take the body out. There are two maids I trust. They won't say anything. You may need...to...um..."

"To tip them? Not a problem. You too. Just let me know how much to make all this go away."

The porter casually looked at JP's lifeless body, then at the blood on the floors and walls. It was obvious it wasn't his first rodeo. "Oh, maybe two hundred thousand pesos each. We will also clean out his room like he was never here. Any cash or anything of value we find, I will split with the others."

Jana was getting better at the conversion rate. Two hundred thousand pesos was about fifty US dollars. It was probably the equivalent of a week's pay for the housekeepers, but not very much for making a body and a crime scene disappear. She dug into her purse and pulled out eight Benjamins which she handed to the porter. "This is two hundred US dollars each. You'll give them their share, won't you?"

"Sí. I will. Count on me. Gracias."

"Thank you," Alex said, his voice strained. He held a towel to his head, trying to staunch the bleeding. "We're going to move all our stuff to the room next door. When our friends return, we'll check out and leave. You'll take care of this for us?"

The porter's eyes flickered around the room. "Leave. You were never here." He looked at Alex who was still holding a towel to his head. "Do you need a doctor?"

Alex shook his head, wincing as pain shot through his temple. "No, I'm fine. Thanks."

Jana carefully inspected Alexander's head, gently pressing her fingers against the wound. "The bleeding seems to have stopped," she said, her expression now one of relief. "It doesn't look too bad, but it has swollen a bit." She gestured to a nearby ice bucket. "Would you like some ice?"

"Only in a glass filled with scotch."

"But, it's only half-past twelve."

"It's five o'clock somewhere."

ACKNOWLEDGMENTS

I want to thank my friend Debbie (Debra…sorry, a 50+ year habit of calling her Debbie is hard to break) for her undying support. She has encouraged me to keep writing and is always the first to read my draft and give me invaluable feedback.

As always, thank you Bob for the many evenings of "technical support," and for listening to the many hours of me talking about the book but not wanting to give you any spoilers.

A very special thank you to my daughter Robin, whose help on this novel was immeasurable.

I'd like to take this opportunity to give a special thank you to everyone who has purchased my books, read an eBook, or asked for a copy at their local library. I especially want to thank those who bought a copy from Amazon and posted a review. You will never know how truly appreciative I am of those reviews.

In August 2023 our daughter Julie Eaton lost her eight-year battle with cancer. Julie lived life to the fullest every minute of every day. If you ever traveled with her, you know why we called her "Tour Guide Julie." Never did a weekend go by without multiple activities planned. It's a cliché, but Julie truly never met a stranger.

Two weeks after Julie passed away, Jimmy Buffett died of cancer. I wouldn't say Jimmy influenced my life as I am pretty sure I was wearing Hawaiian shirts, boiling shrimp, enjoying boat drinks, and dreaming about living on a sailboat before I was a Parrothead, but he certainly reinforced the lifestyle. I don't remember the exact date of my first JB concert, but I know it was in the late seventies at the old Sam Houston Coliseum in Houston. Since that first show, I must have seen him in concert thirty times. Like Jana in this book, the last few times he came to town, I said, "I'll go next year."